A Hag Rises from the

This is a work of fiction. Names, characters, organizations, places, events, and incidents are either products of the author's imagination or are used fictitiously. Any resemblance to actual persons, living or dead, or actual events is purely coincidental.

Copyright © 2021 Douglas Lumsden
All rights reserved.
ISBN-13: 9798731771412

No part of this book may be reproduced, or stored in a retrieval system, or transmitted in any form or by any means, electronic, mechanical, photocopying, recording, or otherwise, without express written permission of the publisher.

Cover design and art by Arash Jahani (www.arashjahani.com)

A Hag Rises from the Abyss

By

Douglas Lumsden

To Teri and Karen: Best Wishes Always

Books in this Series

Alexander Southerland, P.I.

Book One: *A Troll Walks into a Bar*

Book Two: *A Witch Steps into My Office*

Book Three: *A Hag Rises from the Abyss*

Table of Contents

Chapter One 1

Chapter Two 12

Chapter Three 27

Chapter Four 39

Chapter Five 51

Chapter Six 62

Chapter Seven 73

Chapter Eight 88

Chapter Nine 99

Chapter Ten 108

Chapter Eleven 116

Chapter Twelve 126

Chapter Thirteen 134

Chapter Fourteen 144

Chapter Fifteen 153

Chapter Sixteen 164

Chapter Seventeen 177

Chapter Eighteen 190

Chapter Nineteen 201

Chapter Twenty 213

Chapter Twenty-One 222

Chapter Twenty-Two 235

Chapter Twenty-Three 245

Chapter Twenty-Four 260

Chapter Twenty-Five 268
Chapter Twenty-Six 278
Chapter Twenty-Seven 292
Chapter Twenty-Eight 304
Epilogue 313
Acknowledgements 324
About the Author 325

Chapter One

One look at the luxury sedan squatting on the street in front of my office like the queen of all black widow spiders made me wish that I'd been born on a different day. I had turned thirty years old sometime that morning, and I'd celebrated the momentous occasion with my favorite birthday feast: a high-priced bottle of single-malt avalonian whiskey. I spent the evening bellied up to the bar at the Black Minotaur Lounge, knocking back shots and watching the joint fill up a few people at a time until it was packed. No one in the crowd knew that I had just left my carefree young adult years behind and was now staring at the onset of middle age. That was jake with me. I hadn't told anyone that it was my birthday. It was nobody's business but my own.

When my bottle was empty, I'd slipped away and started the eight-block walk to my apartment, telling myself that I'd only aged a day, not a decade. I hadn't noticed any more stray white strands in my dark head of hair that morning than I had the day before. My face, which no one had ever called handsome anyway, was no less, shall we say, rugged looking. I could still empty a glass with the best of them. In my twenties, a bottle of good hooch left me plastered. Now that I was thirty, I was soused. Maybe that was the difference.

It was one of those beautiful Yerba City summer nights, where the moon and the stars disappear and re-emerge behind the rolling low-hanging clouds, and cold gusts of wind whip through the streets and laugh at your feeble attempts to keep the chill from penetrating to your bones. I'd been hoofing it down the sidewalk for the past thirty minutes, hoping to sober up in the cool night breeze. A wisp of fog blew by, and I savored the tang of sea salt as I breathed in the moist air. The troll who had followed me out of the Black Minotaur was still about twenty yards behind me, matching my unsteady steps with his measured ones. He was wearing a tailored gray suit that probably cost more than I typically grossed in a month of investigative work, and I would have bet a c-note that at least two full-grown cows had sacrificed their hides in the production of the troll's enormous leather overcoat. Five would get you ten he worked for the bigshot who owned that shiny black car in front of my office and that his job was to make sure I met the shadowy figures cooling their heels inside it.

When I caught my first glimpse of the luxury sedan, my befuddled brain concocted the absurd notion that someone important had come to acknowledge my rite of passage into the world of thirty-something. Maybe we were going to have a birthday party! Sure we would. The doors to the sedan would open, and the dark figures inside would emerge wearing party hats and holding floating balloons by their strings. They'd bring out a cake, and....

It occurred to me that my evening stroll had done a piss-poor job of clearing my head. That's the thing with avalonian. It's like cozying up to a dazzling uptown dame. You know she's out of your league, and you'd call it a triumph if she just accompanied you to the dance floor for a couple of twirls, but she's silky smooth, she fills your senses, and the next thing you know you she's dragging you to a glitzy all-night after-party when all you really want to do is bury yourself under your own snug woolen bed covers and saw logs until noon.

When I reached the black sedan, the passenger window slid down. I smiled at the shadowy lug inside. "Good evening," I said. "Wonderful night, isn't it?"

"Get in the car, Mr. Southerland." The shadowy lug's voice was neither pleasant nor menacing, but it was filled with the assumption that it would be obeyed. The door behind the lug opened, and the tallest troll I'd ever seen stepped out of the back of the car. For one brief moment, I imagined that the troll was in fact wearing a party hat. I felt the beginnings of an involuntary gasp of delight. But then I realized that the headgear was an ordinary fedora. Oh well. The troll held the car door open and gave me room to enter.

I looked up at the troll. Way up. Despite standing a shade over six-one in my stocking feet, I had to crane my neck in order to meet his red eyes, which glowed like hot coals beneath the brim of his fedora. Even without the hat, he would have been at least eight feet tall. I looked at the shadowy lug in the passenger seat. He gestured with his chin toward the back. I looked over my shoulder at the troll who had been following me. He was broader than the tall troll with the fedora, broader, in fact, than the average troll. I noted that he was not wearing a hat, party or otherwise, and that he was now close enough to reach out and nab me with his four-fingered taloned hands if I was thinking about beating feet.

I climbed into the back of the black sedan with all the dignity I could muster, sliding all the way across the seat to the driver's side of the car. The tall troll slid in beside me and pulled the door shut. The stocky troll opened the driver's side door and stared me down with his glowing peepers until, with a heavy sigh, I relented and scooched myself over to the center of the seat, allowing the troll to lumber in beside me. Though I was now pinned between two trolls, the interior of the sedan was spacious enough that I wasn't too uncomfortable. Even the tall troll was able to stretch his legs, most of the way at least. A smoky glass partition separated the back seat from the front, and looking through it I saw that a third troll was behind the wheel. I smiled. Maybe he was going to drive me to the party!

***

I must have dozed off during the drive, because the next thing I remember was being shaken awake by the stocky troll that had followed me out of the Minotaur. He seemed to want me to follow him out of the sedan, and, since he looked to be nearly six hundred pounds of cold fury, I did what he wanted. I found myself in an enclosed parking garage. The sedan that had brought me there was one of six identical luxury cars clustered in a designated parking area near an unadorned steel wall with an elevator at one end. The rest of the spacious garage was empty save for a few scattered vehicles in parking slots here and there. I drew in a slow deep breath, trying to clear away the alcohol fumes that were still clinging to my brain like barnacles. Despite my nap, the avalonian wasn't going to release its grip without a fight.

"This way," said the shadowy lug, who wasn't quite so shadowy now that we were out of the sedan. In fact, he looked pretty fucking substantial! He wore a brown wool top coat that appeared to be tailored to his bulky frame. His upturned collar framed a round balding head and an iron-jawed mug. His cold dark eyes, thin lips, and weak chin gave his face a shark-like appearance. He had the self-assured demeanor of a man who could take a punch and return it with interest. He stood two or three inches taller than me with a broad chest, massive arms, a long flat torso, and thick bowed legs. I'm a tough guy, two hundred ten pounds of granite.

I'd been trading knuckles with other tough guys since I was a kid, and I'd been forged into a fighting machine by the military. No one would ever mistake me for a pushover. I'm also pretty good at sizing up an opponent. This bruiser in front of me? One look at him told me that I could knock him down with a lead pipe if it was heavy enough and if I was lucky enough to catch him by surprise, but I doubted that I'd be able to get in more than one shot.

The tall troll with the fedora moved up to join the bruiser, and the other two trolls positioned themselves on either side of me. We all headed for the elevator together, just one big happy family. I had no idea where I was or what I was doing there, and no one offered to clue me in. I didn't bother to ask. I'd find out soon enough.

The elevator ride was short, just up a single floor. From the elevator, the bruiser led us to the right down a short hallway and then to the left down a longer one. With a start, I realized that I'd been down this longer hallway before. Forcing my alcohol-soaked neurons to function was like trying to start a fire with wet kindling, but when we stopped at an office door and I read the nameplate, I finally knew where I'd been brought. I was standing in the inner recesses of City Hall, outside the office of Mr. Lawrence Fulton, attorney and security advisor to Darnell Teague, Mayor of Yerba City.

When I read the nameplate, my brain began to defog in a hurry. The hairs on the back of my neck began to straighten, and I felt beads of sweat forming on my forehead, as the last of the avalonian began to beat a hasty retreat through my pores. Fulton was Mayor Teague's fixer, the man charged with working behind the scenes to keep our charismatic and self-indulgent mayor shiny and clean in the public eye by cleaning up the messes he created with his many private indiscretions. Pardon me: *alleged* indiscretions. I had been brought to his door against my will. True, no one had laid a glove on me, but I had no illusions about that. The bruiser and his three laughing boys represented an overwhelming force that I'd be powerless to resist. Actually, I was a little flattered. With this amount of overkill, Fulton was showing me a huge amount of respect that I wasn't sure I deserved. The hallway outside Fulton's office was deserted. I hadn't seen a clock, but I judged that midnight wasn't far off. I'd been led into City Hall through a back entrance. This was going to be a secret meeting with one of the most powerful men in the city, a man I'd hoped I would never run across again. A man, I reminded myself, who had no reason to like me. I was alone, unarmed, surrounded by an elite corps of professional muscle, and still half in the bag. Happy thirtieth birthday, Southerland. I hoped it wouldn't be my last.

The bruiser opened the office door, and we all walked into Fulton's reception room. The lights were off, and no one was there. The bruiser crossed the room to the door leading to Fulton's inner office and rapped at it with his knuckles. Without waiting for a response, he opened the door halfway and leaned through. Light from the inner office poured through the opening and lit up half of the reception area. I heard the bruiser say, "Southerland is here."

"Okay, let's have him," said a quiet voice from within. The bruiser opened the door all the way and looked back at the rest of us. The troll in the fedora put his paw on my shoulder and urged me toward the door. I brushed his arm away and gave him my best steely glare. Then I straightened my coat, brushed off my collar, and breezed my way past the bruiser into Fulton's lair with what I hoped was a manly swagger.

"Ah, Mr. Southerland." Fulton rose from his seat and walked around his desk, extending a hand. He wasn't a big man by any means, but he was the kind of guy who seemed to physically dominate any room that he was in. It had something to do with the assertive manner with which he carried himself, as if he'd never been in a fight that he hadn't won. He had a round, pug-nosed face, and dark eyes that glowed with an inner intensity. His lips were set in a smile that was more professional than friendly. As I grasped his hand in a firm shake, I noted the two ruby-studded gold bands on his middle and ring fingers. Everything about Fulton, from his thick gray-streaked black hair that appeared to have been scissor-clipped and styled earlier that day, to his impeccably hand-tailored suit, to the thin clear lacquer on his evenly trimmed fingernails, spoke of money, style, and authority. It was all I could do to meet his eyes without glancing away. He wasn't showing me anything except courtesy, but I felt more danger radiating from this average-sized high roller than I had from the big bruiser and the three trolls that had brought me to see him.

"Mr. Fulton," I said. "If I'd've known you wanted to see me I would've freshened up."

Fulton's nostrils flared as he drew in a quick sniff. "Hmph. I'd offer you a drink, but I think you're a little ahead of me."

"How about a cup of coffee. Black."

"Commissary's closed for the night, Southerland. Please, have a seat." Fulton indicated an armchair near his desk. I noted that Fulton's guest chairs were a lot more comfortable than the cheap chairs in my own office. Well, he was probably used to entertaining a higher class of clientele than I was. On most nights, at least.

Turning to the bruiser, Fulton said, "Gordon, you can send the fellas home now. I want you to stay with me." The bruiser—Gordon, apparently—stepped into the next room for a moment before returning and lowering himself into a chair near mine. Fulton leaned back against the edge of his desk, but remained standing, commanding the high ground.

"It's been a while," Fulton told me, staring at me with cold eyes.

I stared back. It *had* been a while. About ten months or so.

Fulton met my stare without blinking and continued. "You should have taken that check."

I nodded. "Probably."

The check Fulton was referring to was for more money than I'd made in my entire eight-year career as a private investigator. In exchange for the check, I was to give Fulton a mysterious metal box containing a substance unknown to either of us at the time. In addition, Fulton would ensure that a couple of high-ranking police officers responsible for the murder of an adaro girl would receive their just punishments. It had been a good deal all around. For reasons of my own, I had walked away from it. Fulton had not been pleased.

"You still owe me."

I stretched out my legs and sunk back into my seat. Damn, this really *was* a comfortable chair! "How do you figure? I didn't take your money."

Fulton kept his voice level. "You gave me your word."

"I told you that I would run your offer past my lawyer and get back to you."

"You implied that it was a done deal."

I shrugged. "I'd say that you jumped to a false conclusion."

Fulton reached up and scratched at the wiry stubble on his cheek. It had probably been eighteen hours since he'd shaved, and he'd have a full beard if he let it go for another two days. "Be that as it may, I didn't get what I wanted. That was…disappointing."

I shrugged again. "Things came up."

"Things came up," Fulton repeated in a voice I could barely hear. He sounded sad, but I felt more menace in that quiet voice than if he had been screaming in my face. He met my eyes and his lips spread in what appeared to be a friendly smile. I smiled back. I couldn't help it. I guess I'm a friendly guy.

"Do you mind if I call you Alex?" Fulton asked me in an easy tone.

"Fine with me…. Larry."

Fulton's smile faded by a degree, but his face remained relaxed. He waved his hand in the air as if he were brushing something aside. "Well, Alex, here's the way I see it. I say this, and you say that…. We could argue about it all night, I suppose. But it would be a waste of time, and I don't like wasting time, especially my own. The problem you're having, Alex, is that you think your side of the story matters. It doesn't. I say you owe me, and you do. Practically speaking, that's really all there is to it."

I started to respond, but stopped when Fulton raised a hand. "But I'm willing to set it aside and let bygones be bygones. What's done is done." He gave me his friendly smile again. I didn't return it this time, but he went on anyway. "I need your help, Alex. I need an investigator who isn't afraid of shadows. I hear you did some work for Madame Cuapa a couple of months ago. I'm impressed! That couldn't have been easy."

He was right about that. Madame Cuapa, known as the Barbary Coast Bruja, was the most powerful witch in western Tolanica. Working for her had almost finished me for keeps. In fact, the Madame herself had tried to kill me on two different occasions. It was the only time that one of my own clients had tried to knock me off in the middle of a case. The Madame hadn't been in control of herself either time, and she had pulled me back from the edge of death the second time she'd attempted to do me in. Sometimes when I'm thinking about it late at night, I suspect that I actually *did* die after that second curse, and that the witch brought me back to life. I was grateful for that. I hadn't much cared for the dark place I'd been headed for.

After a pause, I said, "The Madame is…interesting. I guess I shouldn't be surprised that you know I was involved in that case."

Fulton shifted to his tight, professional smile. "Not much goes on in this town that I don't find out about."

I nodded. "From what I hear, Larry, not much happens in this town that you don't *want* to happen."

Fulton sighed. "If only that were true. If you ever had to spend much time with our mayor...." He shook his head. "You have no idea how fragile the bonds are that hold this city together, or how close it's all come to falling apart. The mayor is a fucking bull in a glass factory. And that's where I come in. I try to keep the glass from shattering, and I put the pieces back together again when it does."

"Why do you let him roam around the glass factory in the first place?" I asked.

Fulton shrugged. "That's what he pays me for."

I nodded. Say what you want about Fulton. A local journalist had once referred to him as a spider lurking beneath the mayor's throne in the center of a web that stretched through every district of the city. When he spoke, you listened. When he snapped his fingers, you came running. The fact that I was there sitting in his office instead of home sleeping off a drunk testified to that. If you called him a ruthless cold-hearted son of a bitch with the morals of a tiger shark, he'd be the first to agree with you. But the way I saw it Fulton was neither good nor evil. Bottom line? He was a willing and capable operator doing a dirty job. When you put him on your payroll, he gave all of what passed for his heart and soul into getting the job done, no matter how unseemly or downright messy that job might be. Someone once told me that he'd punch his own mother's ticket if she was standing in his way. When it came right down to it, you couldn't ask much more from a man than that.

"You say you need my help?" I prodded.

Fulton straightened himself and walked around his desk to a high-backed leather rolling chair. He sat down, opened a drawer, and pulled out a manila folder, which he placed unopened on his desktop. Locking his eyes with mine, he asked, "What do you know about the Sihuanaba?"

Something that felt like an electric current ran up the back of my neck to the top of my head and shook the last vestiges of the avalonian from my brain. I was wide awake now, all systems firing. "The Sihuanaba? I know enough about her to keep my distance."

Fulton's dark intense eyes were still locked with mine. "Go on," he prompted.

I looked away from Fulton and considered my response. "I heard stories when I was in the Borderland."

"Did you ever see her?"

My throat suddenly seemed to be dry as chalk. "I'm still alive, aren't I?"

Fulton leaned back into his desk chair and stared at the unopened manila folder for a few seconds as he considered my answer. Then he blinked and looked up with a smile. "Where are my manners? Would either of you like a cigarette? Gordon?"

"Sure Mr. Fulton." The bruiser had been silent up till now, and I'd almost forgotten he was there.

"Thanks anyway," I said. I was aware that every muscle in my body had grown tense. I let my forearms rest on the arms of my chair, crossed my feet at the ankles, and made a conscious effort to relax, starting with the arches of my feet and working my way up, one muscle at a time.

"That's right," said Fulton, opening a polished wooden cigarette box on his desktop. "You don't smoke, do you Alex."

"I hear it stunts your growth," I said.

"I thought that was supposed to be coffee."

"I might have got it mixed up. Mind if I take off my coat? I get the feeling we may be here for a while." Fulton grunted at me, and, taking that for an affirmative, I stood up and pulled off my overcoat. After hanging the coat over the back of my chair, I sat down again and waited while Fulton and Gordon jolted their systems with nicotine.

After he was re-settled in his desk chair, Fulton got back to business. "Tell me about the Sihuanaba."

I made a show of appearing to think about the question while I focused on tightening and relaxing individual muscles, one at a time, and keeping myself calm. "I can only tell you what I've heard. The men in the Borderland get drunk and scare each other with stories about the 'woman in white.' They say that she's some sort of avenging angel for wronged women. She supposedly takes on the form of a beautiful woman and lures wayward men to their deaths. According to the stories, no one who sees her face lives to tell the tale." I shrugged, releasing tension from my shoulders. "It sounds like a lot of hooey to me. I mean, if she doesn't ever leave any witnesses, then how do we know she's real? It's likely just a folk tale. But they take her pretty seriously down there."

Fulton placed his unfinished cigarette in an ashtray on his desk, leaving it to smolder. "You were in the Borderland about ten years ago, right?"

I nodded. "Yes sir. Fighting Lord Ketz-Alkwat's war against Lord Manqu's Qusco insurgents."

"Two-year stint in-country? With the twenty-seventh infantry?"

"Yep."

"You spent a lot of time with the natives?"

"When I wasn't fighting, sure. A lot of good beer in the bars of Zaculeu."

Fulton flashed an easy smile. "I was there about ten years before you. The beer was good then, too."

"That war just goes on and on, doesn't it." I loosened the knot of my tie. The air in Fulton's office had become stifling. It was as if my memories of the Borderland were drawing some of its tropical heat into the room. Or maybe it was just the cigarette smoke.

Fulton opened the manila folder. "Do you remember a man named Kaabiil? Maybe you knew him as 'Cable.' I believe that the men in the twenty-seventh used to drink at a bar he ran in Zaculeu near your base. A hole in the wall called The Silver Mine."

My temples began to pound and a roar filled my ears as blood poured through my head, bringing buried memories along for the ride. "That was a long time ago." I drew in a slow, measured breath. "And another world. I don't think a lot about those days anymore."

"But you remember Cable, don't you," Fulton persisted. "Nice likeable fellow, they say. From what I hear, he was sort of a favorite uncle to the boys of the twenty-seventh. Always good for a laugh. But he had a thing for the ladies. A real skirt-chaser. Had a pretty little wife back home, too, but I guess he couldn't help himself."

"I remember Cable," I said, feeling chill bumps forming on my forearms at the memory. I tensed my arm muscles for five seconds, and then let the tension flow away with a slow exhale.

Fulton continued as if I hadn't spoken. "And then one morning his broken body was found lying on the sidewalk outside an old rundown four-story apartment building. Four stories may not sound like much, but statistics show that a fall from a four-story height—roughly forty-eight feet—has a fifty-fifty chance of being fatal. According to the reports, Cable broke his neck when he hit the sidewalk and died on impact. No one knew for sure what he'd been doing in the building. He didn't live there. But, given his lecherous habits, it was assumed that he was there because of a lady. Maybe this lady pushed him out an open window. But who knows? Maybe there was no lady. Maybe he climbed to the roof and jumped. The police wrote it off as an accident. But the locals all insisted that Cable had been lured into the building by the Sihuanaba. He chased after one woman too many, they said, and she punished him for his transgressions."

"Well, you know how people talk."

Fulton turned over a sheet of paper in the folder. He looked up and met my eyes again. "After the incident, a Sergeant Alexander Southerland from the twenty-seventh infantry was questioned by the local police. According to them, he was the last person to see Cable alive. Is that true?"

"Could be," I said, keeping my voice steady. "I'm not sure. If he was pushed out of a window, then no. If he had an accident, or jumped, then, yeah, maybe."

Fulton nodded. "And did you see anything else the night he died? Anything out of the ordinary?"

I drew in a breath and smiled. My military training had given me a number of skills, and not all of them were related to killing. Secretive men from government agencies I hadn't known existed and still can't identify had taught me how to stand up to questioning by enemy interrogators. It had proven to be a useful skill even after I completed my military obligation. I still practiced the breathing and relaxation techniques that I'd learned back then. So when Fulton asked me what I had seen the night Cable had been murdered by the dark-haired woman in the white dress, I was able to meet Fulton's icy cold stare and state with complete and total conviction, "No, Larry. I didn't see a thing."

Fulton held my eyes for several long moments. "I see," he said at last. Then he looked back down at the folder. "And what would you think, Alex...." He raised his eyes back up from the folder. "What would you think if I told you that the woman in white—the Sihuanaba—has come here to Yerba City?"

Chapter Two

"Well, Larry," I said. "If that's not a hypothetical question, then I'd say you married men ought to be minding your 'P's and 'Q's."

Fulton made a grunting sound that was not quite a laugh. He reached into the manila folder and drew out a printout of a photograph. He turned it around and pushed it toward my side of the desk. I pulled my armchair up close to the desk and leaned forward to get a good look at the photo. It had been taken at night, probably from a cell phone with a dual-LED flash. The details were hard to make out, but the photo showed the shore of a lake from maybe thirty or so yards away. A full moon hung low in a clear sky, and in the moon's light I could just make out the suggestion of a human figure dressed in what might have been a white dress or robe.

I looked up from the photo. "Really?"

Fulton nodded toward the bruiser. "Gordon took this picture last night on his phone. I know that it's not much by itself, but it's only part of the story." Fulton lifted his cigarette out of the ashtray. It had gone out, and he took the time to relight. Once he had the pill fired up, the mayor's right-hand man began to tell me why he'd had me plucked off the street in the dead of night and brought to his office.

"As I'm sure you're aware, this is an election year," Fulton began. "Mayor Teague is seeking his third term, and he's heavily favored to win. His victory would be good for the city, and it would be good for me, which, if we're being honest, is what concerns me most. It's not that Teague is anything special. If you want to know the truth, he's a pompous, self-righteous prick with the intelligence of a turnip and the libido of a jackrabbit. But he's got a handsome face, a powerful speaking voice, and enough spark to light up a ball park. People *like* the son of a bitch! He makes them feel good, no matter how little he actually cares about their problems and no matter how incapable he is of doing anything about them. His one saving grace is that he has no illusions about himself. He knows that when it comes to actually governing this city he's in way over his head. But he likes appearing in public and seeing his handsome face in the newspapers and on television, and he's more than happy to hand the responsibility of running the city to people who are smarter than he is. He lets them make all the decisions, and, for the most part, he does what he's told. He's willing, in short, to be the face and the voice of the mayor's office, while leaving others to do all the important work behind the scenes. And it works! He makes an appearance here, gives a carefully prepared speech there, and the people in the shadows keep the city running."

"And you are one of those shadow people, right?"

"Of course! But I'm not one of the policy makers. Policy doesn't interest me. It's all bullshit. Lord Ketz has his LIA agents planted in City Hall, and nothing happens without their approval. The real job of the mayor's office is to give the people of this city the illusion that one of their own is watching out for them and keeping them safe. Oh, we handle the everyday piddly shit on our own, but all the *important* decisions come from the Dragon Lord's stronghold in Aztlan. Problem is, Lord Ketz is too remote for the average citizen. Have you ever seen the mighty Lord Ketz-Alkwat up close and in person? Of course not. Neither have I. Nor would we want to. We ordinary citizens are beneath his notice, and we know it. He'll do the occasional flyover, just to remind us that he's there, and that he's a hundred feet of immortal fire-breathing awesomeness, but that's it. When we need something fixed, we don't call on *him*. He's got bigger fish to fry than anything we could possibly toss his way. So we need *local* authorities, people we can relate to. People with firm square jaws who will look us in the face with concerned eyes and at least pretend to listen to us. People like Mayor Teague."

It was a nice speech, but Fulton wasn't telling me anything I didn't already know. "I hope you're going somewhere with all this, Larry," I said. "If all you wanted was my vote, you could have mailed me a flyer."

"I'm getting to it." Fulton picked up his half-smoked cigarette, but it had gone out again. He crushed it into his ashtray rather than relight it. Then he sat back in his chair and continued his speech. "My job consists of keeping the mayor from fucking up his life so that he can continue to be reelected, and, believe me, he doesn't make it easy. The core of his appeal is that he is the embodiment of the Tolanican Dream. He's a sharp-dressed golden boy with chiseled features and shiny toys. He's got a smart, attractive wife who dedicates her life to him. He has two charming children studying at top universities so that they can keep his legacy alive. He's the very image of success and personal fulfillment."

Fulton let out a contemptuous chuckle. "But there's the rub," he continued. "It's that *image* that the people are voting for. If the image falls apart, and the good citizens of Yerba City ever get a good look at the man himself, they'll kick him to the curb and move along to the next guy in a flash. The opposition has a strong candidate this time around: Montavious Harvey. He's a respected businessman who's made a fortune in commercial real estate, and he's got a thick head of white hair, hard brown eyes, and a serious face that makes people want to trust him with their life savings. Unlike our boy, Harvey's got a sharp mind. He doesn't just speak in generalities; he gets to the heart of issues, and he calls up supporting statistics with the precision of a computer. He comes across as a man of substance, whereas our boy, as I said, is all image. It's a great image. People love it, and they'll vote for it, no matter how competent Harvey seems. But if you look at it too close, you realize that it's all smoke and mirrors. It's my job to make sure that no one looks too close. Keeping that image intact is a *bitch*! No matter how much I do to keep him clean, our golden boy insists on jumping into a pool of shit every single day. And then I have to scrape the shit off his face and clean him up for public consumption before he goes and dives right back in." Fulton shook his head. Then he leaned forward and met my eyes with his piercing stare. "And this time, Alex, he's in the deep end of the shit-pool, way over his head. And I need you to help dig him out."

I didn't say anything. I didn't have any interest in helping the mayor's fixer with his dirty work. I'd never voted for his boss. Hell, I'd never voted! What was the point? Powerful people were going to do what they do, and, as Fulton had noted, the Dragon Lords had been running everything since they emerged from Hell thousands of years before I was born. The world was what it was, and I wasn't going to change it with a vote. I considered getting up and leaving Fulton to his troubles. He'd sent his trolls home, and I didn't think that he would order his bruiser to stop me from walking away. I was certain that he could find some other sap in his contact files who'd be more willing to help him out with his phony golden boy than I was. Nuts to the whole thing! I was indifferent, tired, and due for a massive hangover, and a warm bed was waiting for me at my apartment.

But I didn't leave. The truth was that Fulton had grabbed my attention the moment he mentioned the Sihuanaba. At some point he was going to tell me what the Sihuanaba had to do with Teague, and I wanted to hear about it. Whether I liked it or not, I knew that I was hooked.

Fulton seemed satisfied enough with my silence to continue his story. "This past Sunday afternoon, Teague called me at home. He was as excited as a fox in a hen house. He told me that he'd taken his wife to the Country Club for a Saturday evening dinner, and that when he was leaving the restaurant he saw this gorgeous dame standing just outside. He only got a side view of her, so he didn't get a good look at her face, but he said that she had long wavy black hair and that her body was so sexy it brought tears to his eyes. She was wearing a slinky white dress that, as he put it, made him want to rip it off her skin with his teeth. According to him, the woman gave him a subtle little sidelong glance and slowly ran her hand over her hip and down her thigh in a way that convinced him she was sending him an invitation. Then she turned and gave him a good look at her ass as she slowly walked away. He told me that he couldn't do anything with his wife around, but that he wanted me to track this mystery woman down and set up a meeting."

"Our mayor's quite the boy."

Fulton grunted. "I told the mayor that I had better things to do than hunt down every pretty twist that caught his eye. He had to give an important press briefing in the morning and I told him to get on with his preparations." Fulton paused to collect his thoughts before continuing. "Then on Monday morning, Teague was waiting for me in my office when I got to work. He'd seen the woman again, but this time he'd been looking out his living room window and she'd been standing in the street in front of his house. The wind was blowing her hair around, so he still couldn't get a good look at her face, but he says that she was wearing the same slinky white dress that she'd worn the night before, and that there was no mistaking the curves that filled it out in all the right places. When she saw him staring through the window at her she waved for him to come outside. But his wife came down the stairs, and he closed the curtains so that she wouldn't see the doxy in the street. By the time he looked out the window again, the doxy was gone."

Fulton shifted in his seat. "I thought we might have a stalker on our hands, so I told Gordon here to put his team together and keep an eye out. This was Monday. The day before yesterday, I guess, since it's past midnight now. Anyway, Gordon and his team stayed with the mayor all day. That evening, the mayor went out to the Country Club for a few drinks with some campaign contributors. Just a social thing, nothing formal. Gordon drove Teague to the club himself, and then drove him home at about two in the morning. He let the mayor out of the car at his house and then took up a post down the street to watch the premises until his backup arrived. The mayor was home for no more than two minutes when Gordon sees him come out his front door and head up the street toward the lake."

I interrupted. "What lake would this be?"

"Huh? Oh, sorry," said Fulton, waving a hand in the air. "Ohlone Lake. The mayor lives in the Galindo District up by the lake when he's not staying in his downtown apartment. Nice area!"

That was an understatement. Galindo was an upscale district in the southwest part of the city, and I knew it only by its reputation. Common working-class stiffs like me weren't welcome there, and I'd never set foot in it. The district's main hub consisted of a gated and guarded residential community inhabited by Yerba City's upper crust, the exclusive Galindo Downs Country Club featuring fifty-four holes of world-class golf, and the private Ohlone Lake, available only to the members of the club.

"The Country Club you've been talking about is the Galindo Downs?"

"Yeah, that's right."

I nodded at Fulton to continue. He, in turn, nodded at the bruiser. "Gordon, tell Mr. Southerland what happened next."

"Sure, Mr. Fulton." Gordon shifted in his seat so that he was facing me. "I followed the mayor on foot, staying close but hanging back to see what he was up to. Mr. Teague walked to the end of the street, hopped the fence, and kept on going right out to the lake. I followed close behind. When I got near the lake, I saw a good-looking dark-haired dame in a white dress waiting for Mr. Teague. Mr. Teague approached her, and when he got close, she raised her arm toward him. Mr. Teague dropped to his knees, and I thought that the woman might have a gat, so I drew my own heater and shouted, 'Freeze, lady!'"

Gordon mimed pointing his handgun at me with a two-handed grip. "She totally ignored me. Didn't even turn her head. But as I got closer I could see that she wasn't holding a weapon after all. I felt silly pointing my piece at an unarmed frail, so I put my rod in my holster and pulled out my phone."

I studied the picture again. I hadn't noticed before, but now that I was looking for it I could see that the white blur was pointing downward

16

at an indistinct blob that *might* have been a crouching man-sized figure. Or it could have been a boulder, or a bush. Even with the flash and the full moon, the image was too dark and too indistinct to make out anything for certain.

After I leaned back in my seat, Gordon continued. "It was dark, but the moon was bright enough to give me a good look at the woman's hand poking out from the sleeve of her dress. It was weird looking, thin and bony, and there was this claw at the end of her finger that had to be two inches long. Her hair was blowing in the wind, so I couldn't get a good look at her face. But I could see her open her mouth, real wide, like a snake about to gulp down a rat. It looked to me like she was screaming bloody murder, and the mayor was laying on the ground with his hands over his ears, like he couldn't stand it." He shook his head. "But I couldn't hear a thing. Not a damned thing."

After a long pause, I asked, "What did you do?"

Gordon frowned. "I aimed my phone and took the picture. When I looked again, the woman was gone. One second the dame is standing there, pointing at the mayor with that claw, her mouth open, screaming a scream I can't hear…. And the next second—" He snapped his fingers in the air. "She's just gone! Damnedest fuckin' thing I ever saw. I reached the mayor and helped him up out of the mud. He was crying like a baby. And one other thing. He had a stream of blood coming out of his ears. Both of them. I figured that I couldn't take him home in that condition, so I cleaned him up best I could with my handkerchief and called Mr. Fulton."

Fulton picked up his cue. "And I had Gordon bring the mayor straight to his downtown apartment."

I sat back and considered the bruiser's story. I had no reason to doubt any of it, and plenty of reasons to believe that I was getting the straight scoop. "Is the mayor still in his apartment?" I asked Fulton.

"Yes, he's been there all day," Fulton said. "I've got a couple of people with him to make sure there's no trouble. But the man is a mess! I was waiting at the apartment when Gordon brought him in, and right off he starts babbling at me. He told me that he'd seen the lady standing outside the club that night. She was facing away from him, but he knew that body, and she was still wearing the same white dress. When he got a chance, he went out to talk to her. She didn't turn around as he approached, but I guess she knew that he was there. Teague says that she asked him to meet her at the lake later that night. She told him where she'd be waiting for him, and then she walked away. After Teague went home, he checked on his wife, who was sleeping. So he snuck out and went to go meet the lady."

Fulton paused then. He started to open his cigarette box, but then thought better of it. I guess he didn't need one, or maybe, knowing that I didn't indulge, he was trying to be polite. He turned back to me and said, "I'm not sure what happened after that. Teague was incoherent. He kept muttering a bunch of hooey about angry women and how sorry he was. And something about a horsehead skull." Fulton shook his head. "Don't ask. Oh, and a bunch of gibberish about screams that he couldn't hear. I don't know what our boy has got himself into, but I've never seen him so skittish. The whole time I was talking to him, he was shaking like a leaf."

My heart pounded, and I could feel the hairs rising on the back of my neck, but I forced my breath to stay even. "Horse skulls? Screams that he couldn't hear? Sounds pretty melodramatic."

Fulton shook his head. "He was extremely agitated. I was afraid that he was going to have a heart attack or a stroke or something! I gave him some pills to calm him down and get him to sleep. We've cancelled his meetings for the next couple of days, but this bullshit has to stop! We've got to prop him back up and put a smile on his face so that business can go on as usual. I just hope that it's not too late. It's a good thing Gordon showed up before things got too out of hand."

I nodded. "So where do I fit in?"

"After Teague was asleep, I did some research. Something about Teague's ravings rang a bell. That whole thing about a ghostly woman in white who teases and terrorizes men seemed familiar to me. I searched online for information that fit the pattern. When I ran across a reference to the Sihuanaba, it clicked. I'd heard something about the Sihuanaba during my own tour of the Borderland, but I didn't know much about her. I never paid the stories much attention. So I learned what I could on the internet, and then I did some digging in my own files, looking for data on the woman in white. After several hours of searching, I came across a copy of a newspaper article about a bar owner in Zaculeu called Cable who some people claimed had been killed by the Sihuanaba. It was an intriguing story. Imagine my surprise when I ran across your name."

My plush seat suddenly seemed as comfortable as an electric chair. "Those are some impressive files."

Fulton laughed. "You can't begin to imagine. Anyway, I'd like to hire you to check out this broad in the white dress. She's probably just some twist with a grudge against our mayor. There's plenty of them out there. Maybe she's a loony. I think that the whole thing could be some kind of hoax. Most likely, she's a plant from Harvey's people. But in the unlikely event that she's really the Sihuanaba, I want to know about it."

I lifted a hand to indicate the bruiser sitting next to me. "Why me? Why not Gordon here? Seems he's already on it."

"I want you to work with Gordon. Like I said, the woman is probably nothing worse than a crazy stalker, but when it comes to the mayor I don't take chances. Maybe we've got ourselves a genuine 'avenging angel,' as you put it. The Sihuanaba, or something like her. I need a little extra perspective to handle something like that. And, besides…." Fulton narrowed his eyes at me. "I think that you have more experience with the Sihuanaba than you're letting on." I started to object, but Fulton plowed right over it. "That's okay. Keep your secrets. Let's just say that I think you're the right joe for this job."

I made a show of stalling. "What specifically would you want me to do?"

"For now I want you to go home and get some shuteye. Sleep as long as you need to. I want you outside the mayor's house at five p.m. sharp. The mayor will be home with his wife by then. Meet up with Gordon when you get there and go with him to check out the lake area where Teague saw the woman. See if there's anything to find, anything we might have missed. When it gets dark, I want you and Gordon's team to sit outside the house and do some surveillance. Keep watch all night if that's what it takes. If the woman shows up, or the mayor leaves his house, then do what you need to do in order to put a full stop to this nonsense before it can hit the media and become a story. I want this shit stopped and buried before Harvey hears about it, if it's not already too late."

"I see. And what's in it for me?"

Fulton's lips parted in a smile that didn't extend past his jawline. "You'll get half your standard rates plus approved expenses."

I returned Fulton's smile with one of my own. "You offered me a lot more the last time you wanted me to work for you."

"That was a one-time offer. And you turned it down."

"And what makes you think I'd work for you now, especially at half price?"

"Because, like I told you when you first walked in, you owe me."

I made to get up to leave. "I don't see it that way, Larry."

"Sit down and relax, Southerland!" Fulton's tone was icy. "There's another part to this story, and you need to hear it."

I hesitated, let loose an exasperated sigh, and leaned back into my chair. "Okay, spill."

Fulton took the time to light another pill for himself. I guess he needed one after all. He offered one to Gordon, who took it and fired it up. Fulton blew out some smoke and waved it away from me, which I thought was a classy gesture on his part. Futile, maybe, but considerate. "Are you familiar with a nightclub singer called Zyanya?"

"Of course!" I said. "Do you think I live in a cave? She was a cute little canary. Sweet voice. I saw her a couple of times at the Gold Coast Club about two years ago when she was just getting started there, back before she got so popular that I couldn't afford the price of admission to her shows anymore. She died way too young. Tough break."

Fulton reached into his manila folder and drew out a sheet of paper. He laid it on the desk for me to see. It was an advertising flyer for the Gold Coast Club featuring a photo of Zyanya singing on a stage in front of a seven-piece band. A spotlight highlighted the singer, who was wearing a tight-fitting gossamer gown that displayed the soft curves of her hips and breasts. She held the mike stand close to her body with both hands, lips open and almost touching the padded microphone as she crooned some sad torch song. Her signature violet eyes sparkled in the light as she scanned the couples hugging each other on the dance floor, swaying back and forth just enough to convince themselves that they were dancing. It was a nice photo, and it hinted at the singer's incredible appeal, but no photo could capture the burning radiance of Zyanya when she was performing live. Each time I'd seen her, it had seemed to me that she was suppressing an inner fire that, if uncontained, would vaporize a city block. The entire city had been stunned by her sudden and premature death.

I looked up from the photo. "Yeah, that's her. So?"

Fulton drew out another photo. It was also a picture of Zyanya, but this one had been taken by a police photographer. Zyanya was lying on her back on ground that appeared to be wet. Her violet eyes were open, but dull, and her lips sagged in the way lips do when their facial muscles are no longer working. Her dark hair was wet and splayed about her head.

A blanket covered most of her body, but I could see that she was wearing a light blue blouse, and it appeared to be soaked.

"She was found floating just off the shore at Ohlone Lake two months ago. Just up the shore, as it happens, from where Gordon took that photo of Teague and the woman in white. According to the coroner's report, she drowned. The water in her lungs matched the water in the lake. Officially, her death has been ruled an accident."

I waited. Fulton had more to tell me, but he was taking his time, asserting his authority by controlling the room. It was something he did without thinking about it. After leaving me hanging for another handful of moments, the fixer reached back into the folder and pulled out another photo. This one showed the bodies of two children, a boy and a girl. The oldest one—the boy--looked to me to be no older than three, but I couldn't be sure. I don't have a lot of experience with children. The two toddlers were lying face up with eyes closed. Like Zyanya, their hair and clothes were drenched.

"These are Zyanya's two children. Their bodies were found near hers. Details about their deaths have not been released to the public. Not many people knew about them." Fulton paused to pull some smoke from his cigarette. "Even fewer people knew that Darnell Teague was their father."

I stopped staring at the photos and sat back in my chair. "Let me guess. Accidental deaths?"

Fulton nodded. "Officially."

"And unofficially?"

Fulton put his cigarette on his lip and let it hang there. "Bruises on the kids suggest that they were held under the water until they drowned. Scratches on Zyanya's arms suggest that at least one of the kids put up a fight as she held them under."

I considered Fulton's words for a few moments. "You thinking that Zyanya murdered her children and then killed herself?"

Fulton smiled. "Looks that way, doesn't it." He laid his cigarette in the ashtray and watched a thin wisp of smoke rise from the tip. It swirled a bit and merged with the dim gray fog that filled the room. "Teague met Zyanya about a year after he was elected to his first term," the fixer said. "He saw her singing one night in a little bar downtown and invited her over for a drink. She was Jenny Hermosa back then. One thing led to another, and they developed a relationship. Teague's the one who gave her the name 'Zyanya,' which is the Nahuatl word for 'forever.' Very romantic. He's also the one who got her started at the Gold Coast and engineered her rise to stardom. Along the way, she gave birth to the two kids."

"Does his wife have any idea about Teague and Zyanya?" I asked.

"She knew all about it. It's been my job to deal with that." Fulton's pained expression showed me how difficult that little chore had been. He shrugged it off and continued. "A few other people know, too, but not many, and I've managed to keep the relationship under wraps. But you can't keep something like that secret for long. For years I've been trying to convince Teague that his thing with Zyanya was political suicide. Finally, about a month ago, Teague broke it off with Zyanya. I'd like to take credit for that, but it was Teague's own idea. Frankly, I'm surprised that he stayed with her as long as he did. He worked harder to maintain two separate households for the better part of five years than he ever did trying to run this city. In the end I think he just got tired of all the responsibility. She was a gorgeous doll, but she was what you'd call 'high maintenance.' And he wasn't any more faithful to Zyanya than he'd been to his wife. The canary was a hot-blooded broad, and the two of them fought like crazy. Teague eventually got fed up." Fulton's lips curled into a half smile. "Zyanya was not pleased about being tossed aside. She refused to accept it. Success had turned her into quite the little princess, and she had a drug habit that made her even more difficult to deal with. She also had a violent temper. I have no doubt that she killed the kids and herself to get back at Teague."

"Pretty extreme, even for a jilted lover," I said.

"True, but it fits her character, especially when you factor in her increased drug use. She was out of control toward the end."

I nodded, but I felt like I was still missing some larger point. "Okay, that's a tragic story, and I can't say that I'm not moved by it, but what's all this got to do with why I'm here and not home stacking up 'z's? Is there some connection to the Sihuanaba that I'm missing here?"

Fulton put his elbows on the desktop and folded his hands in front of his chest. "You're a smart boy, Alex. Think about the optics. You'll get it."

"Oh, I get it just fine. The Sihuanaba isn't that well-known up here in Yerba City, but she's a familiar figure in the Borderland. Everyone there grew up hearing stories about her, so she's part of the culture. And every year, more men from up here are coming back from the Borderland, and most of them are at least aware of the stories. There's also a sizable number of people moving north from the Borderland to the provinces to escape the violence. Mostly to northern Azteca and Texas, but a good number of them are winding up here in Caychan, and Yerba City has received a good number of these refugees. The story of the Sihuanaba is coming up here with them. If it gets out that the mayor is being stalked by a ghostly woman in white, some bright boy will make the connection. It's not much of a secret that the mayor is a womanizer, and if it gets out that he had a second family that he was keeping under wraps, then a lot of people are going to put two and two together and conclude that your boy is being stalked by a monster who punishes shitheels who cheat on their wives and girlfriends."

Fulton nodded. "You see the problem here. It's a real bad look. When Harvey's people get their hands on this stuff, they'll use it to shatter Teague's 'golden boy' image. They'll spin it so that Teague comes off as a debaucher of women who's getting what's coming to him. They'll point to the Sihuanaba as proof of the mayor's true character. They'll re-brand him as a bigamist! That's a tough label to overcome. The fickle citizens of this city will leap off his bandwagon like rats abandoning a sinking ship. Harvey will become the new face of Yerba City, and I'll be out of a job."

"I'm sure you'll land on your feet."

Fulton spread his arms wide and smiled. "I'm comfortable here. I've got the office broken in just the way I like it. It'd be a shame to have to uproot myself and start over somewhere else."

"Yeah, I can see how that would be inconvenient for you." I stared at Fulton, and kept staring until Fulton got irritated.

Fulton held up his palms. "What?"

"I don't know, Larry. It doesn't add up. I get the feeling that you're holding something back."

Fulton chuckled without humor. "You're a suspicious bastard, Southerland."

"I wouldn't know. But a suspicious bastard might be a little curious about the death of that nightclub singer. Seems pretty convenient that she removed herself from the picture during an election year just when she might have been in a mood to give your hotshot loverboy some trouble. In fact, it sounds like a problem that the mayor's fixer might have wanted to take care of personally."

Fulton glared at me with his ice-cold eyes. "And the children? You think I might have had something to do with that, too? I know what people say about me, and, hell, most of it is true. But killing innocent children? You really believe I would do that?"

I shrugged. "You or the mayor himself. And either way the truth would need to be buried, wouldn't it."

Fulton glared at me some more and then glanced down at the desk. He let out a breath. "Trust me, I'm clever enough to figure out some other way. But that's the problem. It took you less than five minutes to cook up a couple of conspiracy theories concerning Zyanya's death. What do you think would happen if the media ran with the story of the relationship between her and Teague? What do you think Harvey's people would do with the sort of baseless speculation that you're suggesting? That's why it's got to be stopped in its tracks."

"Sounds like you've got a problem all right," I put my feet under me and prepared to rise out of my seat. "Good luck with it. It's too bad you can't afford my fee. I don't have my car here. Are you planning on having someone drive me home?"

Fulton didn't smile. He didn't call for a driver, either. Instead, he reached back into the manila folder and pulled out another photo. I wondered how many he had in that folder. He placed the photo next to the others. It showed the dead body of Zyanya sprawled in the sand, but in this photo the body was not covered by a blanket, and I could see that a dark bloodstain covered her blouse over her heart.

I jerked my head up to face Fulton. "She was shot?"

Fulton nodded. "In the heart. With a thirty-eight. We released the other photo to the media."

"What are the chances she shot herself?" I asked.

Fulton shook his head. "None."

"Do you know who shot her?"

Fulton smiled, but his eyes seemed sad. "I know a lot of things." He reached into the manila folder and pulled out one last photograph. He glanced at it briefly, then slid it toward me on the desktop. I leaned in to look at it. It was a picture of a thirty-eight caliber handgun. I recognized it immediately. The security guard at the front entrance had taken it from me the last time I had come to City Hall. Fulton had threatened to use it to frame me for the murder of a young adaro woman. It hadn't come to anything at the time, but I could see where this was going.

I slid the photo back toward Fulton. "You've got to be kidding me, Larry."

Fulton's lips stretched into a predatory smile, exposing a mouthful of teeth. "It's no joke, Alex. The details concerning Zyanya's death have never been released. As far as the general public knows, she drowned her children and then drowned herself. Only a handful of people know that someone shot her, and all of them are beholden to me. As far as the rest of it, who can say? Could be that she was shot by this very firearm, which is still registered to one 'Alexander Southerland.' Your fingerprints are all over it."

"And why would I have any motive to shoot Zyanya?"

Fulton shrugged. "I don't know yet. I'm sure that I'll come up with something. What's important is that if Harvey or anyone else were to try to pin Zyanya's murder on Teague, or me, or anyone else connected with the mayor's campaign, I've got a reasonable and persuasive alternative."

"You'd make me the fall guy."

"Not if I don't have to. But the important point is that I could. And I could make it stick."

I pointed at the photo. "You know, I reported that gun as stolen."

"Three times!" Fulton beamed. "Very thorough of you!"

A hollow pit grew in my stomach. I *had* sent in three different reports, each one several months apart. I'd hoped that at least one of them would slip past Fulton. I should have known better. Fulton had his fingers all over the Yerba City Police Department. He'd probably had the reports of my stolen firearm shredded minutes after I'd submitted them. As far as the YCPD was concerned, that heater was still in my possession. If Fulton gave the word, a bullet from that gun would be found that matched the hole in Zyanya's chest. My case wouldn't even make it to trial. Even with a good lawyer I'd disappear or turn up dead before I got the chance to tell my side of the story.

I sighed. "I get the picture. And it was never necessary. I was going to take your damned case. But half my fees? Come on! I'm trying to make a living."

"You'd be living in luxury if you'd taken my check a year ago."

"That's a long time to hold a grudge. Who would've believed you could be that petty."

"Anyone who knows me. It's a definite flaw in my character. I'm working on it. They say that the first step in solving a personal problem is recognizing that you've got one, so I feel that I'm getting there."

"Yeah? Well you've got a ways to go."

Fulton rose from his chair. "Go home, Alex. Rest up. Eat well. You've got a long evening ahead of you."

Chapter Three

Fulton refused to send me home in one of his black sedans. "I don't have anyone available to drive you," he claimed. Instead he called me a cab. He could be sure that I would add the fare to my expense account. In fact, I told the cabbie to double the tab.

It was nearly two in the morning by the time I walked through the front door into my office. I was dead on my feet, but I stumbled across the room to my desk and switched on my computer. When it was ready to go, I double-clicked on the file for my standard contract and typed Fulton's name into the designated space. I left my rates unchanged. If Fulton was really going to insist that I work for half price, then he was going to have to leave the contract unsigned and ask me to send him a new one. Maybe he'd sign this one without reading it, or without knowing how much I usually charged to do a job. Or maybe he was just fucking with me and would wind up paying my standard fare in the end. In any case, I wasn't going to simply roll over and cave in to his demands. I emailed the contract to Fulton and shut down my computer.

I lived and worked in a small two-story stand-alone rental in the economically depressed Porter District just outside of downtown Yerba City, with my apartment on the second floor above my office. My long day done at last, I climbed the stairs that crossed the wall behind my desk. I opened the door at the top of the stairwell and stepped though it into my living room. Before turning in, I chugged some water out of a reasonably clean glass from my kitchen sink in the hopes that it would lessen the hangover that was heading my way as surely as the morning Yerba City fog. After a stop in my bathroom, I slipped into bed, exhausted, and watched the room spin for a few seconds before closing my eyes and letting out a long, slow breath. I was asleep before I'd finished exhaling.

The dream must have started immediately. I saw Cable standing on the other side of his bar. His eyes were wide with fright, and he was trying to tell me something, but I couldn't make out the words. Then his lips stretched over his teeth and he let out a bloodcurdling scream. Suddenly, as it happens in dreams, I was on patrol. A quarter moon cast a dim light through the night, and I could see eyes shining in the brush. My stomach flipped as I realized that I had gone into the jungle without my carbine. I pulled up short when I saw that Cable, no longer screaming, was huddled at my feet. I looked up, and the Sihuanaba stood behind him. She was wearing a long white dress, her arms covered to the wrists with loose-fitting sleeves. Her wild black hair obscured most of her face as she stared down open-mouthed at Cable, who was cowering between us with his hands pressed against his ears, overwhelmed by a sound that I couldn't hear. I realized that we were no longer in the jungle, but on the roof of a building on a moonlit night. I couldn't bring myself to move as the woman reached out with a clawed leathery hand and pointed an accusing finger at Cable. Then she turned her head in my direction, and, knowing what was coming, I tried to wrench my eyes away from her. It was no use....

    I woke up with my heart pounding like a piston in a Formula One racecar. My senses were numb, and my head felt like it was stuffed with cotton. I sat up in my bed, gasping for breath. I was aware of something moist rolling down my neck, and I reached up with both hands to wipe the moisture away. I looked at my hands, already knowing what I was going to find.

    Because of an encounter I'd had with an elf, a creature that most people believed to be extinct, I could "see" in the dark as easily as I could in sunlight. Technically, the elf hadn't altered my vision; rather, as he put it, he had "enhanced my awareness." Afterwards, I became aware of the world around me in some strange way that I didn't understand. My brain didn't understand it, either, so it processed my new awareness as improvements in my familiar senses of sight, hearing, smell, taste, and touch. Among other things, I knew what I was looking at even when it was too dark to actually see it. What I "saw" on my hands at that moment was blood.

    The blood had drained onto my pillow, too. I got out of bed and walked into the bathroom to examine myself in the mirror. Narrow streaks of blood were trickling down my neck and jaws from my ears, but I wasn't too worried about it. One of the benefits of the elf's gift to me was that my body had become much more aware of its own inner workings. What this meant was that I almost never got sick, and my body could heal itself at an accelerated pace. The trickle of blood had already stopped, and after some experimenting I concluded that I hadn't suffered any hearing loss. I cleaned myself up with a wet paper towel and wiped my ear canals out as best as I could with some wadded up toilet paper. After a minute or so, I concluded that I was in no further danger as long as the Sihuanaba didn't enter into my dreams again.

This hadn't been the first time that I'd relived my encounter with the woman in white in my sleep. She'd been a frequent nocturnal visitor over the years. But this was the first time that I'd awakened with blood streaming out of my ears the way it had when I'd first run into her nearly ten years before. I'd hoped that the nightmares would fade over time, but this one had been the worst in years.

Checking the time, I saw that it had only been about fifteen minutes since I had fallen asleep, but I knew that I was done sleeping for the night. I filled my bathroom sink with cold water and added a couple of drops of shampoo. Then I plunged my pillowcase into the water, scrubbing at the fabric with a washcloth in an attempt to remove the blood. After about ten minutes, I was satisfied that the pillowcase was about as clean as it was going to be, and I hung it over my shower curtain rod to dry.

Throwing on a robe, I walked into my living room and sat down in an overstuffed armchair that I'd bought eight years before at a second-hand shop the day I'd moved into my apartment and set up my office. I told myself that, while it might not have cost as much as Fulton's guest chair, it was every bit as comfortable. To me, at least, and that was all that mattered. I used my relaxation techniques to calm my breathing and slow my heartbeat. Using something like hypnosis, my army trainers had taught me to visualize a pleasant and peaceful scene that I could call up in my mind during times of stress. My personal place of peace was a waterfall in the jungle that I'd run into while on patrol in the Borderland. I'd only seen it once, but it had engrained itself in my memory forever. The waterfall wasn't what you would call majestic, and it didn't appear on any of our maps. It was just a narrow stream that fell about twenty feet or so down to the base of a small rocky incline, where the water poured into a dark pool before continuing on its way into the brush. I had seen the fall during a break from a solid week of heavy rains, and I suspected that it was reduced to a trickle most of the year, and maybe even disappeared altogether during the dry months. But I'd been lucky enough to see it at its peak, and I'd spent a solid hour alone listening to the roar of the water and watching the stream roll over the rocky face to disappear into the swirling pool.

I sat in my chair, recalling the image of the waterfall until the last shreds of my dream had drifted away. Then I took a deep breath, cast my memory back to another time and place, and remembered.

***

"You should have seen her face—like an angel!" Cable's lips lifted into a dreamy smile, and his gaze turned inward as he described his latest heartthrob. "So lovely! So beautiful!"

"Right," said Leota, unimpressed. "Just like the last one. And the one before that." He downed a shot and sipped at his beer.

Cable's eyes snapped open. "No, no, my friend! This one was different. Her beauty was like nothing I've ever seen! And such innocence in her eyes! Her body, so, so adorable. Like a painting! Almost too exquisite to touch."

"Uh-huh," I said, laughing. "I bet that didn't stop you from trying, you old goat!"

"Hey, who you calling old, boy?" Cable snorted. "I'm only two years older than you. Three maybe. Four at the most."

"Fu-u-uck," Colby drawled. "You've got a boy nearly our age."

"Yeah, but I've got the body and the face of a young man. And I can tackle more tail in one night than you children could handle in a month!"

"You sure chase it, that's for sure," I said. I swallowed some beer. "I doubt that you catch much, though. You're so full of shit. You do more talking than fucking."

Cable grabbed his heart, like he was having a coronary. "How can you hurt me like that, Southerland! How can you wound me so!"

Leota, Colby, and I shook our heads at Cable's dramatics. The gregarious proprietor was the main reason that we came to The Silver Mine. The beer was strong, cold, and cheap, but nothing we couldn't find in a dozen other bars within easy walking distance. But Cable had a knack for making young soldiers in a foreign land feel like they'd found an exotic second home, at least for a few hours at a stretch. I held on to those hours with Cable like a rock climber hanging on to a ledge with one hand. I needed those hours. In my two years in the Borderland, my hours with Cable at The Silver Mine were the only ones that I remember with any real clarity. The rest is a blur.

Life in the occupied Borderland was a vivid nightmare for us grunts. It was endless days in camp, each one just like the last, bored out of our skulls, sick to death of each other's faces and stories. Time refused to move. We *needed* it to move, and we tried to speed it along by playing cards, rolling dice, and napping whenever possible. Any imagined slight or careless comment found us throwing punches and kicks at each other, or wrestling each other in the dirt, doing our best to beat each other senseless. We couldn't have given you a good reason for it. More often than not we just needed to be doing something to make time pass while we waited to be sent into action. And then the call would come, out of nowhere. Gear up! Report! Prepare to move out! And off we'd go into the jungle, searching for the enemy, trying to kill them before they could kill us. Encounters with the insurgents were frenzied streams of colors, explosions, smoke, shouts, screams, and random motion. When they were over, we'd carry out the wounded, moaning in pain if they were conscious, almost always covered in blood. Sometimes we'd leave pieces of them—arms, hands, legs, feet—behind in the bush. We'd carry out the dead bodies so that they could be counted and shipped home in wooden boxes to be buried or burned. I never could figure out why we couldn't just leave them in the jungle to feed the jaguars, coyotes, vultures, beaver rats, army ants, and worms, or to rot into the soil to fertilize the bushes, vines, and trees. What was the point of hauling them away? The people who lived in those bodies were gone; what they left behind was nothing but weight. After my first couple of battles, I would ask, did we win? I never could tell. Nothing seemed different afterwards, except that the faces around me would change. Eventually, I learned the answer to that question. After I was promoted to sergeant, the fresh recruits under my command would ask me that same question. "Did we win, Sarge? Did we win?" I'd tell them that we lived through it, and that meant we'd won. Survival was victory. Nothing else mattered.

The only escape from the nightmare was The Silver Mine. Clint Colby had been in-country for two months when Joe Leota and I arrived together, green as grass and innocent as newborns. Colby showed us the ropes and escorted us to The Silver Mine, which the twenty-seventh had claimed as turf. He introduced us to the affable Cable, who served as our host and honorary morale officer. Whenever we had permission to leave the base—and more than a few times when we didn't—the three of us hurried off to the little dive bar to get drunk on local brew and enjoy some native hospitality.

The hospitality not only included Cable's amiable congeniality and bullshit stories, but also, from time-to-time, the companionship of a variety of hot-blooded Zaculeu street girls who loved men in uniform and weren't too particular about which of the Dragon Lords they fought for. Some of these gals were more hazardous than the enemy, and stories of naïve soldiers who had wandered off with some sweet thing only to be found the next day drugged, beaten, and robbed, if not worse, were part of in-country culture. But Cable was protective of his boys in the twenty-seventh, and we always looked to him for a knowing nod and smile or a stern shake of the head whenever some doe-eyed honey would hit us up with a "Hello soldier boy—buy me a drink?"

I remembered the time Cable had frowned and stepped out from the bar to drive away a lovely young doll who was giving me the come-on. I'd been a little pissed off.

"What's your problem with her?" I'd asked. Leota and Colby were smirking at me behind their beers, not bothering to hide their amusement at my frustration.

Cable was still staring at the door, as if he wanted to make sure that the doll wasn't coming back. "She's trouble. Trust me."

I didn't want to trust him. I wanted the doll! "What do *you* know about it!"

"I know plenty!" He'd responded. "Some of those women are devils in disguise! I have a nose for it!"

"Fuck your nose, I'm going to go get her." I was half out of my seat.

But Cable had pushed me back into my chair with a strength I wouldn't have guessed he had. "Sit down, you young fool! I'll bring you and your friends another round of beer. On the house."

He'd come back with the beers, including one for himself, and he sat down at the table with us. "Not all women are to be trusted."

Leota had laughed. "Trust isn't exactly what we're looking for."

Cable had slammed his mug on the tabletop, startling the three of us. "You know nothing!" He'd lowered his voice then. "Do you know of the Sihuanaba?"

"Sure," Colby had said. "She's some kind of folk tale they tell around here."

Cable had shaken his head at the three of us. His eyes, usually lively and filled with amusement, were cold. I'd never seen him more serious. "The Sihuanaba is no tall tale, my friends. She's real. Very, *very* real. She seeks out stupid doll-dizzy young men like yourselves, looking for good times. She tells you sweet things, makes sweet, sweet promises. Then she takes you somewhere secret. She turns to kiss you, and you prepare to kiss her. And then you see that her face is ugly—an old hag's face! Dead-looking, horrible, with teeth like a monster's! And she says, 'Do you still think I'm pretty?' And your heart bursts, or you go mad! And you're never seen again. That's the Sihuanaba! She roams the streets at night, always wearing white. That woman who was just in here, she was wearing a white dress. Stay away from women in white, my young friends. They are not who they seem to be."

I remember that I'd shaken my head, still pissed. "That's it? You chased her out of here because she was wearing a white dress? Lots of the women in this town wear white dresses. They can't *all* be this Sihuanaba. And besides, she had a face like an angel's, not like a monster's!"

"I have a feeling about that one. I make it a point to study women. They are my, what do you northerners call it.... My hobby. More than that—my passion!" Cable's tone had become lighter then. "I study women every chance I get. It's research for my passion! Now, please. Drink up, my friends! I'll bring you more when you want it." He'd smiled his charming smile, and everything was okay again. I figured there'd be other dolls.

I'd wanted to write off Cable's Sihuanaba as a local superstition, but it wasn't easy. I asked around and heard more stories about her from some of the seasoned grunts at the base. I discovered that the 'woman in white' was a popular legend in that part of the world. Although the stories varied widely in the details, one common theme ran through them. A beautiful woman dressed in white would lure men into a quiet place and reveal herself to be a monster. She would drive the men insane or kill them. The victims in the stories were always louses who had cheated on their wives or girlfriends. It seemed to me that the stories were spread by women in order to keep their husbands under control. But I'd seen a lot of terrors in the jungles of the Borderland, things I don't like to think about. A demon taking the form of a beautiful dame didn't seem to be out of keeping with the place. But compared to some of the things I'd seen, a vengeful woman in a white dress didn't strike me as much to worry about. It didn't take me long to put the whole incident out of my mind.

The problem with Cable is that he took his "research" too seriously. Though he often bragged that the mother of his children was the most beautiful and devoted wife any man could possibly desire, he couldn't help pursuing other opportunities when they presented themselves, and, as the proprietor of a drinking establishment, they presented themselves with some frequency. His own lurid tales of his carnal feats, always narrated with wild enthusiasm, kept the rest of us well entertained, though the veracity of many of these stories was always suspect, to say the least. Cable was a charming old rogue, no doubt about it, but how many licentious and desirable twin girls with an eye for older men could possibly live in any one city? Still, we had no doubt that he was, as he liked to put it, "a man of much proclivity," and, in the end, his proclivities cost him everything.

It didn't take long for the Borderland to hammer the stuffings out of even the hardest battle-scarred vet. I'd arrived there believing that I was hot shit and that nothing could touch me. I was going to be the baddest motherfucker the insurgents had ever run into. They were going to sit around their fires in the jungle and scare each other with stories of the phantom warrior who cut through their ranks like a machete through the brush. War was going to be fucking glorious, and I was going to be a fucking hero. That all ended when Leota died. His death knocked me off my high horse, but good. My best buddy bought it early at the end of our first month in-country, blown apart by an IED during a routine patrol. Even though I'd seen others die, it wasn't until I saw Leota's leg fly off in one direction and the rest of his body in another that I lost faith in my own invincibility. Until that moment, I'd believed that no matter how much devastation I walked into, I'd somehow make it out okay. After scooping up Leota's remains, I never again went into a battle believing that I would live through it.

Colby and I went through Leota's belongings the day his ticket got punched. Leota was a notorious mooch, and we wanted to make sure that we had a chance to reclaim anything of ours that he had borrowed. At least, that's what we told ourselves. As we were digging through his things, I ran across a necklace that Leota had made by stringing together twenty-one steel-jacketed thirty-caliber shells on a leather thong. Leota had loved that necklace and believed that it was a good-luck charm. I told him that he would have had better luck by loading the rounds into his carbine, but he insisted that as long as he was wearing the necklace, nothing could harm him. Maybe he was right. For some reason, he had left the necklace behind the day he walked into the path of a roadside bomb just as it was detonated. Maybe the necklace would have steered him down a safer path. I kept the necklace and wore it constantly until the day my tour of duty expired and I was rotated out of combat.

The war claimed Colby sometime after Leota. Months after, maybe. I don't know. After Leota, I had stopped counting the days. I didn't see what hit Colby. We'd both been promoted to sergeant, and he had died while leading his unit on a patrol. I was alarmed at how little I was bothered by Colby's death. By then, the Borderland had numbed me to death and suffering. I figured that my own departure was imminent, and that didn't bother me, either.

I'd gone through Colby's gear, too. All I kept was a picture of a smiling teenaged Clint Colby wearing a fedora. The picture was taken by Colby's grandmother. I called on old Mrs. Colby after I'd finished my service. She wound up being a big influence in my post-war life, helping me get into the P.I. business and renting me my apartment and office. She'd also given me Colby's fedora. I kept it in my closet for years, unused, but had put it on some months back when I was trying to conceal my identity. It kind of grew on me, and I started wearing it as a matter of routine. It gave me a link to a more innocent Colby who had been untouched by the tragedy of war, and it hid the increasing number of white hairs that were starting to find a home on my head.

Some uncountable weeks after Colby's death, I wandered into The Silver Mine, alone. By then, the familiar bar was giving me no pleasure. I kept coming anyway, sometimes with one or more of the men from my unit, more often by myself, but more out of habit than for any desire for comfort. Cable's stories no longer titillated me, and he became more of a familiar and reliable presence than a roguish host. All I knew is that when I wasn't drinking in The Silver Mine, I felt like I was standing in a long line leading to the final sentry post, shuffling forward one step at a time, waiting to be processed and admitted to the land of the dead.

When I walked into the bar this time, Cable beamed like a traffic light when he saw me. "Ahhhh, Sergeant Southerland! Just the man I want to see. Sit! Sit! You want a beer, right? And whiskey? I'll bring you a bottle of my best rye! Nothing but the best for you tonight, my friend! Nothing but the best! And no charge—on the house!"

I'd seen this show before. "Let me guess. You met a woman."

"Not a woman—a vision! Truly, she is an angel!" Cable grabbed two bottles of dark ale from beneath the bar and held them up by their necks with one hand. "See? We drink the best tonight!" He pulled a bottle from the shelf and raced around the end of the bar to a table. "Sit! Sit! And I'll tell you about my beauty!"

I plopped into a chair and Cable opened the bottles of ale. He set one bottle in front of me and held the other in the air. "A toast! A toast to beauty, goodness, and passion!"

I picked up the bottle and tilted it in his direction. "Why not? I haven't seen much of that lately."

We each swallowed some of the warm ale, which I had to admit was damned tasty. "All right," I said without much enthusiasm. "Tell me all about her."

"Such a body! Such lovely curves! Breasts like melons!" He cupped his hand like he was weighing a cantaloupe. "And her thighs, firm and smooth, like marble!" With half-closed eyes, he ran his hand down curvy imaginary flesh. "And her hair," he continued. "Dark as a raven's feathers! So thick and full! Like a waterfall!"

"Yeah?" I'd heard all this a thousand times. "And her eyes? Let me guess—dark and sparkly, like black diamonds?"

Cable opened his eyes. "You scoff! You think maybe she's like all the rest. This one is different! I've never seen anything like her!"

It had been a dreary day, and, despite Cable's characteristic enthusiasm, I wasn't in the mood. "What is it with you, Cable? You've got a wife at home who you say is a lovely woman. Don't you love her? You've got two kids, including a boy almost old enough for the army. You've got a good business. I don't get it. Isn't it enough for you? Because I'd trade my life for yours in a heartbeat!"

Cable responded by opening the bottle of whisky. He took a pull and passed me the bottle. His eyes gleamed in the low light of the bar, lit by a row of bare bulbs hanging from the ceiling. He gazed at me and favored me with a serious smile, looking like a worldly uncle instructing his sister's only boy. "You ask if I love my wife. Of course I do! She's the mother of my children, and she's never given me a moment's complaint. Oh, we have our arguments, like all couples, but she knows who I am, the good and the bad, and she loves me anyway. She's my rock! My anchor! When I'm home, I'm hers. But when I'm not at home—then I'm a man of the jungle! And she is not part of that. In the jungle, a man is not the same man as in his home. He is, how do you put it…. He is like a man at the dawn of time! A natural man! And even though we no longer live in the jungle, even here in the city, we are still men of the jungle. And we live by the rules of the jungle. The rules of nature! Do you understand?"

I didn't. It sounded like hogwash to me. "Neither of us lives in a jungle."

Cable grabbed the bottle from my hand and took a deep drink. "You northerners. It's been too long since your fathers saw the jungle. But here in what you call the Borderland, the jungle is always near. We feel it in our bones! We hear its call in our dreams! We know what it means to be a *natural* man! Maybe it's been forgotten up there in the provinces." He slammed the bottle back onto the tabletop.

I picked the bottle off the table and took a swallow. Who was I to tell Cable how to live his life?

Cable took the bottle from me. "But anyway, enough of that." His smile broadened and his eyes lit up. "This angel, she's meeting me tonight! But…." He paused, as if he couldn't think of the words.

"But?" I prodded.

"I am nervous!" Cable sputtered.

"Huh?"

"I mean that I am a little afraid." Cable smiled and looked embarrassed. "My angel, she is so beautiful. But she is a mystery! The first time I saw her, I was closing up the bar. She was standing across the street in the shadows, staring at me. I saw her and waved. She lingered, like she was waiting for me. I thought to myself, 'What a body that one has! Like a goddess!' I started to cross the street, but she moved away. I watched her go around the corner. And then I forgot her."

Cable took another swallow from the bottle. He set the bottle down and wiped his mouth with the back of his hand. "The next night, when I'm closing the bar, I see her again. She is once again across the street, in the shadows. She looks at me and smooths her hands down the sides of her dress, like she is trying to get me excited. And, yes—I get excited! She is so lovely! And she looks so eager! I shout at her: 'Good evening! Are you looking for company on this fine night?' And I bow a little, you know? I give her a smile. I ask her: 'Won't you come over for a drink?' But she laughs, a low, sweet laugh, like little bells. 'Tomorrow,' she says. 'I will come for you tomorrow.' And now tomorrow is tonight!" Cable sat back and rubbed his hands together.

I shrugged. "Okay. Then what do you need *me* for?"

Cable's smile faded. He put his hands on the table and leaned forward. His jaws were tense, and his eyes open wide. "Southerland, my friend. My angel...." He lowered his voice to a near whisper. "She wears white!"

I stared at Cable for what must have been a dozen heartbeats. And then I burst out laughing. I couldn't help it. I laughed and tears came to my eyes. I couldn't remember the last time I had laughed like that. Cable just watched me, nodding and looking sad. When I could speak, I said, "You've got to be fuckin' kidding me! All those times you've warned us northerners away from women in white. Telling us that they were man-hating demons, and how they were going to drag us off into dark alleys and finish us off. And now, what, some twist in a white skirt winks at you and your stories are all bullshit?" I laughed some more, but now I was feeling bitter.

"No, my friend," said Cable. "It is because my stories are *not* bullshit that I need you tonight. When my angel comes tonight, I will go off with her. I have a good feeling about her in my stomach. She shines like an angel, I think. She does not give off the stench of a demon. My nose, my stomach, they tell me she is no monster, but a natural woman! But, just in case my nose and my stomach are deceived, I want you to follow—at a discreet distance, of course!—but keep me in your sight. Just to be sure. If everything goes like it should, then you go off, find your own little angel. But...." He paused and looked uneasy. "If things do not go so good, and I am wrong about my angel, then it will be a nice idea to have a brave soldier at hand, no?" He winked at me. "In case I need reinforcement, right? You'll do this for me?"

I shook my head, but said, "Hey, you're buying the drinks, right? Sure, why not. I'll be your wingman, buddy. Until you don't need me anymore, of course."

Cable let out a nervous laugh and held out his beer bottle. "To my wingman!"

"To my *main* man," I said, and I chugged the rest of my brew.

Chapter Four

I stayed at the Silver Mine until closing time, nursing drinks and watching the crowd both inside the bar and in the streets outside. I saw plenty of women in white dresses, but none of them showed more than a casual interest in Cable. Or in me, for that matter. I was drinking alone, and I must have been giving off some kind of vibe that I wanted to keep it that way. People who spend much time hitting up bars can tell. Eventually, Cable chased the last of the crowd out of the place and locked up. He had been giddy all night, and now he was in a hurry to meet his angel.

"How do you know she's not going to stand you up?" I asked him when he cleared my table.

"She'll be here! You'll see." He hummed to himself as he carried away the empty bottles. The night was still warm, and I wiped sweat off my face with a napkin as I climbed out of my seat.

"Stay back," Cable said as he opened the front door. He peeked outside, and the broad smile on his face when he turned back to me told me all I needed to know. "She's here! Across the street, waiting! My angel!" He held up a set of keys. "See this? This is the key to the door. Watch us through the window. Don't let her see you! When you see that we are walking away, come out, lock up, and follow us. Stay close—but not too close! Do you understand me? Be near at hand—but be discreet!" He was as jumped up as a teenager going on his first date.

He went out the door and I moved over to the window. I peeked through the shutters and saw a woman in a white dress standing under a street light. It was about three in the morning, but these were the tropics, and the air was warm and humid. The woman's dress was made of a gauzy, almost sheer material, and, though it covered her from head to toe, it did little to conceal the curve of her full breasts and the length of her shapely thighs and calves. Luscious waves of black hair poured down the sides of her head. She was turned a little sideways with her head down, so I couldn't get a good look at her face. Still, I had to admit that Cable's "angel" was as pretty as he had said.

Cable all but ran across the street to her, shouting a greeting. The woman peered sidelong through her hair at Cable and began to turn away from him as he approached. The old rogue hesitated, but the woman's eyes lingered on him as she turned, and, although she walked a half-step in front of Cable, her swaying hips invited him to follow. And follow he did, chattering at her a mile a minute as they walked.

I let them get to the corner before I stepped out through the entryway, locking the door behind me and pocketing the keys. I saw Cable attempt to take her hand in his, but she pulled her arm close to her body, preventing him from grabbing hold. Cable stopped in his tracks, confused, but the woman half-turned toward him and waved him on. He fell back in with her, remaining half a step behind her swaying hips, continuing to chatter.

I followed them into an unfamiliar part of the city, staying a half-block behind the pair. The woman didn't seem to be in a hurry. She walked with a casual grace, seeming to enjoy the stroll through the still night, content to fill Cable with anticipation. Cable filled her ears with his excited babble the entire time, laying on the charm. If she spoke at all, I didn't hear her. As we walked, I noticed a change in the character of the city. The Silver Mine was located in a bustling commercially-zoned working-class neighborhood far from the glittering lights of the modern downtown district. The atmosphere was lively and down-to-earth. The wealthiest citizens of Zaculeu wouldn't be caught dead in that neighborhood, but no one who spent time there wanted them around anyway, so it worked out well for everyone. Within minutes, however, our walk took us into a darker, less vibrant part of the city. We passed into a sector where all of the streetlights were burned out or broken, and only a few of the buildings along the street had any light at all trickling through their grime-stained windows. Many of the ramshackle shops appeared to have been abandoned years before. We passed by a narrow pitch-black alley, and I saw two pairs of predatory eyes reflecting starlight from the darkness within. I'd seen eyes like that in the jungle while on night patrol, and I reached up and rubbed one of the shells from Leota's necklace, hoping that it was as lucky for me as he claimed it had been for him. I'd been brought up in a rough neighborhood, one that swallowed its inhabitants whole if they couldn't scheme or fight their way out of it, but what I was experiencing that night in the depths of Zaculeu was something altogether different, something primitive and alien. In my mind, I heard the voice of Cable telling me that we northerners were far removed from the jungle, but that the men of the Borderland still felt the jungle in their bones. I was beginning to understand what he meant.

At long last, the couple reached a shabby wooden apartment building, one of those places that had been built to store away the city's impoverished and disadvantaged. It was essentially a slum neatly packed inside one four-story structure. Without hesitation, the woman walked through the front door of the building into its murky interior, and, after a short pause and a quick glance in my direction, Cable followed her inside.

I stopped, unsure what to do next. Did Cable expect me to follow the two of them off the streets? And then what? How far were my wingman responsibilities supposed to take me? The woman hadn't lured Cable into a dark alley, but this gloomy building seemed even more dangerous. Fuckin' Cable! I ran to the doorway and slipped inside.

The woman was leading Cable up a staircase. I crossed through the darkness and waited for the two of them to gain some distance. But I didn't follow right away. Instead, I took out a pocket knife that I always carried with me and began to scratch a set of lines on the wooden wall. When I was done, I put my will into the sigil that I had created, and waited.

I can't remember a time when I wasn't able to summon and command air elementals. Not many people have this ability. You have to be born with the skill, and, for no reason that anyone has ever been able to discover, it first manifests itself at different times in different random people. But for me, it was always there, and, once I started school, my teachers took pains to hone my skills. Because of their teaching methods, the pains tended to be mine rather than theirs. At first, they tried to beat instruction into me. When I got older, they added electric shock and waterboarding to their instruction. They didn't reserve such treatment for me, of course. That was simply how things were done in school. But I suspect that I would have been a more receptive student if my teachers had been more interested in making an effort to *teach* me the craft of summoning and less inclined to jam it down my throat in the least amount of time and with the least amount of effort possible. Or maybe I'm just trying to justify my own recalcitrance. In any case, I was more stubborn than most students, and not the most accomplished. I had a lot of natural ability, and I never had a problem summoning and commanding small air elementals, but any funnel of wind more than a foot tall presented me with a serious challenge. Controlling them usually took more exertion on my part than I was willing to expend. Anything really large ignored me with impunity.

Military training improved my skills with elementals, but I was still limited to the relative small fries. On a good day, I could command a six-foot elemental, at least for a little while, but anything bigger than that was out of my league. Like most summoners, I was limited to one element. I could do air, but fire, earth, and water were out of my skill set. Some elementalists can handle multiple elements, or large elementals, or both. The seven Dragon Lords are supposed to be able to control all of the elements, no matter how large, but I don't know if that's true. From a young age, I resolved to stay beneath the notice of the rulers of the seven realms. It's always been hard enough just getting by in my own neighborhood.

A few seconds after carving the sigil and powering it up with my will, a small swirling funnel of air, about the size of my thumb, blew into the room and hovered in front of me.

"Greetings, elemental," I said. "Are you ready to serve?"

"Greetings, master," whispered the tiny air spirit. "This one serves."

I pointed up the stairs. "Two people climb. Follow them. Do not let them see you. When they stop, or when they pass through a door, come back to me. Do you understand?"

The elemental swirled in silence. I groaned to myself. Most elementals have, let's say, limited intelligence, and this one appeared to be slower on the uptake than most. I remained patient and explained my instructions with as much care as I could, using common words and phrases. It got "follow" and "return," but it stumbled over "when they stop," and the concept of doors. Finally, after a frustrating minute or so, the tiny spirit whispered, "This one understands."

I sent it after the couple and climbed the stairs myself, advancing with the same care that I employed in the jungle. When I reached the fourth floor, I began to worry. Had the elemental misunderstood my instructions? Had Cable already followed his angel into a room on the second or third floor? The worm-eaten walls of the building were thin, and, despite the late hour, it seemed like half the occupants in the building were up and about. I hadn't encountered anyone on the stairs, but I could hear all manner of noises coming from rooms outside the dimly lit stairwell. What I couldn't hear was Cable's voice. Had the four-story climb exhausted him? It hadn't bothered *me*, but I was in far better shape than the old barkeep. After walking through the city for miles and tackling these stairs, I wondered how much Cable still wanted his "angel." I found myself hoping that she would make all his exertions worthwhile.

As I paused on the fourth-floor landing, the elemental zoomed in from somewhere. I couldn't see it in the darkness, but I could sense that it was near. "Report!" I commanded.

"Top of building," it whispered.

"They climbed up to the roof?"

The elemental considered my question before repeating, "Top of building."

"What are they doing?" I asked, but the elemental remained silent. "Never mind. I release you from my service."

I didn't see the tiny spirit go, but I sensed that it was no longer with me. One more flight of stairs took me to the roof, and I took them two at a time until I reached the door that led out to the rooftop. I tried the doorknob, but it was locked. Damn! It was a simple lock, and I could have picked it if I'd had something to pick it with, but I didn't have anything at hand. I didn't have anything to shoot if off with, either. I felt the door with the palms of my hands. It didn't seem any sturdier than the rest of that rundown building. But knocking a door off its hinges isn't nearly as easy as they make it look in the movies. I gave the door my steeliest glare, but that didn't work, either.

Suddenly, a strangled yelp sounded through the door. It sounded like a man's voice. "Cable!" I shouted. I heard the scream again, louder this time. I banged on the door. "Cable!" I kicked at the door, and I felt the wood panel splinter. I kicked at it again, and my foot burst through the panel. I pulled my foot back, and pieces of door came back with it. The wooden door had survived decades of tropical rain and humidity, but not without damage. I kicked some more, and rotted wood flew off in chunks, leaving a hole behind. When the hole was big enough, I pushed my way through it.

A full moon illuminated the rooftop. I saw Cable on one knee near the edge of the building, his hands covering his ears. He was screaming like a wounded coyote, his face twisted in agony. A stream of blood leaked from under his hands and down the sides of his face. The woman he'd followed up to the rooftop stood a few feet from Cable, her back to me. She was pointing at him with a skeletal finger. As I watched, horrified by the sight, the woman took a step toward Cable and threw back her head, as if screaming.

Cable cried out. "No, please! Stay away!" He scrambled backward toward the edge of the building.

"Cable!" I shouted. I rushed across the rooftop toward the woman.

"Stay back! Get away from me!" Cable scrambled back another step, then another—and plunged over the edge of the roof! One moment he was there, the next he wasn't.

"Cable! No!"

The woman turned and faced me.

As I watched, the woman's lustrous black hair transformed, becoming colorless and hanging lifeless over her face. She shook her hair away from her brow to reveal the hideous face of an ancient hag. Her wrinkled skin hung like old dried parchment from an unnaturally long, horse-like mug. Two enormous canine teeth rose out of her mouth from her lower jaw and extended over her upper lip. Spittle dripped from the corners of her mouth and down the sides of her elongated chin. A gray wart sprouted from the side of her nose like some kind of fungal growth, and a tuft of black hairs sprung from a mole the size of a small mouse on the side of her jaw. Except for her coal-black eyes, which glared at me with a lunatic's burning intensity, she had the appearance of something that had died ages ago. When I saw that misshapen face, I froze. Her lips parted, and a rasping voice that seemed to emerge from a well—or from deep within a crypt—asked me, "Do you still think I'm pretty?" Then the hag's mouth opened wide, and she let out a shriek, like a hundred thousand screams. But it was a shriek I could only feel, as if the sound was beyond the range of human hearing. The vibrations from the shriek rattled the bones in my temples, behind my ears, and at the base of my skull, and I felt as if my brain was being shredded by a billion microscopic bits of metal. I went down on one knee, closed my eyes, and clapped the palms of my hands over my ears. I could feel blood pushing past my hands and down my cheeks.

I must have passed out, because the next thing I remember was lying on the rooftop in dead silence, alone. The sides of my head throbbed, and the back of my neck burned where Leota's necklace touched skin. Blood covered my hands, and for a second I believed that I had gone deaf. But then I heard a scream from the base of the building. I crawled to the side of the rooftop and looked down over the edge. Cable's body was sprawled on the sidewalk, fifty feet below. A man and a woman were standing over his body, avoiding the widening pool of blood that surrounded it, and other people were coming out of the front of the building to get a look. Someone pointed up in my direction, and I backed away from the edge. Cable was dead, the woman had vanished, and I couldn't do anything to change what had happened. It was time to get back to the base.

But I wouldn't get there right away. The local cops put the arm on me as I was walking out of the building. They took me downtown and made me tell them my story, which I did without holding anything back. When I was done, one of the cops nodded and, looking a little sad, spoke a single word: "Sihuanaba." That seemed good enough for the other cops, but they held me overnight anyway for no good reason. M.P.s showed up the next morning and brought me back to the base.

And that had been it. Except, of course, for the recurring nightmares that were still going strong ten years later.

***

In the end, sleep found me after all, a dreamless one, thankfully, as far as I could remember, and sunlight was streaming through my window into my face when I woke up in my chair. My head felt like someone had hammered a nail through my forehead, my stomach rumbled like a cement mixer, and my mouth tasted like I'd been eating vulture food, but other than that I felt…well…to be honest, I felt like I'd gone all in with a pair of aces and been ambushed by a royal flush. Had I really let myself be extorted into providing my professional services to the corrupt mayor's even more corrupt fixer? To investigate the possible appearance of a monster that had been haunting my dreams for ten years? For half my standard rate??? What kind of sap did that make me?

I groaned out loud when I stood up from the chair and stumbled into the kitchen to find a cold bottle of beer. I thought about frying up some eggs for breakfast, but when I saw that it was a little past noon, and, therefore, time for lunch, I popped a frozen pizza into the microwave, instead. I probably would have had the pizza for breakfast anyway. It went better with the beer.

When the pizza was ready, I pulled it out of the microwave and carried it into my living room, where I put it down on a TV tray. I stared at it without eating, pondering the predicament that I'd found myself in. I wasn't nuts about working for Fulton at *any* price, much less the cut-rate fare that he was forcing on me. But I didn't have much of a choice as long as the son of a bitch was holding my thirty-eight. I knew that the predatory shark had no qualms about using it as false evidence to implicate me in a murder. It didn't even have to be Zyanya's murder; he could use my piece to hang a frame on me any time he pleased! Somehow, I needed to get the firearm out of Fulton's possession.

Maybe my friend Crawford could help. Unknown to his neighbors, Crawford was a were-rat, a shapeshifter who could transform himself into a swarm of rats, or, technically speaking, a *mischief* of rats, as Crawford liked to remind me. He'd helped me steal an item from the YCPD's downtown headquarters right out from under the nose of a police captain. Fulton had been there, too. It's amazing how useful a bunch of rats linked by a group intelligence can be, and Crawford had helped me out on several occasions, including with the Shipper case. But, I reminded myself, that case had been especially hard on Crawford, and I wasn't sure that he'd be up for any similar capers just yet. He'd still been a little shaken up when I'd called him a couple of weeks earlier.

I thought about ways I might be able to use an elemental to help me out. Maybe I could send one to search for the handgun. Trouble was, the piece could be anywhere. Fulton might not even have it at City Hall. For all I knew, it was in a storage locker somewhere, or a safe deposit box. It might not even be in the city! I knew that I was going to have to get creative, but, for the moment, I had nothing. Throwing my hands up in surrender, I dug into my pizza. It tasted like cardboard and lodged in my throat, but a bottle of beer helped guide it to where it needed to go.

It was while choking down my lunch that I realized what I was going to have to do. I didn't like it, but I was backed into a corner and short on options. Problem was, Fulton was out of my league. It was a blow to my pride to admit it, but that fact was slapping me in the face, and all I could do was stand and take it like a man. Fulton was a shark who swam in deeper waters than I could navigate without help from another shark who knew the neighborhood. Swallowing my pride the way I'd forced down that cheap pizza, I found my phone and hit the number at the top of my speed-dial directory.

After one ring, my call was answered by a sunny female voice with a huskiness that betrayed a carton-a-day nicotine habit. "Robinson Lubank's Law Office."

"Hi Gracie. You alone?"

"Sorry, baby," Gracie cooed, her voice apologetic. "Robby's in the office today." Then she brightened. "But I can check and see if the break room is available!"

"Thanks, doll. But for now I need to talk to your hubby."

"Awww.... You're no fun! Are you in trouble again, honey?"

"Who—me? You know I'm all about the straight and narrow."

"Sure, baby! That's what interests me about you—your straight and narrow!"

Gracie was an outrageous flirt, and she'd been giving me the tease since we first met. But it wasn't serious. At least I didn't *think* so. Sometimes it was hard to tell. But while Gracie and Rob Lubank might be an unusual couple, and not just because she was human and cute as a kitten, while her husband was an ugly, foul-mouthed, ill-tempered gnome with the ethics of a rattlesnake, they were as close a couple as I'd ever met. For my money, Lubank was the slimiest, most corrupt attorney in Yerba City, with blackmail files on every important dignitary in the metropolitan area. But he doted on Gracie, the only person he loved more than himself. And Gracie was his committed partner in every way. You'd never know it to hear her talk, though!

"What am I going to do with you, Gracie."

"Surprise me, sugar—I can't wait to find out!"

"Right. Next time for sure."

"Sure thing, baby! Robby just got off the phone. I'll put you right through. And, sweetie—you know you can "pop" in here anytime!"

I shook my head and smiled.

The next voice I heard nearly blew out my eardrums. "Alkwat's balls, peeper! What the hell do *you* want! I've got *important* people to talk to today. You know, people with *money*! Unless this call's billable, I ain't got time for it! Talk fast, I'm about to hang th'fuck up!"

"I need legal advice."

Lubank shifted gears faster than a stock-car driver coming out of a turn. "We-e-e-l-l-l-l! That's another story, my friend. The meter's on, so start talking. And take your time—I've got all afternoon!"

As it turned out, it didn't take all afternoon. In fact, it didn't take much time at all. I gave him the skinny on my assignment from Fulton and described my dilemma with the handgun. When I was finished, Lubank was incredulous.

"That's it?"

"Well...yeah. Pretty much."

"Alkwat's flaming pecker, Southerland! I knew you weren't the brightest bulb in the chandelier, but I didn't realize you were a fucking idiot!"

"You've got a solution?" I must have sounded a little dubious.

"Have I got a solution? Of course I've got a solution, you numbskull! This one's easy! It's so fuckin' easy that I feel like I'm fuckin' stealing your money! That won't stop me from billing you for my time, of course. Full rates, too. Unlike some people I know, I'm a professional, and I take *pride* in my work. I don't fuckin' sell out for half price to *nobody*!"

"Well? How long are you going to keep me hanging?"

Lubank's chuckle was evil. "Long enough to make you feel good and stupid once I tell you what you need to do."

I waited, knowing that patience wasn't one of Lubank's few virtues.

"All right, all right! I'll tell you. Your problem is that you're basically a snoop and a sneak. You can't think beyond finding out where Fulton is holding your heater and then sneaking in and stealing it away from him. But you're missing the fucking point! The reason that Fulton can hold the gun over your head is that it's registered in your name! All you need to do is eliminate the entry in the Central Firearms Registry! If the roscoe ain't registered to you, then it ain't your roscoe! Problem solved!"

I thought about that and found a few holes in it. "My fingerprints are all over the piece."

"Fingerprints—phooey!" Lubank's voice was filled with contempt. "I can get around fingerprints. All they indicate is that you might have handled the gun at some point. They don't prove that you killed anyone with it! Where did they find the gun? How long after the songbird's murder was the gun discovered? How many people could have tampered with the firearm during that time? Could the prints have been planted?" Lubank let out a dismissive snort. "Don't worry about fucking fingerprints. They don't prove squat!"

"Okay, but that leaves the matter of breaking into the registration database. I have no idea how to do something like that. This is a government registry we're talking about. Security's gonna be tighter than an underground vault! Who can bypass something like that? You?"

"Why Mr. Southerland!" Lubank exclaimed with manufactured outrage. "I'm offended that you would make such a suggestion! Don't you know that hacking into a government database is a crime? I wouldn't even begin to know where to find someone who would be capable and willing to commit such a breach of law no matter how much he was paid to do so, unless perhaps he was a member of one of the city's noted crime syndicates. Especially one with an interest in unseating our current mayor. Funny thing: there's an article in today's newspaper that you might find pertinent to the matter. But as a respectable representative of the law, I don't want to strain the bounds of attorney/client privilege by hearing about any transgressions you plan to commit, or to have others commit in your name." Lubank broke into a laugh. "I've opened the window for you, kid. What you do now is up to you."

***

After disconnecting my call with Lubank, I thought about the devious gnome's advice. Eliminating the pistol from the Central Firearms Registry just might be the solution I was looking for, provided that I could pull it off or find someone who could. Lubank knew that I had an in with the Hatfield Syndicate, the most powerful criminal organization in the city, and it was obvious that he was suggesting I make use of that connection. He was also telling me that the Hatfields might have an interest in working against Teague. But I'd have to be truly desperate to go to the Hatfields for a favor. Any service they provided would come with a high price, and I didn't mean money. They would want a service in return, and I'd be obligated to provide it. No, the last thing I wanted was to be indebted to an organization as shady as the Hatfields.

But what if it was the only thing I had left?

Tightening my robe so that I was more or less decent, I went downstairs and opened my front door, hoping that no would-be clients were waiting for me on the doorstep. As I had hoped, nothing was waiting for me outside my door except the morning paper. I brought it in and, keeping my 'Closed' sign in place, locked the door behind me.

It didn't take me long to find the article that Lubank had alluded to. At the bottom of the front page was a press release from the mayor's office containing a bunch of hooey about the mayor's plans to curtail the growing influence of organized crime in Yerba City. It looked to me like something Fulton had cooked up to hide the fact that the mayor was currently hiding out in his home having a nervous breakdown after an encounter with a spirit of vengeance set on punishing him for his dissolute ways. The interesting part of the release was a section claiming that Teague was going to ensure that criminal organizations would be prohibited from making large donations to the ongoing mayoral election campaigns. Teague was quoted as saying, "It would be detrimental to the city if my opponent won the election with a campaign largely underwritten by an organization, such as the Hatfield Syndicate, that would leave the new mayor beholden to nefarious underworld bosses." The implication was obvious. Fulton wanted the public to believe that the Hatfields were supporting Teague's opponent. It might or might not be true, but, if it was, the Hatfields might be willing to help me get out from under Fulton's thumb if I could help damage the Teague campaign in the process.

I swept the newspaper into my waste paper basket. The day I became a patsy for the Hatfields would be a dark one indeed. I'd have to find another option.

In another couple of hours, I would be meeting with Gordon and his team of trolls. I needed to shake off the remains of the previous night and morning and get myself combat ready. I chugged the remainder of my beer and headed for the bathroom. I brushed my teeth and shaved the stubble off my chin. Then I stood under the shower until the hot water ran all the way out. I remained standing under the freezing cold water until my whole body went numb. By the time I'd dried off and dressed, I was wide awake and ready to rumble.

Chapter Five

    Fulton had told me to meet up with Gordon and his team at five, so I pulled up to the guarded gate at the entrance to the exclusive Galindo Estates residential community at four p.m. sharp. When I'm on the job, I make the rules. The sentry guarding the gate gawked wide-eyed at my car, a monstrosity I liked to call the beastmobile. It had been sold to me by a mob-affiliated owner of a high-end escort agency, and, although I'd had a detailer remove the purple racing stripes, along with the decal of the naked winged sprite rising from purple flames on the automobile's enormous hood, and even though I'd had him repaint the jet black exterior an innocuous brownish color officially named "deep taupe," my beastmobile still cruised the streets like a caricature of a pimp's ride. The car was wrong for me in every imaginable way. Private dicks need to be inconspicuous. Driving in the beastmobile was like standing under a spotlight in a dark theater. I was by nature a private person. I lived and drank alone, and that was the way I liked it. The beastmobile set off radar blips for miles around. My apartment and office were filled with bland second-hand furnishings. I liked to meet the world in a suit and tie, but the suit was off the rack and the ties came from a thrift store down the street. The beastmobile sported a garish red leather interior that I'd elected to keep for reasons that I couldn't begin to explain. A friend of mine named Gio, who ran an auto repair shop a block from my apartment, kept the car parked in his lot, and his son, a high-school kid named Antonio, tended to the beastmobile as if it were their own adopted child, keeping the exterior and interior in spotless condition and the four hundred forty-two horsepower eight-cylinder engine running like, well, like a beast! I justified ownership of the ridiculous vehicle with the idea that it was as reliable under pressure as the sunrise, and, if times got rough, I could move into the thing. The trunk of the car was large enough to hold everything of importance that I owned with room to spare, and I had once enjoyed a restful night's sleep in the car's spacious back seat at a time when I really needed it. Bottom line, it was my car, and anyone who didn't like it could piss the hell off.

I stopped at the gate and rolled down my window. The sentry ran his peepers over the length of the beastmobile and stared at me with disapproval. "You lost?" he asked me.

"Nice day isn't it?"

The look of disapproval on the sentry's face deepened, and, despite the fact that it was indeed a lovely day, with puffy white clouds drifting past the sun and a cool ocean breeze pushing fallen leaves down the street, he didn't answer my question. I guess he wasn't a chatty fellow.

So much for pleasantries. "Gordon from Lawrence Fulton's office is expecting me."

The sentry nodded, gave my car one more dubious look, and stepped into his guard station. He picked up a microphone and began speaking to someone, Gordon probably. After a brief conversation, the sentry put the microphone down and shouted at me through the open window. "Are you Summerland?"

Close enough, I figured. "Yeah, that's me."

"He says you're early."

I nodded. "It's true. I'm early."

The sentry let out a breath. "He says you can go through, though." He seemed disappointed.

"I suppose I'd better go on through, then."

The sentry took a final look at the beastmobile, shook his head, and pushed a button. The gate swung open at a snail's pace, and I resisted the temptation to gun the engine before it was fully open and flip the sentry off as I squeezed through. Sometimes it feels good to be snarky, but it's not professional. As this case developed, I'd probably need to get through this gate again, and, in that event, I wouldn't want to have to deal with a hostile security guard. So I waited for the gate to come to a full stop, thanked the sentry, and eased the beastmobile into the neighborhood.

I'd looked up the directions to Teague's house on my computer and written them down. I could have entered the address into an app on my phone and let the pleasant robot's voice guide me to my destination, but I didn't allow anything on my phone that could be used to pinpoint my location. I'd not only disconnected the phone's GPS device, but also any app or feature that could allow the phone to be tracked. This included the barometer, altimeter, gyroscope, accelerometer, and magnetometer, all of which come standard in most cell phones, and which can be used by authorities to track a phone if it's turned on and moving from one location to another. Eliminating these features made my cell phone less "smart," but I didn't mind trading some convenient artificial intelligence for a little peace of mind.

The broad residential streets of the Galindo Estates took me past locked gates blocking private driveways that led through a carefully maintained wilderness to mansions that rose above the bushes and trees like private fortresses. The magnificent and imposing structures, whose stylish and beautiful exteriors had been designed by the leading architects of the realm, invited admiration, but only from a distance. I spotted one of Fulton's vehicles—probably the same one that had brought me to his office the night before—parked near the mayor's house. My own luxury transport looked like it might get along with Fulton's shiny sedan, and I parked behind it. As I stepped into the street, I told the beastmobile to behave and not do anything that might make the smaller, more refined automobile uncomfortable.

I took in a moment to scan my surroundings. So this was where the upper crust laid their weary heads after a day of consorting with their peers in luxury offices, in the boardrooms, and in the nineteenth hole after a day on the links. This was where they unwound after implementing schemes, determining fates, and moving unimaginable sums of imaginary money through the ether. Or whatever rich people did with their time. I had no way of knowing. It seemed like a pleasant neighborhood, but maybe it was just the weather. It was a little too quiet for my tastes, though. I missed the constant sound of traffic: rumbling engines, screeching tires, blaring horns, the occasional gunshot in the night, and the ubiquitous wailing of sirens. I settled my gaze on the mayor's home. Teague's residence was one of the more modest ones in the neighborhood, probably no more than a dozen or so rooms, and it was set closer to the road than the others. He would have had a good view through his living room window of a beautiful woman in a white dress standing in the street in front of his house, maybe a hundred feet away across an impeccably arranged rock garden with enough stones to construct a building the size of the one I rented.

I reached under my shirt and fingered the shells on Leota's necklace. I don't know why I had slipped it on before leaving my apartment. Maybe it was because I'd been wearing it ten years ago in Zaculeu, the last time I'd seen the Sihuanaba outside of my dreams. I'd met her, and I'd lived. That had always been a puzzle to me. Why hadn't she killed me that night? Why had she left me on the rooftop? It wasn't that I had any burning desire to find out, especially if learning the truth meant another run-in with the avenging angel, or whatever kind of monster she was. I could go my whole life without that. But if I'd learned anything in my thirty years it was that you play the hand you're dealt, and if Teague's mystery woman was indeed the Sihuanaba, then maybe it was right that I would be facing her down again. Maybe, one way or the other, it would end the nightmares once and for all. That would be jake with me.

***

Gordon and all three of his trolls got out of the black sedan to greet me. Gordon walked toward me, and extended his hand.

"Afternoon, Southerland. Welcome to the team."

I gave the proffered hand a shake. "Afternoon, Gordon."

"Call me Gordo. Only Mr. Fulton calls me Gordon. Even my wife calls me Gordo."

"Gordo it is, then."

Gordo turned to the trolls. "You've met the fellas, but let me make with the formal intros. This is Stormclaw. He may be old, but he's the best wheelman in the business." The old driver, red eyes glowing through a pair of sporty dark glasses, nodded at me and grunted. Gordo then indicated the troll that had followed me out of the Minotaur on the previous evening. "This is Ironshield." The barrel-chested troll jutted his chin in my direction, barely moving his head. "And this is Thunderclash." The eight-foot troll with the fedora moved toward me like a walking skyscraper and extended his knobby four-fingered hand. I clasped it with my own and was grateful that he didn't crush it into a pulp.

Like all trolls, these three were hairless from the neck up, with large pointed ears, leathery gray faces, thick ruddy lips that, when parted, revealed an intimidating set of pointed ivory teeth, and eyes that glowed like burning coals. All three trolls were dressed in tailor-made navy blue suits with pale blue shirts and blood-red ties. They all wore ankle-length leather overcoats that I was certain concealed loaded shotguns inside their inner linings. Thunderclash was the only one wearing a head piece, which looked to be a size twelve and some change. He had a hawk nose and a long jawline that made his face seem to droop from the ears down. Ironshield was built like a tank. Trolls are known for their size and strength, but this one looked like he could uproot an oak tree with one hand and use it as a backscratcher. His face was broad and somewhat square, and his upper lip seemed to be twisted into a permanent sneer. Stormclaw appeared to be older than the other two trolls by several decades. He had deep wrinkles in his face and a noticeable stoop in his stance. Trolls have longer lifespans than humans, and I guessed that this old one had made it past his second century. His watchful eyes never stopped moving behind his shades, as they continually scanned the street from one end to the other. From the way Thunderclash positioned himself in the group, I got the sense that he outranked the other two trolls. Gordo appeared to be something like the lieutenant in the unit. Thunderclash was the sergeant, and Stormclaw and Ironshield were the soldiers.

Introductions out of the way, Gordon—Gordo—turned to me. "I wasn't expecting you for another hour."

"I wasn't busy. Thought I'd get a jump on things."

Gordo scratched at his ear and looked me up and down. "Well, not much happening at the moment. The mayor is inside, probably sleeping. He was in no shape to work today, so Mr. Fulton pumped him with enough sleepy-time powder to bring down a moose and had us bring him home to his wife. He should be out for another couple of hours."

That suited me fine. "How 'bout we look over the place by the lake where you saw the woman in white?"

Gordo seemed pleased by this suggestion. I had no doubt that he'd been camped in the black sedan for hours watching a quiet house sit off the street and do nothing. "Sounds good. Thunder and I will come along. Stormclaw and Ironshield will stay here and keep a watch on things."

I nodded. "Have you been down to the lake since last night?"

Gordo shook his head. "Not me. But Mr. Fulton sent a forensics team there this morning."

"They find anything?"

"Not much. Footsteps where you'd expect to see them, but that's about it."

"The woman's footsteps, too? Any indication where she disappeared to?"

Gordo sighed. "Well, that's kind of odd. The forensics jeebos seem to think that she ran down to the lake and dove in. But I think I would have noticed that happening when I was there."

"It was pretty dark," I reminded him.

"Yeah, I guess it was." Gordo sounded doubtful.

We walked in silence the rest of the way to the lake, Gordo next to me and Thunderclash, who had lit up a fourteen-inch cigar, trailing a couple of steps behind, his eyes scanning the area as we moved. We stepped through some trees into the area where Teague had met the woman in white, which was marked off with crime tape. No one else was around. I stopped to take in a sweeping view of Ohlone Lake. A sleek speedboat bounced across the pristine silver-blue surface of the water far off to the south, but otherwise the lake appeared to be deserted. I saw a parking lot to my left on the north side of the lake where a boat ramp slanted down into the water, but I only spotted two vehicles in the lot, a four-door familymobile with a boat trailer and an old white van that needed a wash. The light shining from the late afternoon sun at my back caused the ripples in the lake to glitter like a field of diamonds. I thought of the thousands of Yerba City citizens who would have enjoyed a sunny June day picnicking, barbecuing, swimming, boating, and waterskiing in one of the most beautiful spots in the city, but the lake was open only to the well-heeled members of the Galindo Downs Country Club, and, from the looks of it, they had better things to do.

I walked up to the crime tape and stopped without going beyond. Gordo and Thunderclash pulled up close behind me, probably wanting to see what kind of operator I was. I didn't blame them. Gordo had welcomed me to the club, but that didn't mean I was one of them. I wondered if Gordo was a little sore that his boss had dumped a new face into his squad. The bruiser seemed friendly enough on the surface, but I didn't know what was going on inside him. The trolls had greeted me with an air of detachment expected of seasoned professionals, and they had spent the previous evening sweeping me off the street and whisking me away to see the big boss. They'd done a neat job of it, too. They probably thought of me as some kind of patsy, if they thought anything about me at all. That was fine. I wasn't there to impress anyone.

I pointed toward a spot near the lake. "Is that where you saw the mayor?"

"Yep, right up there near the shore." Gordo indicated a spot closer at hand. "And over here is where I was standing when I snapped that photo."

I ducked under the crime tape and stepped inside the perimeter. Gordo did likewise, and Thunderclash stepped over the tape. The two of them gave me room while I examined the path leading down to the lakefront. It didn't take a specialist to trace the two sets of footprints that led from the end of the street and down the soft sandy surface, or to see where the larger set of footprints had lengthened into a run and then come to a stop before continuing on.

I looked behind me toward the trees between us and the street, and then back ahead of me toward the lake. I turned to Gordo. "The mayor walked through here to the lake. You followed him, then ran this far with your pistol in hand. You stopped here, put the gat away and took out your phone for the pic."

I paused and looked at Gordo for confirmation. He nodded. "Yeah, that's right."

I looked toward the lake. "So you're, what, about thirty yards away at this point? Maybe twenty-five?"

Gordo nodded again. "Thirty yards at the most."

"That pic doesn't tell me much. I'm sure you saw more than the pic shows."

"I did. The photo didn't pick up any details. But I could see that the woman didn't have a weapon, except for that vicious-looking claw coming out of her finger."

"And you said that the hand had an odd appearance?"

The big bruiser grimaced. "It was creepy all right. Thin, like it was all bone, but covered with leathery-like skin. Like a lizard's foot. Or maybe a rooster's claw."

I took a look around. "I'm not picking up the woman's footprints yet. Any idea where she might have come from?"

Gordo shook his head. "She was there when I got here."

"Okay, let's take a look."

Thunderclash stayed behind, keeping watch, while Gordo and I moved closer to the lake, making sure that we didn't disturb any traces or overlook anything that the forensics team might have missed. Those guys almost never leave case-breaking clues behind for intrepid private dicks to discover, but it never hurts to look.

When we reached the spot where the mayor was cringing at the feet of the woman, I stopped and gave the ground a thorough examination. The forensics team had walked through the scene, but I assumed they hadn't disturbed anything important. I could see where the team had taken plaster casts of footprints, one from the mayor, one left by Gordo, and one of a bare foot that might have been left by the woman in white. I bent down to take a close look at the track, using all of the enhanced awareness given to me by the elf. There wasn't anything special about the print. It might not have even belonged to the woman that Gordo had met. It could just as easily have been left by some rich man's daughter on some previous occasion. But Gordo had seen the woman and taken a snapshot. I looked for more prints of bare feet, but didn't find many. I saw tracks leading toward the water, which is probably why the forensics people had suggested that she had run to the lake and jumped in. But it's not the job of forensics to make conclusions. Their job is to gather evidence, and as far as the woman in white was concerned, the scene wasn't offering up enough to tell much of a story. I examined the area carefully, but when I was done I couldn't tell where she had come from or where she had gone. Maybe that in itself was evidence of something.

I stopped my search and turned to Gordo. "What do you make of it?"

Gordo sniffed. "I don't like it that we don't see more prints for the woman."

I nodded. "Pretty sandy here. The wind would have covered most of the prints." I stared at the prints leading to the shore. "Those prints don't go all the way to the water."

Gordo looked out over the lake. "The wake from a boat could have washed away anything close to the shore."

"See a boat out there last night?"

Gordo shook his head. "Nope. It was dark, though. Still, I think I would have noticed if a boat was close."

A ring tone sounded from behind me. I turned and saw Thunderclash pull a troll-sized cell phone from the inside of his coat. The troll grunted once and called out, "Some trouble back at the house. Sounds like we'd better head back."

Gordo sighed. "Guess we'd better check this out. We can come back and finish up here later."

I took a quick look around. "All right. I'm not sure there's much to see here anyway."

As I turned to head back to the road, I had a sudden sensation of something out of place, as if I'd detected a subtle motion at the edge of my vision. I stopped where I was and began to scan the grove of cypress trees that separated Ohlone Lake from the neighboring Galindo Estates residential area.

Gordo noticed that I'd stopped. "What is it?"

I ignored his question and concentrated my attention on the trees. My pulse quickened as I experienced a strong sensation of being watched. My elf-enhanced awareness was picking up something, but I couldn't tell what it was. Suddenly, in the same way that one notices the steady ticking of a clock only after it stops, I became aware that something that I'd been looking at in the grove of cypresses had vanished. I marked the location and started to head in that direction.

Gordo walked with me. "See something?"

I kept my eyes on the trees. "Maybe. I want to take a look."

"We need to check on the mayor."

"You go ahead. I'll just be a second."

Gordo veered away from me. "All right, but don't be long."

I crossed the distance to the trees, keeping my attention on the spot where I thought something had disappeared. When I reached the spot, I stopped and examined the grounds. Nothing jumped out at me, and I was about to give up and go find out what was happening with the mayor, when I spotted a tiny gray lump sitting on top of a fallen leaf. Knowing that I was going to be visiting a crime scene, I'd brought a couple of evidence bags with me, just in case. With great care, I lifted the leaf and poured the gray lump into one of the bags. It appeared to be fresh ash from a cigarette, or, given the size of the lump, more likely a cigar. Someone had been standing in that spot, smoking a cigar and watching Gordo and me. And then he'd vanished without a trace. Frustrated that I didn't have the time to do a broader search, I put the evidence bag in my pocket and hurried off to rejoin Gordo's team.

***

When I reached the mayor's house, I saw that Teague had backed his car out of the garage and into the driveway, but Stormclaw and Ironshield were standing behind the car and blocking his way to the street. I glanced from the medium-sized sedan to the two full-grown trolls and concluded that the car wasn't going anywhere if the trolls didn't want it to. Ironshield probably could have picked it up and carried it back into the garage if he felt like it. Mrs. Teague was leaning into the driver's side window pleading with her husband. Gordo was watching from a few feet back, and Thunderclash was standing at the foot of the driveway, cigar clamped in his teeth as he scanned the streets.

Thunderclash was closest and seemed to be the least busy, so I walked over to him. "What's up?"

The troll kept his eyes on the street as he answered me. "The mayor decided that he wanted to take off in his car. He told the missus that he wasn't safe here, and that if she didn't want to come with him, then he'd leave without her. He packed a suitcase and tried to drive away. Mr. Fulton's orders are to keep him here."

The mayor and his wife were shouting at each other. He sounded scared. She was in tears. I looked up at Thunderclash. "Gordo said he'd be knocked out for another couple of hours."

Without looking down, the troll blew cigar smoke out the side of his mouth. "He was mistaken."

I nodded and walked up the driveway. I listened to the mayor and his wife argue for a few moments and then turned to Gordo. "Okay if I talk to Teague?"

Gordo's brow arched over one eye. "Better you than me."

I raised my voice so that it could be heard over Mrs. Teague's sobs. "Mr. Teague! Can I ask where you are going?"

The mayor leaned toward the open window and stared up at me. The muscles on the left side of his face twitched and pulled at the corner of his mouth. His eyes were wide open, and his pupils dilated, almost obscuring the irises surrounding them. An angry network of red veins ran through the whites of his eyes. He looked like a man who had seen a ghost, or maybe an avenging angel, and wanted to be somewhere else before it returned.

Teague's mouth opened, closed, then opened again. "Who the fuck are you?"

"My name is Alexander Southerland. I'm a private detective. Lawrence Fulton hired me to help you with your problem."

Teague appeared to be having trouble processing this information. He stared at me for a few moments, then gave his head a vigorous shake, as if he were trying to wake from a dream. "I don't know what you're talking about. It's not safe here! I— I need to leave!" He tore his gaze from me and looked at his wife. "I need Tracy to come with me. Gordo! Get Mrs. Teague into the car! We've got to leave! Now!"

Mrs. Teague reached for the car's door handle. "Please, Darnell! Please come inside."

"Let go of the door, Tracy! If you won't come with me, then I'll go without you!" Teague looked back over his shoulder through the back window, and I knew that he was on the verge of taking his chances with the trolls behind the car.

I kept my voice calm. "Mr. Teague, you're as safe here as you would be anywhere. Safer with these mugs watching out for you."

Teague whipped his head in my direction, eyes so wide that they looked as if they'd fall out of their sockets. "You don't know anything about it, mister! Tell those trolls that I'm going to flatten them if they don't get out of my way."

"Those trolls aren't going to be bothered by a little car like this, Mr. Teague. Stay here and let them protect you and your wife."

Flecks of foam sprayed from the corner of Teague's mouth. "They can't protect me from…from..."

"From the woman in white?"

The mayor's mouth dropped open. "How do you know about…"

"I've run into her before, Mr. Teague." I was aware that Gordo had turned to stare at me. "I know what you saw. And what you heard."

Teague's eyes narrowed. "You…. No, you're lying to me! You're fuckin' lying!"

"I'm not lying, Mr. Teague. Let's go into the house and talk about it. You'll be safe, I promise. Your wife will be safe, too. Come on, Mr. Teague. Your house is the safest place you can be right now."

Teague's face twitched like something was crawling around inside it. Then he lowered his eyes and let out a sigh. "All right. I…" He shook his head. "All right." He looked up at me again. "What did you say your name was?"

"Southerland. Come on, Mr. Mayor. Let's get you and your wife off the street."

Chapter Six

The trolls resumed their surveillance from the black sedan while Gordo and I walked the mayor and his wife through the garage and back inside the house. On our way inside, Gordo leaned toward me and whispered, "Did you really meet that woman before?"

"Later," I muttered back.

Gordo and I followed Mayor and Mrs. Teague into a living room that had made a number of appearances in magazines and local TV programs devoted to home care and interior design. Mrs. Teague sat beside her husband on a long living room sofa, her arm curled beneath his and her fingers clutching his bicep. Long horizontal shadows streaked over the two of them as the sun tried to fight its way through half-opened window blinds. Even under the circumstances, Tracy Teague was a striking woman, well into her forties and aging like fine wine. Her thick dark auburn hair was streaked with thin strands of silver and hung in waves to the top of her shoulders. She was the kind of thin that came from hours of aerobics and healthy eating habits. With the exception of a tiny smudge of mascara that had been left at the corner of her eye when she'd wiped away a tear, the mayor's wife was the picture of grace under pressure. I wondered how often she'd had to be a source of strength for her husband. More often than she'd wanted to, probably. Gordo and I pulled chairs up close enough to the sofa that we could chat with the couple in comfort and prevent Teague from trying to do a runner if he became so inclined.

The mayor had succeeded in composing himself, and his face had re-settled into the photogenic countenance that made him such a media darling. I marveled at his ability to flip the switch from terrified mouse to regal lion in an instant. His face had stopped twitching, and his eyes weren't even red anymore. Only his still dilated pupils revealed any evidence of the fear that Teague was working hard to suppress.

Teague looked up at me. "You say you've met the woman?" When I glanced at Mrs. Teague, the mayor waved a hand. "It's okay. I've told my wife everything." Mrs. Teague lowered her eyes and looked uncomfortable.

Rather than answer his question directly, I leaned in toward the mayor. "Tell me what you saw at the lake. Tell me about her face."

Teague's mouth widened into the smile he uses when the cameras are rolling. "Well, it was pretty dark. I can't really say that I got a good look."

I stared at him until his smile faltered ever so slightly. "Is that what you told Mrs. Teague?"

The mayor's wife tightened her grip on her husband's arm, and he glanced over at her.

I sat back in my seat. "What did you see, Mr. Teague? You want help? Then cut the bullshit. I'm not one of your flunkies, and I don't need anything from you. You tell me the truth or I walk out and leave you to your demon."

The mayor looked up at that. "Demon?" He tried to chuckle, but I could hear the strain in it. "Surely you don't mean that in a *literal* sense."

I shrugged. "Would you prefer 'avenging angel'? That's probably more appropriate given your proclivity for the ladies, don't you think?"

Teague's expression darkened and he sat up straight, "Now wait a damned minute!"

"Shut up, Teague!" I felt Gordo flinch a little, but I plowed ahead. "Five minutes ago you were a puddle of quivering goo flying off in a blind panic to who knows where, and ready to desert your wife in order to get there. Don't try to convince me that you've suddenly grown a backbone. I can help you against the woman, but, to be honest? I'm not convinced that I want to. Maybe I'll just leave you to her. You've seen her. Talk to me now and I'll help you. Otherwise deal with her yourself."

Teague's mouth worked, but the twitch in his face was back. He collapsed into the sofa and lowered his forehead into his hands, even as his wife maintained her grip on one arm. When he looked up at last, his eyes were red again, his swagger gone, but he seemed more sad than panicked. When he spoke, his voice shook. "She was…old! So old, like a corpse that had been buried and dug up again. And ugly! Her face…. It was weird! Like it had been…stretched!" He shook his head. "I know it sounds crazy, but it reminded me of a horse's skull."

I nodded. "And did she say anything to you?"

Teague seemed confused. "What?"

"What did she say after you saw her face?"

Teague lowered his eyes and glanced at his wife, who wasn't looking at him. He looked back up at me and blinked. "She said... She asked me if I thought she was pretty." Mrs. Teague looked over at her husband. I had the impression that this was the first time that she'd heard this part of the story.

I locked my eyes on Teague's. "Is that what she asked? Think, Teague. What were her exact words?"

Teague tried to turn on his smile, but it didn't work. I wondered if I'd broken his switch. He sighed, instead. "She said, 'Do you *still* think I'm pretty?'" He looked over at his wife, who held his eyes for a moment, let out a sigh, and looked away. She tightened her grip on his bicep, and it seemed less like she was hanging on to him and more like she was trying to inflict pain.

I nodded at Teague and cleared my throat in order to hide the fact that a chill like tiny needles had run up my spine when I heard him repeat the woman's words to him at the lake. It was the same question that Cable's "angel"—the Sihuanaba—had asked me on the rooftop in Zaculeu, and that she'd been asking me in my nightmares ever since.

I shook off the chill and gathered the strength to ask my next question. "And after that? What did you hear?"

Teague squeezed his eyes shut and raised the back of a clenched fist to his mouth. He chewed on a knuckle, as if part of him wanted to prevent the memory from escaping into the world. But another part of him wanted to come clean, and he managed to force himself to speak through his hand. "No words...a scream! Or more like screams, hundreds, maybe thousands of them all at once. But screams I couldn't hear. I *felt* them! It was like an explosion with no sound. Like the wail of a siren blaring right in my ear, but a sound that was so loud.... It was like my ears couldn't handle it, and my hearing just shut down. It...it still hurts to remember!" He shifted his hand from his mouth to his ear, as if the siren blast still echoed in his head. "And...and...."

I leaned forward. "And what, Mr. Teague?"

"Judgment!" Teague blurted out the word. "I felt like I was being judged by every woman who had ever been hurt by a man." He shook his head, keeping his hand clapped over his ear. "That's what the scream was. It was women, thousands of them, *millions* of them, shrieking with pain! And I could feel that pain, the pain that all of them felt when a man cheated on them, or used them and tossed them aside when they were done with them. Or worse!" He glanced at his wife, who was still squeezing his arm. When he spoke again, his voice had sunk to a near whisper. "It was a trial. They accused me and judged me, and they found me guilty. And I'm so sorry.... Sorry about all of it." Teague jerked his head up at me, eyes wide and mouth twitching. His voice started soft, but grew louder as he spoke until he was shouting. "She's going to come back! The woman! She's coming back! She's not finished with me! The last thing she told me was that she was coming back for me. The trial isn't over! You've got to keep her away from me! Keep her away!"

Mrs. Teague had had enough. "No more! Can't you see he's delirious? He's not thinking right. It's...." She shook her head. "It's the pressure that he's under. His job and the election. He needs rest, that's all. He'll be fine. He just needs a good night's sleep." She looked from me to Gordo and back again. "He'll be okay now. You can go. I'll take care of him tonight. I'll see that he gets the rest he needs." She reached up with her free hand and gently pulled her husband's hand off his ear. "You two can see yourselves out, can't you?" She looked up at Gordo, beseeching him with her eyes. "Please, Gordon. I promise that I'll call Lawrence if I need any help."

Gordo and I looked at each other. I shrugged, and we stood. Gordo turned to Mrs. Teague. "We'll have a team outside the house all night. If you need anything, just give us a holler, okay?" But Teague had buried his face into his wife's neck, and she was busy comforting him. Gordo nodded at me, and we found our way back out to the street.

Once outside, Gordo took out a pack of cigarettes and offered me one. I shook him off, and he lit one for himself. After a puff, he shook his head. "What do you make of all that? Has he lost it?"

I shrugged. "Not for me to say."

Gordo raised an eyebrow. "No? I was watching you in there. What do you know about this woman in white? What did Mr. Fulton call her? The Sihuanaba?"

I gave the neighborhood a quick scan, looking down both ends of the street. "Too much, and not enough, Gordo. Let's get back to the lake while we've still got some daylight. I want to make sure we didn't miss anything."

***

On the way to the lake, I told Gordo and Thunderclash about my glimpse earlier of someone or something in the trees and showed them the ash in my evidence bag.

Thunderclash removed four inches of cigar stub from his mouth and handed it to Gordo. Then the troll took the bag from me, and his eyes glowed with a deep red light as he studied its contents for several long moments. Finally, he grunted. "It *looks* like cigar ash, but that's not from any cigar I've ever seen. I don't think it's tobacco." He opened the bag and held it up to his nose. "No, not tobacco. Not marijuana or hashish, either. Not even cornsilk. It's nothing I've ever smoked." He closed the bag and took his cigar stub back from Gordo.

Gordo turned to me. "Mind if we keep that and send it to a lab?"

"Sure, as long as you let me know what it is as soon as you find out."

When we reached the trees, I pointed out the spot where I'd found the mound of ash. Thunderclash crouched and studied the ground. "He was probably standing on this flat rock here where he wouldn't leave any footprints." The troll took a couple of steps back so that he could examine a wider area. He shook his head and grunted. "He could have run off in any direction without leaving prints. This area is just too rocky." Thunderclash looked my way. "Wanna take a look?"

"No, that's all right. I've got something else that I want to try, though. I'll need another couple of minutes." Gordo arched an eyebrow at me. "I'm waiting for something," I told him.

Gordo glanced at Thunderclash and then turned back to me. He opened his mouth to say something, but at that moment a gray two-inch funnel of swirling air darted through the trees and lit on my shoulder. A hissing whisper emerged from the funnel: "Greetings, Aleksss! How's trickssss?"

Gordo's eyes opened wide, and Thunderclash took a step backwards. I smiled at the tiny whirlwind. "Hello, Smokey. Ready for some action?"

"Smokey is ready to rumble!"

Gordo laughed. "Is that an elemental?"

"He's my *main* elemental. Isn't that right, Smokey?"

The funnel of air hopped from one of my shoulders to the other. "Smokey is happy to serve!"

Thunderclash stared through a puff of cigar smoke. "Well I'll be damned!"

I'd sent out a summons for Smokey when we'd set out for the lake. It was several miles from the little elemental's haunts in the smoke-filled rafters of the Black Minotaur Lounge to Ohlone Lake, and it had taken nearly fifteen minutes for it to navigate the wind currents and get to me. My skills with elementals had come a long way since my time in the Borderland. In fact, since my encounter with the elf, I'd developed abilities that I'd never known were possible. Unlike any other human elementalist that I knew of, I no longer needed to draw or scratch out a summoning sigil when I wanted the service of an elemental. The enhanced awareness that I'd received from the elf had given me a better understanding of the spirits of the air, and I could now call an elemental simply by picturing the appropriate sigil in my mind. I'd given Smokey its name, which allowed me to summon it specifically when I needed its services, rather than having to take my chances with just any random air spirt that happened to be nearby. I'd worked with Smokey on many occasions, helping it to enlarge its vocabulary and to practice certain skills, and the little fellow had proven to be a reliable asset. The so-called "experts" on the subject continued to insist that elementals were semi-intelligent natural spirits that could mimic words and phrases and follow routine instructions, but that they were not truly sentient creatures. It was clear to me, however, that Smokey had a distinct personality, experienced genuine emotions, and was able to respond to patient teaching and learn new concepts. If that didn't constitute sentience, then I didn't know what did. The more I worked with Smokey, the more convinced I was that there was a lot that I could teach to the "experts," including all of my former teachers. Maybe I'd call on a couple of them someday. I might enjoy using some of their own tried-and-true teaching methods on them.

"Smokey, I want you to fly through this grove of trees, from one end to the other. I want you to fly around every single tree. I want you to search for two-legged creatures taller than this." I indicated a height of about two feet off the ground. "If you see one, I want you to come back to me and tell me. Keep searching until I call you. Does Smokey understand?"

The elemental bounced on my shoulder. "Smokey understands! I see two creatures now! A human and a troll!" Smokey leaped into the air and circled Gordo and Thunderclash before returning to my shoulder.

"That's very good!" Elementals tended to take a literal approach to their tasks, but I wondered whether Smokey had just attempted something like humor. I shook the idea off for the moment. "Go search for others. Off you go now!" The elemental stretched itself into a long, thin whirling tube and zipped away into the trees.

Thunderclash shook his head. "I'll be damned." Gordo chuckled.

I started out of the trees. "Come on. If anyone is watching us, Smokey will find them. Let's finish checking out that lakefront."

***

A half hour later, Gordo and I reached the same conclusion. The barefoot prints that probably belonged to the woman in white came from no place and went nowhere.

Thunderclash had only spent a brief time examining the scene before taking up a post just outside the space marked off by the crime tape. I gathered that the troll's primary duty was to make sure that no one disturbed Gordo or me while we were working. Gordo, who had been crouching over a print that was pointed toward the lake, stood and scratched his head. "It's like she flew in and then flew out again. Maybe the woman is some kind of air spirit. That would put her in *your* world, wouldn't it?"

I shook my head. "Not in the neighborhood *I'm* from. I'm just a working-class summoner. If she's an air spirit, then she's from the equivalent of Galindo Estates. They don't allow mugs like me to loiter in their streets. We spoil the view."

"And yet, here you are." Gordo's lips curled into a smile. "Hanging out with the mayor and his missus in their own lovely palace."

"Yeah. This is definitely out of my comfort zone." I poked at the sand with the point of my shoe. "I think we've seen everything we can here."

Gordo circled, giving the lakefront area one last going over. "And here's me thinking that we'd trip over a hidden clue that would lead us straight to that mystery woman."

I gave the area one last going over of my own. "Funny how it never seems to work that way." A thought struck me as I prepared to head back to the mayor's house. "Zyanya died somewhere around here, right?"

Gordo hesitated for a moment before pointing his chin northward in the general direction of the boat launch. "Yeah. Her body and the bodies of her children were found right up that way somewhere." Gordo's voice sounded a little flat and subdued to me, and I got the sense that he was reluctant to discuss the matter, or admit that he knew anything about it.

"Let's go take a look."

Gordo scratched his chin. "You sure? Her death doesn't got nothing to do with the woman in white, and, anyway, I don't think there's nothin' to see there."

"Probably not. Let's do it anyway."

"The sun will be going down soon."

"Not for another hour. It'll only take a minute."

Gordo looked like he was going to object further, but then he shrugged and forced a smile on his face. "Sure, why not. Long as we're here, right?" He waved at Thunderclash to get his attention and let him know where we were going, and the two of us walked along the shore toward the spot where Zyanya's body had been discovered two months before. We walked in silence until Gordo turned toward the lake and lifted a hand to indicate the water in front of him. "Her body was found floating right about here, maybe ten or twenty yards off the shore. The water doesn't move much, but her body probably drifted in from a little farther out."

"And the children?"

Gordo pointed. "They popped up out in the lake a few yards up that way."

I looked out over the lake, watching how the waters moved. This wasn't the ocean, but the peaceful lake's surface rippled in the wind, and tiny waves lapped the shore. I nodded toward the parking lot. The car with the trailer was gone, but the old white van was still there. "Do you know how many boat launches there are on this lake?"

Gordo shrugged. "Three, I think. There's this one, and there's one farther north. Maybe two, I'm not sure. And there's one on the south tip of the lake. This one here is the most popular one, though. You can access it from the main road leading out of the Country Club and from the Galindo Estates."

"Only three boat launches? Maybe four? It's a big lake."

Gordo chuckled. "Yeah. But the whole north and east sides of the lake are bordered by golf courses, and they don't want you launching boats near them. The noise would disturb the golfers."

I stared at the white van, focusing on it in a way I could not have done before the elf had buried a magic sliver of crystal in my forehead. I saw a wooden rack on the roof of the vehicle with hooks and ropes. It looked like something that might be used to tie down a small boat. "Do people fish in this lake?"

Gordo nodded. "Sure. The country club restaurant serves rainbow trout fresh out of the lake. Costs an arm and a leg, but it's worth it! For a fee, you can take a fishing boat out to a couple of quiet spots on either end of the lake that they've roped off for recreational fishing. Most of the fishermen use the other two launches, but the one south of here isn't far off, and you can get there from this launch pretty easily."

I was still looking out over the lake when a tiny whirlwind landed on my shoulder. I heard Smokey's excited hissing whisper: "Smokey sees someone!"

"Where!"

In response, Smokey stretched and leaned back toward the trees.

"Back where we started?"

"Yesss! Creature with two legs is where Smokey came to Aleksss."

I resisted the temptation to look in the direction that Smokey had indicated. If someone was watching, I didn't want to let him know that he'd been discovered. "What kind of creature? Human?"

"No. Smokey doesn't know what it isss."

That was odd. Smokey was familiar with every species of being, sentient and otherwise, that walked through the doors of the Black Minotaur, and that place attracted all manner of creatures. "Big as me? Bigger?"

"No. Smaller."

"Like a gnome? Or a dwarf?"

Smokey hesitated before answering. "Tall as gnome. Not gnome. Wider, like dwarf. Not dwarf. Something different. Something Smokey never see."

Odder still, especially since Smokey was as old as the wind itself. "Okay. Go back to the creature and watch him. Don't let him see you. If he moves, follow him. Go!"

Smokey zipped off, and I turned to Gordo. "Let's get Thunderclash."

Gordo nodded. "What do you think it saw? Small as a gnome but wider? But not a dwarf?"

"Beats me!" As we strolled toward Thunderclash, casual as a couple of tourists enjoying the quiet of the late afternoon, I scanned the tree line, using my elf-enhanced senses to try to catch a glimpse of our watcher. Nothing, nothing, nothing…. There! Had I seen something? I let my eyes roll past the spot and then roll back again. Yes! I could just make out the shape of a figure standing still as a statue in the shade of the cypress trees. His dark brown clothing blended into the darkness, making him almost impossible to detect if he didn't move, and I'd needed all of the elf's gift to me in order to spot him. As it was, I could just make out his silhouette, gnome-like, but different in some way that I couldn't yet discern. I needed a closer look.

We caught up to Thunderclash, and Gordo walked up next to him. "Southerland's elemental found someone right on the spot where he found the cigar ash. Says he's about the size of a gnome, but not a gnome." Gordo stretched and pointed at the parking lot. "Why don't you head for the boat launch. Walk like I've just given you a reason to check it out. Before you get there, cut into the trees and double back. We'll head toward the street and then veer back over to where he's standing. If he sees us coming at him, maybe he'll run into your arms. Let's see what the little fucker is up to."

It sounded like a good plan to me, so I went along with it. Thunderclash nodded at Gordo and set off for the boat launch, not running, but covering ground in a hurry with his long strides, as if he were on a mission. Gordo and I continued toward the path that took us through the trees to the Galindo Estates. The watcher never moved, except to rotate inch by inch as he tracked us. I tried to keep him in the corner of my eye without giving away the fact that I was aware of his presence. As we got closer, I noted that Smokey's description of the fellow hadn't been far off. He was no more than three feet tall, and probably a little less. That's about a foot shorter than the typical dwarf. Gnomes *can* be that short, but only rarely, and this creature was much bulkier than any gnome I'd ever seen. Gnomes are spidery-looking creatures with round torsos, sunken chests, thin necks, and spindly arms and legs. This creature was as round as a gnome, but even through his clothes I could see that his chest was broad and his arms and legs were thick and muscular. If he had a neck at all, I couldn't see it under his hooded sweatshirt. Nor could I see if he had the distinctive large rounded ears of a gnome. As for his face, I couldn't make it out at all with my sidelong glances. I needed a more direct look.

When we had drawn parallel to the creature, Gordo nodded with his chin to our right. We made a sudden turn and, picking up our pace, headed straight for the creature, who was staring right at us from about thirty yards away. Gordo yelled, "Security! Stay where you are!"

The creature didn't move as we closed the distance in a hurry. I looked into his hooded face—and saw nothing! Then I became aware that the creature was wearing a black mask that completely obscured his features. I saw Thunderclash—surprisingly stealthy for a troll—approaching the creature from behind. We had him pinned in.

In the blink of an eye, the creature leaped high into the air and grabbed a branch extending from eight feet up the trunk of a cypress tree. He planted his feet on the side of the tree trunk and, with an explosive crack that sounded like a clap of thunder, snapped the branch right off the side of the trunk. He pushed off the tree, flipped through the air, and landed on his feet, brandishing the branch—six feet long and half a foot wide at its base—like a club.

Gordo and I pulled up short, amazed at the creature's superhuman strength and agility. Even Thunderclash stopped in his tracks, momentarily stunned. The creature darted toward Gordo and me, and we each took an involuntary step back the way we had come. The creature then whirled with blinding speed and swung the tree branch at Thunderclash, who was running at him from behind. The branch caught Thunderclash smack on his left thigh, and, with a roar, the troll toppled to the ground in a heap.

Gordo pulled a pistol from the inside of his coat and shouted, "Freeze, motherfucker!"

As Gordo and I watched, too dumbfounded to move, the creature dropped the branch and leaped ten feet into the air. Graceful as an acrobat, he arced his body into a swan dive and launched himself headfirst at the flat rock where he'd been standing while he'd observed us. To our utter astonishment, he plunged straight into the surface of the rock, as if it were the deep end of a pool, and disappeared without a trace.

Chapter Seven

"Well, I'll be damned." Thunderclash was the first to break the silence.

Gordo ran over to Thunderclash. "Alkwat's balls! You okay, Thunder?"

Thunderclash climbed to his feet. "I'm fine. The little motherfucker caught me off balance." He tested his leg and, limping just a bit, walked over to get a closer look at the flat stone.

I raised my hand, palm up. "Smokey? You up there?"

The elemental zipped down from somewhere overhead and hovered above my palm. "Smokey is here."

"Aces! Take a look at that stone. Tell me what you see."

Smokey lowered itself until it floated a few inches above the stone where we'd seen the creature disappear. The elemental whirled for several seconds without saying anything.

"Smokey?"

"Smokey sees rock."

"Alex sees rock, too. Is there anything special about it?"

"Special?"

Communicating with elementals, even a smart one, like Smokey, is always a tricky business. I chose my words with care. "Is there anything that makes this rock different from other rocks?"

The funnel of air continued to whirl in silence for a few more moments. Then the elemental lowered itself until it was touching the surface of the rock. "Rock is rock. Something was inside rock."

I let out a breath and tried not to express any of the frustration that was building inside me. "Yes, Smokey. The creature that you spotted for me jumped inside."

"Smokey saw. Something else was inside rock."

That caught my attention. "Something else?" Gordo stepped a little closer to Smokey, listening with interest.

"Yesssss. Elemental of earth was here. Smokey seesss…. Smokey doesn't know how to say what Smokey sees. Smokey knows elemental of earth was in rock."

Finally we were getting somewhere. "That's great, Smokey! You did good!"

Smokey whisked itself away from the rock to hover on my shoulder. "Smokey is happy to serve Alekssss!"

I couldn't help smiling at Smokey's eagerness to please. "Nice work, little fellow. You deserve some rest and relaxation. I release you from your service for now. Have fun at the Black Minotaur!" Smokey stretched itself until it was the size of a six-inch rotating straw and launched itself into the breeze.

Gordo raised an eyebrow at me. "That's some pet you've got there!"

"Smokey's no pet. It's more of an associate."

"Well, give her a raise!"

I chuckled at that. "Her? Elementals aren't made that way."

Gordo winked at me. "If you say so. So what did your associate say about an elemental in that rock?"

I nodded. "An earth elemental. It makes sense. Earth elementals are outside my ability to summon and command, but I know a little about them. They travel through the earth, and they can bring along cargo, or passengers. I think that our watcher is an elementalist, and that the elemental was his getaway vehicle."

Gordo nodded. "So that...thing, whatever it is, he could be anywhere now. Is that what you're saying?"

I thought about it. "Something like that. It depends on how long that creature can hold his breath."

"Then we'd better get back to the mayor's house as quick as we can. Thunder? You ready to move?"

Thunderclash did a knee bend and grunted. "I'll live. Let's go."

We started off for the path back to the residential area when I pulled up short. "Wait!"

Gordo and Thunderclash stopped and stared at me, questions in their faces.

"Do you two hear that?"

Gordo frowned, listening. Then he shook his head. "I don't hear anything."

Thunderclash cocked his head. "Just the wind in the trees."

I continued to listen. "You two go on. I'll join you in a few minutes. I need to check something out."

Gordo shrugged. "Again? What is it with you?" He sighed. "Okay, but watch out for that critter. From what you say, he could pop up anywhere. Holler if you need help." He waved Thunderclash toward the path. "Let's go."

I waited until the two of them were out of the cypress grove and back on the street. When they were out of my sight, I started walking through the trees toward the boat launch, trying not to make any noise. Though Gordo and Thunderclash couldn't hear it, my enhanced senses had picked up a faint sound, so soft that it might have been mistaken for the murmuring of small waves as they rolled onto the shore of the lake. But, as I focused my senses on the sound, I heard something distinct from the splashing of the water. I heard the anguished sobs of a woman in pain.

When I drew parallel to the spot where Zyanya's body had been found, I stopped behind a cypress and peered around it at the lakefront. Even though I was half expecting to see her, my breath caught in my throat as I found myself gazing at the woman in white—the Sihuanaba! She looked just as I remembered from the streets of Zaculeu, just as I'd been seeing her in my nightmares ever since, except that her long black hair and white dress were drenched, as if she had just emerged from a swim. She stood facing away from me and staring out over the lake. Her arms hung at her side, and drops of water dripped from her fingertips and from the strands of her hair. Every few seconds, her body would shake, and I would hear a strangled sob escape unbidden from her lips. A normal woman would have been freezing in the late afternoon breeze, and I found myself wanting to emerge from my hiding place, drape my coat over her shoulders, and comfort her.

But I shook off the urge, which felt to me like a witch's spell, something I knew about from firsthand experience. I didn't know exactly what the Sihuanaba was, but I didn't believe that she was natural to this world. If she'd ever been human, she was something else now. Whatever she was, I'd seen her face, and I knew that her outward beauty and apparent vulnerability were illusions. It was impossible for me to think of her as anything but an unearthly, inhuman hag.

As I watched her, trying to figure out what to do next, she turned without warning. I ducked behind the tree, hoping that I was hidden by the shadows and the gathering darkness, fearing that she could see in the dark as well as I could. A surge of panic ripped through my body. My heart hammered in my chest, and my stomach tried to climb into my throat. Fighting hard against the urge to lam out of there as fast as I could, I willed myself to stand firm. My feet betrayed me, however, and before I could stop myself I took an involuntary step backwards. I caught an exposed tree root with the heel of my shoe, and, flailing my arms in a futile attempt to catch my balance, I fell backwards and tumbled into the underbrush. As I scrambled to retrieve my hat and regain my feet—along with some shred of dignity—I lost sight of the hag. I hurried out of the trees, but by the time I emerged into open ground she was nowhere to be seen.

"Hey!" I yelled. I jogged toward where she'd been standing, swiveling my head back and forth to see if I could catch a gander of her anywhere on the lakefront. All I could see was my own long shadow, cast by the last glow of the setting sun and stretching to the surface of the lake. When I reached the spot where I'd last seen the hag, I observed that the sand was soaked all the way to the lake, but I detected no hint of any footprints leaving the area in any direction. I avoided the wet sand. I'd once had an ugly experience with a water elemental after stepping into what I thought was nothing more than a puddle, and I'd been wary of anything resembling a pool of water ever since. I kicked dirt into the wet area. Nothing happened. I didn't think it would, but, on a day when I'd seen a strange masked creature in a hooded sweatshirt dive headfirst into a rock, I felt like I couldn't be too careful.

I took a few moments to gaze out over the lake, watching the wind ripple its glassy surface as the last traces of sunlight disappeared. It was quiet. Too quiet. I shook my head. I was getting jumpy. Too jumpy. I decided that it would be a good idea to see what the rest of the team was up to. Taking one last look around at the deserted lakefront, I pulled my coat close against the wind and hurried to the path leading out of that patch of wilderness and back to civilization.

***

I didn't tell Gordo that I'd seen the Sihuanaba. The bruiser struck me as a decent joe, and his team of trolls seemed professional enough, but they all worked for Fulton, and I knew better than to trust that sharper. Smooth operators like Fulton tell you only what they want you to know, and only a fool would assume that they are always on the level. I would give him an honest day's work, but I had no qualms about holding back on anything I uncovered until I knew for sure what I was into. Besides, I hadn't received a signed contract from that weasel yet. He'd only offered to pay me half my rates, and I'd be damned if I was going to give him anything for free.

We were all sitting in the black sedan, positioned in the same way that we'd been the night before: Stormclaw behind the wheel, Gordo riding shotgun, and me between the trolls in the back seat, Ironshield on the driver's side and Thunderclash, his fedora brushing against the roof of the car, on my right. I was part of the team, at least for now, and these were going to be our spots. We'd have had more room in the beastmobile, but, knowing that it wouldn't have been accepted, I didn't make the offer. For one thing, I would have insisted on being behind the wheel, and that would have upset the team dynamic.

We were preparing for the long night of surveillance by chowing down on the food we'd brought with us. I was working on a frozen roast beef sandwich that I'd microwaved just before leaving my apartment and stuffed into an insulated lunch box. I also had a thermos of black coffee that, if not exactly hot, was at least still warm. Gordo was munching away on a submarine sandwich with all the trimmings and drinking from his own thermos. The trolls were holding odd-shaped wooden bowls with handles on their sides and using knives to pick chunks of raw meat from a vile-smelling cold stew of some sort. Pork or beef, I hoped, but I knew better than to ask. A troll's food is his own business.

The partition was down, and Gordo looked back over his shoulder from the front seat. "Hey Thunder! How's your leg?"

Thunderclash swallowed a mouthful of bloody flesh. "It's good. Not a problem."

The bruiser took a drink from his thermos. "You ever seen anything like that before?"

"Nope! Never. Damnedest thing, wasn't it?" Thunderclash plucked another chunk from his bowl with his knife.

Ironshield raised his bowl to his lips and slurped up some of the broth. He lowered the bowl and wiped a trickle of dark scarlet off his mouth with the back of his hand. The stocky troll looked over my head at Thunderclash, and his upper lip pulled back into a sneer. "You say it was a little fellow?"

Thunderclash nodded at him. "Yeah, the motherfucker couldn't have been more than three feet tall."

"And he knocked you down with a stick?"

Thunderclash scraped meat off his knife with his carnivore teeth. "It wasn't a stick. It was a motherfuckin' tree!"

From the front seat, Gordo snorted. "It wasn't a whole tree. It was a fuckin' *branch*!"

Thunderclash rubbed his leg where he'd been struck. "A *big* branch. Practically a tree."

Ironshield shook his head, and his sneer grew more pronounced. "Lord's balls! I don't know, man. It's a sad day when big bad Thunderclash starts letting himself get trashed by some gnome."

"I lost my balance! He stuck that branch in front of me and I tripped."

Gordo laughed. "That's not the way I saw it. He whacked you good! Chopped you down like a fuckin' redwood."

Thunderclash stabbed at one of the chunks in his bowl. "Yeah, well that wasn't no gnome, I'll tell you that."

"No, it wasn't," Gordo agreed. "Its arms were huge! What do you think, Southerland? Could it have been a dwarf?"

I shook my head. "My elemental said it wasn't. And I've never seen a dwarf that short."

Gordo nodded. "And I've never seen one jump around like that." He turned back to Thunderclash. "Could you have torn a branch that size off a tree?"

Thunderclash shrugged. "Sure, no problem. But I couldn't have jumped up, grabbed the branch, planted my feet on the side of the tree and snapped off a branch that size, and then pushed off the tree trunk, flipped in the air, and landed on my feet. And I don't know anything that can!"

Stormclaw, who had been listening while keeping his eyes focused out the window of the car, spoke without turning his head. "I might have some ideas about that."

We all looked at the driver. Gordo raised an eyebrow. "Enlighten us, old-timer."

Stormclaw took a sip from a troll-sized flask as big as a pineapple, swished it around in his mouth, and swallowed, all without turning his gaze from the street. "I've heard some stories about little folks who are stronger than you'd expect. They call them by different names in different places, but you hear about them in all seven realms. Some of them are magical. They don't take well to cities, but you can find them in forests and jungles. Mountains, too, maybe. Depends on how many of those stories you're willing to believe."

Ironshield snorted. "Sounds like bullshit to me."

Thunderclash turned to glare at him over my head. "You'll see how real he is when he pops up out of the street in front of you. Southerland here says he could be anywhere, traveling under the ground."

Ironshield turned his glowing eyes on me. "Th'fuck you sayin'?"

I took a bite of my sandwich and met his stare while I chewed. Gordo spoke for me. "Southerland says that the little fucker has himself an earth elemental that carries him around underground. The three of us saw him dive straight into a rock and disappear. Southerland here says he's probably still around and could come up anywhere at any time."

Ironshield took an involuntary look at the floor of the sedan.

"Anywhere out of the ground," I clarified.

"Lord's fuckin' balls!" Ironshield's eyes grew wide. "Can it come up through the street?"

I thought about that. "I don't see why not. Asphalt is made of sand and ground up rocks, all held together with bitumen. That's all natural earth-type stuff, so an earth elemental should be able to carry the creature through it without any trouble."

Ironshield scowled and began chewing on another chunk of meat. "This job just keeps getting better and better." He looked out his window to study the street with renewed attention.

Gordo swallowed another bite of his sandwich and looked up at Stormclaw. "Anything happening out there?"

Stormclaw shook his head. "All quiet. No little folks popping up nowhere, and no little ladies in white dresses trying to snatch away the mayor."

Gordo wiped his mouth with his sleeve. "Gonna be a long night of nothing, I think."

Ironshield sat bolt upright in his seat. "Wait a second! I think I've got something!"

We all turned to look at him. "What is it?" asked Gordo.

Ironshield opened his mouth and let out a thunderous belch that lasted for five full seconds and filled the inside of the car with the stench of rotting meat. When he was finished, he half closed his eyes, put a contented smile on his face, and relaxed back into his seat with a satisfied, "Ahhhhhhh…."

Gordo groaned. "Lord's balls, Ironshit! You're a fuckin' asshole!"

Thunderclash shook his head. "Feel better?" he asked.

"Sure do!" Ironshield's smile broadened. "I think I've got room for the rest of my dinner now." He raised his bowl and took a big gulp of the bloody broth.

By now, the air inside the car was thick with the mingled smells of stale coffee, dead meat, both raw and cooked, the odor of sweating bodies, both human and troll, and breath so foul that it would send a seasoned dental hygienist into another line of work, like collecting garbage. In other words, it was the typical working environment for a surveillance team. I shrugged and finished my sandwich.

Ironshield shifted in his seat. "So what's up with this bim? I hear she's a dish!"

Thunderclash groaned. "You thinkin' you might get yourself laid by this chick in white?"

Ironshield's sneer straightened into a grin. "Hey, would it surprise you?"

Thunderclash glanced down at me and then back at Ironshield. "To be honest? Probably not. But you want no part of this one, loverboy! Don't you listen to the briefings anymore?"

Ironshield leaned his shoulder against the car's window and crossed his ankle over his knee. "Yeah, yeah. She's supposed to be one crazy bitch. But she's never climbed the Iron Pole!" The troll grabbed his crotch. "It's got a way of making the scariest dame get *re-e-e-al* friendly!"

I saw Gordo roll his eyes. "You're so full of shit."

Ironshield's grin grew wider. "I'm full of something, all right. It's called my big dick! And it's out of control!"

Thunderclash nudged me. "You wouldn't believe how much tail that ugly pug pulls in."

Ironshield chuckled. "And it's not just trolls and adaros, either. We're talking about some fine human femmes! I like 'em big and soft." He reached out and cupped his hands around imaginary butt cheeks and mimed pulling them into his hips. He looked down at me, his mouth parted in a sneering leer. "And let me tell you, pal. Those human sluts are *begging* for my meat! You puny human men don't have enough between your legs to satisfy them." He threw his head back and released a guffawing laugh from deep in his chest. "Haw haw haaaaaw! What can I say? Chicks *dig* me!"

Thunderclash threw a chunk of his dinner at the leering troll. "That's 'cause they don't *know* you, you asshole."

Ironshield's grin widened. "They don't have to *know* me to *blow* me!"

Thunderclash groaned and waved a dismissive hand. "Some skirt will be the death of you someday."

"Maybe. But what a way to go!"

Gordo turned to get Ironshield's full attention. "Careful what you say, hot shot. If Mr. Fulton is right, this might not be your ordinary frill. She could be some undead spirit that kills crazy poon-hounds like you."

Ironshield scoffed at Gordo's warning. "Hey, undead's better than dead, right? Especially if the broad's got a big ass!"

At that point, a long low rumble that sounded like a lawnmower engine rose from the front seat. It reached a thunderous crescendo and then sputtered to a halt. Gordo whipped his head around to glare at Stormclaw. "Alkwat's flaming pecker, Stormclaw!"

Thunderclash scrunched his nose and fanned his fedora in front of his face. "Th'fuck, man! Give us some warning next time! Phew! What'r ya eating—week-old road kill?"

Ironshield slapped Stormclaw in the back of the head. "For fuck's sake, roll down the windows!"

The expression on Stormclaw's wrinkled face never changed, and his eyes remained on the street. After a few moments, he reached to the door controls and flicked at a switch. All four windows lowered about half an inch and then stopped.

Ironshield straightened up in his seat and took a deep breath of fresh night air through his barely opened window. "Gee, thanks, asshole!"

Thunderclash put his hat back on his head and smiled down at me. "Welcome to the team, Southerland. Hope you're enjoying your first day."

I looked up at him. "It's had its ups and downs."

Ironshield slapped at my shoulder with the back of his hand. "Hey, Southerland! You're not married are you?"

I didn't rub my shoulder. I realized that the boisterous Ironshield had just been trying to get my attention, but that didn't mean a slap from the troll wouldn't leave a mark. I looked up at him and put a smile on my face. "Nope. Single and free."

Ironshield smiled back at me. "You and me oughta hit some clubs some time. Gordo and Thunder are taken, and Stormclaw's too old to get it up anymore, but you and I could do some serious scoring."

"Sounds like I'd just get in your way."

The troll peered down at me. "Naw, man. Let me give you some pointers and you'll be picking up more prime pussy than you can shake a stick at. Here's what I like to do. I find me the prettiest little lady in the place. I walk up to her and say, 'Hey, babe! Wanna fuck?' Nine times out of ten, she slaps me in the face. But that tenth one...." Ironshield closed his eyes and his face relaxed into a dreamy expression. "Ooooohhh *baby!*"

Gordo shook his head, groaning. "Just ignore him, Southerland. He's an animal, but aside from that he's also a first-class shithead."

The smile never left Ironshield's face. "Awwww, Gordo. You're so cute when you're jealous."

Gordo smirked at Ironshield, then turned to me. "He has no clue. I married my Nysha thirteen years ago, and it was the smartest thing I ever did. Ironshit runs through them like cheese slices at a buffet table, but he'll never know the pleasure of having a good woman at your side supporting you through thick and thin." Gordo nodded at Thunderclash. "He knows what I'm talking about. How long you and Lucretia been married now?"

Thunderclash scratched at his long jaw. "Let's see now. We've got an anniversary coming up pretty soon. Our seventy-sixth, I think. Seventy-seventh maybe."

I did some mental calculations in my head. If Thunderclash had married at a typical age for a troll, then he would be about one hundred twenty, give or take ten to twenty years. Roughly the human equivalent of about forty. I looked up at him. "Sounds great! It just hasn't happened for me."

Thunderclash's long face split into a grin. "Let me show you something."

Ironshield groaned. "Here it comes."

Thunderclash reached into his coat and brought out a wallet. He opened the wallet and turned it so that I could see a photo displayed in a transparent cover. "That's me, of course, and that's Lucretia. And that there is little Marco."

I leaned in for a closer look. I'd never seen a baby troll before. Trolls were not a prolific species, and maybe only one in ten troll couples gave birth to children. Baby Marco, nestled in his mother's arms, looked to be about four feet tall and probably a hundred fifty pounds. His face was dominated by his large pointed ears and red eyes that smoldered beneath a thick bony ridge. He looked like a demon from Hell, which, of course, is where trolls had emerged from in the first place.

I leaned back and smiled up at Thunderclash. "Cute kid."

Thunderclash beamed as he put away his wallet. "Lucretia did me real proud, giving me a son like that. I was afraid it might be a girl, but Lucretia's a good wife. She wouldn't've done that to me. Now Marco can carry on the Thunderclash name. You bachelors are really missing out. There's nothing like having a good woman to cook your dinner every night and sew a new button on your shirt when you lose one."

Ironshield snorted. "Hngh! I've got nothing against married women. Long as they're not married to me!" He let out a guffaw and clapped me on the shoulder. "That's why Gordo and Thunderclash never invite me over to their houses. They're afraid that if their wives get a good look at me, they'd never be satisfied with their ugly husbands anymore."

Gordo shook his head. "Ironshit, you're such a knucklehead. Not that I'd have anything to worry about. My Nysha only has eyes for me. That's what I love about her. She's totally mine."

I looked up at Thunderclash and gave a brief nod toward Stormclaw. Thunderclash glanced at the driver and back at me. He narrowed his eyes and gave his head the tiniest of shakes.

Stormclaw's gaze never left the street, but he spoke as if he'd heard my unspoken question. "It's been seventy-three years since I lost my Flavia, but she gave me the eighty-one best years of my life. I was never interested in anyone after her."

"She must have been pretty special," I offered. Stormclaw took a drink from his flask and said nothing. I gathered that as far as this topic was concerned he'd contributed all that he was going to.

Ironshield crossed his arms. "You old ladies are about as much fun as a temperance meeting. I'm going to get some shuteye. Let me know if any gnomes pop out of the dirt or any hot chicks show up. Sounds like you'll need me to handle both of them for you." The sneering troll closed his eyes, slumped in his seat, and stretched out his legs. Within a minute, his snores were reverberating through the inside of the sedan like a symphony of malfunctioning chainsaws.

***

We continued our surveillance of the mayor's street until well past midnight. Teague never emerged from his house, and when Gordo checked on him at ten he was sleeping like a kitten. His wife, Tracy, said that she'd given him one of the sleeping pills that Fulton had provided her, and that he wasn't likely to wake until sunrise. No strange ladies stalked the streets, and no unnaturally strong little demons clawed their way up into the mayor's front yard or through the asphalt into the street. That's the way it goes with surveillance. Ninety-nine-point-nine percent of the job is just killing time, and usually nothing much happens during the remaining point one percent, either.

A couple of hours after falling asleep, Ironshield woke up and regaled us with stories about his time as a student at Angel City U., where he'd spent his days studying criminology and his nights partying like there was no tomorrow. Most of his stories were dubious, to say the least, but I had to admit that his enthusiastic renditions of his shameless and tawdry debauchery kept the rest of us entertained as the minutes drifted by like a thick fog on a windless day. I would have preferred a nice quiet game of poker, but card games are too distracting for surveillance work. So we laughed and groaned at Ironshield's outrageous bunk and kept our attention on the surrounding night.

As we frittered away the hours, I learned a few things about my new crew. Gordo had spent his mandatory service years as a bodyguard at the Tolanican embassy in Indraprasthra, the capital city of Sindhu, which is where he'd met his wife, Nysha. He was fluent in the Sindhu language and had a deep knowledge and appreciation of its culture. It just goes to show: the bruiser may have looked like a ham-and-egger, but he had a head on his shoulders. After his three-year mandatory, Gordo left the service and took up prizefighting, racking up a dozen victories without a loss until he ran into a real buzzsaw one night who put him down for the count in the eighth round. The fight had taken place in Yerba City, and, as it happens, Fulton had been watching from a ringside seat. Despite the fact that Gordo had finished the fight on the canvas, Fulton liked the bruiser's grit. He approached Gordo in the locker room after the contest and offered to put him on his security staff if he would agree to give up the ring for good. Gordo, concluding that his pugilistic career had peaked and that further fights would only scramble his brain cells, accepted

Fulton's offer on the spot. That had been eleven years ago, and Gordo had been grateful to Fulton ever since.

I learned that Thunderclash was an ex-cop who got drummed out of the YCPD some seven or so years back after breaking a table over his sergeant's head in a stationhouse dustup. The way Thunderclash told it, the sergeant had been in the pocket of the Hatfield Syndicate. Thunderclash and his partner, a human named Mapletree, had refused their boss's order to turn their backs when a Hatfield torpedo was attempting to erase an eager young newshound who was digging a little too deep into the family's business. Soon afterwards, Thunderclash and Mapletree had been dispatched on a domestic disturbance call.

"The call stunk," Thunderclash said. "Me and Tree suspect a trap as soon as we get the call, so we put on vests. We get to the house and knock on the door, and we hear a woman screaming. We had to enter the premises, right? But we go in with weapons drawn. Five loogans were waiting for us, and they start slingin' lead as soon as we step in. We get plugged right away, but we're wearing vests, so we're okay. We take out three of them, and the other two run. I'm about to pursue, when Tree drops to a knee. Blood is pouring from his neck right above his vest. He's still breathing, so I apply pressure to stop the bleeding and call for backup." Thunderclash paused. "No one shows up. Tree doesn't make it."

Thunderclash returned to the station and brained his sergeant with the table. The blow would have killed the sergeant on the spot if he'd been human, but he was a troll, and as a result he'd only lost most of an ear and suffered a sizable bump on the noggin. Thunderclash lost his job, but Fulton scooped him off the scrapheap, gave him a position in his security force, and made sure that the YCPD and the Hatfield family let him be. A few weeks later, the sergeant was found dead in a sleepy-time girl's crib, victim of a hot-shot of skag, the needle still hanging from his arm. It might have been a coincidence.

The car was quiet as Thunderclash told his story, even though the others had already heard it. "Tree was a good man," Thunderclash concluded. "Left behind a wife and three children. When I caught up to the two loogans who got away, I cut off their ears after I finished them. I've cut off six pairs of Hatfield ears since. Fuck the Hatfields."

I was surprised to hear that Ironshield had been born into an upper-crust Angel City family. His father was a respected judge, and it was due to his influence that Ironshield had been accepted at ACU's prestigious School of Criminology. To the consternation of his old man, Ironshield, as he himself admitted, squandered every dime of his hefty allowance on "booze, broads, and bribes," the latter to his professors in exchange for passing grades. Unable to find enough corrupt professors to advance past his second year, he'd given up college and entered into his mandatory government service. His father had exerted more influence, and Ironshield found himself posted in downtown Tenochtitlan as a martial arts instructor with the rank of lieutenant. According to Ironshield, his exploits in the swinging nightclubs of Tenochtitlan were still the subject of song and legend. When his term was up, he'd moved to Yerba City with the intention of opening up his own gym. He was in City Hall checking boxes and filling out forms in one of the bureaucratic offices, when Fulton had walked in out of nowhere, strolled straight up to him, and, without so much as a "Hi, how you doing?" asked him if he wanted to be a part of his security team. Ironshield had laughed when he told me his story. "I don't know how, but the son of a bitch knew my whole fucking history. I figure my old man must have had something to do with it, riding in on his white horse one more time to rescue his only son from permanently fucking up his life. Good thing, too! To be honest, running a gym was already sounding like too much damned responsibility for a good-lookin' jasper like me. I don't know why I was even considering it. Even filling out the forms seemed like a lot of work. Fulton's offer was just what I needed—a chance to pound some heads every once in a while and plenty of free time in between jobs for hittin' the clubs! I've been with Fulton for five years now, working with these three losers. They'd be lost without me!"

Stormclaw was the mystery man of the team. I picked up that he'd been with Fulton longer than any of the rest of them. He rarely spoke, but when he did it was worth hearing, and everyone listened. He'd apparently traveled all over the world, but not even Gordo knew why or under what circumstances. Stormclaw himself offered no hints. He stared out the window, his wrinkled face expressionless, and said nothing, even when others discussed him openly or speculated about his background. Ironshield never wasted an opportunity to rib him about his age, implying that the old troll was impotent, decrepit, and senile, and that he stunk up the car with his old-man smell, but Stormclaw just let it all ride. I had the feeling, though, that no one, including Ironshield, wanted to tangle with him. He had that look about him that invited you to take your bellicose bullshit elsewhere.

    As the morning wore on, we stopped gabbing and grew content to stare into the night and keep further thoughts to ourselves. A relief crew would arrive at about two, and Gordo told me that he'd call me sometime around noon with further instructions from Fulton. Gordo's crew seemed like a solid team, and being with them reminded me of fighting shoulder to shoulder with my unit in-country. Some of those memories were good. The camaraderie and trust among members of a team fighting to keep each other alive is impossible to replicate. But most of my memories from those times were the stuff of hellish nightmares, and I didn't like recalling them. Too many of the men I'd fought with were dead, and, despite earnest and heartfelt promises, I'd lost contact with the ones who'd made it home. I'd wanted to sever all of my links to the Borderland, even at the expense of maintaining connections to the people that I'd served with there. Maybe that was a failing on my part, or the result of a flaw in my character. I don't know. If it was, it was a flaw I could live with. In any case, I'd been working solo since leaving the service. That night, after sitting with these men and helping them keep a lookout on the quiet street outside the mayor's house for an entire evening, I found myself growing comfortable in their company. But I knew that I could never truly be a part of their team. I could eat and drink with them, bullshit with them, and help them do a job, watching their backs while trusting them to watch mine, but I would always be an outsider. I had a few folks who I liked to think were friends, even if they weren't really *pals*, and I enjoyed the occasional poker night with the boys. But I knew who I was at heart: a solitary lug who liked drinking alone in a corner booth at a crowded bar, observing the exchanges, the back-and-forth, the hustling, the seductions and rejections, the whispers and shouts, the actions and reactions, and all of the playacting and drama, observing the whole messy theater of life from the balcony and keeping my opinions to myself. And I was fucking jake with that, copacetic as a pig in shit.

Chapter Eight

It was almost three in the morning when I walked up the stairs into my apartment, too tired to even brush my teeth. I had just managed to slip off my overcoat when I was startled by a raucous clanging coming from somewhere in the alley behind my building. Looking out my window, I saw that an aluminum garbage can had tipped over, and that something had crawled most of the way inside and was digging through its contents. Probably a raccoon, I thought. It wouldn't be the first time. This one was making a *huge* racket as it thrashed around inside the can. Must be a big one, I thought.

I knew I'd have to scare the critter off if I was going to be able to get the sleep I was needing, so I put my overcoat back on and prepared to go into battle. Getting to the alley from my apartment required climbing the stairs down into my office and going through a side door into a hallway that led to a back door. A laundry room that I had partially converted into a homemade gym sat off the hallway to the left. I went into the laundry room and grabbed a broom, planning to use it to drive the raccoon away. Then I continued down the hallway, opened the back door, and stepped out into the alley.

The critter was still rooting around inside the fallen garbage can, and the metal container made an awful clatter as it rolled back and forth over the asphalt. I made some noise of my own. "Hey!" I yelled, and started banging the broom handle on the asphalt as I made my way toward the garbage can. "Hey! Scram! C'mon—git!" When I reached the garbage can, I began striking it with the broom. "Come on out of there! Git!"

The thing that backed out of the garbage can was not a raccoon. I didn't know what it *was*, but it definitely was *not* a raccoon. I thought at first that it might be a goat. It had the head of a goat, complete with a long, thin goat's beard and two large curved horns. But I'd never seen a goat with glowing red eyes that burned like a troll's. Nor had I ever seen a goat with a row of thorny spikes that ran down the length of its spine. And no goat that I'd ever seen had a long hairless rat's tail, or humanlike feet with razor-sharp nails extending from the tips of its stubby digits like claws. Truth be told, I'd never actually seen a goat at all, at least not live and in person, but I'd seen pictures, and I'd seen goats in movies and on television. Still, limited as my knowledge of goats might have been, I was pretty sure that the creature I was looking at was something other than a goat. Then, as we stared at each other in shocked silence, the creature did something that I was fairly certain a goat couldn't do. It stood on its hind legs and began walking toward me with a purpose.

I took a step backwards and poked at the creature in the center of its chest with the broom handle. With a swipe from its taloned hand, the creature knocked the broom out of my grip. It snorted and opened its jaws, revealing a terrifying set of pointed teeth. Drool dripped down the sides of its snout as the creature met my eyes with its glowing red ones. I found that I couldn't look away. All at once, I was overwhelmed with the nauseating odor of dead flesh. My stomach lurched, and sweat began to pour down my forehead. My legs grew weak, and I felt like I was going to wretch.

With an effort, I wrenched my gaze away from the creature's eyes and staggered backward. Although the stench that had threatened to overcome my senses didn't fade, the sensation of nausea that had gripped me so suddenly now began to subside. I forced myself to face the creature and prepared to defend myself against an attack.

The creature didn't move. It seemed startled. I wasn't an expert in interpreting the facial expressions of goats, but the creature's eyes were wide and it no longer seemed aggressive. In fact, it appeared to me that the creature was, well, maybe not afraid of me, but cautious. Deciding to test my theory, I made a quick threatening move in its direction. It dropped to all fours and drew a few short steps back from me. I advanced another stride, and it backed away some more. By now I had reached the broom, and, carefully, without taking my eyes off the creature, I bent down and scooped it up. The creature held its ground, watching me with what I thought was a wary expression.

Rather than charge at the creature, I took some time to study it. On its hind legs, it had stood about five feet tall, and with its red eyes, its teeth, its talons, and its spikes, it had been a chilling sight to behold. But now that I was able to take a better look at it, I could see that the creature was not in good shape. Despite the darkness of the early morning, my elf-enhanced awareness allowed me to see that the creature's skin was infected with mange, and that the fur on the spots that weren't bare was wiry and matted. The thing was also so emaciated that its ribs and spine looked like they might rip through its skin at any moment.

"What the hell are you?" I asked it.

It cocked its head in reply.

I shook my head at it. "You're hungry, aren't you."

It crouched until it was lying on the ground with its feet tucked under its bony body. The spikes on its spinal ridge lay down until they were almost flat on its back. It looked up at me, the glow in its red eyes muted, and whined like a sick dog.

I'm not an animal lover. I'd never had a pet, and I'd never missed having one. But I knew misery when I saw it. I had no idea what to do with this creature, though. It smelled like a week-old corpse, and I had no inclination to bring it anywhere near where I slept. But I couldn't let it bang around in the trash cans, not if I wanted to get any sleep before Gordo called me at noon. I had no alternative. I steeled myself to chase it out of the alley and into the street.

"C'mon, you mangy alley rat. You've got to go." I poked at it with the broomstick. The spikes on its spine sprang upright, but otherwise the creature didn't move. "Go on! Git! Go prowl around in somebody else's garbage!" I poked at it some more.

The creature raised its head and gave me a mournful look. It climbed to its four feet, turned, and shambled away down the alley. As I watched it go, it turned once and looked back at me with an accusing glare, its eyes glowing through the darkness with a dull light. Then it turned away and walked on until it disappeared around the corner of the alley.

"And don't come back," I muttered under my breath. "Fuckin' overgrown alley rat." After picking up the fallen garbage can and setting it back in place, I stumbled back to my apartment, and, feeling like a heel, fell into bed at last.

***

My alarm woke me up at ten thirty, and by the time Gordo called me at noon, I was in my office and ready to roll. I learned from Gordo that the rest of the morning had passed without incident, and Fulton had ordered his operatives to transport the mayor to his downtown apartment for the day.

"Me and the rest of the team are with him now," Gordo told me. "The mayor and Ironshield are swapping war stories, by which I mean stories about their sexual conquests. It sounds like a lot of hooey to me, but those two animals are like peas in a pod. At least the mayor is in better spirits today. I expect that by tomorrow he'll be back to giving speeches and kissing babies."

"Do you want me to join you?" I was sipping on some coffee, debating with myself whether to kick it up a notch with something from a bottle.

"That's up to Mr. Fulton. He wants to see you this afternoon at three. He'll be at Wally's. You know where that is?"

"Wally's Tap Room? Sure. It's where all the bigshot politicians go to meet, greet, and collect their suitcases full of dough. Any idea what he wants with me?"

"Maybe. He was pretty disturbed about our ruckus with that little fellow. Mr. Fulton calls him an 'earth demon.' I don't know about that, but I think he wants to talk to you about him."

I poured a finger of rye into my coffee. "He's already got me looking into the woman in white. Is he dropping that now?"

"That's between you and the boss. Maybe you're his expert on *all* the out-of-the-ordinary threats to the mayor these days."

"He doesn't need an investigator. He needs a witch! I can recommend a couple to him."

"Well, like I said, that's between the two of you. We'll probably be stuck in this apartment babysitting the mayor through the weekend, and Mr. Fulton may want you to take a shift or two, so maybe I'll be seeing you later."

"Okay, pal. We'll see what the chief has in mind. I'll give you a call if I'm coming."

I started to disconnect then, but I was stopped by a sudden thought. "Gordo! Before you go.... Where does your crew get that slop that they eat?"

"You mean that bloody soup? You can get it at most butcher shops."

"Any place where you can get it for cheap? You know, someplace where the meat isn't necessarily inspected for content or quality? Or species?"

"Hmmm.... There's this market that Stormclaw goes to where he gets it for cheap. Thunder and Ironshield are always giving him shit about it, not that the garbage they eat is much better. It's in the Porter District on the corner of Wool and Summer. Kind of a shady neighborhood. I wouldn't go there at night without a fully loaded roscoe."

I chuckled. "I live just inside the Porter. I know the place you're talking about. It'll do. Thanks!"

Gordo hesitated, and I sensed that he was weighing his words, trying to be diplomatic. "You know, if you wanted to make some *real* money, I'll bet Mr. Fulton could find a place for an operator like you on his staff. If you want me to put in a good word...."

I chuckled again. "Don't worry, the food isn't for me. And I live on the *fashionable* end of the Porter. Anyway, I like running my own business. Thanks, though."

"Well, it's your life. I hope you didn't take what I said the wrong way."

"Not at all. It's all jake. I'll probably be seeing you and the boys later, depending on what Fulton has in mind."

"All right, buddy. Keep walking the sunny side!"

"You bet!"

After we disconnected, I downed my juiced-up coffee and pondered making another call. Decision made, I punched a private cell number into my phone, leaned back in my chair, and propped my feet up on my desk.

Detective Laurel Kalama connected after two rings, her voice sounding weary. "Hello, gumshoe. What's up?"

"Cheating spouses, runaway daughters, you know, the usual. How are things in homicide? People still killing each other?"

"Every chance they get! Talking out your problems is a lost art these days. This a social call?"

"Of course, Detective! I wasn't doing nothin' and I thought I might call me a copper and shoot the breeze for a while. But as long as I've got you on the line, I've got a work-related question for you. You know, one investigator to another."

"You mean amateur to pro, don't you? Well, shit. You know how it is with us *real* cops. We've got nothing but free time on our hands. Go ahead and ask your question. I'm always willing to educate civilians with inquiring minds."

"Thanks, pal. Did homicide get involved with the Zyanya death?"

"Zyanya? The singer? I hear that she drowned herself. See, the way it works at the YCPD is that homicide investigates murders."

"It was a suicide? You're sure about that?"

"That's what they tell me."

I hesitated, pondering the detective's choice of words. "That's what *who* tells you?"

"Oh, you know. The old wise men upstairs who park their asses behind their shiny desks and tell us soldiers when to run and when to grovel."

"Oh, *those* guys." I took my feet off my desktop and straightened up in my seat. "I hear they're pretty smart."

"Sure they are. Smart enough to protect a songbird's reputation from a bunch of nosy homicide dicks and kick the matter of her death over to the people in expensive suits who know how to handle crimes involving people who matter."

"Is that bitterness in your voice? Detective, I think you're trying to tell me something."

"You're mistaken, gumshoe. This is a social call. Which we should continue some other time. When I'm not working at the office. Say, over a drink? Soon?"

"That could be a problem. My current job is taking up a lot of my hours and I'm not sure yet what my calendar looks like for the near future." I hesitated. "I've got a free hour right now…. You got time to drop by my office for lunch?"

"Whatcha got to eat?"

"Nothing you'd want, and I just had breakfast. Why don't you grab yourself a burger on your way over?"

I heard the detective sigh. "Sure, sure. It's not like I'm doing anything anyway. I probably don't have more than a half a dozen open case files on my desk, each one stamped 'urgent' for some reason. They'll probably solve themselves. Sometimes I think I'm just stealing my salary, which comes right out of the taxpayers' pockets. It's a crime! Don't go anywhere, gumshoe. I'll be right there."

The call disconnected and I put my phone down on my desk. I hadn't known Detective Kalama long. She and I had found ourselves working with each other a couple of months earlier after a mortgage company executive named Donald Shipper had been killed in a spectacular fashion by a witch's curse that Madame Cuapa, the infamous Barbary Coast Bruja, had been compelled to launch against her will. In the few days that the detective and I had teamed up, she had impressed me with her intelligence, honesty, and professionalism. She'd also proven to be a reliable partner when the shit was flying. I preferred working alone, but if I ever needed someone to watch my back I could certainly do worse than the detective.

I'd called Kalama on a hunch, and because of a nagging tingle on the inside of the back of my neck, a prickling sensation that was all too familiar to me because I'd been experiencing it all my life. More often than not, that annoying prickle meant that I was about to land in a pool of shit up to my eyeballs. It was an overwhelming impulse that made me want to ask inconvenient questions, like "Why…?" and "How...?" and "What's down that unlit alley that I was warned never to walk into after dark?" This time, the prickle was telling me that I needed to discover everything I could about Zyanya's death, no matter what the consequences might be for yours truly. According to Fulton, the singer had been murdered, shot in the chest, and he had a crime-scene photograph to prove it. But Kalama, a homicide detective for the YCPD, was under the impression, along with the rest of the public, that Zyanya had drowned, and the department had written it off as a suicide. It was clear that she wasn't satisfied with that explanation, however.

And there was something else about Zyanya's death that didn't sit right with me. It had bothered me from the beginning that the Sihuanaba had led Teague to the lakefront where Zyanya's body had been discovered. Sure, it could have been a coincidence. Unlike a lot of people, I believed that coincidences happen all the time. And there was the fact that Teague lived within easy walking distance of the quiet lakefront, so it was a logical place for the Sihuanaba to lure the mayor and inflict her punishment on him. But I'd heard the Sihuanaba crying at the exact spot where Zyanya's body had been fished out of the water. Maybe there was nothing to it, but the prickle in my neck was forcing me to find out for sure. I needed to know about the singer's death, and it sounded like Kalama might be able to shed some light on it.

***

Kalama stepped through my office door a half hour later and plopped down in the armchair across the desk from me. "We've gotta make this quick. I'm double-parked."

I shoved a hot cup of coffee—cream, four sugars—across the desk. "No burger?"

"I ate it in the car on the way over." She picked up the cup, tested the coffee for temperature, and then drank down a healthy gulp.

I hadn't seen Detective Kalama in more than a month, since just after the Shipper case. She'd been in bad shape then, but I could see that she'd recovered nicely. Kalama was probably a real looker when she was done up and dressed to please. I'd never seen her that way, though. What I saw was an attractive cream-colored face with hard edges, no makeup, and no-nonsense dark eyes. Her hair was dark, thick, and cut midway down her neck. I knew that she was a couple of years shy of forty with a nineteen-year-old daughter, but her fit athletic figure made her look at least five years younger. Her plain shirt and slacks were pure business. I didn't know who she was after hours, but when she was working she was all cop.

She put her cup down and got right to it. "You're looking into Zyanya's death?"

"It's related to a case I'm working on. I can see myself drifting in that direction."

She nodded. "Good. Keep me in the loop."

I took a sip of my own cup of coffee, black, because I like my coffee to be coffee. Except, of course, when I needed a little extra jolt to it, but I'd already had a finger of booze earlier, and I wanted to have a clear head when I met with Fulton later that afternoon. "You've got something to tell me about her death?"

"Not officially, but, yes, I do. You're aware that the singer's two kids were discovered along with her body?" I nodded, and she continued. "When the call came in, we didn't know if the canary had committed suicide or been murdered, but two dead children were involved. The captain's first thought was that the mother had drowned the kids. That made it a probable homicide, and I got the assignment. I made it almost all the way to the crime scene before I was yanked off the case."

"What happened?"

Kalama's lips twisted into a scowl. "Leea!"

Leea. The Lord's Investigation Agency, or the LIA. Leea. Lord Ketz-Alkwat's own department of justice, and the highest law enforcement agency in Tolanica. Although they were not officially designated as such, everyone knew that the LIA was the Lord's internal spy service, too, his own personal police force. They were his eyes, ears, and hands. A secretive organization with no oversight except the Dragon Lord himself, they were everywhere, they saw and heard everything, and they could make anyone in Tolanica disappear as if they had never been born. When leea showed up to a crime scene, the local cops were reduced to errand boys. Either that, or they were simply told to pick up their notebooks and go home. Some cops loved it when leea showed up, because that meant one less job for them. But serious cops—cops like Kalama—had a different outlook on the elite investigative unit. They considered the leea agents to be intruders, prima donnas in expensive suits who built big reputations for themselves and their agency by hogging all the glory cases and leaving the mundane crime for the locals to deal with.

I knew why leea had nabbed the case. "Mayor Teague and the songbird were an item."

Kalama nodded. "And those kids were probably his. But it's a local case, and it belongs to YCPD."

I picked up my coffee cup. "Not anymore."

"Yeah? Well I don't like being brushed away from an important murder case like I'm some kind of amateur. No offense."

"Why should I be offended? I'm as much a professional as you are. And I get to be my own boss, which means I get to make my own decisions."

"Sure, but do you get benefits? Insurance? Paid vacations?"

"I try not to need insurance. And when's the last time *you* ever took a vacation?"

One side of Kalama's lips lifted into a half-smile. "Kai keeps asking me the same question. He says that the worst part of being the husband of a cop is that he only sees me for a couple of hours at a stretch." Her smile broadened. "But those hours are intense! Speaking of which, how's *your* love life coming along?" Her eyes drifted to a painting that hung on my wall above some file cabinets. Two feet tall and six feet wide, it was too big for my office, and the subject matter, a mysterious black bird sitting on a mesa overlooking a haunting desert landscape, seemed a little elegant among my secondhand furnishings, like a tuxedo jacket over a flannel work shirt. Kalama looked back at me. "Didn't that painting used to be in the Widow Shipper's living room?"

"Let's talk about something else." I took a long sip of my coffee.

Kalama's eyes softened and her expression took on a motherly tone. "Poor baby. It's your own fault, though. You're not a *bad*-looking guy. Some women like that hardened weather-worn look. You just need to make yourself more available."

I put my cup down on the desk. "Right. So you said something about the LIA?"

The intensity returned to Kalama's eyes and the scowl to her face. "They've scooped up the Zyanya case, and they're going to bury it. Someone up high doesn't want Teague's dirty laundry exposed, especially during an election year. Teague gets protected, and Zyanya gets forgotten. So much for justice."

I frowned. "Does she deserve justice? She killed her own children, right?"

"Probably," Kalama admitted. "But did she kill herself?"

I hesitated. I wasn't ready yet to tell the detective about my encounter with Fulton. Maybe I was a little embarrassed about it. Besides, if I told Kalama that Zyanya had been shot, she would raise a stink about it with her superiors, and I didn't think that would go well for her. So I hedged. Maybe I was wrong not to trust her to take care of herself, and I'd no doubt have to come clean at some point, but, for the moment, I decided to dummy up. "Kind of looks that way," was all I told her.

"But we don't *know*, do we! Because no one is investigating her death! And, for that matter, we don't *know* that she killed her kids! And, if she did, why? Shouldn't somebody be finding out about that?" Kalama picked up her coffee cup and put it down again without drinking from it. "There's something going on behind all this. And it all points to the fuckin' mayor. He's covering up his girlfriend's death because too much attention to it would make him look bad during an election year, and Ieea is helping him do it." She shook her head and crossed her arms. "I don't like it."

I tapped one-handed at my desktop with my fingertips. Kalama was probably right. If an inquiry into Zyanya's death was going to implicate Mayor Teague in some way, then Ieea was more likely to bury the case than investigate it. Teague was the kind of pliable politician that the Dragon Lord's inner circle liked to see running things at the city level, especially in a major metropolis like Yerba City. Political scandal invited reform, and reform was almost always anathema to the tradition-conscious leaders at the higher levels of the Tolanican government. After all, Lord Ketz, the ruler of Tolanica, had been in his position for six thousand years! His highest priority would always be stability. If it came to a decision between keeping a corrupt, but cooperative, mayor in office, or making sure that some local nightclub torcher received justice, well, the choice was obvious.

"You want me to dig into the songbird's death, don't you."

"Yes, I do."

"And keep you informed."

"Yes. And don't you dare start yappin' to me about fuckin' fees!"

I smiled at the detective. "Don't worry. I'm pretty sure that my current case is going to require me to take a look at what happened to Zyanya." For half-price, I reminded myself, but I didn't mention that to Kalama.

Kalama drank down the last of her coffee and stood. "I've gotta go. Nice to see you again, gumshoe. Be careful with the agency. They won't like you butting in."

I stood. "You know me. I'm as cautious as a moth in a lighter factory."

Chapter Nine

After Kalama left, I logged on to the internet and did some cursory research on Zyanya. Fulton had said that it was Teague who had given her the "Zyanya" moniker and set her up in the Gold Coast Club, and I found nothing to contradict that story. Details of Zyanya's history prior to her two-year run at the Gold Coast were scarce, but I managed to come across a brief bio of the singer that revealed a few details from her early life. According to the bio, the singer's given name was Jennifer Hermosa, and she'd been born in Yerba City. Her parents had moved north from Azteca right after they'd married, and Guillermo Hermosa had left his wife, Tayanna, for parts unknown two months before she'd given birth to Jennifer, the couple's second child. Tayanna delivered two more children after that, but the bio didn't name the father, or fathers, nor did it give the names of Jennifer's two younger siblings. The bio claimed that baby Jennifer began to sing before she could walk, and that she'd started singing for dough at weddings and in local bars when she was still a teenager. When she was fourteen, her mother died of cancer, and her older sister, Edith, took over as head of the household. I left myself a reminder to do more research on Edith when I had the time.

Satisfied for the moment, I leaned back in my chair and recalled the two times that I'd seen Zyanya perform. I'd been star-struck by her sweet, emotion-packed voice, her stunning beauty, and her ability to dominate the stage in front of a band of talented musicians. The word 'charisma' gets batted around a lot, but, if anyone had it, Zyanya did. Despite her powerful presence, she'd always seemed a little sad to me. Maybe it was the fact that most of her songs seemed to be about lost love and heartbreak, or maybe it was the effect of the spotlight on her large violet eyes. She had begun to make a name for herself in Yerba City, and it seemed inevitable that her star would continue to shine. The prevailing opinion was that Zyanya owed her success to Mayor Teague. He had opened the gates for her and engineered her rise to the highest levels of the Yerba City music scene, and then she'd brought her tragic end upon herself with her own self-destructive impulses. I wasn't so sure. I couldn't help but think that someone with her kind of talent and stage presence would have found her own way to stardom somehow without the help of someone like Darnell Teague.

At two-fifteen, I switched off my computer and left my office to go meet Fulton. Traffic was no worse than usual as I made my way downtown, but parking was an issue, and it was about twenty after three by the time I walked into Wally's Tap Room. I spotted Fulton with his back to the wall in a corner booth at the rear of the lounge and crossed the room to join him. I passed by clusters of cheery swells drinking martinis or gin and tonics or whiskey sours, lips stretched into smiles as they clamped down on cigars with their teeth or let cigarettes dangle from the corners of their mouths. Here and there, the rare broad was mixed into the cluster, forced to make herself a little more attractive in order to be accepted, to drink a little harder in order to be respected, and to speak a little louder in order to be heard. According to the newspapers, more political decisions were made in this room than in the offices of City Hall.

Fulton saw me coming and motioned me to a seat across the table from him. "Sit down, Southerland. You're late! You started drinking yet?"

"Not so's you'd notice."

He waved to a waiter, who veered away from the table he was heading for and made a beeline for Fulton. "Give this man what he wants," Fulton told him.

I looked up at the waiter. "Whiskey and soda. No ice." The waiter hustled off without a word.

The glass in front of Fulton was nearly full. It looked like a whiskey on the rocks, and I noticed that the ice had begun to melt. Apparently, he'd been waiting for me to arrive before starting on his drink. As I settled into the booth across the table from him, he took a long sip and set the glass down on a paper coaster.

"Tell me about this earth demon." Having waited twenty minutes for me, I guess he wasn't in the mood to waste time on small talk. I described the encounter to him like a reporter with a deadline, giving him as much detail as I thought necessary.

"And your elemental said that the creature definitely wasn't a dwarf or a gnome?"

"That's what it told me."

Fulton shook his head. "And it used an earth elemental to make its escape? I don't like elementals. Creepy things. Pretty handy, though, I guess. Right?"

I shrugged and said nothing. My drink arrived, and I sampled it. I was pleased to find that the whiskey was damned good! I expected no less from the famous Wally's, but sometimes the most exclusive watering holes could be the most disappointing.

I put a "this drink ain't half bad!" expression on my face, and Fulton responded with the briefest of smiles. "I understand that you had Gordon take you to the place where the songbird's body was found."

I nodded. "I did."

"Why?"

"I was curious." I took another sip of my drink.

Fulton locked his eyes on mine. "Let me be clear, Southerland. Your job is to investigate the woman hounding our mayor. I want to know if she's really the Sihuanaba or just some crazy stalker. And keep an eye out for this earth demon. He might be connected with the woman in some way. Even if he's not, I want to know if he's a threat to the mayor." He pointed a finger at me for emphasis. "Leave the Zyanya case alone. She went cuckoo, drowned her kids, and then drowned herself. End of fucking story. The LIA looked into it, and that's their conclusion. It's my conclusion, too, and I don't want anyone coming up with any conclusions that are different from mine, if you get my drift." His eyes didn't leave mine as he lifted his drink and took a healthy sip.

"And that's how it really happened?"

Fulton set his drink on the coaster with just a touch more force than necessary. "I don't want her death surfacing with all this other bullshit that's going on. I told you before, the optics are bad. If the press gets wind that I've got someone poking around at this songbird's corpse while he's investigating a stalker, someone will try to put two and two together and make a story out of it. That hurts Teague in an election year. We can't have that. We *won't* have that! Am I clear?"

I knew that arguing with Fulton would be a mistake. "Sure, Fulton. No problem."

Fulton continued to stare at me, trying to read my face. I let him. Finally, he nodded, sat back in his chair, and picked up his drink. "Good. The mayor's in his apartment. I've got Gordon and his team with him 'round the clock, and if they can't keep him safe, no one can." He stared at his glass and frowned. "The damned fool mayor wants to go golfing on Sunday, and I can't talk him out of it. He's lined up three of his biggest boosters for a morning tee time at Galindo Downs."

I turned my glass around on its coaster without lifting it. "You can't stop him?"

Fulton glared at me. "I could shoot him in the head. That would stop him."

I thought for a moment. "Have you considered it?"

"I think about it every damned day! He's a pain in the ass! But..." The fixer shrugged. "I'm paid to keep him alive."

I picked up my drink. "Too bad."

Fulton grunted and shook his head. "You play golf, Alex?"

"I tried it once. It didn't take."

"It's a good game. A gentleman's game, though not everyone who plays it is a gentleman. The links are a great place for making deals. There's plenty of free time for friendly negotiation. That's why so many bigshots like to play. Golfers tell themselves that they're getting some exercise because they're out in the open air all morning, but mostly they drink beer, swing a club between seventy and a hundred times, depending on how good they are, and ride around in those fuckin' little electric carts. You get more exercise here at Wally's walking to the men's room every five minutes to piss away the booze you've been drinking." As if to emphasize his point, Fulton downed his drink and stood. "Hold my seat. If the waiter comes by, tell him I want more of the same."

I nursed my drink while Fulton was gone, and I made sure that he had a fresh drink waiting for him when he returned. I thought it might be a good idea to let him get a little ahead of me while we were talking.

Fulton came back after a few minutes. He sat and tossed back half his drink before setting the glass back on the coaster. "The mayor wants you to caddy for him on Sunday," he told me. "One o'clock tee time. Be there at noon."

I couldn't stop my surprise from showing. "Why me?"

Fulton shrugged. "He likes you for some reason. You can help keep an eye on him."

"What about Gordo and his crew?"

"I've been riding them hard, and they're going to need a day off. But Thunderclash will be there with you. That bastard never rests! The two of you should be able to handle things." Fulton pushed his empty glass to the center of the table. "I don't think that the Sihuanaba is likely to show up. Her mode of operation is to lure men off to some lonely spot during the night and then do her voodoo on them. I don't think she'll make a play in a public place in broad fuckin' daylight." Fulton tapped the edge of the table with one of the large rings he always wore on his fingers. Those rings would do serious damage if he ever decided to take a poke at someone. That was probably the reason he wore them. "I'm more concerned about this earth demon. Gordon says that you told him he can travel underground, and a golf course is nothing *but* ground. That little motherfucker could pop up anywhere!"

"True," I agreed. "But to my knowledge he's never made a move on the mayor. It seems to me that he was there watching us investigate the lakefront, and he ran off when we came at him. I think he was just a bystander. I don't see where he has anything to do with the mayor."

"No?" Fulton frowned and set his jaw. "Well, you might be right. But I don't know anything about him, and I don't like it that he was in Teague's neck of the woods last night." He looked up at me. "I want you to find out whatever you can about what kind of creature he might be. I want to know every fuckin' thing there is to know about him before the mayor sets foot on the golf course on Sunday. Maybe there's some kind of connection between him and the woman. If there is, I need to know about it. Maybe he's got other reasons for hanging out at the lake, but, if he does, I want to know what they are. I doubt that he lives there. You're an investigator—investigate him! You've got the rest of today and all day tomorrow and Saturday. I don't want any surprises on Sunday."

"Okay."

"Any questions?"

"Yeah. What does a caddy do?"

Fulton's face lit up in amusement. "When the mayor wants a beer, give him a beer. When he asks for a three-iron, give him a fuckin' three-iron. If he asks you for advice on his swing, tell him to stop thinking and stay in rhythm. Any more questions?"

"Just one. You sign my contract yet?"

The fixer's face tightened. "I'm having my accountant go over it. There seems to be a problem with your stated fees, but I'm sure we'll have it ironed out before the weekend."

Fulton seemed done with me, so I downed half my drink, left the rest on the table, and started to slide out of the booth.

But Fulton stopped me. "Not so fast, Southerland. There's something else I want to discuss with you."

I settled back into my seat and said nothing.

After some hesitation, Fulton looked across the table at me. He seemed a little uncomfortable. "What do you think of Gordon and his team?"

I shrugged. "They seem like a good crew."

Fulton considered this non-answer for a moment. "Did you pick up anything…unusual? About any of them?"

"Like what? Stop being coy, Fulton. If there's something you want to know, ask me."

"I want to know if they're loyal. Or if any one of them might be *dis*loyal."

I was taken aback by the question. "Seriously? I just met them. How would *I* know!"

Fulton frowned and leaned across the table to get closer to me. When he spoke, his voice was little more than a whisper. "Harvey's got a sharp operator working for him. Man named Benning. He does for Harvey what I do for Teague."

"You mean he's Harvey's fixer?"

Fulton's smile didn't reach his eyes. "If you want to call it that, sure. He's an attorney, like me, and, also like me, he protects his client any way he can. Now, I've got a couple of people in Harvey's organization, and I assume that he has a couple in ours. But I haven't rooted them out yet."

"How do you know they're there?"

"Because that's what guys like me and Benning do."

I thought about it. "And you think that one of Gordo's guys is a mole?"

Fulton shook his head. "Not necessarily. But I have to assume that anyone in our camp could be working for the enemy. To be frank, that's one of the reasons I brought you in. You're an outsider, and you haven't been on Benning's radar, although you will be now."

"Terrific. Well, what do you expect me to do about it? Am I supposed to be your spy now?"

"Stop being a sap! I just want you to keep your eyes open, that's all. You'll be working with Gordon and his team until we've straightened out this mess with the woman in white. If you see anything that seems funny to you, let me know."

The waiter came by then and placed a fresh drink in front of Fulton. He looked at me, but I shook my head. Fulton stared at his drink until the waiter left. Then he raised his eyes to meet mine. "Benning works for the Hatfields. The Hatfields own Harvey."

I mulled that over in my mind and then shrugged. "So?"

Fulton's face tightened. "That's why Teague needs to win this election! You think he's incompetent? You think he's morally repugnant? You think he's bad for this city? Just wait till you see what this city will be like when it's run by an organized crime family!"

I shrugged. "Would I notice the difference?"

Fulton picked up his glass and took a slow sip. When he put the glass down, his face was relaxed. "You're just like all the other chumps in this city, Southerland. You think that all politicians are crooks. Well, maybe there's something to that. Any politician who tells you that he isn't in it for the power is lying through his teeth. He wouldn't *be* in this racket if he wasn't grabbing for some juice. He'd be running a fucking charity, or a non-profit foundation. So, sure, Teague wants to continue being mayor because he likes the perks and the respect that comes with the job. But you know what? Teague *loves* this city! And so do I. We were both born and raised here. Sure, it's got its problems. It's dirty, dangerous, and as corrupt as a dockside whorehouse. Believe me when I tell you that this city busts my balls every single day. There are times when I wish I could pull the handle and flush the whole filthy dump into the bay. But it's *my* city, and, for my money, Yerba City is the greatest fuckin' city in the whole fuckin' world, and I'll break any man's teeth who says different!"

I stared at Fulton for a couple of seconds before asking, "Is this the part where I take out my checkbook and donate to the cause?"

Fulton glared at me over his drink. "Funny guy. I get it. You don't think much of Teague. You don't think much of me, either. But anyone who believes that this city would be better off in the hands of the Hatfields, a bunch of drug-peddling, gunrunning, lowlife pimps with no respect for the city's political traditions…well, that person would be a fucking fool. And, unless I'm seriously underestimating you, I don't think you're a fucking fool."

"I don't know, Fulton. You might be overestimating my intelligence."

Fulton set his drink down on the table. "Yeah? Maybe. Well let me put it this way. Teague and I want this city to survive and flourish, if for no other reason than for our own benefit. We have a vested interest in the health of this city. If it does well, we do well. But the Hatfields? They don't care about this city. They don't care about anything but the family business. They talk a lot about wanting respect, but for them it's really all about the dough. They will rob, fuck, or murder anyone at all just to pile up more for themselves. Give them the opportunity, and they will drain this great city of everything it has. They'd squeeze it dry until it was nothing but broken-up concrete and rust. Then they'd pack up and move on to greener pastures."

I downed the remainder of my drink. "Even if I believed this campaign rhetoric you're slinging my way, you're still asking a lot from a hired gun that you aren't willing to pay."

Fulton's lips parted in a tiger's smile. "There's more to life than money."

"Yeah? Like what?"

"Like being free to work in this town as a licensed private eye and not getting nailed for murder. Stop yanking my chain, Southerland! Find out all you can about the woman and about that earth demon. Get in touch with me if you run across anything important. Unless you hear otherwise, plan to meet up with the mayor at noon on Sunday at the Galindo Downs clubhouse. I'll see that you have a signed contract and a retainer by then. Hell, do a good job for me and I might even open up a full-time spot for you on my staff. You'd earn more in a month working for me than you make in a year as a private dick."

I had nothing to say to that, so I stayed mum. Fulton leaned back in his seat and picked up his drink. "I don't know why, Southerland, but I like you. You're tough, sure, but I've got a lot of tough guys working for me already. But none of them stand up to me like you do. It's good for a guy in my position to have someone around him who is willing to spit in my eye if he doesn't like what I'm tellin' him. Keeps me in line. Right now you're small potatoes. Minor league. Think of this job as an audition for a spot in the majors. Now fuck off and go get the skinny on that dame and the runt." He tossed back the remainder of his drink and turned to look for the waiter.

I suddenly felt forgotten and invisible, so I stood and stepped out of the booth.

Fulton stopped me. "Southerland!" I waited, and the fixer raised his eyes to meet mine. "I meant what I said about Zyanya's death. Stay away from it! That story is dynamite. People in this city loved her, and if the press starts painting her up to be a victim, the city is going to need someone to blame for her death. Someone they can hate. Well, that someone's not gonna be Teague. That story's got to stay buried. But if you keep scratching at it, and it blows up, I'll see to it that the people of this city get their fall guy. You understand what I'm sayin'?"

    I got it. It couldn't have been clearer. I turned away without a word, and none of the cheery men and women sipping civilized drinks from their ice-cold glasses while planning the city's future so much as glanced at me as I walked out of the bar.

Chapter Ten

A black cloud cast stormy shadows inside my head as I sat behind the wheel of the beastmobile and prepared to head into the afternoon traffic. I was accustomed to making the rules when I was on the job. I wasn't used to taking orders from a client as if I were still in the service and the client was my superior officer. But, as long as Fulton had possession of my handgun, I knew that he had me over a barrel. I told myself once again that I was going to have to do something about that.

The traffic had picked up while I'd been away, and as I fought my way through the congested streets of downtown Yerba City I thought about the circumstances surrounding Zyanya's death. It left Fulton with a problem, a problem that needed to be fixed. Although he'd covered up the relationship between the mayor and the songbird as best he could, it was an open secret at best. Fulton had to assume that Montavious Harvey knew about it. He was too well-connected not to, and, besides, his fixer had probably planted a mole or two in Teague's camp. So Fulton had to ensure that Zyanya's death didn't become a bigger story than it already was. He used his influence to have the case turned over to the LIA with the understanding that the agency would declare the matter closed. The death was a tragedy, but not a mystery. Nothing to see here. Move on.

I understood Fulton's position. Hell, I sympathized with it. The last thing Fulton needed was for some clumsy private dick to come stomping in with his work boots and start kicking up the dirt that was burying the case. Not because the dick would uncover anything suspicious, but because any new attention to the singer's death could be used by Harvey's campaign to generate troublesome conspiracy theories and strip away the flimsy golden-boy persona that kept Teague, and, by extension, Fulton, in power.

Still, I couldn't stop the questions from forming in my head. Fulton was just a little *too* determined to keep me out of the Zyanya case. What if Zyanya had been threatening to make trouble for Teague while he was trying to get himself reelected? What if Teague had panicked and killed her, possibly even by accident? Or what if Fulton had permanently silenced Zyanya, or had it done? Fulton needed to keep the singer's death from exploding in Teague's face. Well, why should I stand in his way? The YCPD had been chased away from the case. Kalama believed that the LIA had closed it, and she was probably right. No one, including my client, had hired me to look into it. Kalama wanted me to, but so what? I respected the detective, but I didn't owe her anything. The smart thing for me to do was to focus on the Sihuanaba and the "earth demon," or whatever he was. That's what I'd been hired to do, even if at a reduced rate. Digging into Zyanya's death would only lead to trouble.

The problem was obvious. The Sihuanaba had appeared to Teague soon after Zyanya's death, and the vengeful spirit had lured the singer's ex-lover to the site where she had died. I'd seen the Sihuanaba, crying, on the exact spot where Zyanya's body had washed up from the lake. It strained the bounds of credulity to believe that Zyanya and the Sihuanaba weren't connected in some way. Fulton wasn't stupid. He had to know that the jilted lover and the spirit of vengeance were linked. Fulton wanted me to investigate the one, but to stay clear of the other. The fixer had looked me straight in the eye and ordered me to lay off the Zyanya case. How did he expect me to do that? He hadn't asked, and he hadn't said "please." That had been rude. I don't like rude. Rude pisses me off.

A cacophony of horns snapped me out of my reverie. I gunned my way through the green light so that I could stop behind the line of cars waiting for the next one. I wasn't going to be able to do much about Zyanya at that moment, but at some point I knew that I would have to at least talk to some of the people who had been close to the singer when she died. It occurred to me that Gordo, or someone on his team, might have some insight. I'd have to be careful what I asked them, though. I didn't want my inquiries getting back to Fulton, not while he could use my heater as manufactured evidence against me. I'd have to tread carefully and take advantage of any openings that came my way.

I didn't know what to make of Fulton's suspicions concerning a mole operating within his organization. I thought that Fulton was right to assume that Harvey's man, Benning, would at least try to plant someone in Teague's camp, or to turn someone who was already there. Could Gordo or someone on his team be working for the Harvey campaign, and by extension, if Fulton was giving me the straight dope, the Hatfield Syndicate? It was possible, of course. But I hadn't seen any indication of it. And if one of them was a plant, so what? How far was I willing to go to stooge for Fulton just because he had the power to take away my investigator's license or frame me for murder? That was a question I didn't want to ask myself, because I didn't know what I would answer. I decided to let it be for the moment.

Traffic relented only a little as I left the central downtown area and entered into the Porter District. On my way home, I swung by the corner market on Wool and Summer. The place was barely more than a shack. It didn't even have a sign. But behind its large picture window facing Wool Street I could see at least a dozen customers walking the aisles and another half dozen lined up at the single checkout counter with their baskets of groceries. The store even had a parking lot. No one slot was wide enough for the beastmobile, but I was fortunate enough to find two adjacent slots whose combined width provided me with the room I needed.

The meat section was in the back of the store, and a troll in a white cloth butcher's hat and a bloodstained apron the size of a sail stood behind the display of meats, a lit cigar dangling from his lips. When I got close, he asked, "Help ya?"

"I'm looking for that troll soup, whatever it's called. The one with raw meat soaking in blood."

The troll nodded. "Ya want yonak? Large, medium, or small?"

"How big's a large?"

"Feeds two."

I assumed that he meant two trolls, since no one else was likely to touch that stuff. "How big's a small?"

"Half the size of a large."

"That should do it."

The butcher scooped the yonak out of a thirty-gallon metal cauldron into a glossy cardboard bowl, managing to keep ash from his cigar from falling into the soup. He held up a couple of unlabeled shakers for me to see. "Ya want me to spice it up for ya?"

"No thanks. I'll take it plain."

"Suit yerself." The butcher put a lid on the bowl and taped it shut. "Pay at the counter. Next!"

When I got back to my apartment, I considered whether or not to refrigerate the yonak. I wanted it to be about room temperature, and I didn't care if it got a little gamy. The problem was that it smelled like roadkill, and, with the way the odor was already spreading, I calculated that my apartment would be unlivable in about fifteen minutes. My solution was to carry the soup down to my laundry room and cover it over with a canvas tarp. That kept the stink down to a minimum, especially after I closed the laundry-room door.

Back at my desk, I forced myself to think about Fulton's leverage over me. Lubank was right: stealing my gun back was not an option. I didn't know where he was storing the piece, and I had no way of finding out. Could I use an elemental to find out? Even if I planted Smokey in his pocket, I had no reason to believe that Fulton would ever mention the location of the gun or put himself in the same room with it. Eliminating the entry from the registry was a great idea if I could figure out a way to do it. Lubank had pointed me toward the Hatfields, but if I allowed them to help free me from Fulton's grip I'd be putting myself at the mercy of the Syndicate. I'd never be my own man again.

I thought and I thought. I took out my phone, punched in a number, and then stared at the screen without connecting the call. It was a slim hope. I didn't like the odds. I stared at the screen some more. It wouldn't hurt to ask. I raised a finger and let it hover over the call icon. I could think of a hundred reasons why I shouldn't go any further. I let my finger hover. I stopped thinking, took a deep breath, and, feeling like the ground had just crumbled beneath my feet, made the call.

After the third ring I was met by a sudden burst of words. "Tom Kintay! Speak to me I'm all ears!"

"At ease, Corporal. You sound a little frayed at the edges."

The voice lapsed into a hopped-up impression of a famous old-time movie gangster. "You got the wrong man, copper!"

"Oh, you're the wrong man, all right. What's doin', Corporal?"

"You know me, Sarge, workin' like a dog."

"How long have you been awake? You should get more sleep."

"Sleep? What's that? This is an election year, and that means fund-raising dinners and secret meetings. The demand for quality product goes up and up, and they all want something more special than the last pill they popped or the last crystal they burned in their water pipe. Good thing I'm a genius!"

"When are you going to take all that talent and put it to work for the good guys?"

"Good guys! Who are they? You must be talking about chumps with no dough, because let me tell you, Sarge, if they can afford what I'm designing, they're buying it!"

"Ever think about designing a cure for the common cold?"

"What for? You cure the cold, you kill the demand for your product! Then what? Economically, it's a dead end." Kintay's voice began to race like a sports car on the open highway. "Anyway, people don't want a cure for their colds—they want a cure for their boring lives! They want excitement! They want sensation! They want their wires fired and their minds blown! They want to be gods, even if just for a few hours. I can give them that. And you want me to fuckin' give them chicken soup? Fuck that! If I'm going to design a cure for something, it'll be for the clap! In fact, that's not a bad idea! My bosses could use that—and how! You shoulda seen—"

"Whoa—slow down, Corporal! You haven't been sampling your own product, have you?"

"Hey, someone's got to test it! I take pride in my work. I would never let the bosses flood the streets with something I haven't stamped with my own seal of approval!"

"Well, whatever you're working on now, you might want to dial it back a bit."

"You think? Hmmm. You might be right about that. I've broken three test tubes in the last half hour. Hang on! I'm gonna pop a couple of reds."

"Wait! Kintay? You still there?" I could hear him muttering to himself over various muffled noises.

Tom Kintay worked and practically lived in a lab in a nearly deserted industrial park where he designed exotic and expensive drugs for the Hatfield Syndicate, who distributed them for an obscene profit to the more well-heeled residents of Yerba City. Technically speaking, these designer drugs were illegal, but the Hatfields operated as if they were exempt from government authority, no doubt because they diverted a sizable portion of their profits into the pockets of anyone who might otherwise object to their way of doing business. I'd heard that the Dragon Lord himself allowed the existence of an unregulated underworld for his own obscure purposes. I'd also heard that the Hatfield Syndicate was secretly run by Lord Ketz himself! That seemed a little far-fetched to me, but there were times when I wondered. Whatever the truth might be, I knew that when dealing with the Hatfields it was a good idea to treat the organization as if they existed outside the legal system, which was true in every way that counted.

But I was hoping that I wouldn't actually have to deal with the Hatfield Syndicate itself. Kintay and I had our own personal relationship that preceded his involvement with the Hatfields, and my hope was that I could come to a private arrangement with him that wouldn't involve his bosses. It was a long shot, but at that moment it was the best shot I had.

After a minute, Kintay's voice sounded in my ear. "You there, Sarge? I'll be better in a few minutes. What's on your mind?"

"I've got something you might be able to help me out with."

"Ahhhhh—someone special? You need to boost her drink a little? Put her in the right frame of mind?"

"Nothing like that, you perverted punk."

"Because I've got something I've been working on. Makes them want it—bad! I haven't had time to try it out on a *real* girl yet, but it's worked wonders with the mice! The females are wearing the males out!"

"Can it, Corporal! Focus!"

"Sorry, Sarge. The reds will kick in momentarily."

"Let me know when you're down from the mountain."

"I'm about halfway there. Got a problem you say? Go ahead and lay it on me."

So I explained to the jacked-up underworld chemist how Fulton was holding my piece to my head to extort professional services from me, and what I wanted to do about it.

Kintay let me finish and responded in a voice that sounded close to normal speed. "You want me to hack into the Central Firearms Registry and eliminate the entry for your piece?"

"Is it doable?"

"You mean, by me?"

"You're good with computers. You taught me how to access the shadow web, and I figure you've done some hacking.

"Maybe I have and maybe I haven't, but I don't have the chops to break into a site like the Central Registry. You know how it is. Dragons are natural hoarders. Lord Ketz allows his treasures to circulate, but he wants to know where everything is at any given time. That's why it's better to get items like firearms from people like the Hatfields. Once we sell it to you, it's off the books. We don't record the sale, and we don't care what you do with the product once you've got it. But anything you buy from a licensed outlet is going to be recorded in a government ledger. You bought a fucking candy bar from a licensed supermarket? That transaction is recorded in a government database somewhere, and some clerk in the Dragon Lord's administration can call up data showing exactly how many candy bars you've legally purchased in your life. And those records are kept under some serious lock and key!"

"So you're saying that there's no way into those records?"

Kintay hesitated. "Nothing's impossible. I'm sure that the Syndicate's got some jeebos who might be able do it. I can ask around if you want."

"I was hoping that we could keep this between you and me. You sure you can't do it yourself? I'll owe you."

"It's the Central Registry, Sarge! I'm good, but not *that* good. You want a recreational pharmaceutical that will combine intense sexual pleasure with cosmic enlightenment, then I'm your guy. But computer hacking is just a sideline for me. Breaking into government databases is the big leagues. Let me run this by the bosses for you. I'm sure they could help you out."

"Sure they could. But they wouldn't do it for nothing. I don't want to be in their debt. I'd rather owe you."

I could almost hear Kintay shrug. "Sorry pal. No can do."

I thought for a few moments. "Okay. Do you know anyone from outside the Syndicate who might be able to help without putting me in debt to your bosses?"

After a pause, Kintay sighed. "Maybe. I'll make some calls. You'll owe me for that."

"Thanks, man."

"Don't thank me yet. I'm not making any promises."

"Do what you can. I appreciate it."

"I'll get back to you. It might take a few days."

"All right. Sooner the better."

"Sure, sure. Listen—I'm serious about that mood enhancer! I can get you a free sample for field testing. Just say the word!"

"Hey, Corporal—remember when I had you arrested for stealing pharmaceuticals from the field hospital?"

"Of course, Sarge! You brought down a sweet little racket."

"How in the hell did you ever get out of jail!"

Kintay laughed. "It was a bum rap, flatfoot! You M.P.s had nuthin' on me!"

"Right."

"Besides, I think that the army'd had enough of me. And, just between you, me, and the lamppost, the Hatfields may have had something to do with it. They recruited me right out of the military prison gates!"

"Figures."

"Yep—getting arrested was the best thing that ever happened to me! It got me noticed! And the Hatfields have been good to me. That's why you've been my pal ever since."

"That's a heartwarming story. Makes me want to cry a little."

"Yeah? Sarge, I've got a pill that will have you fuckin' laughing again in no time flat!"

Chapter Eleven

Fulton had told me to investigate the woman in white and the earth demon from the lake. He'd told me to lay off the Zyanya case. I had other plans. After disconnecting my call with Kintay, I turned back to my research on Zyanya, picking up where I'd left off earlier that afternoon. I wanted to see if I could dig up anything on her older sister, Edith. If she was still in Yerba City, she'd be a good person to talk to. But searches for Edith or Edie Hermosa got me nowhere. I figured that she was married now and had adopted her husband's last name. I did a phone directory search for Hermosa, hoping to find a potential younger brother. The search gave me fifty-four entries, and a handful of them looked promising. I followed these up with phone calls, but none of the Hermosas had an older sister named Jennifer or Edith, or a mother named Tayanna. One had a father named Guillermo, but the ages didn't match up. After two hours, I called it quits and started thinking about dinner.

Before I could get out of my chair, the ring-tone on my cell phone went off, and I saw Detective Kalama's name at the top of my screen. I put my dinner plans on hold and connected the call.

"Hi Detective. What's up?"

"You started looking into the songbird's death yet?"

"A little. Why?"

"Funny thing. I just got out of the lieutenant's office. Someone up high sent word down through channels. To me, specifically. I've been told that you might try to hit me up for info on Zyanya. If you do, I'm to tell you that I don't know squat, and then I'm supposed to inform my lieutenant that you made the attempt."

"Huh. That didn't take long."

"What do you mean? What'd you do?"

"I met with Lawrence Fulton this afternoon."

"Shit! Why?"

"I'm forbidden by the ethics of my profession to tell you that he's my client and I'm working a case for him, which means that you found out about it some other way."

"You're working for that sleazebag? Lord's balls, Southerland! I knew you were a whore, but I thought you had *some* standards!"

"He's very persuasive."

There was a pause on the line while Kalama considered this. "Either he's paying you a fortune, or he's got something on you."

"I'm working for half my usual rates," I admitted.

"For fuck's sake, gumshoe! And here I thought you were a smooth operator."

"I'll work my way out of it. I've got a few things going."

"I'll bet! Hey, if he's putting the screws to you then maybe I can do something to help you out. Unless you're too fuckin' male to be rescued by a frail."

"I'll humble myself if necessary. Just don't make me beg."

Kalama chuckled at that. "Might be fun! So what happened with Fulton?"

"Zyanya's name came up in my initial conversation with Fulton. He ordered me to leave it alone. I told him I would, but he probably didn't believe me. Besides, he's a guy who doesn't like leaving anything to chance. I'm guessing that he dropped word to someone at the top of the YCPD—maybe the commissioner himself—that I might be making inquiries about Zyanya, and to make sure that I got nowhere near it."

"And they know that we worked together on the Shipper case and figured that you'd come to me for info."

"That's my guess."

"So…. *Is* Zyanya's death related to the case you're working on?"

I hesitated. "I'm leaning in that direction."

"You think that Fulton had something to do with her death?"

"Good question. I don't know. Even if he didn't, he benefits by it, and he's got good reasons for wanting her death to be as quiet as possible. His boy's up for reelection, and he's afraid that the Harvey campaign will do something with it if they get the opportunity."

"It's an interesting angle, that's for sure. So are you backing away from looking into Zyanya?"

"That'd be the smart thing to do."

"It would."

"I guess I'm not that smart."

"That's what I've always said. So how far are you into the case?"

"Not far." I hesitated, and then came clean. "I know that Zyanya was shot and that she didn't do it herself."

"Fuck! I knew it!"

"Don't stir things up, Detective. You'll be writing parking tickets if you do. Or worse, considering that the LIA has this thing locked up tight. Let me handle this. I'll fill you in on anything interesting."

"Fuck!" Kalama was silent for a couple of breaths, and then I heard her let out a sigh. "Okay, gumshoe. I'll sit tight for now. What's your next step?"

It sounded like the detective might stay on the sidelines, at least for the moment, and I felt some of the tension I'd been holding float away. The last thing I'd wanted to do was to drag Kalama deep into a quagmire that might threaten her career. I also liked the idea that she might be able to toss me a lifeline if I got in over my head.

"I need to talk to someone who was close to her," I told Kalama. "I've been looking into her family. I know that she was born Jennifer Hermosa, second child to Guillermo and Tayanna Hermosa. Her father left her mother for parts unknown right after baby Jennifer was born, and her mother died of cancer when Jennifer was a teenager. I know that she had an older sister named Edith and two younger siblings whose names and genders I don't know yet. I haven't been able to turn any of them up."

"Good thing you know a cop who's willing to talk to an amateur like you."

I sat up in my seat. "You've got something?"

A pause. "Maybe."

"Don't be a tease, flatfoot! I'll call Kai and tell him what an evil copper you are."

"Oh, he knows, he knows. He thinks it's part of my charm."

"Yeah? Well I'm not feeling it. I've been at this for hours!"

Kalama chuckled. "You should have called me."

"A bigshot homicide dick like you? You wouldn't have taken my call."

"Probably not."

"C'mon, Detective. What have you got? Spill!"

Another pause. "Say 'please.'"

"Please." I tried to make it sound sincere.

A longer pause, and then, "Say 'pretty please.'"

I think I might have growled. "Would you like me to buy you some fucking flowers?"

"That might do it."

"Detective!"

"Okay, okay. You're no fun. Edith Hermosa is a singer. Apparently, musical talent runs in the family. She goes by Nina, doing the one-name thing, like her sister. She performs locally, just not anywhere classy like the Gold Coast. Check the club listings in the entertainment section of the paper. You should be able to find out if she's appearing somewhere this weekend."

"That's great stuff! How did you manage to get it? I thought you'd been banished from the case?"

"Probably best you don't ask."

I heard a voice on Kalama's end of the call, and she told someone that she'd be right with them. After a moment, she came back on the line. "We need to meet somewhere quiet, gumshoe. Sooner the better."

"Okay," I agreed. "Sometime tomorrow afternoon should be good. I'll have to wait and see how things go."

"Call me when you know. I'll shake myself free. Gotta go!"

***

I went upstairs and threw a frozen pizza into the microwave. Fuckin' Fulton! He hadn't wasted a moment trying to barricade me from the YCPD, even after I'd told him that I would stay away from the Zyanya death. I'd been lying, of course, but I was still offended that he hadn't taken my word for it. And it sounded like he was serious about paying me half wages, too. Lord Alkwat's flaming pecker! I didn't need Fulton's money, and I told myself that I would shove it in his face when he tried to pay me. It wouldn't be the first time that I'd rejected his dough.

As I chewed on my pizza, I opened the morning paper to the entertainment section and found a column listing the acts currently appearing in the area's night spots. Yerba City had enough of these to fill a couple of pages. The larger venues had splashy ads at the top of the page with individualized logos and photographs of the performers. Nina wasn't appearing at any of these clubs. The rest of the night spots were listed alphabetically in small print with the performers indicated in even smaller print. I scanned through more than two dozen clubs until I found Nina on the second page. I was in luck. Nina was headlining that night and through Saturday night at a place called The Turbo Lounge, which was located in Placid Point. Not the best neighborhood in the city, but not the worst, either. It was still early evening, and I had plenty of time to drive out and catch her act. If my luck held out, I'd be able to introduce myself to her during one of her early breaks and ask some questions about her sister.

As I was refolding the paper, I caught sight of a short article on the back page of the local news section. The headline read, "Rare Beast Spotted in Porter." The article consisted of one short paragraph: "The Department of Animal Control reported Wednesday that a rare and potentially dangerous animal was spotted roaming through an alley in the Porter District during the early hours of Tuesday morning. The animal was described as resembling a goat with a long hairless tail and a row of spikes running down its spine. It also had glowing red eyes. A spokesperson from Animal Control warns that the animal could be an ancient semi-sentient beast last seen in the Province of Texas and thought to have died more than a century ago. The spokesperson warns that the animal should be considered dangerous and should not be approached. Anyone seeing the animal should stay clear and notify Animal Control." The article included a phone number and a web address for the agency.

So, that foul-smelling beast I'd seen scrounging in my garbage can had attracted enough attention to make the papers. That meant that the beast wasn't just your run-of-the-mill overgrown alley rat. According to Animal Control he was "semi-sentient," whatever that meant. And he was "ancient"? If so, the beast had seen better days. Animal Control also said that the creature should be considered dangerous. He was ugly, and I'd experienced a wave of intense nausea when I'd first spotted him, but other than that I hadn't felt all that threatened by him. Truth was, I felt a little sorry for the mangy critter. That's me, just a big bundle of sentimentality.

I put the paper aside and climbed down the stairs to my office. It occurred to me that with my attention diverted to the Zyanya death, I hadn't spent a minute that day looking into the Sihuanaba or the strange little hooded fellow. It was Thursday, and Fulton wanted answers by Saturday morning. I started to initiate an internet search of little creatures capable of chopping down a troll with a tree branch, but then I said "fuck it" and starting searching for stories about Nina, instead.

There wasn't much to see. Zyanya's big sister had no social media presence that I could find, which was strange. In my business I'd had to search for a number of missing persons. Typically, a quick search through the various social media sites would lead me right to their doorstep. It seemed that most folks couldn't order a meal in a restaurant without taking a picture of it and displaying it to the rest of the world. I didn't get it. Did they think that being served food on a plate was some sort of unique experience? Was this the first time they'd ever seen a tuna salad spread over a bed of lettuce? Nobody hid anything about themselves anymore. Even people who didn't want to be found would leave a trail through various social media sites that anyone could follow. But not Nina. I didn't find a trace of her in any of the usual websites. I figured that someone in the entertainment business would want to be as accessible as possible, but apparently Nina was one of those rare birds who valued her privacy.

Nina's name began to pop up when I started searching clubs and bars. She hadn't reached the bigtime, but she seemed to draw steady work at small to medium-sized venues. I searched for recorded material, but found none. Apparently, she was strictly a live act, at least for the time being. I looked for reviews and found a few one-sentence summaries. "Enjoyed the sultry sounds of a singer named Nina (no last name)," read one of them. "The four-piece band was fronted by a songbird calling herself Nina, a good-looking dame with a pleasing voice," read another. "The joint was raucous, too raucous for the singer, a cute little number named Nina, to make herself heard over the clamor," read another. Not exactly the kind of buzz that would elevate someone to center stage.

After about an hour of this, it was time to get myself to the Turbo Lounge. Placid Point wasn't far as the crow flies, but I knew that it would take me at least forty-five minutes to fight my way through traffic to get there, even skirting the edge of downtown. Yerba City is sprawled over forty separate hills that cover the tip of a peninsula like a lumpy thumbnail. Over the years, the city expanded a piece at a time, and, in an ill-conceived compromise arising after a lengthy and contentious deliberation inside a smoke-filled conference room, each of the city's thirty formal districts had been given responsibility for its own transportation infrastructure. The result was a confusing mishmash of twisting roadways that follow no discernable plan and serve only to ensure that getting anywhere in Yerba City requires the determination of a bulldog and the patience of a vulture.

As it happened, it took me almost an hour to find the Turbo Lounge, a nondescript club in a row of other, seedier-looking clubs, gin mills, restaurants, and other commercial establishments. The club had no public parking lot, and every spot on the street was occupied. The nearest parking garage was two blocks away, and it was full. The next nearest parking garage was another two blocks away, and it was also filled to the brim. Cursing non-stop, I managed to find a garage with available spots some eight blocks from the Turbo. The flat rate that the lot charged for the night would have got me an overnight stay in one of the nearby flophouses. I slid my credit card through the slot and hoped that my balance would cover the parking fee and still leave me enough to pay the cover charge at the club.

The streets of Placid Point were darker than those of central Yerba City. The corner streetlights were clouded, burned out, or broken. The neon signs that flickered over the entryways of gin mills and hash houses did a poor job of lighting the night. The few pedestrians making their way over the cracked sidewalks had their hats pulled down to their eyes and their hands pushed halfway to their elbows in the pockets of their cheap overcoats. They moved like wraiths, kept their eyes fixed on the sidewalk three feet in front of them, and said nothing.

As I was passing by the door of a gin mill, the door flew open and three tough-looking brunos in black leather coats and newsie caps spilled through it onto the sidewalk. One of them veered into me, and, without thinking, I put a firm hand on his chest to prevent a collision. The bruno, a rough pug with a head of dirty blond curls that hung down from his cap to his collar, reacted to my touch as if he'd been jabbed with a cattle prod.

I pulled my hand away. "Careful, pal."

The bruno's head swiveled, and I found myself staring into a pair of bloodshot eyes the color of hazelnuts. He made a startled sound, and I nearly gagged at the stink of rotgut on his breath. He pushed at me with enough strength to back me off a step.

I raised up my hands, shoulder height and palms out. "Easy fella. No disrespect intended."

One of the other pugs nodded in my direction. "What have we got here?"

The first bruno continued to glare at me. "Asshole put his hands on me!" He reached inside his coat, pulled out a knife with a broad twelve-inch blade, and held it in front of my face.

The bruno probably just wanted to put a scare into me. He and his pals were most likely out on the town looking for kicks. I'll bet he had a line for the occasion, something like, "You want a piece of me? How 'bout I cut a piece outta you!" He'd probably practiced that line, or one like it, in the mirror a few dozen times as he brandished his blade. Maybe he'd even used it on a few live suckers. Maybe it was even a pretty good line, one that I might want to use myself on some occasion. Problem was, I wasn't interested in hearing it.

I lived the first eighteen years of my life in a tough working-class neighborhood in a river town in eastern Missouri Province. My old man was a factory worker when he was working, which wasn't often. When he didn't have a job, he was a mean drunk. Truth be told, he was a mean drunk when he was working, too. My mother was the wife of a mean drunk, which is a full-time job in itself. I was an only child, and I always had the impression that as far as my parents were concerned I was one child too many. I can't complain. I think they tried to be good parents, and they weren't any worse than the other parents in the neighborhood. But it didn't take me long to figure out that the less time I was with them, the better we all liked it. I spent a lot of time out in the neighborhood with other kids like me. We did what aimless tough kids do, and I learned to fight. I liked fighting, and I got to be pretty good at it.

After my eighteenth birthday, I joined the army and was shipped off to basic training. I thought I was the cock of the walk. It didn't take me long to find out that I was just another wise-ass punk who fancied himself a rough customer. That didn't stop me from responding to every slight—real or perceived—with flying fists and scrapping at every opportunity, until one day a sergeant told me that if I was going to roughhouse I'd better learn how to do it right. Next thing I knew, I was yanked out of basic and shoved into a "special unit" that I didn't know existed. For the next ten weeks, a dozen of us—ten men and two women—were put through an intensive martial arts program that transformed us from undisciplined brawlers to dangerous weapons. It was by far the most exhausting ten weeks of my life. We trained for eighteen hours a day, every day, and we spent the other six hours eating and sleeping in isolation. Every day, I was battered, bruised, and beaten, but I gave as good as I got. I never learned the names of the other eleven members of my unit, or what became of them. On the last day of the program, we were put through a number of formal matches and judged by a panel of officers that I'd never seen before or since. Of the twelve, I graduated sixth in my class.

I was offered further training but turned it down. Funny thing: the more skilled I became, the less I wanted to fight. For some reason that I can't explain, knowing what I was doing took the fun out of it. But the lessons I learned during my training stuck with me. I was taught, for example, that when someone pulls a weapon on me, I should assume without question that they intend to use it. I also learned that speed and determination trump size and strength. I heard it every day for ten weeks until it was burned into my brain: strike first, strike often! I learned that thinking stopped when the fighting began and that mercy was for losers.

When the bruno showed me his knife, a switch flipped and my training took over.

As soon as I saw the neon light reflect off the bare blade, my arm shot out as if of its own accord, and I buried my stiffened thumb into the pug's eye. My training had programmed that reflex into my synapses. Go for the soft spots: the eyes, the throat, the ears, the solar plexus, the groin. The bruno almost stabbed himself as his hands flew up to his face. After the soft spots, attack the joints: the elbows, the wrists, the fingers, the knees, the insteps. I grabbed the arm holding the knife with both hands, stepped in, and twisted. I came down on the back of his elbow with my shoulder and heard a snap, which was followed by a clatter as the knife hit the sidewalk. I shoved the bruno into one of the other pugs and swooped down to pick up the knife. The third pug had started to close on me, but found himself eating sidewalk after I kicked him in the shin and brought the hilt of the knife down on the tender spot behind the base of his ear.

A slide step brought me back to the tough customer who had drawn the knife on me. I put the point of his knife under his chin and forced him to stand up straight until he was on his tiptoes. Then with my other hand, I reached under his coat and found a sheath that looped over his belt and was held in place by two snaps. I had no trouble removing it.

The four of us stood frozen for a moment. "Maybe you should all go now," I told them. They all agreed, and within seconds I was alone on the sidewalk.

I studied the knife in my hand. It was well-maintained, with a polished steel blade, thicker at the end than at the grip, like a machete, though not quite so heavy. Its soft leather-covered handle felt comfortable in my grip, and its razor-sharp edge looked like it could peel a grape. I could see why someone would have been reluctant to part with the weapon. The sheath was made of stiff leather and fit close against my right hip after I snapped it in place over my belt. I wasn't really a knife man. I'd had some training in the military, but I was much more comfortable with a roscoe. Still, this was a serious knife, one that could do heavy damage in close quarters. If my instincts hadn't kicked in the instant I'd seen it, the bruno could have sliced me to ribbons with that blade. Did I have the right to take it from him? Under the circumstances, I thought that I did. The world seemed safer with the blade in my hands instead of in his.

With no further deliberation, I put the knife in the sheath, pulled my coat closed, and continued on to the Turbo Lounge.

Chapter Twelve

A dozen or so humans, a couple of gnomes, and a lone dwarf were lined up outside the Turbo Lounge when I got there. A bored-looking troll admitted them one at a time after giving them a cursory onceover. When I reached the door, the troll looked me up and down. "Check the weapon when you get inside," he muttered without much interest. I hadn't thought that my sheath would show through my coat, but maybe it did. Either that, or the doorman took one look at my face and guessed that I was armed. Either way, he was good.

The troll opened the door for me, and I stepped through into a reception area where a cute young dish stood behind a counter. She probably had a nice face, but my eyes were drawn like magnets to the two bulges of flesh that were straining to burst out of her low-cut blouse. I didn't think it would take a lot of effort to give them their much-desired freedom.

"Would you like to check your hat and coat?" asked a cheerful voice that tinkled like silver bells.

I tore my eyes from her struggling breasts, and the dish did indeed have a nice face. I gave her my hat and coat, along with my sheathed knife, and paid the cover. To prove that I wasn't too much of a creep, I kept my peepers fixed on hers and smiled. "When does Nina go on stage?"

"You're just in time. She should be starting in a few minutes."

I thanked the sweet young lady and, allowing myself one last quick peep at her moneymakers, stepped through a swinging door into the lounge.

The joint was nicer than I'd expected, but I hadn't been expecting much. The lights were dim, but not so dim that I couldn't have navigated my way through the patrons and past the tables even without elf-enhanced night vision. I breathed in and savored the sharp scent of whiskey and the bittersweet odor of beer, which drew me to the bar stretching off to my left. As I made my way to it, I picked up the refreshing tang of lime and the greasy-fish odor of deep-fried calamari. My stomach growled, and I realized that I was hungry as well as thirsty. I passed by a group of laughing patrons and my nose twitched at the intermingled fragrances of cologne and perfume. I found an empty stool at the bar and glided onto it with the practiced efficiency of a veteran barfly.

A bartender with a handlebar mustache and receding hairline questioned me with his eyes. "Beer and a shot," I told him.

I turned my back to the bar and took in the room. The joint was lively and borderline casual. My button-down shirt and tie were okay if I loosened the tie and rolled up my sleeves. I thought that might be a good idea once I settled in. The cocktail waitresses and cigarette girls weaving their way through the tables weren't as pert or pretty as the doll at the front counter, but they made up for it by wearing revealing scoop-necked blouses, skirts short enough to show plenty of thigh, fishnet stockings with bows on their garters, and pointed shoes with three-inch heels that must have left the girls soaking their feet for hours when they were finished with their shifts. The stage at the end of the room was large enough for a small combo, and the dance floor at the foot of the stage was small enough to encourage couples to dance in each other's arms without moving around too much.

My beer and shot were waiting for me when I turned back to the bar. The whiskey was no better than average, but I thought it was swell, especially after I washed it down with the ice-cold beer. My glass was still half full when I heard scuffing and bumping noises from the back of the lounge. I turned and saw four scruffy customers in black suits taking their places on the stage. The patrons, more interested in their drinks and each other, barely noticed as the band members began getting their instruments ready to play. So far, Nina was nowhere to be seen.

The band noodled for a while and then went silent. The longhaired piano player signaled the others, and they broke into a quick jazz/rock fusion number that got immediate attention from the patrons. The chatter didn't exactly cease, but it became more subdued, and most heads turned to face the stage. The musicians were more enthusiastic than skilled, but I thought they sounded all right. Compelled by the beat, I tapped my foot against the side of my barstool as I sipped my beer.

I clapped along with the crowd when the number ended, and without waiting for the applause to die down, the bearded guitar player struck up a slow bluesy riff. After a couple of bars, the rest of the band jumped in. Then a door opened from behind the stage and Nina walked through to a burst of renewed applause. The overhead lights dimmed as a spotlight sliced through the darkness and followed her progress. I sat up to get a good look as the singer climbed the steps to the stage and moved to the waiting microphone.

It wasn't that Nina was beautiful by traditional standards, but she was striking. Her thick black hair was parted on one side and swept over dark eyes the size of old gold coins. Her scarlet lipstick gleamed in the light of the spot, making the rest of her face seem pale as cream in contrast. She didn't smile. She wore a sleek sleeveless black dress that hugged her hips and hung to the tops of her high-heeled shoes. A large teardrop-shaped opening in her dress exposed much of her torso from a point between her breasts to a wide expanse below her beltline. After focusing for a bit, I realized that an elaborate spiderweb was tattooed on her midsection, and that a dark-colored gem was set in her navel, right in the center of the web. I not only found myself titillated at the sight of her tattooed torso, but much more aroused than I would have expected. Was the gem in the center of the web shaped like a spider? It was too small and I was too far away to tell for sure, even with my enhanced vision. As Nina moved behind her microphone, I found myself wanting—needing—to trace the webbing on the naked skin of her midriff and to study the tiny gem set in the middle of her belly. I shook my head. Thirty years old, and I was still discovering things about myself that took me by surprise.

Nina's voice was pretty good, I guess. I mean, what did *I* know about music? I didn't have a favorite band. I would have had a hard time telling you what type of music I preferred. If pressed, I probably would have shrugged and answered "Something hard, dark, and snappy with a driving bass." This music was soft and sultry, a torcher's crooning over gentle strains from a band content to provide support from outside the spotlight. I liked the sound of her singing, and that's all that mattered.

Halfway through Nina's first song, a few couples got up from their seats and made their way to the dance floor. By her second number, the floor was filled. I sat on my barstool and ordered a whiskey and water. I was still nursing it when the band took a break. I was surprised to discover that it was already twelve thirty, and they'd been at it for more than an hour and a half. It had seemed like just a handful of minutes to me.

I took one of my business cards from my shirt pocket and asked the handlebar-mustached bartender for a pen. When he brought one to me, I wrote a message on the back of the card: "Nina. I'm enjoying your performance. When you get a chance, I'd like to ask you a couple of questions about your sister. I hope you will oblige. Alex."

I asked the bartender to give the card to Nina, and he took it without a word. After serving a couple of customers, he walked to the back of the lounge and disappeared through the door behind the stage. I finished my drink, and when the bartender returned a minute later, he gave me a quick nod and went back to work. I left a couple of bills under my empty glass and ordered a refill when the bartender came to collect it.

When the bartender brought me my drink, I saw his face turn toward the back of the club. I followed his gaze and saw Nina making her way through the lounge, her eyes studying me as she moved in my direction. She was wearing a loose gray wrap that crossed over the front of her dress and covered her bare midsection. The bartender picked up a rag and began wiping down the bar in front of me, giving him an excuse to stay close.

When she reached me, Nina glanced over at the bartender. "Give me a shot, Eric." She turned back to me. "That's all I've got time for. You're a cop?"

"Private. Like it says on my card."

"All the same to me." Nina took the shot glass from the bartender, emptied the contents with one gulp, and put the glass down on the bar.

I talked fast before she could leave. "I'm looking into the death of your sister. I think that there might be more to it than the police are letting on. I was hoping that you might be able to shed some light on it."

Nina stared at me with her large unsmiling eyes. Up close, I could see lines in her forehead beneath her makeup. Her nose was a little sharper than it appeared onstage, and pointed just to the right of center. I could also see the trace of an inch-long scar under her left eye that her makeup didn't quite conceal. "Why?" she asked me. "What do you care?"

I shrugged. "I liked her singing. And I don't like our mayor."

Her eyes narrowed as she processed my answer. Then she asked, "Are you working for the Harvey campaign?"

"I most definitely am not," I responded.

She stared at me for a few moments, and I let her. She looked me up and down without speaking. She met my eyes, as if searching for something. Then her face relaxed by a degree. "We finish up at two. Come see me in the back when we do."

I nodded. "Okay."

She started to turn away, but then stopped. She almost smiled, but couldn't quite manage it. "Enjoy the show, sugar." She walked away then, intent on getting back to business. I watched her go, admiring the snug fit of her dress on her swaying hips. I didn't stop watching her until the door behind the stage closed behind her.

***

The last set ended exactly at two, and I followed the band as they left the stage. Nina was waiting for me just beyond the door. Her eyes were beaming, still charged by the energy from her performance and from the enthusiastic ovation she'd received after her last number, but she still didn't smile. "Come on, big boy. They've given me an office to use as a dressing room." She turned and walked, and I followed.

She reached a door and held it open for me. "Wait inside. I've got to go powder my nose."

I entered an office the size of a walk-in closet that was probably used by a bookkeeper during the day. I flipped a wall switch, and the overhead light was blinding after the low light of the lounge. The office had just enough room for a desk, one chair, and some file cabinets. A computer on the desktop had been pushed to one side to make room for a tube of lipstick, several containers of makeup, a hairbrush, and a portable mirror. An ashtray on the desktop was filled with butts, and a half-empty pack of cigarettes lay next to it. A half-filled bottle of rye and an empty glass sat behind the ashtray. My card was tucked under the glass. Across from the desk and in front of a row of file cabinets, a casual dress and her gray wrap hung from a portable clothes rack. A pair of comfortable-looking shoes lay on the floor beneath the dress. A gym bag was propped up against the file cabinets.

I was standing in the center of the room behind the desk chair when Nina came in. There wasn't anywhere else to stand. She smiled just a little when she saw me. "How do you like this star treatment? I'd offer you the chair, but I need to get off my feet." She plopped into the room's only chair and slouched, stretching her legs and giving me a good look at the spiderweb on her torso. I saw then that the black gem in her navel was indeed carved in the shape of a spider.

"I enjoyed the show," I told her.

She looked up over her shoulder at me. "Did you really?" She glanced down the length of her body and then back up at me. "Some people come for the singing and some for the view. What did you like most?"

Something about the spider-shaped gem pricked at my subconscious for an instant, like the gentle scrape of a kitten's tooth, but Nina's eyes caught mine and the sensation vanished. "I liked both very much," I said. "But I came to ask you some questions."

She smiled then, the first genuine smile I'd seen from her, though it lacked heat, like the last bit of sun at the end of a winter's day. She sat up in her chair and said, "Hand me my shawl, will you?"

I turned to retrieve the gray wrap from the hanger. When I turned back, I saw that Nina had stood and was facing me. In that small room, we were only separated by a few feet. I took a step toward her and wrapped the shawl around her shoulders. The top of her head came up to my chin. Tiny beads of sweat had formed in the part of her hair, and they glistened in the overhead light. I breathed in a combination of musky perfume and perspiration that made my stomach flutter in a pleasant way. Nina pulled the shawl across her dress and looked up at me without smiling. "Thank you," she said, her voice low and gentle. "Would you like a drink?"

"No thanks. Are you done for the night?"

"I'm done working, but if you want to buy me a drink I can stick around for a while."

"I just want a few minutes of your time. Like I said, I've got some questions I'd like to ask you. It won't take long."

Nina smiled, reached up and put a finger on my cheek, and I felt a surge of electricity in her touch. "Sure, sugar. Whatever you say."

She sat down then and folded her hands on her lap. "Fire away, copper."

I walked around her and leaned against the side of the desk. "You're Zyanya's sister, right? Edith Hermosa?"

Nina sighed. "That's right. It's no secret."

"You don't exactly broadcast it though."

Nina looked up at me. "What am I supposed to do? Bill myself as the next best thing to the fabulous Zyanya? You can't afford her so come see her big sis instead?"

I shrugged. "Drawing on the connection might get you some bigger venues. Couldn't hurt."

Nina's eyes flared. "I've got talent, mister! I can stand on my own two feet!" She sat up straighter in her chair. "Say, what are you—a copper, or some sleazy promoter?"

"Okay, okay. No need to get sore."

Nina let herself relax a little. "Yeah? Well if you got some questions about my little sister, you better get around to asking them, buster! I ain't got all night, you know!" She grabbed the bottle from the desktop and took a quick slug without bothering to pour it into the glass.

I was kicking myself for my clumsiness. Nina was an artist, and, although she was still riding high on adrenaline, I knew it would only be a few minutes before she crashed. I should have realized that her nerves would be raw before I reached out and poked at one. I needed to smooth things out—fast! I tried to make my voice as conciliatory as possible. "I'm sorry, Nina. I didn't mean to offend you. You've got a swell act. I wasn't lying when I said I enjoyed it. I don't know enough about the music business to tell you how to run your career. I was just curious, that's all. You're doing me a favor by answering my questions, and I won't take up much more of your time. Forgive me, please."

Nina glared at me for another moment, and then burst out laughing. "Oh, sugar! You're so damned cute when you're begging for forgiveness! You've really got that sincere thing down cold, don't you?" She laughed a bit more, and her shawl fell open, exposing the gem in her navel. Again, something about the gem seemed…unusual…but before I could figure out what it was, Nina pulled the shawl closed. "Go ahead, dear. What do you want to know? Make it quick, though."

I took a deep breath. "I really only have one question. Do you think that your sister took her own life?"

Nina's face hardened and her eyes lit up. "Absolutely not! Anyone who says that she did is a dirty liar!" She looked into my eyes like she was trying to look into my soul. "My sister was murdered! And I know who did it! Or leastways who was behind it."

"Darnell Teague?"

At the mention of the mayor's name, Nina's eyes widened and her mouth parted in surprise. "Yes, that's right! Or one of his goons."

"Lawrence Fulton?"

The widened eyes narrowed. "Maybe. Say, what's your game, anyway, mister? Is this some kind of trick? Those people would kill me if they knew I was talking like this." She looked at the bottle in her hand and set it back down on the desk. "You're not wearing a wire, are you? If anyone says that I told you what I just told you, I'll say you're lying!"

"It's okay, doll. I happen to think that you might be right."

"Yeah? So what are you, LIA? Are you going to arrest Teague?"

"No, I'm just a private investigator, like I told you. I can't arrest anybody."

Nina looked down at her hands, and her voice sounded tired. "Then what good are you? Why are you asking me about Jenny?"

"I'm just looking for the truth," I told her.

She looked up at me, and I could see the bitterness in her eyes. "The truth? What good is the truth, mister? What's the truth going to do for Jenny? Or me?" She looked down again. "You better leave now. The manager don't like me to bring visitors back here."

I nodded, though she wasn't looking at me. "Okay, Nina. Or should I call you Edith?" She didn't look up. "Or Edie?"

She looked up then, and I thought that she was suppressing a smile.

I stood away from the desk. "I'd like to talk to you again, if that's okay. Maybe over a cup of coffee?"

She hesitated, studying me, and then nodded. "Okay. Sure. Why not?"

"You've got my card. Call me."

She nodded again, and I started to leave. "Hey, doll—I really did like your show. You've got talent!"

She smiled and stood, brave and brazen. "You bet I do, sugar!"

When I reached the door, I heard her voice from behind me, a little tentative now, the bravado absent. "You can call me Edie."

I turned and saw her standing, arms folded across her breasts, staring up at me from behind the long lashes of her half-closed eyes, her lips slightly parted.

I put a hand on the doorknob. "Hello, Edie. I'm Alex. Call me tomorrow before you go to work, okay? Let's meet for coffee. I think we can help each other." She pulled the shawl tight across her dress, as if fighting off a cold breeze.

Chapter Thirteen

When I returned to the lounge area, a jukebox was playing some slow jazz to cool down the after-hours crowd, and I considered having one more whiskey and soda for the road. A joint like this would typically stay open until after three, but I suddenly felt exhausted, so I decided to head home to get some sleep, instead. I had a lot of questions for Nina—Edie, that is—but I wanted to ask them in a more relaxed setting, when her emotions weren't flying like a kite in a tornado. She had asked me if I was with the Harvey campaign. I found that curious. Had one of Harvey's people been in contact with her to find out what she could tell them about the relationship between her sister and the mayor? I'd be surprised if they hadn't. She hadn't asked me if I was working for Teague, and I wondered why not. Maybe she was familiar with all his people, and I was a stranger. In her "dressing room" she had treated me at first as if I were a star-struck fan. Maybe I was. But that had changed when I started asking her about her sister. She'd become defensive, and even hostile when I'd suggested that she might be able to capitalize on her sister's name. I wondered if there was some sibling rivalry at work. Maybe she was jealous of her sister. She considered herself talented—she *was* talented—but Zyanya had been a headliner at the swankiest club in town, and she was working in the outlying districts of the city, striving to succeed on her own merits. Her anger had turned to fear at the mention of the mayor and his fixer. "Those people would kill me if they knew I was talking like this," she'd told me. Then bitterness when I'd told her that I was searching for the truth, and hopelessness when I told her that I couldn't arrest anyone. And, as I was leaving, "You can call me Edie." Opening herself to me and asking me to treat her with kindness.

Or was I reading too much into the tilt of a head, the position of her arms, a gentle tone in her voice? I swore at myself. It had been too long since I'd "made myself available," as Kalama had put it. I couldn't deny the attraction I felt for Edie. Was it mutual? It had seemed so at first, but I reminded myself that Edie—Nina—was a performer, and that she'd been riding the high of a big ovation from an appreciative crowd. She'd been friendly as I was leaving. What had she been telling me with that look? She'd seemed almost shy! That spiderweb on the skin of her midsection.... I was surprised by its effect on me. If someone had asked me what I liked in a woman, the tattoo of a spiderweb on her stomach is not something that would have occurred to me. And that gem, that tiny spider.... Something was odd about it. It wasn't attractive in itself. In fact, it was something of a horror. Black with a hint of dark green...a mouth full of fangs...something growing out of its head—vines maybe? I remembered tiny leaves on thin strands. And eight limbs that curled...up?...outward?

That was it! That's what had been nagging at me! I expected that the spider would be perched face down on the web, but this spider was lying on the surface of the web, stomach exposed, legs curled outward, its open mouth facing the onlooker, fangs exposed. It wasn't a natural position for a spider, unless it had fallen on its back into the web and was struggling to free itself. Was that what the position signified? Was that the message that Edie was trying to convey? I shook my head. Artists. Who knew. Maybe I'd ask her about it when I saw her again. Against my better judgment, I found myself smiling at the prospect. Smiling like a seventeen-year-old. Or like a middle-aged dope.

Traffic was relatively light going home, and I made the trip in under forty minutes. The first thing I did when I got to my door was to check out the alley behind my building. The garbage cans were upright, and nothing appeared to have disturbed them. I went into my laundry room and dug around in some storage boxes until I found a cheap remote surveillance camera that I'd bought on impulse a few years earlier and never got around to using. I grabbed some tools, walked back to the alley, and attached the camera to the wall next to my alley door. I'd also brought out the troll food that I'd bought the previous afternoon, and I set the cardboard bowl on the ground within view of the camera. The bloody meat stew had been sitting at room temperature for hours, and it smelled like ripe carrion. If this didn't attract the overgrown alley rat that Animal Control was after, who knew what it might bring in. I went to bed pondering the possibilities.

***

I dreamed about tiny spiders and giant spiderwebs. I dreamed about the way Nina's arms had felt under the palms of my hands as I had smoothed her shawl over her shoulders. I dreamed of the teardop opening in her dress behind the microphone as Nina swayed to the gentle rocking of a blues beat. I dreamed of large sad eyes, a scar obscured by makeup, a sharp nose that leaned just a bit off-center. I dreamed of a voice saying, "You can call me Edie," and the sound of that voice made my heart pound. I dreamed of a spider with vines growing out of its head descending on me from above, giant now, a slot in its gruesome face opening to reveal a mouthful of fangs that dripped poison, its curled limbs reaching for me. The music that had been playing in my head began to change. The gentle blues began to pound, the notes rose in pitch until they became a screech—the shriek of the Sihuanaba!—too intense for my ears to hear any longer, but the pounding persisted, grew steadily louder and faster, threatened to crack my skull and burst out of my temples…. And then the hideous face of the hag, her eyes, the eyes of madness, burning into mine, and her voice, the dry rasping voice from the grave, "Do you still think I'm pretty?"

 I woke, groaning, my heart racing. But then the sound of slow blues and a low sultry voice, a little sad, but hopeful somehow, filled my head and calmed the beating of my heart. I fell back to sleep and dreamed of falling waters, dark rippling pools, and sparkling lights.

 Beams of light streaming through my window blinds woke me sometime after sunrise. I pulled my covers over my head and attempted to crawl my way back into dreamland, but the gates to that realm were closed and locked up tight. Giving up, I rolled out of bed and prepared to meet the day.

 It was Friday, and Fulton had left me to my own devices. I wanted to continue investigating Zyanya's death, and my hope was that Edie would call and arrange to meet with me to talk about her sister. Fulton wanted me to find more information on the Sihuanaba and the earth demon, and I hadn't done anything about it the day before. First step would be to find out what kind of creature the earth demon was. I'd start with an internet search and then go from there. After a shave and a shower. And breakfast, of course.

 As I was walking into my kitchen, though, I stopped and sniffed at the air. I'd caught a whiff of something foul, and it occurred to me that I'd been subconsciously aware of the odor for some time. It was faint, and I probably wouldn't have noticed it at all if it weren't for my enhanced senses, but it was growing stronger. I sniffed again and wondered if a mouse had died during the night somewhere nearby.

I remembered my alley scrounger then, and wondered if he'd found the yonak. If so, my surveillance camera should have recorded the footage. I ran down the steps to my desk, opened the camera software on my computer, and called up the remote recording. Since the camera was motion-activated, I didn't have to wait long for some action. As soon as I activated the play button, I saw an image wander into the wide-angle camera range from the right side of my screen. My camera used a cheap night-vision technology, and all I could see was a poorly lit green-tinged silhouette, its shape distorted by the wide-angle lens. Despite the recording's flaws, I knew that I was viewing the same critter that I'd seen before. The horns and the row of spikes along the spine were a dead giveaway. As I watched, the goat-like creature walked straight to the troll food, lowered his snout into the cardboard bowl, and began munching away with obvious relish. After a few bites, the creature lifted the bowl off the alley floor with his two humanlike forepaws and stood on his humanlike hind feet. He raised the bowl to his snout, threw back his head, and, in an all-too-human fashion, poured the contents of the bowl into his open mouth. Then he licked the bowl clean with a long, thin tongue.

When the creature had satisfied himself that there was nothing more to be had from the bowl, he tossed it into the alley. To my surprise, the creature then looked straight into the camera with his glowing eyes. After staring into the lens for several seconds, still standing on his hind legs, he reached for the knob to my back door and pushed the door open. He glanced directly at the camera one more time—and then disappeared through the doorway into the back of my building!

I jumped out of my chair and hurried to the door that led from my office to the rear hallway. When I opened the door, the faint dead animal stench that I'd detected assaulted me like a left jab to the snout. Right away, I noted that the door to my laundry room was wide open. I stepped into the room and stopped dead. Curled up in a laundry basket half filled with the clothes that I was intending to wash the next day, sleeping like a baby, and smelling like week-old roadkill, was the mangy alley scrounger.

My first question was, "What the fuck?"

My second question was, "Wait—wasn't my back door locked?"

I stepped past the laundry room, moving with caution and trying not to wake the creature, and crept down the hall to the back door. The deadbolt was in place, and it could only be unlocked from the outside with a key. So how had the creature been able to get in? As intriguing as that question was, it was overshadowed by an even more pressing one, namely, what the hell was I going to do with him now that he was inside my house? His stomach-churning stench filled the hallway and was drifting into my office. If for no other reason than that, he had to go—now!

I hustled back to the laundry room. The creature was still curled on my clothes, and now he was snoring like a buzzsaw. I was kicking myself for whatever impulse had caused me to put food out for the scrounger. He'd seemed so skinny and pathetic, but I'd only meant to feed the beast, not invite him to move in with me! I realized what a sap I'd been. Had I really believed that the animal would enjoy a free meal and then go on his merry way? That's not how it works with strays. Once they figure you for a soft touch, they never leave you alone. Well, nuts to that! Animal Control was on the lookout for the beast, so all I needed to do was give them a call and let them pick him up.

I returned to my office and called the number from the newspaper article. An officious female voice came on the line.

"Animal Control."

"Hello. I read in the paper that you're looking for a goat-like beast with spikes down its spine and a tail like a rat. I've got it trapped in my hallway."

"You've got it? Where?" The voice was excited.

"Yeah, I guess so. It matches the description that was in the paper."

"How are you feeling, sir? Are you all right?"

"Huh? I'm fine. Why do you ask?"

"Did the creature see you? Did you look into its eyes?"

"Its eyes? Sure. They're red and they glow, like a troll's."

"And you say you're okay? You're not feeling sick?"

I couldn't figure out at first why I was getting the third degree, but then I remembered the wave of nausea I'd felt the first time I'd encountered the creature. "I'm fine. I felt a little dizziness when I first saw him, but it passed. Why? Is the creature carrying some kind of disease?"

"Just stay away from it, sir. Give me your address and we'll send somebody out there right away."

Fifteen minutes later, a van double-parked in front of my building. Five men in protective gear and wraparound sunglasses flew out of the vehicle and ran up to my front door like they were storming the gates of an enemy stronghold. Four were carrying tranquilizer guns, and the other was carrying what appeared to be a medical bag. I let them in before they kicked in the door.

The man with the bag came in shouting. "Where is it!"

I pointed to the hall door. "Through there. He's in my laundry room. I think he's sleeping."

"Go! Go!" The man waved the others toward the door, and they marched through it double-time, like soldiers on a drill ground. I pegged their leader for a deskbound blowhard who had seen too many war movies. When his soldier boys had been appropriately dispatched, the blowhard jerked his head in my direction. "Sit over there!" he demanded, pointing at one of the armchairs that I keep near my desk for clients.

I didn't move. The blowhard grabbed me by the arm and tried to pull me into the chair. At about two-ten, I figured I had the man by maybe twenty pounds. More than that if you eliminated the flab and only counted muscle mass. When I didn't budge, the blowhard reached out with both hands and tried to push me into the chair. "Sit down!" he screamed.

I grabbed the blowhard by the collar with one hand, dragged him to the chair, and forced him into it. "You need to learn some manners," I told him.

The blowhard got red in the face. "You've been exposed to the…to the creature!" He'd been about to say something else, and I wondered about that. Before I could ask him about it, he reached up and grabbed my elbow. "I need to examine you!"

I shook myself free. "Are you a doctor?"

"As far as *you're* concerned I am!"

I decided to be polite, so, without rancor, I asked him, "Why don't you go fuck yourself?" I started off for the hallway without waiting for an answer.

"Halt! You can't go back there!"

Just then, one of the blowhard's soldier boys popped back into the office. "It's not here," he announced.

The blowhard shot up from the chair. "What?"

"We looked everywhere. There's nothing here."

I swept past the soldier boy and made my way to the laundry room. The other three soldier boys were standing in the room waving their tranquilizer guns around as if they could use them to force the creature to show himself. The creature had left a dent in the bundle of clothes in my laundry basket, and I could still detect his putrid scent, but he was nowhere to be seen. I went down the hall and checked the back door. It was locked. I flipped the switch to release the deadbolt and pulled the door open. I scanned the alleyway in both directions but saw no sign of the critter.

"Looks like he's flown the coop. Sorry boys."

The blowhard was apoplectic. "How could you have let it get away!"

I shrugged at him. "Last I checked, he was sleeping in the laundry room. The back door was locked, and I've been in my office since I called your agency. He had nowhere to go. Beats me how he got away."

The blowhard's eyes narrowed. "Is this some kind of hoax? He was never here!"

"Come on. You can still smell him, can't you?"

The blowhard sniffed the air and wrinkled his nose. He looked at his soldier boys. They shrugged.

The blowhard gave me what I guess he thought was a fierce glare through his wraparounds. He waved his arm at his pals in a circling motion and pointed toward the front door. "Let's get out of here!"

"You want me to call you if he comes back?"

No one answered. They marched single-file out my door without saying goodbye.

***

Alone in my house again, I opened the windows to let the foul air out and the fresh air in. I summoned a half-dozen elementals to speed up the process, and in fifteen minutes the place was smelling better than it had in months. I studied the surveillance video again, puzzling how the critter had managed to open my locked door. He'd somehow locked it behind him when he left, too. Neat trick! I wondered if he could teach it to me. It would come in handy for a man in my racket.

I popped a couple of frozen waffles into my toaster, and when they were ready I covered them with banana slices, peanut butter, and chocolate syrup. It was a meal fit for a king! I brought the dish downstairs to my office and fired up the coffee machine. While I polished off my breakfast, I started searching the internet for information on dwarflike creatures with the agility of a monkey and the strength of a troll.

The well-traveled and laconic Stormclaw had told us that stories of creatures matching that description had been told in all seven realms. I found references to many of them online, most of them in the form of folk tales. The details in the tales varied, but they shared many common elements. The creatures were sentient and intelligent, or at least as intelligent as humans, and ranged in size from six inches to three feet tall. They were abnormally strong and agile, and they could move like lightning or disappear in the blink of an eye. One other disturbing commonality in the folk tales is that the creatures tended to be meat-eaters with a craving for human flesh. None of the tales indicated that these creatures could control earth elementals.

Outside of the folk tales, I found a handful of references to known populations or sightings of undersized sentient creatures in Tolanica, including a cultural survey with a photograph. According to the article, a species of small humanlike creatures called "nirumbees" had once thrived in the Baahpuuo Mountains in Lakota Province, but had dwindled in number with the coming of the industrial age. The article stated that the nirumbees "shunned cities," but small villages of these little people could still be found tucked away in the lightly populated highland forest areas of western Tolanica, where their isolation was threatened "by the increasing encroachment of the timber and oil industries." I looked at the grainy black-and-white photo of three pudgy men, each about thirty inches tall, standing next to a beaming normal-sized human in a three-piece suit, and staring with vacant eyes at the ground in front of them. The three nirumbees were half dressed in animal skins and feathers and holding crude spears, probably at the request of the survey team that had found them. They appeared to be wishing that they could be anywhere except in front of the camera. None of these sad-looking little villagers looked like someone who could fell a troll with the bough of a tree or leap ten feet into the air and dive into a rock, but maybe the survey team had caught them on a bad day.

By noon, I was feeling cooped up and restless. Edie hadn't called yet, and I suspected that she was still sleeping. Given her working hours, I doubted that she saw a lot of morning sunshine. I decided that I needed to go back to Ohlone Lake and look for signs of the earth demon or nirumbee or whatever he was. Maybe he had left some trace of himself that would help me figure out what I was dealing with. Who knows, maybe he was camped somewhere by the lake. Someone who "shunned cities" might find few other areas within Yerba City to be as appealing.

I swung by a bakery on the way out to the Galindo District and picked up half a dozen doughnuts. I was halfway through the second one when I pulled up to the gates of the Galindo Estates. The sentry I'd encountered on my previous visit peered out the open window of his booth, eyeing the beastmobile with suspicion.

Before the sentry could say anything, I held up the box of doughnuts. "Hey, pal. Can you do me a favor? I bought more of these doughnuts than I should have, and I've got four left. Think you can take them off my hands? They're pretty good. Still fresh, too." I bit off a piece of the doughnut that I was working on and held the box out my window for the sentry to take.

The sentry frowned at me. "You're working with Mr. Fulton's crew, right?"

"That's right. He sent me here." That was almost true. Fulton had told me to get information on the Sihuanaba and the little fellow, and this is where my investigation had brought me.

The sentry frowned down at the box of doughnuts. "What kind are they?"

"Let me see. I bought a variety pack. I think there's a coconut crème, a chocolate glazed, something with raspberry filling, and I'm not sure about the other one. Maple maybe. Yeah, maple."

The sentry's frown disappeared. "I like maple. I like chocolate, too."

I held the box out closer to him. "Take them all. I've had all I need."

The sentry hesitated, then took the box. "Thanks, man. If you're coming to see the mayor, he's not home. His wife is out, too. The mayor is probably downtown. His wife drove herself out late last night and hasn't come back yet, so maybe she's with him."

"Fulton wants me to make sure everything's secure. I'll be out at the lake. Don't worry, I won't disturb the neighbors."

"Better not. Maybe you already know about it, but cops are in the neighborhood. Something must be up. They came in early this morning and are still here."

I shrugged. "Maybe somebody's cat went missing."

The sentry considered this. "Yeah, could be. Someone misplaces an earring and they fuckin' call the cops. They get mad if the cops don't get here quick enough to suit them, too. Hey, what's your name? I'll need to write it into the records."

I reached into my shirt pocket and pulled out a card. "Call me Alex." I handed him the card.

The sentry glanced at it and pushed a button to open the gate. "I'm Devon. Bring me a chocolate maple bar next time. That's my favorite."

"You got it, Devon." I waved at him as I drove through the gate and into the Galindo Estates.

Chapter Fourteen

The mid-afternoon sun was streaming through thin wisps of clouds when I emerged from the trees separating the residential area from the lake. I lowered the gym bag that I'd brought with me to the ground, loosened my tie, and rolled up my sleeves. I was overdressed for the lake, especially on a summer day, but I wasn't there for recreation.

Others were. Several power boats raced across the lake, and a group of teenagers in bathing suits were wading in the water or sunning themselves on the shore near the stretch where Zyanya and her children had washed up. Feeling conspicuous, I picked up the gym bag and, staying close to the trees, made my slow way toward the boat launch.

Several cars with boat trailers were parked in the lot at the launch. So was the white van that I'd seen earlier. I'd thought that it might be, and I'd come prepared.

"Still there Smokey?" At the sound of my voice, the elemental descended from somewhere over my head until it was hovering a few feet in front of me.

"Smokey is here."

"Good! You remember the two-legged creature about this tall that we saw over in those trees before?"

"Smokey remembers."

"Keep watch over this area. If you see him, come to me fast and tell me. Understand?"

"Smokey understands. Smokey will watch for creature." The elemental shot into the sky and disappeared from view.

As I approached the van from the passenger side, I could see that no one was sitting in the front seat. I went to the front of the van and noted the Lakota license plates. The white surface of the van was streaked and spattered with the dust and mud from roads leading through several of Tolanica's provinces. Shattered and smashed remains of flying insects covered the front grill of the vehicle and the surface of the headlights. The windshield had been wiped clean when the van had last passed through a filling station, and I peered through the glass to see past the front seat. As far as I could tell, the vehicle was unoccupied. I moved to the driver's side of the van and looked inside. I could see that the driver's seat was padded and that the pedals for the accelerator, brake, and clutch had all been bolstered with blocks so that a very short person could operate the vehicle. Rob Lubank's car had been modified in this way, but these blocks were larger. Lubank was about three and a half feet tall, more or less. The driver of this car had to be at least half a foot shorter than that. About the size of a nirumbee.

Next, I examined the rack on the roof of the van. It was a homemade job, constructed of unfinished wood and strands of hemp rope that looked to have been twisted by hand. The roof was scratched and scarred, but I couldn't tell what had been tied to the rack. A small rowboat would have fit there, but so could a number of other things.

I looked back through the driver's side window and confirmed that the lock was pushed down. It was an automatic lock with a control console on the inside of the door. I dug inside my gym bag and took out two wedges, a hammer, and a two-foot length of stiff wire. After laying these objects out on the asphalt, I picked up the wedges and inserted them into the lining of the upper part of the window, taking care not to leave any scratches. I tapped on them with the hammer until I'd created an opening large enough for the thick wire. Then I pushed the wire through the opening, angling it downward until the end of the wire reached the control console. I maneuvered the wire until I was able to push on the button that unlocked the doors. When the locks popped up, a high-pitched two-toned alarm began to wail. I pulled the door open, slid quickly into the driver's seat, and pried open the fuse box at the base of the steering column. This wasn't the first time I'd ever popped a car, and I had a good idea which fuse was connected to the alarm. I pulled out the most likely one, and the alarm went silent.

I stepped out of the van and stood near it, minding my own business. I waited for half a minute. Smokey didn't appear, so I walked around the van to the passenger side, opened the door, and slid inside. The alarm had sounded for only a few seconds, and, with luck, the nirumbee had been too far away to hear it over the racing boats, shouting teenagers, and other noises from the surrounding city. Anyway, who responds to car alarms? They go off so often that no one pays any attention to them. Still, the alarm had been loud, and I didn't want to waste any time.

The floor on the passenger side of the front seat was littered with cardboard food cartons with the remains of something that smelled like dead animals. Labels on the cartons showed that they'd all come from a grocery store in Crow Rock, the capital city of Lakota Province. An empty grocery sack was crumpled up among the cartons. I opened it and found a receipt for six cartons of yonak dated six days earlier. A sealed carton was on the seat within reach of a driver, and it felt half full. I took off the lid and smiled at the chunks of flesh swimming in the blood-based broth. Yonak! The carton contained the same troll dish that I had left out for the giant alley rat! The driver of this vehicle was no troll, but yonak seemed to be the preferred fare for all sorts of meat-eaters. I resealed the package of foul-smelling stew and put it back on the seat where I'd found it.

The glove compartment was empty, which surprised and disappointed me. I was hoping to find a registration tag, but no dice. An open ashtray in the dashboard was filled to overflowing with the butts of what looked like small cigars. Quite a few of the butts had spilled out of the ashtray to litter the floor of the van. The ash looked like the same stuff I'd found by the rock that had swallowed up the nirumbee. I scooped up a few of the butts and put them into a plastic evidence bag that I'd brought with me.

I climbed out of the van and reentered through the rear door. The back seats had been removed from the van, leaving all the space behind the front seat open for storage. A child-sized sleeping bag was unrolled on the floor, a sewed canvas bag filled with feathers at the head. A metal toolbox, filled with well-used tools, was bolted to the floor on one side of the van. It appeared that the nirumbee did his own car repairs. Sitting next to the box was a canvas bag. I looked inside and found a stack of large dried leaves. I pulled one of the leaves, thick, almost leather-like, from the pile. I was no herbalist, but I knew what a tobacco leaf looked like, and, while these leaves had a similar appearance, they weren't tobacco. I held it to my nose and breathed in. The leaves had an earthy scent that I couldn't identify. I rubbed the leaf with my fingertips and felt an oily film. I sniffed my fingertips and detected something faint and bitter. The leaves had been cured in something, but, again, I didn't know what. I was out of my depth. Collecting two of the leaves in a plastic baggie, I closed up the canvas bag and continued my search.

I found some spare clothing, and most of it seemed to have been handmade in a villager's hut from tanned hides, feathers, and twisted hemp threads. Hanging from a hook on the wall of the van, however, was a tiny, but elegant, two-piece suit inside a plastic drycleaner bag. A matching tie hung out of one of the suit's outer pockets. On the floor beneath the suit was a pair of expensive leather shoes, about size four or five, and wide. Custom made, I thought. Relative to his height, the nirumbee's feet were huge. A pair of dark socks were stuffed inside one of the shoes.

I'd been in the van long enough, but I took a little time to cover my traces. It was bad enough that I was breaking and entering. I didn't want to leave a mess behind. That wouldn't have been polite. All I needed to do was re-install the fuse.

As I was fitting the fuse back into place, I noticed a second closed compartment on the other side of the steering column. Curious, I flipped it open. A pain shot through my eyes, as if I had stared into the sun, and I quickly jerked my head to the side. Taking care, I eased my eyes back toward the compartment. No light was emerging from it, and nothing lit my hand when I moved it over the opening. I reached into the compartment and felt something small and smooth, like a pebble, lying inside. It didn't feel hot to the touch. I lowered my head to look inside, but the stabbing sensation returned and I had to pull my head away. Whatever was inside did not want to be seen.

I thought for a second, and then I took out my phone. I activated the camera app, held the screen in front of the open compartment, and snapped a photo. Nothing exploded. Everything seemed fine. I closed the compartment and put my phone in my pocket without looking at the screen.

I was about to leave the van, but on impulse I pulled out one of my business cards and left it on top of the half-eaten carton of yonak. Then I closed the door, remembering to lock it, and walked away from the vehicle.

Smokey had still not appeared by the time I stepped out of the parking lot and into the sandy lakefront. The boats still raced across the water, and the teenagers were still enjoying the summer sun. I walked into the trees with my gym bag until I was halfway to the path leading back to the Galindo Estates. Then I stopped and summoned Smokey, who came whizzing through the trees a moment later.

"No sign of the creature?"

"Smokey doesn't see two-legged creature."

"Okay, buddy. Thanks for your help."

After I released Smokey to return to the rafters of the Black Minotaur and bask in the fumes of whiskey and beer, I took my phone out of my pocket and called up my last photo, narrowing my eyes to slits and preparing myself for blinding pain. I glanced at the screen and jerked away. No pain. Feeling silly now, I opened my eyes and looked at the photo on my screen. It was an oval-shaped gemstone of some sort, smooth as a pebble in a riverbed, translucent, like frosted glass, with pink and red veins running through it. The stone was clearly visible, and my phone seemed no worse for having captured its image. The stone hadn't seemed to object to the artificial lens of a camera the way it had to my own gaze. Odd. Some strange voodoo was at work here. I'd look into it later, but for now I put the phone back in my pocket.

I pondered my next move. My search of the van had been revealing, but, even apart from the mysterious gemstone, I was still looking at a lot of questions. It was evident that the van belonged to the nirumbee. According to the article I'd seen, the nirumbees lived in villages in Lakota Province, and the van had Lakota plates. Circumstantial evidence maybe, but good enough for a working hypothesis. The drive from Lakota to Yerba City couldn't have taken less than three days, even with little sleep. The state of the vehicle told me that the nirumbee had come in a hurry. He had bought yonak for the trip and eaten while he drove, chain-smoking during the entire drive without bothering to empty his ashtray. He'd slept in the back of the van, probably for short breaks before resuming the drive. And he'd ended his trip at Ohlone Lake. Why there unless it had something to do with either Zyanya or the Sihuanaba? He'd brought along business clothes. Had he planned to meet someone in the city? I still had more questions than answers.

When had the nirumbee arrived? I'd counted six containers of yonak, five empty and one half full. A receipt showed that the nirumbee had bought the yonak six days earlier on Sunday, and he was now halfway through his last container. Assuming that he'd set out on Sunday, and that he went through one full container of yonak per day, then he'd probably arrived late on Tuesday, the night before Gordo, Thunderclash, and I had seen him watching us from the trees. He'd have to drive fast and almost non-stop to cover the distance in that amount of time, but it was doable. Teague had first seen the woman in white on Saturday. Had that sighting triggered the nirumbee's journey the next morning? How could it? Or was it Zyanya's death that had sent the nirumbee to Yerba City?

I gave up. I was making a lot of shaky assumptions based on little evidence. For all I knew, the nirumbee was in Yerba City for some other reason altogether, a reason that had nothing to do with my investigations. It seemed unlikely, but, after all, the universe didn't revolve around me and my interests. Maybe something else was going on.

I was thinking that I should have had Smokey widen its search of the forested area around the lakefront. The nirumbee's van was in the parking lot, and I reasoned that he must be somewhere near. I was surprised that he hadn't shown up when the van's alarm sounded. Perhaps an earth elemental had taken him to another part of the lake, but earth elementals have finite territories, and they only travel within their established borders. Of course, it was always possible that he'd met someone at the lake and been driven somewhere else. Truth was, he could have been anywhere. But my gut feeling was that, having driven all the way from Lakota Province to Ohlone Lake, he must still be somewhere in the area.

A scream jolted me from my thoughts. Another scream joined the first, along with shouts. I ran out of the trees in the direction of the teenagers. They were staring at two objects that two of the boys were dragging out of the lake. I was still a hundred yards away when I saw that the objects were the bodies of two children. I didn't have to get any closer to know that they were dead.

***

I had just finished giving my statement to an officer when I saw Detective Kalama heading across the lakefront in my direction. She glanced at the photographer taking photos of the two bodies from different angles, and she slowed to take a good look at the bodies themselves as she passed by. When she reached me, the detective nodded once and turned back to watch the forensics team do their work.

After a few moments, Kalama sighed and turned back to me, frowning. "You were here when the bodies were discovered?"

"I was back in those trees." I pointed. "I heard the teenagers screaming and came out to see what the fuss was about."

"Solve the case yet?"

"It's early."

"Right. Anything you want to tell me?"

I thought about it. "There's a white van in the parking lot over there. It's been there for three days. Lakota plates. The driver is a strange little creature, smaller than a dwarf, but strong as a troll and quicker than a cat. He's all kinds of suspicious, but I have no idea if he's connected to any of this. Still, you might want to check that van out and get whatever you can on the owner."

Kalama's eyebrows raised. "You search the vehicle yet?"

"Maybe."

"Fuck, Southerland. I'd arrest you for breaking and entering, but I got this thing over here to deal with."

I paused for a moment. "So this is a homicide?"

Kalama sighed again. "We don't know. Coldgrave called an emergency 'all hands on deck' for this one. He thinks that Ieea will grab it away from us any minute now, and he wants us to have as much intel as we can get before they do."

I nodded. "You don't seem surprised to see me here."

"I had a chat with the sentry at the gate as I was coming in. He warned me that a suspicious mug who looked like an underworld button man was driving a tank through the neighborhood, and he showed me your card. He heard about the dead kids, and he thinks you did it. He's feeling bad because he let you bribe him with some doughnuts."

"Great. He'll never let me past the gate next time. Not for less than a dozen chocolate maple bars."

Kalama's smile lasted for less than a second. She turned again to gaze back at the crime scene. Kalama was a tough broad. Male or female, you didn't last in homicide for almost a decade by being soft. But she was also a mother who loved her daughter. I'd be lying if I said that I knew how she felt standing a few yards away from the lifeless bodies of two children barely out of diapers, but I knew that it had to be messing her up pretty bad. She reached up and pushed a strand of black hair off her forehead. "Hard to see children like that. And these are just babies. The boy is only six. The girl's five. I sure *hope* it's not a homicide, but when a couple of fully-dressed children come washing up out of a lake, it's hard to think it could be anything else."

"A boy and a girl," I said.

Kalama nodded. "Brother and sister."

"Drowned."

"In Ohlone Lake, near the Galindo Estates."

"They're going to have to stop advertising this neighborhood as a nice place to raise kids."

Kalama looked up at me. "Think we can rule out coincidence?"

I shrugged. "Coincidences happen."

Kalama's brief chuckle contained no humor. "Sure they do. Happen all the time."

Zyanya's two children had washed up in this same part of the lake just two months earlier. The oldest had been a boy, the youngest a girl. They were younger than these two, but not by much. They'd been murdered. A lot of people like to say that they don't believe in coincidences, but the universe is a big place. Statistically, coincidences are inevitable. In this case, though? The odds that two sets of children, a boy and his younger sister, just happened to drown in the same part of the same lake a mere two months apart? Laying money on coincidence would be the mother of all sucker bets.

Kalama agreed. "The deaths are connected. Have to be."

"Zyanya killed her kids. She wasn't around to kill these two."

"We think she killed her kids. We don't know for sure." Kalama nodded in the direction of the bodies. Nearby, a woman was being consoled by two police officers. "That's the mother?"

"Right. She lives in the neighborhood. The father is out of town. He owns some kind of computer software…hardware…wetware, I don't know. Not even thirty and he's one of the richest men in Caychan. Guess I should have gone to college."

Kalama snorted. "Computer jeebos like that don't go to college. College grads work for jeebos like that."

"Well, I hope your people got her story." I nodded back at two men in dark suits, fedoras, and sunglasses walking in our direction from the boat launch parking lot. "If those sharpers aren't leea, I'll give up booze for a year."

Kalama's face tightened. "Shit!"

"Yeah. I don't want to deal with those mugs. I'm gonna skedaddle."

"Go. I'll call you later."

"Affirmative, copper. Hey, don't forget about that van."

Kalama glared at the approaching LIA agents. "Might be too late for that, gumshoe. I think we're about to lose this case."

***

A black luxury sedan was parked in front of my office. Twice in one week! If word got back to Mrs. Colby that I was seeing a higher class of clientele, she might raise my rent! The sedan wasn't the same model as the one that Fulton had sent for me, and the well-dressed troll waiting by the passenger door wasn't part of Gordo's crew. As I strolled down the sidewalk toward the car, I started whistling one of the tunes that I'd heard Nina sing the night before. It was after five, and she hadn't called me yet. Should I have been worried? I decided not to dwell on it. Now wasn't the time. A troll was waiting for me.

"Get in the car, Mr. Southerland. Someone wants to see you." The troll held the passenger door open for me. I was going to get to ride shotgun!

"What if I don't want to see him?" I asked.

"Don't be a wise guy, peeper." The troll sounded bored.

"What about my gym bag? Can I leave it inside my office?"

The troll frowned, and then nodded. "Okay, but be quick."

The troll followed me and watched as I opened my office door and slid the bag inside. "Mind if I get my roscoe?" I asked, just to be funny. I was disappointed when the troll didn't laugh. That was my 'A' material!

I followed the humorless troll back to the car and slid through the passenger door into the creamy soft leather seat. I felt richer just sitting there.

The troll walked around the front of the car and climbed in behind the wheel. He was alone. Whoever I was going to see didn't think it would take more than one troll to handle me. He was right, but I still felt insulted.

"Who are we going to see?"

The troll ignored my question and started the car. That was all right. I would find out soon enough.

Chapter Fifteen

The troll took me to a quiet residential neighborhood just outside of the Midtown District. He pulled up to a gated driveway and punched some numbered buttons on a security call box. The gate slid open, and the troll drove us up a brick driveway to a modest one-story stucco house. When we got to the front door, the troll opened it and ushered me inside to an entrance hall with a tile floor, where he patted me down. Satisfied that I wasn't packing anything more serious than some nail clippers and a set of lock picks, he told me to take off my shoes and leave them on the floor near the door where several other pairs, including three pairs of child-sized shoes, were already stashed. He took off his own shoes and left them there, as well, where they towered over the other sets like schoolyard bullies. Then he told me to have a seat in an armless padded chair in the hallway and disappeared into the back of the house, leaving me to contemplate my stocking feet.

The troll returned five minutes later and motioned me to follow him. He led me down a carpeted hallway to an open doorway, but he stopped me before I could enter. "I'll need to hold on to your cell phone." He held out his hand. "You'll get it back when you leave."

I handed him my phone, and he stood aside to let me enter. I was greeted by a thin silver-haired sharper in a gray suit with a bushy salt-and-pepper mustache that covered his upper lip, a diamond stickpin in his tie, and a fucking white carnation in the buttonhole of his lapel. He stood shoeless in front of a polished mahogany desk, holding a glass of something dark over ice.

"Mr. Southerland!" The sharper held out a hand. "So pleased to meet you. I'm Anton Benning." He glanced at the troll. "That will be all for now, Bronzetooth. Please close the door."

I grasped Benning's hand and he gave mine a shake that was firm enough, but with no attempt to intimidate. "Would you like a drink? I've got some genuine shawnee whiskey that I think you'll like."

"I might at that, Mr. Benning."

He stepped over to a liquor cabinet and poured some of the Province of Sawano's leading export from a half-filled bottle into a glass. "Ice?"

"Please. It's a warm day."

He handed me the glass and watched me sip from it. He smiled when he saw my reaction to the whiskey. "Smooth, right? Distilled from sixty-five percent corn and aged in charred oak barrels for six years. No added coloring or flavoring, just pure, eighty-proof shawnee, the drink of gentlemen."

I took another sip and let out a slow breath, savoring the warm sensation in my throat as I exhaled. "I don't know if I'm what you would call a gentleman, but I could get used to this."

Benning's eyes lit up. "I daresay you could, my boy! I daresay you could! Now, please, have a seat." He placed a hand on my elbow and guided me to a leather sofa near his desk. He sat in a high-backed desk chair and wheeled it around until he was facing me.

Benning took a sip of shawnee and placed the glass on his desktop. "I'd offer you a cigarette, Mr. Southerland, but I understand that you don't smoke. Is that correct?"

"It is, although I'll puff on a good cigar on occasion."

Benning raised an eyebrow. Just one. I'd always wanted to be able to do that, but never figured out how. Maybe you had to be born with the ability. "Let's hold off on cigars for the moment. Maybe we'll have the occasion to light a couple up when we've concluded our business."

"And what business would that be, Mr. Benning?"

"Yes, let's get to that." Benning leaned forward in his chair. "You're working for Fulton."

It wasn't a question, so I didn't answer. I sipped my shawnee whiskey, instead, and listened to the pleasant tinkling of the ice cubes on the sides of the glass.

"He wants you to investigate a certain woman in white and make sure that she doesn't bring any harm to the mayor, or, more precisely, hurt his chances for reelection."

I still hadn't heard a question. I twirled the glass in my hand so that the water from the melting ice cubes would cool the whiskey.

Benning continued. "As you no doubt already know, I'm a legal advisor for the Montavious Harvey campaign. I'm interested in knowing about this woman who is troubling the mayor."

I shrugged. "I don't know much. She's quite a mystery."

Benning's eyebrow shot up again. "Is that so! Hmmm. Well, I know that she's been stalking the mayor, and that she put some kind of scare into him a couple of nights ago."

"Sounds like you know as much as I do."

Benning let out a sigh, and his mustache stretched over a forced smile. "Possibly, but I'd be disappointed in you if that were true. You and I both know that this woman in white might be a supernatural creature known as the Sihuanaba. They tell a lot of stories about her in Azteca and the Borderland. In northern Qusco, too. She has never before been sighted in this part of the world, however. Any idea what has brought her to Yerba City, and, more specifically, why she has targeted Mayor Teague? That's what Fulton wants you to find out for him, isn't it? I'd like to know about that, too."

I tried to keep a poker face. Benning seemed to know quite a lot about what Fulton had hired me to do. It sounded like Fulton was right to suspect that Benning had planted a mole in his organization. "The thing is, Mr. Benning, Fulton is paying me good money to find out things for him. You seem to want this same information for one drink of good whiskey."

Benning's smile pushed the end of his mustache up on one side of his face. "Would you like another glass? I'll give you a bottle to take home with you. I've got plenty. And I'll give you a lot more money than Mr. Fulton is paying you. I mean, he's only paying you half your normal rates, right? Now, now, don't look so stunned. I know quite a lot about what goes on in Mr. Fulton's office. He thinks he's a smooth operator, but he's not nearly as smooth as he thinks he is, or as smart, either. He is certainly not an *ethical* man."

"I see. And the Hatfields are ethical?"

Benning put his hands on his knees and leaned a little closer to me. "It's true that the Hatfields are helping to finance Mr. Harvey's campaign. But I work for Montavious Harvey, and it is in that capacity that I wish to employ your services. Montavious is an ethical man, a good man. Work for me, and you'd be working to elect a *competent* mayor who would be *beneficial* for this city, a mayor with solid business sense and strong moral fiber, one with genuine family values. One who, in contrast to our current mayor, is neither a bigamist nor a murderer."

"Murderer? Who'd he murder?"

The ends of Benning's mustache rose. "We know quite a lot about our esteemed mayor. His relationship with that lovely singer, Zyanya, was hardly a secret, even from most of the general public, who laughed it off as a harmless joke. And although Mr. Fulton has done his best to keep loose talk of Zyanya's children out of the media—on the 'down low,' as it were—well, that kind of information can't be kept hidden from anyone with the resources to uncover it. As for the singer's untimely death, no one with a half a brain accepts the official verdict of suicide. No, Mr. Teague's relationship with poor Miss Zyanya had grown too volatile. Mr. Fulton repeatedly warned the mayor that his liaison with the singer threatened his chances for reelection, but the situation had grown to the point where merely severing the relationship would no longer suffice. What would she do to retaliate against Teague once their relationship ended? And, besides, the mayor had grown very weary of Zyanya's...shifting moods, let's say."

Benning shook his head before continuing. "No, I'm afraid that the singer had to go. Whether the idea was Teague's or Fulton's, they are both equally guilty. Someone in their organization 'did her in,' as they say, but it is the men at the top that bear the ultimate responsibility for her death."

Benning met my eyes, letting me get a good look at the solemn expression on his face. "Is that the kind of people you want to be working with, Mr. Southerland?"

It hit me then. "You want me to find proof that Teague or one of his people murdered Zyanya! That's what you're really interested in, isn't it."

Benning shrugged. "Could you do it?"

"Maybe."

"Would you do it, if I asked you to? See to it that Teague and the members of his corrupt little cabal receive justice for their crimes? That's what *you're* interested in, isn't it? Justice?"

"Sure I am. I'd like to see every bigtime criminal in this city get what he deserves. And then the rest of us could live happily ever after. I'll wave my magic wand and make all the bad guys disappear."

"You can make *some* of them disappear. With our help."

"And who would replace them?"

Benning pursed his lips until they were hidden beneath the bush under his nose. "Fulton is a murderer, Southerland, or he's covering up a murder. And for what? For political gain. It's petty, really. A small and mean little man who became a big wheel by dazzling the public with someone else's pretty face. But underneath the makeup, that face is an ugly mass of pits and scars. And now Fulton wants you to help him smooth it over and keep it looking pretty for the public."

"And what are you offering as an alternative? The Hatfield Syndicate? An underworld crime family that peddles dope to addicts, prostitutes to degenerates and the desperate, and gambling to poor saps who can't pay their rents or put food on the table?"

Benning waved a hand in the air. "Oh, people will always have their vices. That's just the nature of sentient beings. If you try to outlaw the things that people desire, then you can't be surprised when outlaws will spring out of the very earth to meet the need for these desires. You can't eliminate desire, Mr. Southerland. And that's where the Hatfield family comes in. They satisfy desires."

Benning leaned forward in his chair and lowered his voice like he was about to give me a hot stock tip. "Mr. Southerland, I'm going to let you in on something that Mr. Fulton would never tell you, even if he knew about it. The Hatfield family has come to an agreement with Mr. Harvey. When he is mayor, the Hatfields will allow their activities to be moderated by reforms instituted by Mr. Harvey."

I reached for my drink. "That right? What are they going to do—go legit?"

Benning snorted. "Legit! What does that even mean? You think that there is a difference between large legitimate corporations and the Hatfield Syndicate? They're two sides of the same coin, and, believe me, they operate under the same principles. Only the product is different."

Benning folded his hands in his lap as he settled into his pitch. "There will always be an underground market for things that people desire. But under Harvey's carefully crafted reforms, these desires will be satisfied in a way that is reasonable, businesslike, and, above all, peaceful. Gone will be the days in which gangs of lowlife thugs compete with each other, often violently, to supply low-quality product. Instead, in Harvey's administration, violent amateur organizations will be eliminated, and the Hatfields will run the entire under-market as a regulated business, not as a street gang. Products will be safe and safely distributed in a controlled manner. Disputes arising from unsatisfactory arrangements will be dealt with peacefully for the most part, with restrained violence used only in the most extreme circumstances. For all intents and purposes, the undermarket will be legitimized and organized under the control of professionals."

I took it all in, sipped my drink, and didn't say anything.

Benning sat back in his chair and lifted his glass off his desktop. "Come work for me, Mr. Southerland. At, shall we say, triple your standard rates? Plus more respect than you'll ever get from that double-dealing snake in the grass and his puppet mayor. Help me put a murderer away for good. Let's put a good man, a decent man, like Montavious Harvey in charge of Yerba City. If we work together, we can make a difference. Harvey will rein in the crime syndicates and make this city a better place for the 'average joe' and the 'average jane' to live, a city where emerging entertainers aren't violently taken from us for the crime of threatening the status of a corrupt politician, a place where justice can prevail. What do you say? Shall we break out a couple of cigars to go with these drinks?" He beamed at me like I was his favorite nephew, and his mustache stretched from ear to ear as he raised the glass to his lips.

I swirled the remains of my drink around the bottom of the glass. "I appreciate the shawnee, Mr. Benning. I appreciate your offer, too. I can't take you up on it, of course, but that doesn't mean I don't appreciate it."

Benning placed his glass back on the desktop. "I'm disappointed to hear that, Mr. Southerland. May I ask why?"

I set the glass down on the end table. "First, I'm already working for Fulton, and it would be a breach of ethics to contract my services to his professional rival." Benning looked like he was about to raise an objection, but I continued. "Second, I don't wish to become a tool in the hands of the Hatfield Syndicate."

Benning shook his head. "As I told you, I am employed by the Montavious Harvey Campaign."

"You work for Harvey to ensure that he plays ball with the Hatfields. Harvey doesn't have the juice to regulate the Hatfields. The Hatfields don't just contribute to Harvey's campaign, they own him. And if I take you up on your offer, they'll own me, too. Quit trying to kid me with all that 'you'd be working for the Harvey Campaign' crap. If I were to work for you, I'd be working for the Hatfields. And once the Hatfields have their hooks in you, you're part of their gang whether you want to be or not. But I don't have to tell *you* that, do I?"

Benning's face tightened, and I thought that he was going to get steamed. But he was too cool a customer for that. He collected himself in an instant, twisted his face into an appreciative half-smile, and raised an eyebrow.

"Touché, Mr. Southerland! It would be useless for me to deny that although I am, in fact, employed by the Harvey campaign, the Hatfield family is my principal client, and, as such, the primary source of my income. And I will admit that the Hatfields tend to place a high value on continued loyalty from anyone whom they employ. And you're right. If you work for me, you will be, indirectly at least, working in the interests of the Hatfields."

Benning raised a finger and shook it a little. "But, is that really so bad? My boy, you're working for Fulton! Believe me, that piece of excrement places the same value on continued loyalty as the Hatfields do. Tell me that he doesn't behave as if he owns you, even while insulting you by refusing to compensate you for the full value of your services. Why do you put up with that—unless he has some kind of hold on you?" His eyes widened and he leaned back in his chair. "Ah, I can see by your face that this time it is I who have hit the mark. Let me assure you that whatever it is that Fulton has on you, the Hatfields can free you from it, for good!"

Apparently my poker face was still a work in progress. "I don't doubt that for a second, Mr. Benning. But then I'd owe them, and the interest on that debt would always be just a little more than I could pay off."

"And you'd be no worse off than you are now, except that you would owe your debt to the Hatfields instead of to Fulton." Benning leaned forward again. "And so it comes down to this. Would you rather 'play ball,' as you put it, for Fulton, or would you rather switch teams and work for the Hatfields. My boy, it's going to be one or the other. I have no illusions about the Hatfields. I know that they will do whatever is necessary to ensure that the family continues to thrive. But are you so naïve as to believe that Fulton is any different? That his hands are cleaner than the hands of the Hatfields? You can't possibly believe that, can you? No, I'm afraid that both teams play fast and loose with the rules. Both sides are equally ambitious and both can be equally unscrupulous when they run out of other options. But, Mr. Southerland…" Benning paused to make sure that he had my attention. I was listening. "The difference is that the Hatfields won't insult you by paying you less than your just price for any service you might render on their behalf. They will treat you like the professional that you are. The Hatfields *want* their people to succeed and to enjoy the rewards for that success. Mr. Fulton would rather bully you into working on his behalf." He raised a fist in the air and tightened it. "Squeeze your services out of you until he's drained you of everything he can get from you, and then toss you aside when you are of no further use." He opened his hand and waved it, as if flicking mud off his fingertips.

He sat back in his chair and fingered the carnation in his lapel. "And make no mistake, my boy. Do this job for me and when you're finished you'll still be the same man you are. You'll be free to continue operating in the manner in which you've grown accustomed, to take whatever case you want, as long as you don't work against the interest of the Hatfields. Yes, the Hatfields demand loyalty, but, unlike Fulton, the Hatfields believe that loyalty is a two-way street. Help them out this time, and the family will direct cases your way. Lucrative cases from a respectable base of clientele. And you'll have resources available to you that even the police are unable to provide. You'll never have to worry about where your next meal is coming from, or whether you can pay the next month's rent." Benning clapped his hands together. "So, what's it going to be, Mr. Southerland? Are you going to continue allowing yourself to be used by that loathsome extortionist, these murderers of innocent young women, or are you going to let yourself be rescued, and to be free to succeed and flourish? Here's my hand, sir—take it!"

Instead of taking Benning's extended hand, I reached over and picked up my glass from the end table. I leaned back into the sofa and sipped the smooth shawnee. After a moment, Benning withdrew his hand.

I put the glass back down on the table and turned to Benning. "What if I said that I need to think about it? Would you allow me to leave?"

Benning harrumphed. "Of course, dear boy. Take a look around you. Does this look like the home of a hoodlum? But what is there to think about? You have questions? Feel free to ask. You'll get nothing but honesty from me."

Like hell I would! According to Benning, my future consisted of two choices: working for a shady political power broker who was strong-arming me for my services and treating me like a chump, or working for a regulated underworld organization that would treat me like a professional and show me as much loyalty as I showed them. But I didn't buy the premise of his argument for a moment. Fulton was a hard number, but he and the Hatfields operated on different scales. Benning had told me that Fulton would squeeze me and toss me aside. Maybe so. But Fulton had told me that the Hatfields would squeeze the entire city and leave it behind, and I didn't doubt it. Maybe Fulton had been playing me for a sucker with all his talk about loving the city. Put that aside. But I remembered Fulton's indignation when I had suggested that he might have something to do with the death of Zyanya's children. It had seemed genuine to me. That didn't mean that Fulton wouldn't stoop to having children rubbed out if he believed deep down that it was necessary, but I thought that he might at least be troubled by the decision. The Hatfields wouldn't bat an eye. Nothing was beneath them. And no elected official was going to control them, either. The idea that the Hatfield Syndicate was going to transform itself into some kind of do-gooder agency dedicated to the public welfare was a giant load of hooey, and not even the most polished and articulate pitchman could make it any less of a load. The Hatfields were the lords of the underground, and they would sink to unimaginable depths to acquire what they desired. Including *my* services, I suddenly realized. That thought made my skin tighten, like a plastic wrapper in a microwave oven.

And then there was the other part of Benning's argument, the assumption that I had only two choices. There was always another choice if you had the guts to take it. My problem was that I didn't know what that other choice might be, short of sticking a gat in my mouth and eating a bullet. I was too young and too stubborn for that, but I was going to need to find another option, fast.

I took one last slug of shawnee, emptying the glass. "I'm all out of questions, Mr. Benning. I've heard what I need to hear. You've got a real gift—you could sell hair tonic to a troll! And I'll admit that a lot of what you say makes sense. But how long do you think I'd stay in business if word got out that I gutted a client? The only customers I'd be able to get would be the ones that the Hatfields sent my way. You say that I'd be free to do business as usual as long as I didn't inconvenience the Hatfields. Maybe that's how it would start. But as time went on I'd be doing more and more work for the family and less and less for anyone else. That's not what I call freedom. As for Fulton, he's slick and he's tough, and I might be in over my head. He's a big, vicious dog. But the Hatfields are a pack of wolves. A big pack, with a loyal soldier in every shadow. I might have a chance with Fulton. With the Hatfields, I'd be nothing but dog meat."

Benning leaned back in his chair and sighed. He raised his eyes to meet mine. "As you wish. I think that you're making a mistake, but I can see that you're a man who is not prone to changing his mind once he has made a decision, misguided as it may be. But I want you to think about something. You say you'd be dog meat if you agreed to work on behalf of the Hatfields. What makes you think you wouldn't be if you don't?"

Something cold formed in the pit of my stomach and began to spread into my chest. I could feel the hairs standing up on my arm and on the back of my neck. "I assume that's a threat."

"Just a friendly warning, Mr. Southerland. Just a friendly warning. You won't accept my offer of employment? That's fine. I won't put you on the payroll. But if you find proof that Teague or Fulton or one of their associates murdered that poor singer, give me a ring. Anytime, day or night. Do it as a favor. I'd be…appreciative. Or do it because the singer will receive the justice that she isn't going to receive otherwise. Shall we leave it at that?" He stood then, and I followed suit. He pulled a business card from his shirt pocket and handed it to me. Then he reached across his desk and pushed a button on his phone console. "My man Bronzetooth will drive you back to your office."

I thought about that. Benning wouldn't allow any violence in his home. This was a man who required visitors to remove their shoes before walking on his carpets. I was sure that the idea of bloodstains on those carpets kept him awake at night. But once I was in the black sedan with his troll? This was a horse of a different color.

"Thanks, but don't bother your associate. I'll call a cab."

Benning raised his eyebrow. It was always the same one. "Nonsense, my dear boy! I had you plucked off the street, and it's only right that I put you back where I found you."

The door to the office opened, and the troll walked in. Benning glanced his way. "Mr. Southerland will be leaving now. Drive him back to his office or wherever he wishes to go. And drive carefully, Bronzetooth. Until you deliver him safely, he's still our guest. See that he comes to no harm."

"Thank you, Mr. Benning. It's been an interesting visit. I'm sorry that we couldn't make a deal, but you've given me a lot to think about."

"I wish you luck in your investigations. And if you need anything, feel free to call. I hope to see you again."

I left feeling certain that my life would be swell if that never happened.

***

Bronzetooth never said a word on the drive back to my office. He didn't try to kill me, either, so I felt doubly blessed. As I was about to slide out of the passenger's seat, the troll turned his burning eyes in my direction. "We're watching you, Mr. Southerland. You should have taken the boss up on his offer."

I put on a smile. "Stop by anytime, Bronzetooth. I've got yonak in the refrigerator. Extra bloody."

Bronzetooth made a sour face. "I hate that fucking shit!"

"Right. Nothing but prime rib in the Benning household, I suppose."

Bronzetooth glared at me as only a troll can. "Get out of the fucking car!"

I complied with his demand. He drove away like he was ashamed to be seen in my neighborhood.

Chapter Sixteen

The sun was sinking into a thick layer of fog by the time I entered my office. Leaving my lights off, I sat at my desk and pondered the painting on my wall. The crow's shoulders seemed a little hunched to me, like he was tired. The desert landscape seemed to taunt him, as if secrets were buried under the rocky ground, far from the crow's reach. I stared at the painting until the last of the sun's rays stopped streaming through my window blinds.

I wanted to hear from Edie. It occurred to me that she might have called when I was in my meeting with Benning. I took out my phone, which Bronzetooth, true to his word, had returned to me once I was outside Benning's house. I saw now that it had been turned off. When I turned it back on, I checked for missed calls. Edie hadn't called, but I told myself that she was probably just waking up and that she'd get in touch with me soon. I did have one missed call, though. Fulton had tried to get in touch with me, and he'd left a voicemail message. I listened to it, and Fulton's recorded voice told me to call him back right away.

I wasn't ready to talk to Fulton. Screw him. Screw Fulton and Benning and all the rest of those corrupt power brokers. Why was I mixed up with these unsavory con artists anyway? What was I doing in the middle of their political tug-of-war for the fate of the city? I didn't care about politics! For my money, anyone with the ambition to hold a political office was by definition too attracted to personal power to trust with the responsibility. What the city needed was an ordinary clerk who could keep track of the numbers and the reports and make sure that everything was organized. Any good secretary to any big boss in any large corporation would be able to handle the job, and the city would be the better off for it. Fucking political horseshit! Every time I talked to smarmy jokers like Fulton or Benning I felt like I needed a shower. I found myself longing to sink my teeth into a nice juicy case of insurance fraud, something boring and routine with a hefty payoff at the end of it.

I forced myself to stop stewing and turned my thoughts to Edie. She'd be calling soon, and I had a couple of calls to make before I heard from her. Not to Fulton, though. He could wait. I punched in a number and waited.

Detective Kalama answered on the third ring. She sounded as tired as the crow looked. "What do you want, gumshoe."

"Hello, Detective. How's the world treating you?"

"Like shit. But why should today be any different?"

"I take it that you lost another case to Ieea?"

"Yeah. They want to talk to you. They didn't like it that you fled the scene of the crime."

"Did you tell them that I'd already given a statement to the police?"

"I believe that your statement is now in their hands. I don't know if they'll bother to read it, though. They don't seem to think that us local cops know how to properly interview a witness."

"Get a chance to look at that van?"

"Leea wouldn't let us near it. We were told to pack up our gear and go home so that the adults could handle things."

"So what now?"

"Officially? It's out of our hands."

"And unofficially?"

I heard the detective sigh. "I've been over what we managed to get from the scene. It looks like murder. The kids had water from the lake in their lungs, and we've got clear markings on their necks indicating that they were held under the water."

"That's rough. Any suspects?"

"That falls under the category of police business, citizen."

"You mean Ieea business, don't you? As I understand it, the police aren't involved with this case."

"Thank you and fuck you." Kalama paused. "We're still involved. When the mother discovered that her children were missing, she called the department. Our officers were doing a door-to-door when the children washed up out of the lake."

"The gate sentry warned me that cops were in the neighborhood."

"Nice of him. He probably thought that they were after you. Anyway, the point is that we're operating on the presumption that the killer is still in the neighborhood. Leea may have taken over the murder case, but patrolling the streets of a gated residential community isn't their style. They've farmed that task out to the locals, and we've got some officers out there. We're going to keep a police presence in the neighborhood for a few days, through the weekend, at least. Maybe longer unless they get lucky and nail this perp. One of the perks of living in Galindo Estates. Must be nice to be rich."

I didn't say anything, and after a few breaths, Kalama noticed. "Something on your mind, gumshoe?"

"Yeah. Those officers you've got out there in the neighborhood.... They might be in more danger than they realize."

"What do you mean?"

I wasn't in the habit of sharing the details of my cases with the police. When clients hired me, they expected confidentiality. That went double—maybe triple—for a sharpshooter like Fulton. Which is why, up to this point, I hadn't told Kalama about the woman in white. But I wouldn't be able to look Kalama in the face again if one of those cops ran into the Sihuanaba or the nirumbee in the middle of the night without knowing what he was up against. So I decided to open up to the detective.

"You didn't hear this from me," I told her. "This is an anonymous tip from a concerned citizen, okay?"

"Okay, mister anonymous citizen. Whatcha got?"

"Your cops need to be on the lookout for a couple of unusually dangerous characters. One of them is a stumpy little bastard, about two and a half feet tall. But don't let his size fool you. He's strong as a troll and can jump around like a spider monkey. He can also command earth elementals. You getting this?"

"Yeah, I got it. I'm just not sure I believe it!"

"Trust me, I've seen this runt bring down a troll with a club. The other character is even more dangerous. It's a woman with long black hair who wears a white dress. Her usual M.O. is to lure men away to some secluded place, where she reveals herself to be some sort of demonic hag. She either kills the lug or drives him insane."

Kalama made sure I was finished before asking, "You're not pulling my leg, are you gumshoe?"

"It's been a strange couple of days. The woman is known in the Borderland as the Sihuanaba."

"The see-...."

"*Hwan*-aba," I finished. "Also known as the 'woman in white.' She's some sort of avenging demon who takes revenge on men who cheat on or otherwise abuse women."

"I see." Kalama thought about this for a moment. "Are we supposed to arrest her or give her a medal?"

"That's up to you. But you might want to warn your bulls against following good-looking dames in white dresses off into the underbrush."

"Or I could keep quiet and let some of those mugs get what they deserve." Kalama sighed. "Okay, I'll make sure they're warned and hope they take it seriously. Even better, I'll suggest that we send more female officers out there. Maybe team a female up with every male."

"That's a swell idea. Good thinking, copper. I recommend that you keep them in teams of four. These characters are pretty tough."

"You think that one of them killed those kids?"

"I don't know, but it's not a bad assumption."

"So Fulton's had you investigating some kind of mutant dwarf and a demon manslayer?"

"Who, me? I'm just an anonymous concerned citizen, remember?"

I remembered something then. "By the way, Detective. Did your boys happen to swing by the mayor's house?"

"They did. No one was home."

"The mayor was at his downtown apartment. The sentry told me that his wife had been out all night. She hadn't come back yet when I got there."

"That sentry is a chatty guy."

"His name's Devon," I informed her, feeling helpful.

"And he likes doughnuts. You aren't trying to tell me that Mrs. Teague is a person of interest in the murder of those children, are you?"

"Wouldn't that be something? No, but it might be interesting to know where she was all night."

"She part of your investigation?"

I hesitated. "Hard to say. I don't have anything that points to her, but who knows?"

Kalama was silent for a few moments. Then she said, "I don't know. I suppose I could try to talk to her, if Ieea hasn't already shut her down. My gut says that there's nothing there, but it's not like I have much else to do. Outside of the half dozen other cases on my desk, that is. Come to think of it, maybe *you* should talk to her. You're working for her husband's lawyer, right? That gives you a better excuse to question her than I've got."

"Fulton might not want me near her, but I'll see what I can do. I'll get back to you if I dig up anything interesting."

Just then, I heard a buzz on my phone. "Hey, I've got a call coming in. I'd better take it."

"Hot date?"

"Something like that. I'll talk to you later." I disconnected before the detective could respond.

I answered the incoming call. "Alexander Southerland."

"Hi, big man. Are you free for breakfast?" Edie's voice sounded smooth, like a crooner's.

"Little late for breakfast, isn't it?"

"Not for me. You can have a steak if you want."

"Got a place in mind?"

"There's a diner near the Turbo called The Lighthouse. It should be called The Hash House, but it's okay. You can't miss it. It's got a neon sign in the shape of a lighthouse."

"Sounds swell, sugar. I'm out the door. Expect me in a half hour."

"Eager. I like that in a man." She disconnected the call, leaving me to stare at the screen of my phone.

***

I walked up the block to Gio's lot to pick up the beastmobile. Gio spotted me and waved me into his office, where he was sitting behind his desk using one thick finger to enter some data into his computer. He closed whatever file he'd been working on when I entered and pulled a half-smoked cigar out of his shirt pocket. "You missed poker night last night, you prick! You know I always do better when you're there. Kofi about cleaned me out!" He took a matchstick out of a box on his desk and lit up his cigar.

"How much did you lose?" Gio was one of the worst poker players I'd ever encountered. He had a rubber face that gave everything away. Neither he nor the other members of the Thursday Night Poker Gang knew that my elf-enhanced awareness allowed me to pick up all of their tells, and that I wasn't a fair match for any of them. But I was in it for the camaraderie, rather than the money, and I folded a lot of winning hands in order to keep from taking advantage of them.

Gio puffed a cloud of smoke off to one side. "Not enough to keep me from coming back next week. Where were you? Not working, I hope. Tell me you were with a dame!"

I pulled up a stool and sat down. "Both, actually. I was questioning a dame."

"Well, I hope she said 'yes'!"

I laughed. "It wasn't that kind of question. She's quite a lady, though. A singer. I caught her act before I talked to her, and it was pretty good!"

Gio smiled around his cigar. "Oh yeah? Anyone I know?"

"She goes by Nina. She was performing at a place called the Turbo Lounge in Placid Point."

Gio shook his head. "Don't know her. But me and the missus don't get out much anymore, so I'm kinda out of touch." Gio rocked back his desk chair and blew cigar smoke at the ceiling. "I used to be quite a night owl, you know. Me and Connie could really cut a rug back in those days." He slapped a hand on his belly. "That was about fifty pounds and three kids ago." He reached up and rubbed the top of his head with his grease-stained palm. "I had hair back then! Hard to believe it was only fifteen years ago."

I tried to picture a thinner and hairier version of the bald burly mechanic on the dance floor at the Turbo, but my imagination failed me. It was hard to believe that Gio was only about nine or ten years older than I was.

Gio sighed and shook his head. "But that's what happens when the kids come along. It all changes."

"You got a pretty good set of kids, though," I reminded him.

"Yeah, that's all Connie's doing. She does all the work. I just try to keep outta her way."

"That's not true. I've seen you with them. You're a great father. Those kids are lucky to have you."

"Those kids are a pain in the ass. If it weren't for them, I'd still be paintin' the town red on my Friday nights instead of working late to put food on their table." Gio finished off his beer with a gulp and let out a belch.

"Are you telling me that you regret having children?"

"Every damned day!" Gio pushed his cigar back into his lips. "But they're also the best things that ever happened to me. Next to Connie, of course. Antonio is fourteen now. He's practically a man! Sierra is twelve. Boys are going to be following her home pretty soon. Gemma is ten, still a kid, but she won't be for long. Let me tell ya something, Alex. When I look at them, all I see is the babies they used to be. It tears me up inside! Sometimes I can't wait for them to move out of the house and leave me in peace. Other times I wonder why they have to grow up so fuckin' fast."

"What about painting the town red on Friday nights?"

The big mechanic laughed. "You kidding me? That kind of shit is fine when you're young, but there's nothing more pathetic than a screwball my age trying to act like he's still twenty-one. My children keep me on my toes and force me to be responsible. Without them, I'd still be trying to act like a fuckin' firecracker!"

I shook my head. "As long as you're happy."

"Happy!" Gio barked out a short laugh. "Who the hell is happy? Happy is for chumps! I'm *satisfied*. I've got a nice family and I work steady. I can still enjoy a drink and a cigar, and sometimes I win a few bucks at poker. I love cars, and so does my son and one of my daughters. Fuck happy! I'll take satisfaction any day of the week."

I couldn't figure out if Gio was the wisest man in the world or nuttier than a fruitcake. While I was trying to decide, he waved his cigar at me. "So where ya off to tonight? Back to see your canary?"

"I'm meeting her for dinner, actually. I have a few more questions for her."

Gio responded to that with a broad toothy smile. "I'll bet you do! Get it while you can, slugger!"

I groaned. "It's not like that."

"No?" Gio crushed out his cigar stub in an ashtray. "Well you won't get nowhere with an attitude like that!"

Later, as I was driving the beastmobile off his lot, I decided that Gio might be a pretty smart fellow after all. It was a shame that he was so lousy at cards!

***

By the time I fought through the Friday evening traffic and found a place to deposit the beastmobile, I was running about ten minutes late. It was another ten minutes before I walked beneath the neon lighthouse and entered the restaurant. The place was about half filled, and it smelled like deep-fried fish, heavy on the oil. I spotted Edie sitting in front of a cup of coffee in a booth along the back wall. I hung my hat and coat on a rack by the counter and crossed the diner to join her.

"I took the liberty of ordering for you," Edie told me as I slid onto a sea-green plastic-coated bench across the table from her. "I don't have a lot of time before I have to be at the club."

"What am I getting?" I asked.

"Pan fried abalone with rice. Hope you're not allergic to shellfish."

"Not a problem. Kind of expensive, though."

"That's okay. You're buying." She sipped her coffee.

"What did you order for yourself?"

"A bowl of oatmeal. I don't eat much before I go on stage."

"In that case, I guess I can afford the abalone."

A waitress came by and asked me if I "needed" coffee. I told her that I did, and she poured me a cup. I ignored the thin film on the surface of the brew and took a sip.

Edie watched me with interest. "You don't take cream or sugar?"

"Nope. I like my coffee to taste like coffee."

"Does it?"

I shrugged. "It's doing a passable imitation."

Edie was wearing the casual dress that I'd seen hanging on the rack the night before. Her hair seemed a little wet, as if she'd recently showered. "You live near here?" I asked.

"I've got an apartment a few blocks away."

"You live alone?"

"I've got a roommate." She cocked her head and smiled. "She was kicked into the street about a year ago, and I let her move in with me. You might like her."

"What makes you think I'm looking?" I sipped my coffee.

"Men are always looking. Ever been married?"

"Nope."

She pushed a lock of hair off her forehead. "Why not?"

"Haven't met Miss Right, I guess. What about you?"

Before she could answer, the waitress came by with our orders. Edie waited until the waitress had topped off our coffees and left us to ourselves before answering me. "I tried marriage for a while. It didn't take."

"Let me guess. He didn't like your singing?"

Edie stuck a spoonful of oatmeal in her mouth and swallowed. "He loved my singing. He loved it so much that he didn't want me singing for anyone else. He seemed to think that I was cheating on him when I did. Which is hilarious, because he had no problem with cheating on me in the more conventional sense."

I cut a slice of abalone and tried it. It was tender the way boiled shoe leather is tender, but I managed to swallow it after mashing it with my teeth for only a minute or two.

While I was chewing, Edie told me more about her marriage. "I was eighteen and taking care of my two little brothers. Jenny had left home the year before with a pretty jasper who dumped her two months later. She was fifteen and pregnant, but a back-alley butcher with a wire hanger took care of that. She was already earning some real dough singing in bars. I could sing, too, and I hated her because she could work while I had to stay home with our brothers. So when Bear came along and said he'd marry me, I thought he was the key to my freedom."

"Bear?" I'd finally finished off my first bite of the abalone.

"Yes, Bear! You got a problem with that? Anyway, the way I figured it, he could work during the day and watch my brothers when I had a gig. He was a welder, and he made money at it. He didn't drink too much, and he was good with the boys. He was good to me, too, when we were alone at night. So I married him. It seemed like a good idea. Until he told me that he didn't want me singing in public anymore. And then he started sleeping with some little roundheels down the street." She shook her head. "He'd say he was going to the corner market for a pack of cigarettes, and he'd come home an hour later smelling like jasmine and rum. And he thought I wouldn't notice?"

I was getting the hang of the abalone. I could handle it all right if I sliced off smaller strips and softened them with lemon juice. "How long's it been since you've seen him?"

"It's been almost ten years since I tossed him out on his ear. After he'd been gone for three weeks, he came to the house stinko. Drove his car right over my front lawn and up to the front door. He forced his way through the door and tried to…rekindle our romance on the kitchen table. So I stabbed him in the stomach with a steak knife. He probably lived, but I haven't seen him since." She swallowed some coffee. "I haven't been all that anxious to get hitched again since then."

"Can't say as I blame you. How did you manage to get a singing career going?"

"I made a deal with my brothers. I told them that if they didn't burn the house down or kill anybody while I worked nights to put food on their table, I wouldn't drive them out to the desert and feed them to the coyotes."

"How'd that work out?"

Edie put her spoon down in her bowl and wiped her mouth with a napkin. "Not as well as it could have. Luis, the oldest, managed to get through school and make it into the army. They tell me that he died honorably in the Borderland. Miguel, the youngest, tried to rob a liquor store with a thirty-two he'd picked up from somewhere. The clerk had a shotgun under the counter. Miguel's rod wasn't even loaded. But the shotgun was. Stupid little fuck! He was only fourteen." Edie shook her head and shrugged. "I guess I wasn't cut out to be a mother."

I took my time chewing another bite of abalone and gulping it down. It gave me an excuse not to say anything.

Edie smiled at me, and her eyes brightened. "Feeling sorry for me yet? Don't. My father ran out on us when I was two, so I don't hardly remember him much, but my momma said he did us a favor by leaving. According to her, he was a louse, and we were better off without him. My momma died and left me to take care of three kids, but she was a good lady. She taught me how to survive, and even if she didn't make it herself I wouldn't have come this far if it wasn't for her. My brothers and sister are gone now, too. I guess I got family down in Azteca, but I ain't never met them. So I'm the last of us. But I'm still kicking, buster! And I'm free as a bird! I'm making an honest living, and it's only going to get better. I don't know if you noticed, but I can sing! I'm good! And it's only a matter of time before people start to find out about me." She leaned forward across the table. "I'm saving my dough, and soon I'll have enough to take my act to Angel City. That's where the action is! When I get there, I'm gonna show them what I've got! Once they get a load of me, I'll be a star!"

I took a sip of my coffee. "Sure you will. You've got plenty of talent. I hear it's a tough racket, though. Gotta know the right people."

She cocked her head and stared at me. "Like my sister, you mean? She met the right person all right. And look where it got her! That was her mistake. She thought that a man was going to take care of her and take her to the top." Edie shook her head. "Let me tell you something about Jenny.

From the time she was born, she was a doll. Always the pretty one. Those violet eyes that drove men bananas? She was born with those peepers! Her skin was smooth and delicate, like porcelain. She never so much as had a pimple! And her voice! She was breaking hearts with that voice from the time she was four years old. Momma used to say that Jenny was the future of the family. She was going to make millions with that pretty face and that golden voice. Everyone always treated pretty little Jenny like she was made of eggshells, like the slightest slap in the kisser would break her apart. And from the time she was twelve she always had some man who wanted to take care of her, to protect her from the big bad world. So she never learned to take care of herself. And you wanna know something? Those men didn't really want to protect her." She snorted. "Men! Jenny never met a man who cared about what she wanted to do or to be. They just wanted her to belong to them, like she was some kind of prize. My Bear was the same exact way with me. I suppose that's just the way men are. Grasping, greedy pigs who don't care about nobody but themselves." She looked at me dry-eyed, challenging me to argue with her.

I started to slice off another sliver of abalone, but decided that it wasn't worth the bother. I put my knife down on my plate and met Edie's eyes over my coffee cup. "Did you and your sister get along?"

Edie laughed a little. "We fought all the time. You got a brother?"

I shook my head. "I was an only child."

"Lucky you. Jenny and I were at each other's throats our whole lives. But you wanna know something, buster? She was my best friend. And I was her best friend. We loved each other like only sisters can. And I miss her every…single…fucking…day!" Edie's expression was hard, and her eyes grew so intense I thought that they would catch fire. But then she smiled and her face relaxed. "You about done with those abalones? I need to get to the club."

***

I paid the check at the counter and walked with Edie to the Turbo Lounge, a two-block stroll through gusty winds, the moon and stars hidden behind a blanket of low-lying clouds. We were in no hurry, and Edie continued to chat with me on the way. She was a dame who liked to chat, as long as I showed any interest in her. It was hard not to. Edie was an interesting lady. She had suffered her share of hardships, maybe more than her share, but she had never allowed herself to be beaten too far down by them, and she always came up swinging. I admired her resilience. She had no illusions about the world, but she was going to meet it on her own terms. I learned that when I tried to ask her about her sister's death.

"I don't want to talk about Jenny anymore," she told me. "Ask me about my roommate."

"Why?"

"I think you'd like her. She's adorable, and she's available."

"Maybe I like you," I said. "Are you available?"

She half-turned to me, a crooked smile on her face. "Weren't you listening to me back there? I told you what I think of men."

"Sure you did. But you weren't talking about *me*."

She laughed. "Oh, I suppose you're different, is that it? What are you, thirty-five?"

I pulled my hat brim over my eyes. "Ouch! That hurts, lady. I just turned thirty a couple of days ago."

She gave me an appraising look. "You've lived a hard life!"

"Thanks, angel."

"So thirty, then. And never been married? You like women. I can see that by the way your peepers roll all over me. So I'm guessing that women don't like you." I looked at her, and she was smiling. "So, big man, why do you suppose I should think you're different than any other selfish lug I've ever met?"

"You must see something in me," I said. "Otherwise, why would you be so keen to fix me up with your roommate?"

"Because she don't mind belonging to somebody. And she ain't particular like I am."

"Is she pretty?"

"Does it matter?"

"Maybe *I'm* particular."

Edie made a scoffing noise. "Men only *say* they're particular. Give 'em a couple of drinks and suddenly they ain't so fussy."

"So you're looking for a man who will only have eyes for you even when he's loaded?"

"Are you kidding? Mister, I'd settle for a man who only had eyes for me when he was sober!" She kicked at a sandwich wrapper that had blown across the street and settled in front of her. "Fat chance of that ever happening."

I made a show of looking her up and down. "I don't know. You're a real lulu."

She smiled a little at that, but gave me a sidelong glance. "Lots of women are lulus. You'd try your luck with any of them. You and every other man."

I pulled up my collar against a sudden wind gust. "They can't all sing, though."

Edie laughed, looking no less skeptical. "Get a little liquor in you and you'll think they sing well enough. But, say, I've practically told you my life story, and you haven't told me nothing about yourself."

"Why do you want to know about me?"

"Because, you fool, I want to be able to tell my roommate about you." She smiled at me and wrapped her arm in mine. "So spill, big man. Why would Sunny be interested in a mope like you?"

"Sunny? Your roommate's name is Sunny?" I was enjoying the pressure of Edie's arm on mine, and I drew her in a little closer.

"Yes, her name is Sunny, as in the opposite of Moony. It matches her disposition, too, unlike mine. So what should I tell her about you?"

I couldn't help it. I gave her a two-bit tour of my life's story, from growing up slugging it out on the streets, to a brief summary of my tour in the Borderland, to my days as an M.P. rounding up deserters, brawlers, and thieves, to my return to a civilized world that seemed so different from the one that I'd grown up in, and finally to the story of how I found out that one of Mrs. Colby's prospective tenants was a were-rat. By the time I'd reached that point, we were standing at the rear of the Turbo Lounge, where a band was waiting in a van, and Edie told me that she needed to go inside and transform herself into a crooner named Nina.

"Are you going to stay for the show?" she asked me.

"Only if you'll let me see you when you're finished."

She cocked her head back a notch and looked at me sidelong through narrowed eyes. She pursed her lips and crossed her arms over her chest. After studying me for a few moments, she uncrossed her arms, reached up, and patted me on the cheek. "Stick around, champ. Stick around, and we'll see."

Chapter Seventeen

The slivers of abalone that I'd choked down at the Lighthouse Diner had only scratched the surface of my hunger, so I sat at the bar and ordered a cup of clam chowder and a plate of fried calamari to go with my glass of beer. It was ten thirty, and the Turbo Lounge was packed. On stage, a one-armed dwarf in an army jacket was growling out some passable blues rock. He was backed by a tight three-piece band, including a gnome who could tickle some mean ivories. The dance floor was only half filled, and the patrons at the tables seemed oblivious to the efforts of the musicians, but I thought that they were better than decent. I gave the band an enthusiastic ovation after their final number.

I was finishing up my beer when Nina's band took the stage. As they had the previous night, the band opened with an instrumental number. While I waited for Nina to hit the stage, I got a second beer from the same handlebar-mustached barkeep I'd seen the night before. He was more talkative this time around.

"Back again, eh sport?"

I looked up to meet the bartender's curious gaze. "Why not? This isn't a bad place."

The bartender began to wash some whiskey glasses in a sink behind the bar across from where I was sitting. "We get some good acts. You here for Nina?"

"She's a talented little canary." I sipped some of the brew and wiped foam off my upper lip with a paper napkin.

"A real dish, too. She always pulls in a big crowd."

I scanned the packed house. "So I see. She play here often?"

"As often as we can book her. I don't think that will be for much longer, though."

I looked up at the bartender. "Oh? Why's that?"

The bartender pulled at one end of his mustache, smoothing it to a point. "She's too good for Placid Point. Some Midtown club will pick her up pretty soon, if she's willing to do what it takes."

I put my beer glass down on a cork coaster. "Do what it takes? What does *that* mean?"

The barkeep shrugged and grimaced. "Those club owners downtown are assholes. There's only one way that a twist who can sing gets on one of their stages. They've got to pass a backstage 'audition.'" He shook his head.

I watched him wash a shot glass. "I see. So talent and drawing power won't get them past the casting couch?"

Handlebar mustache looked across the bar at me and met my eyes. "There's no shortage of good-looking dames with nice voices in this city. There's a thousand of them sitting at home tonight who would fill a joint like this, or even one of those pricey Midtown venues, especially on a Friday night. It's the ones who are willing to make the bookers and managers happy that get the gigs. That's the way this business works."

"Is that the way it works here, too?" I asked.

The bartender put a clean glass upside down on a towel to dry. "Usually. Not always. The boss likes Nina. I don't know what she had to do to make him like her. Maybe all she had to do was smile and sing a song. It's possible."

My stomach was having a rough time with the calamari that I'd been dumping into it. "Why are you telling me this?"

"It seemed like something you needed to hear."

"You're wrong. I didn't need to hear anything of the sort."

"All right, fine. I like Nina. I think she's a good lady. I don't want some joe to get mixed up with her and then blow a fuse when he finds out what she has to go through in order to make a living in this business. That's all. Better you know going in."

"What makes you think I'm mixed up with Nina?"

Handlebar mustache smiled. "She and I talked a little after you left last night."

"She wants to fix me up with her roommate."

He frowned. "Her what?"

"Her roommate. Some dame named Sunny."

The bartender's frown disappeared as his face lit up with amusement.

I watched him stifle a laugh. "What's the gag?" I asked him, biting back on a rising surge of annoyance.

"Sunny's her cat." Handlebar mustache poured some whiskey into a clean shot glass and set it next to my beer. "On the house," he told me.

Then he stepped away to take an order from a swell in a bomber jacket who had pushed his way up to the bar.

I was pondering this revelation around the contents of the shot glass when Nina walked into a spotlight at the front of the stage. She wore the same dress as she had the night before, and I found my eyes once again drawn like a magnet to the jewel in the middle of her abdomen. I raised my eyes and saw that she was looking in my direction. I tossed a smile her way, but she didn't catch it. Instead, she wrapped both hands around the microphone, closed her eyes, and started swaying to the music, listening for her intro.

Nina crooned the same numbers as the night before, belting out the same notes with the same moves and the same precision, but, somehow, her performance seemed to lack some of the luster that I'd seen the previous evening. If I'd been a critic, I would have called it a workmanlike effort, skilled, but a little forced. The crowd responded to her performance with the same gusto as the previous evening, maybe with even a little of the extra enthusiasm that a Friday night on the town adds in, so what do I know. But to me it seemed that Nina wasn't drawing the same level of energy from her audience that they were taking from her. She seemed remote, as if she were unaware of her surroundings and just going through the motions. It was only when she broke into a sad ballad about a lover who left for the Borderland and never came back that she seemed to put any real passion into her voice. Her heartfelt rendition of that number earned her the biggest ovation that she'd received to that point, but she seemed oblivious to it. I wondered what had put her off her game and hoped that it wasn't anything that I'd said or done. Maybe I'd forced her to relive too many bad memories. She'd seemed all right when I'd left her. Maybe something had happened while she was waiting to go on.

I noticed handlebar mustache watching Nina when he wasn't taking orders and dispensing drinks. His frown told me that he had also sensed something wrong in the singer's performance. At one point, I caught his eye and shrugged at him, palms up. He shrugged back and shook his head. Then a customer called for him, and the barkeep went to take his order.

When it was close to time for the band to take a break, I waved handlebar mustache over to me. I asked him for a pen and wrote a three-word question on the back of one of my cards. I handed the card to the barkeep and asked him to give it to Nina during her break. "Don't read it," I told him, knowing that he would.

The bartender went into the back with my card and, when he came back alone a few minutes later, he walked up to me on my side of the bar. "She told me to tell you that everything's fine. She heard that a couple of kids drowned today. No one she knew, but it upset her a bit. She's all right now, I think. She also said that she wants to see you when she's done." He stared at me, like he was trying to tell me something, or maybe give me some kind of warning. I had the feeling that he thought of himself as Nina's big brother. Some big brother he was. He didn't even know if she had slept with his boss. Or maybe he did, and he just didn't want to tell me. I turned back to my beer.

After a few moments, the barkeep laid something on the bar next to my drink and resumed his place behind the bar. I saw that it was the card that I'd asked him to give to Edie. I read the message that I'd written on it: "Sunny's a cat?" Beneath my question, written in a billowy cursive script, was a response: "Is she? That explains a lot!" I tucked the card away in my pocket and waited for Nina's next set.

***

The magic was back in Nina's performance during the second half of her show. She sang with cool self-assurance, seducing the audience with sultry moans and throaty growls, bopping and twirling during the swing numbers and gently swaying her hips to the slow rhythm of the bluesy torch songs. The dance floor filled, and the audience whistled, whooped, and applauded with vigor after every song.

After the band's final number, Edie and the other musicians waved to the crowd and made their way off the stage to the back door. After the last member of the band had disappeared through it, I gulped down the rest of my beer and crossed the lounge. When I stepped through the stage door, I found Edie in the backstage area exchanging handshakes, fist bumps, and congratulatory hugs with the other members of the band. I stood off to the side, ignoring the occasional curious glances from the musicians. After everyone except Edie had said their goodbyes and scattered either back into the lounge or out the back door into the night, Edie turned toward me and smiled. "Glad to see you stuck around, sugar. You wanna walk me to my dressing room?"

"Sure, doll. You wouldn't happen to have a bottle of rye back there, would you?"

She stepped toward me and reached up to slide her fingers behind my tie, just under the knot. Then she slid her hand down the back of the tie to the middle of my chest. "Sure I do." Her voice came from somewhere deep in her throat. "Come on. I'll let you pour."

She released my tie and started walking away from me, looking back over her shoulder to see if I was going to follow. I thought it would be rude of me not to, so I did. That's how much of a gentleman I am.

Inside the tiny office that served as her dressing room, I found an open bottle and a whiskey glass. "Do you have another one of these?" I asked, holding up the glass.

Edie shut the door. "That's the only one. Pour some of that for me, and you can have the bottle."

I filled the glass and handed it to her. "The second half of your show was terrific," I told her.

She made a scoffing sound. "Is that your way of telling me that the first half of my show was shit?"

I took a shot from the bottle. "I wouldn't say it was shit. It was good. But your second set sparkled."

Her lips curled into something that could have been either a smile or a sneer. "Aren't you sweet. I gave a half-assed performance out there during the first set. My heart wasn't in it."

"The audience seemed to like it."

"They were a nice crowd, but they don't know music from shinola. Lucky for me they were in a good mood. It's not always like that. Good thing I was able to shake it off and step it up after the break. The audience was all good and tanked by then, and the drunker they are, the more they take it personal when they don't think they're getting my best."

I leaned against the side of the desk. "Handlebar mustache told me you heard about a couple of kids that drowned this morning. He said it shook you up a little."

Edie sat in the desk chair and took a small sip from her glass. She slid into a slump and looked up at me, eyes filled with sadness, but with a trace of a smile on her lips. "Handlebar mustache?"

"It's hard to miss."

She chuckled, but the sadness didn't leave her eyes. "His name is Eric. He's a decent lug."

"He seems protective."

Her smile grew. "He fancies himself a knight errant, and he thinks I'm a damsel in distress. Can you believe that shit? Poor sap! He's got no idea!"

I raised the bottle and took another slug. The rye was cheap, but it made up for its lack of presumption by tasting like battery acid. I set the bottle down on the desktop. "Did you know the kids?"

"Huh? No. Tuvi—he's my bass player—he told me about it. It was the first I'd heard of it, and I guess it just struck a nerve. Poor little things."

I watched her eyes grow distant as her thoughts turned inward. "It's understandable that you'd be upset, what with this thing coming so soon after what happened to your sister's children."

She jerked her head around to stare at me, eyes wide and mouth opened. "You know about her babies? They were supposed to be keeping that quiet!"

"They? Who's they?"

She looked away. "Teague. Fulton. Fulton clamped down hard on the press and did what he could to squash the rumors that popped up on the internet. He told me that if I told anyone about what happened, he'd see to it that I never got another gig in this town. He's made it so that most people don't even know that Jenny *had* kids. And he doesn't want anyone to know that... that..."

"That your sister killed her children?"

Edie sat up in her chair and fixed me with another stare. This time her eyes were narrowed. "How do you know about that?" She spat the words through clenched teeth.

I shrugged. "I'm a private investigator."

"Oh yeah? Well you don't know nuthin'! It wasn't her fault! They drove her to it!" Edie's grip on the armrests on her chair was so tight that her knuckles had turned white.

"Teague and Fulton? It's okay. You can talk to me. Nothing you tell me will get back to them. I promise."

She stared at me, trying to make up her mind.

"If it helps," I said, "I know that Teague was the father."

She continued to stare at me, but after a few moments she let go of the chair and dropped her hands into her lap. "I don't want to talk about my sister right now, okay?"

"Sure, doll. We don't have to talk about anything you don't want to talk about. I want to get to the bottom of your sister's death, but it can wait. You can tell me about it when you're ready."

She glared at me, lips pursed. "Oh, I can, can I? Well isn't that swell! What if I don't want to tell you about it at all? Why should I? You're not even a cop! You're just a fucking private snoop!" She grabbed her glass off the desktop and slammed back a slug of the rye.

I saluted her with the bottle. "You're right, doll. You don't have to tell me a thing. I'm no cop. I came here for the music." I raised the bottle to my lips and tipped it.

Edie continued to glare, but then she sighed and I watched some of the tension fade from her face. She braced her elbow on the armrest and held her glass out to me. "Top this off, will ya?"

I poured until her glass was half full. She pulled the glass toward her lips, but held it there without drinking. "Say, who are you working for, anyway? You said you weren't working for Harvey, and you're not working for Teague. Who's trying to get the dirt on Jenny? Some newspaper? The cops?"

I shook my head. "Believe it or not, I'm not working for anybody on this one. Just my own curiosity, which doesn't want to let it go. I get that way sometimes. Something happens, and I gotta know about it."

Edie wet her lips with the rye. "So you're not getting any dough out of this? Well that doesn't make any sense!"

I shrugged. "You're right. It doesn't. Fact is, Fulton told me *not* to investigate your sister's death. He told me in no uncertain terms to stay away from it."

She smiled then. "Let me guess. You're one of those hard numbers who don't like being told what to do."

"Not by assholes like Fulton I don't. With others, I might be more agreeable."

Edie cocked her head up at me and slid down her seat a few inches. My eyes fell on the jewel in her navel, but I gave myself a mental slap in the face and forced myself to look away. The singer's lips curled into a tight smile as she put her glass back on the desktop and pushed some hair, still damp from her performance, off her face. "Did you really like the show?" I met her eyes with mine. A moment ago, she'd been ready to rip the armrest off her chair and beat me over the head with it. The next, she was like an insecure little girl seeking my validation. She was zero to sixty and back again, with sudden unexpected turns and no warnings. If you weren't braced for it, a dame like that could make you seasick!

"I loved the show, baby," I told her. "I could listen to you warble all night."

"And I'm easy on the eyes, too." She reached down with one hand and slipped a finger under the hem of her dress.

"Cute as a button," I agreed.

Edie's smile widened by a degree, and her eyes seemed to brighten. "Yeah? Well you ain't so bad yourself, you know."

"What, with this ol' mug?"

"It's a swell mug. It's seen some action. I like that. Pretty boys aren't my type."

"And what about Sunny? You think I might be *her* type?"

Edie's grin grew sly, and she crinkled her nose. "I'm not sure yet. She's shyer than you might expect. You might have to kinda sneak up on her."

"I can be sneaky. I'm a private snoop, remember?" I let my eyes run down her slumping body, over the swell of her breasts and down to the spider-shaped gem in the middle of her tattooed webbing.

Edie's eyes followed my own, and then she looked up at me. She pointed back to the clothes rack on the other side of the room. "Get me my wrap, sugar. I'm starting to feel a little naked in here."

I pushed myself away from the desk and stepped over to the rack, not without some reluctance. She didn't rise from the chair, and I spread the wrap over her like a blanket, tucking it in a little around her hips. She smiled at that and leaned her head back a notch. "You know, I think Sunny might go for you."

"That's good to know," I said.

Edie's gaze turned soft. "I think I could go for you, too. Why don't you kiss me and see if I like it?"

I bent down and touched her lips with mine, letting them linger for a second before pulling away. I searched her dark eyes for a response. "Well?" I asked.

"Hmm," she said. "I'm not sure. I think you'd better kiss me again."

So I did, longer this time. She reached up and laid her hand on the back of my head so that I couldn't pull it away. That was fine. It was where I wanted it to be.

We held the kiss for a few precious moments, and then she slid her hand off my head so that I could come up for air. She ran her hand over my cheek and down my neck to the knot of my tie. "I think you should walk me home now," she told me, her voice husky. "I want to see if Sunny approves of you."

***

Edie made me wait outside her "dressing room" as she changed out of her Nina costume and into her casual duds. As we walked to her apartment, which wasn't far from the club, my thoughts were lost in the warmth of her body next to mine in the cold night. We didn't talk much, but I listened to the thickness of her impatient sighs as they rose from the depths of her chest. I lost myself in her scent, musky after her three-hour show, and the light in her dark brown eyes as she gazed into mine. That's why I never saw it coming.

"I want my knife, motherfucker!" The voice came from behind me. I turned and stared into the eyes of the bruno with the curly blond hair. His two pals stepped out of the alley we'd just passed and stopped on either side of him. Curly had a shiner on one eye, and one of his arms was in a homemade sling. His other arm was fine, however. All three of the pugs were packing heat, and their rods were pointed at my chest.

I'd been carrying Edie's gym bag, and I let it drop to the ground between us. "Hello Curly. What knife?"

"The knife you stole from me, asshole!" The bruno extended his gun a few inches in my direction to scare me. It was working, but I wasn't going to let him know it. My brain was scrambling for ways to keep Edie from getting plugged. I had a plan, but I needed to stall.

"Oh, *that* knife. Hey, I'd give it to you, but I don't have it on me. I left it at home tonight. Maybe we can all come back tomorrow?"

I thought it was a good suggestion, but it didn't appear that the bruno was going to go for it. His face tightened and his eyes narrowed. "How 'bout I drop you and we search your dead body?"

I thought this was going to be it. I prepared to shove Edie out of the line of fire, but she suddenly threw up her hands and shouted. "No, wait! We've got your knife!" Turning to me, she began to plead. "Darling—please! I don't want to die! Let the man have the knife! It's in my bag, remember? You gave it to me to carry."

With that, Edie bent down and unzipped her gym bag. "It's right in here. Please! Don't shoot me! Please! Here it is! I've got it!"

When she straightened up, she was holding a pistol in a two-handed grip and pointing it at the bruno. "Drop it, mister, or I'll fill you full of holes!"

The bruno blinked. One of his pals started to turn his piece toward Edie.

"Don't move a muscle, motherfuckers!" Edie shouted. "Or Blondie gets it!"

I did the math: three guns against one. I didn't like the results. Everyone had a piece but me. I was feeling left out! But I had something that nobody else had, and the three pugs were about to find out about it. I hoped that it wouldn't be too late.

I heard it before they did, a deep whistling, quiet at first but growing in volume fast, like the sound of an oncoming train. Then the blond bruno heard it, too, and he lifted his eyes toward the sky above the street. He had just enough time to see what appeared to be a small dark cloud descending from the night at breakneck speed when I pointed at it and shouted, "Attack them!" Then I threw myself at Edie and twisted so that she fell on top of me as I tumbled to the sidewalk.

Edie's gun went off, and I heard more flying lead through a deafening roar as a broad funnel of wind touched down in the center of the three pugs like a bomb blast and knocked them off their feet. Three caps rose high into the air, and three guns were flung out over the street to crash through the window of a closed mattress store on the other side. The pugs hugged cement, pinned in place by seventy-mile-per-hour winds blowing straight down on their backs.

Most of the elementals that I summoned were sneaky little puffs of whirling air that I used as spies. The medium-sized whirlwind that I'd named "Badass" was the exception. Badass was the most powerful elemental that I could summon. It varied in size and shape from a spherical blob of slow-moving breezes, about six-feet in diameter, to a funnel standing twelve to sixteen feet tall and two to four feet wide with the velocity of a small tornado. It could shatter a cypress tree with its winds. When it was really trying, it could topple a small car. I used Badass as muscle.

I was on my back, and Edie was sprawled on top of me staring at the whirlwind in front of us. "Holy moly!" she exclaimed, eyes wide with amazement.

"You okay?" I asked her. I had my arms wrapped around her, and, despite the lumps I'd endured when I hit the sidewalk, I was enjoying the weight of her body on mine, probably more than I should have been under the circumstances. I was disappointed when she picked herself off me to rise to her feet.

I stood and called out, "Badass! You can let them up now. Come over here."

The elemental slowed its whirling and drifted to my side.

I looked up. "Nice work, Badass."

A howling moan emerged from the funnel of air floating by my side. "Greetings, Aleksss. This one is happy to serve."

The moment I'd turned and seen that Curly and his pals were flashing iron, I'd called up the appropriate sigil in my mind and called for Badass. The big elemental once told me that it followed me wherever I went and would never be far away when I needed it. From hints that it had dropped, I believed that the elf who had given me the gift of enhanced awareness had appointed Badass to be a sort of personal guardian for me. I had mixed feelings about that. On the one hand, I appreciated having a miniature tornado at my disposal whenever I needed it. On the other hand, my debt to the elf increased every time I summoned the elemental.

I knew that the elf was using me in some small way as a pawn in his quest to overthrow the rule of the Dragon Lords, and the thought of being on the wrong side of those immortal, unkillable, hundred-foot long flying fire-breathing masters of magic made my blood run cold. For my money, the elves had been foolish to oppose the advent of the Dragon Lords six thousand years ago during the so-called Great Rebellion, and they couldn't have been surprised when the Lords attempted to wipe them from the face of the earth in retaliation. The way I saw it, those ancient humans had done the right thing when they abandoned the elves and chose to fight for the Dragon Lords, instead. Thousands of years later, most humans believed elves to be extinct, though alleged sightings of the mysterious elves were common in every culture. In literature, elves were scheming masters of ancient lore who came out at night and preyed on unsuspecting humans. Well, I'd met an elf in broad daylight, and, although he *seemed* to be a nice enough old gee, I couldn't help but wonder if he wasn't setting me up to be a sacrificial victim in some devious plot. I shuddered to think what he had in mind for me, but he'd given me some valuable gifts, and he'd helped rescue me from the threshold of a dark death. Bottom line was that I owed him.

My three would-be assailants were still lying face down on the sidewalk, arms covering their heads. I brushed myself off and called out, "You pugs can stop eating pavement now."

They rose, grunting and groaning, to their feet and shot uneasy glances at each other as they tried to figure out what had happened to them. I waited until they were all staring at the half-seen elemental hovering next to me.

I kept my voice conversational. "In case you haven't figured it out, I'm an elementalist. That means that I have the ability to summon and command elementals. Air elementals, specifically. Like this one. I want you all to know that if I give it the word, this tornado will pick you up and carry you to the middle of the Nihhonese Ocean." Badass intensified its whirling and stretched to a height of nearly twenty feet. The pugs, eyes wide, stared at it in silence.

I raised my voice to a shout so that I could be heard over the sound of the whirling wind. "Fun's over for the night, boys! Best go home and sleep it off!"

The pugs looked at each other and began to slink away.

When they were gone, I turned to Badass. "Just for the record…. Could you really have picked those goons up and dropped them in the ocean?"

"Noooo….."

"I didn't think so. Thanks again. I release you from your service for now." The elemental lifted itself into the air about ten feet overhead and then shot into the night sky where it quickly disappeared from view.

I turned and saw Edie staring in the direction where she'd last seen the elemental. Then she turned to me and spoke in a voice that was little more than a whisper. "Holy moly! That was fuckin' awesome! I didn't know you were a wizard!"

"I'm not. I'm just a two-bit elementalist."

She tilted her head. "If you say so!" Then her eyes narrowed, and she hit me in the shoulder with her fist. "Hey! Why'd you knock me over like that! That hurt!"

I raised my hands in surrender. "Sorry! I was trying to keep you from taking lead. You weren't hit, were you?"

"Me? No." Her eyes widened and she looked me up and down. "How about you? Are you all right?"

I made a show of patting myself on the chest, sides, and hips. "I'm jake. Looks like they missed us both." Then I stared at her.

She raised her eyebrows. "What are you looking at?"

"Were you trying to kill that pug?"

"I was ready to, buster, believe you me! But the gun went off in the air when you bumped me. Hey, how'd you like that gag I pulled? I caught those lugs with their pants down!"

"That was some quick thinking, sister," I told her. "But you can put the iron back in the bag now."

"What? Oh yeah!" She looked at the gun that was still in her hand. "I forgot I was holding it."

"Wait! You mind if I take a look at that?" I reached for the piece.

"Oh sure, go ahead." She handed me the pistol, and I examined it. It was a snub-nosed six-shot thirty-eight caliber revolver with a black two-inch barrel and a brown handle, small enough to conceal and powerful enough to blow a hole in a man's chest from fifty yards away if you knew what you were doing. It looked clean and cared for.

I handed the gat back to Edie. "That's a serious weapon."

"Serious as a heart attack! A girl can't be too careful in a neighborhood like this." She put the pistol back in her gym bag, zipped it up, and handed it to me. Her breathing was heavy and her eyes shining. "Take me home, big man. I need to get you off the street."

Wasting as little time as possible, Edie led me up the block and around the corner to a picturesque hundred-year old house that had been subdivided into apartments. We almost ran up the stairs to the second floor to get to hers. Once inside, we didn't wait for Sunny to make an appearance before getting better acquainted.

Chapter Eighteen

I woke an hour past sunrise after no more than two hours of sleep. I slipped out of bed without waking Edie. An orange and white cat lay curled at her feet. Sunny, I deduced. I hadn't seen her until now. She watched me put my clothes on, but yawned, stretched, lowered her head, and closed her eyes before I was finished tying my tie. Apparently, I wasn't that interesting.

I took a quick look around Edie's bedroom, which I'd barely noticed earlier that morning. I wasn't snooping, I told myself. I just wanted to get a sense of the personality of the gal I'd been holding in my arms for the past few hours. The room projected an aura of stark drama. The walls were painted a pale pink. Black curtains kept any trace of light from passing through her window. Edie was curled up in black silk sheets and covered with a solid pink quilt. A rug the color of blood lay on the black hardwood floor. Her slatted bi-fold closet door was black, as was the door leading out of the bedroom and into the rest of the apartment. On one side of the room was a rose-colored makeup table with lacy black trim on the corners. An oval mirror with light bulbs circling the glass stood on the center of the table, and various containers and tubes were scattered around it.

On one end of the makeup table was something that looked like a miniature pot-bellied stove. It was spherical, black, of course, about six inches tall, and it stood on four short curved legs. The front of the stove was open, and the melted remains of a red candle with a blackened wick filled the interior. I broke a piece of the wax off and sniffed at it, but detected no scent other than scorched wax. The top part of the stove was detachable, and pulling it off exposed a flat grill, blackened in the center and covered with a fine gray ash. I sniffed at the ash and detected a faint floral scent with a metallic undertone. The floral scent might have been burnt incense. The metallic smell probably came from the grill itself, which was coated with chrome. The parts of the grill that weren't blackened still gleamed like new. I gave the outside of the stove a closer inspection. The polished black surface was clean and unscarred, and I concluded that the stove, or incense burner, hadn't been used often. Just once, maybe. I shrugged and looked around for my fedora, which I found on the floor next to the bed.

Before I left, I bent down and brushed the hair off Edie's temple. I kissed her on the forehead. She mumbled something that I couldn't decipher and shifted in her sleep, but her eyes stayed closed. I put my lips near her ear and whispered, "Call me later."

One of Edie's eyes opened just enough for me to catch a sliver of dark brown. "You going?" she breathed.

I nodded. "Not for good I hope. You'll call me when you wake up?"

She closed her eye and smiled. "If you're lucky."

When I was back on the street, I wasn't quite sure where I was. I walked to a corner and checked the street sign. Damn! The garage where I'd parked the beastmobile was six blocks away, and the morning was cold enough that I could see my breath. Or maybe that was the fumes from the beer and rye I'd had the night before. I tried to convince myself that the morning air would wake me up and get me ready for the rest of the day, but all I really wanted to do was get back into Edie's bed where it was warm and wrap myself in Edie's welcoming arms.

I had calls to make, questions to ask, and answers to seek. With one last backwards glance toward Edie's apartment, I marched off to find my car.

***

I knew that something was wrong the minute I walked through my front door. I sniffed the air and nearly retched at the scent of game animal and wet garbage. I made a beeline for the laundry room, but it was empty. I returned to my office and, sniffing like a bloodhound, followed my nose up the stairs to my apartment.

When I opened the door at the top of the stairs, I stopped and groaned. My kitchen had been trashed! The refrigerator doors, both the main door and the door to the freezer compartment, were hanging wide open. The counters and floor were covered with broken beer bottles and spilled beer, broken egg shells and raw eggs, shredded slices of bread, torn boxes of frozen pizza, frozen waffles, and microwaveable roast beef sandwiches, shattered glass bottles of peanut butter, and crushed cubes of butter. Prints of what looked like bare human feet tracked the floor between the kitchen and the stairway door, and the knob of the door was sticky with egg yolk and butter. I'd noticed the footprints on the stairs and in the back hallway, too. Stepping back through the door, I followed them.

The tracks led down the hallway to the back door, which was locked from the inside. I unlocked it and walked out into the alley. The trashcans in the alley had all been overturned, and garbage was spilled everywhere. I didn't linger.

Back in my office, I accessed the app to my surveillance camera and spent the next few minutes watching the video feed from earlier that morning. At three thirty-seven, the giant goat-headed alley rat pulled the lid from my garbage can and began rooting around inside it. He pushed it over when he was finished and passed by my camera to my back door. As he had done the previous morning, he stood on his hind legs, opened the door, and walked through, not at all inconvenienced by the deadbolt that I'd made sure was set in place. The time stamp on the video feed read four eleven when the creature reemerged through the door. He paused to stare directly into the lens of my surveillance camera. I watched him bite into a raw egg and suck the yolk from the shell. Then he turned away, tossed the broken shell into the pile of garbage that he'd pulled from my trash can, dropped to all fours, and disappeared out of camera range.

That son of a bitch! I was going to hunt him down, kill him, and have his head mounted on my wall! But I had something else I'd have to do first. Cursing out loud, I retrieved a mop, broom, and dustpan from the laundry room and headed upstairs to clean up my kitchen.

I was nearly done when my phone chimed. I checked the screen and tapped the "accept call" icon.

"Hi, Gordo. What's up?"

"The usual bullshit. Mr. Fulton wants you to help us babysit the mayor tonight."

"Why? Did something happen?"

"A couple of kids washed up yesterday morning at Ohlone Lake."

"I know. I was there."

Gordo paused for a breath. "That so?"

"Fulton wanted me to investigate the earth demon, so I went back to the lake to try to find traces of him. I found the van that he'd driven here from Lakota Province. I checked it out, but he wasn't in the immediate area. I was still there when the bodies of the two kids washed in. I stayed around to give a statement to the police, but dusted when leea showed up."

"You tell any of this to Mr. Fulton?" Gordo's tone told me that Fulton might be a little miffed that I hadn't checked in with him as soon as I'd seen the bodies.

"Not yet. I was going to call him later today."

"He'll want to know what you know."

"Right now it's not much. I was hoping to get a little more dope before calling him."

"He'll want to know why he didn't hear from you right away."

"Fuck him. If he doesn't like the way I do my job he can fire me."

"Now, now, Southerland. Nobody wants that. Anyway, Mrs. Teague was pretty upset about those kids. They're from the Estates, and she knows their parents. She came downtown this morning to see Mr. Teague and Mr. Fulton. She said that she didn't feel safe alone at the house, and she wanted her husband to come back home and for the rest of us to stay there and protect her. Mr. Fulton nixed that idea. He doesn't want the mayor to leave the apartment until this whole business with the woman in white is over with, and he told Mrs. Fulton that she should stay there with her husband. But Mrs. Teague hates the apartment and won't go there. So Mr. Fulton split the team. He sent me and Thunder to stay with Mrs. Teague at her house and left Stormclaw and Ironshield at the apartment to babysit the mayor."

"Are you with her now?"

"Yeah. She's packing. She called her sister and is going to spend a little time with her. She and her husband have a nice place in the Peninsula. The sister's coming up to get her."

"Is she going to be there for a while? I'd like to talk to her before she leaves."

There was a pause on the other end of the line. "You might want to clear that with Mr. Fulton first."

"Gordo!"

"I'm just sayin'! Mr. Fulton likes to know what his people are doing."

"I'm not 'his people'! He hired me to do a job, but I set my own rules. I'm not going to call him every time I need to take a piss!"

"All right, all right. Mrs. Teague's sister won't be here for another hour or so."

"I'm coming over now. I'm out the door. Don't let her go anywhere until I get there." I disconnected the call.

I was halfway to Gio's lot when my phone buzzed. It was Fulton, of course. I knew that Gordo would call him and tell him about our conversation. I tapped the "decline" button. Fulton could wait.

When I reached the beastmobile, my phone buzzed again. Fulton had left a three-minute voicemail message. After I'd pulled the car into the street, I set the phone to speaker and listened to Fulton's message.

Fulton was livid! He demanded to know why I hadn't called him the moment I'd seen the bodies of the two kids. He wanted to know what I'd told the police. He wanted to know if the Sihuanaba or the earth demon were connected to the deaths of the kids. He reminded me once again to lay off the Zyanya case. He accused me of going rogue and keeping him in the dark, and that he expected to know about everything I was doing the minute I did it, and blah, blah, blah, blah. He told me to stay away from Tracy Teague, and that I was wasting *his* valuable time by going out to see her. He finished by ordering me to call him back as soon as I'd finished listening to his message. Sure I would. I put my phone back in my pocket and drove out to the Galindo Estates, stopping at a bakery on the way to pick up a chocolate maple bar.

***

Gordo let me into the mayor's house. "Her sister should be here any minute," he told me.

"I don't need much of her time."

"She's upstairs. I'll go get her."

I made my way to the living room, where I found Thunderclash seated in an armchair and reading the newspaper. He put the paper aside and stood when I entered. "How you been, Southerland? Staying out of trouble?" He extended a hand.

I gave the hand a brief clasp. "Depends on who you ask."

The troll smiled. "I better not ask Fulton. I might get an earful."

"What do you mean?" I asked, pretending innocence. "Fulton and I are pals!"

"Let's hope it stays that way. You seem like a swell guy, Southerland, but Fulton signs my paychecks." Meaning that if Fulton told him to feed me to a shark, he'd do it without thinking about it twice. But he might drug me first, so that I wouldn't suffer.

"Lucky you. He hasn't signed jack for me yet. Good thing I'm such an agreeable guy."

Mrs. Teague came into the living room then with Gordo following close behind.

"Mr. Southerland? I'm glad you came. I never had the chance to thank you for the help you gave my husband the other day. You were a little harsh with him, but I think that's what he needed."

"Hello Mrs. Teague. I'm glad you're not sore at me. I'm told that I can be a little rough around the edges sometimes."

Her lips curled into the slightest of smiles. "I'd offer you coffee, but I'm afraid that I don't have much time. My sister will be here soon."

"I only have a few quick questions. But I'd like to ask them in private, if you don't mind. Would it be okay with you if I talked with you alone?"

Gordo took a step toward me. "Now just a minute, Southerland. I don't think that's such a hot idea."

Mrs. Teague put a hand on Gordo's elbow. "No, no, Gordon. It's quite all right. I left my suitcases upstairs. Would you and Artemis be so kind as to bring them down to the front porch for me? The two of you can watch for my sister."

Gordo hesitated. "Are you sure, Mrs. Teague? If you're not feeling up to being questioned…"

"I'm fine, Gordon." Mrs. Teague smiled at me and indicated the armchair that Thunderclash—Artemis?—had been sitting in when I arrived. "Please, Mr. Southerland. Have a seat."

Gordo and Thunderclash looked at each other for a moment. Then Gordo shrugged, and the two of them left the room.

I lowered myself into the offered chair, and Mrs. Teague sat down on the edge of the sofa. I kept my voice low so that it wouldn't carry. "You weren't home Thursday night when those two children were killed. Is that correct?"

Mrs. Teague's response was a tight smile.

I waved a hand. "I don't need to know where you were, not specifically. The sentry at the gate told me that you drove yourself out sometime that night and didn't come back the next morning. Where you were is none of my business, but I want to verify that you weren't in the neighborhood at any time that night."

Mrs. Teague sat back into the sofa. "I was elsewhere."

"In another part of town?"

She frowned. "Yes."

"All night?"

"Yes, all night. What's this about?"

"Does your husband know that you were out?" When she didn't answer, I asked, "Does Fulton? Gordo?"

She held my gaze for a moment, then turned away and sighed. "No, and I'd appreciate it if you didn't mention it. To any of them."

"Don't worry, Mrs. Teague. I don't intend to. I have no interest in how you spend your private time, and what they don't know won't hurt them, right?"

She shared a sly smile with me. "Darnell won't care to hear about it, and Lawrence already knows more than he needs to. That man doesn't need to know everything. He only *thinks* that he does. But there's more to it." She paused, gathering her thoughts. "My husband's job requires him to be away from me, sometimes for extended periods of time. During those times, there can never be the slightest hint of impropriety in my activities. My husband's rivals, and the media in general, are at all times desperate to generate a scandal, real or implied, in order to undermine my husband. I would die rather than disgrace him, Mr. Southerland. Anything I do in my private life must be…discreet. Do you understand?"

I nodded. "Perfectly. Okay, one more question. Why are you leaving today? Gordo told me that you don't feel safe here."

Mrs. Teague's smile disappeared. "Those two poor kids lived just a couple of streets over! For all I know, the monster who killed them is still in the neighborhood! I don't want to be here all by myself."

"You could always join your husband downtown."

She shook her head. "No, I can't." She folded her hands in her lap and tilted her head back a little. "That apartment is his center of power. My husband is the mayor of this city. He's in a position of great responsibility. But he's not well suited for the role. Oh, he looks the part, and, when he's in the public eye, he acts the part, but he's not a strong man. I think he's a *good* man, at heart anyway, but a man in his position has to do some bad things, and a weak man in his position often does bad things even when he doesn't have to. My job is to be his supportive wife, and a big part of that means that I have to be ignorant of the bad things that he does, both the ones he has to do and the ones he does because he can't resist the temptations that come with the office he holds. But I'm not going to spend a single night at the place where he indulges himself and others in his indiscretions, whatever form they might take. I will keep the hearth fires burning. I'll always make him welcome in his own home. I will accompany him in public, and I'll hold on to his arm and smile for the cameras. But I will neither be part nor parcel to the corruption that goes on behind the throne, whether it's professional or personal. I hope that I am making myself clear."

I studied her for a few moments, then leaned forward in my chair. "Why do you do it? After all he puts you through. Why do you stay with him?"

She raised her eyebrows. "I'm the wife of the mayor of this city, Mr. Southerland. Do you think I'd be happier if I went to business school and learned data entry?"

"Who knows? The data entry clerks I've met seem happy enough."

She smiled a little at that. "I daresay. But then they've never been the wife of the mayor of Yerba City. Believe me, the position has a lot going for it."

I leaned back again. "Yeah, I guess so. So that's it? You don't want to be by yourself in this house because of what happened to those children? There's an extra detail of cops patrolling the streets. You've got private security to keep out the riffraff. Despite the recent troubles, this is the safest neighborhood in the city. Maybe in the entire province."

Mrs. Teague looked down at her hands. She didn't say anything at first. Then, without lifting her eyes, she said, "There's something else." She paused, and I waited for her to arrange her thoughts. "I talked to Loretta. That's the woman whose children were.... Well, I went to see her at her house yesterday after she was done talking with the police. I made her some coffee and offered to let her stay with me for a few days if she wanted. But she said that Richard, her husband, was flying in that evening, and that she'd be okay until he got home. Anyway, while I was talking to her, she told me that she'd heard a woman crying that night through her open window. She said that they were cries of great sorrow from a woman who was obviously distressed. According to her, the sound came from the lake, although I'm not sure how she would know that for sure. She was adamant about that, however. She said that the crying had a weird echoing quality to it, like it was coming from a distance. The sobbing woke her up. The first thing she did was to go check on her children, and that's when she discovered that they were missing."

"Did she tell this to the police?"

Mrs. Teague shook her head. "No. I asked her the same question. She said that she thought the police were already judging her harshly." She raised her eyes to meet mine. "Do you have children, Mr. Southerland?"

"No. Never had the pleasure."

"Then you can't possibly know what that poor woman is going through. She's suffered the worst loss that any woman can suffer, and she's putting one hundred percent of the blame on herself for not being able to prevent it from happening. She believes that if she had tried to tell the police officers a story about hearing distant cries from a woman in distress, they would have thought that she was either making it up or that she was not in her right mind."

I shrugged. "She should have told the police anyway. But you're probably right. Like you said, there is no way that I can fathom what the woman is going through. And maybe the crying woman is incidental to the whole thing anyway. Just because the sound woke her up doesn't mean that she was the one who…took her children from her."

Mrs. Teague nodded. "When she told me about the crying woman, that was *my* reaction, too. That the woman had nothing to do with her children. But I don't think so anymore."

Mrs. Teague paused, eyes still downcast. I waited for her to continue. Finally, she raised her head and gazed upward and off to one side, remembering. "Last night, or rather early this morning, at a little past four, I, like Loretta the morning before, was awakened by the sound of a woman crying. I lay in my bed, terrified! I couldn't move! The crying lasted until just before dawn. It wasn't just sad—it was horrible! The woman was obviously miserable! But…. There was something strange about it. I don't know how to describe it except to say that it had an eerie sort of quality. It scared me nearly to death! And that's why I have to get out of this house. I can't spend another night alone here."

She looked down at her hands again, and I thought about what she'd told me. "Did the sound come from the lake?"

She shook her head. "I'm not sure. And that's the thing. I couldn't tell where it was coming from. Nothing made sense! It couldn't have come from inside the house. I was the only one here. I know that. I was alone last night, and the house was locked up tight. All my windows were closed. Sometimes, when the wind is right, I can hear people down by the lake at all hours of the day or night. But only when the windows are open. Our windows are double-paned. They're very secure. When they're closed, the house is practically soundproof! And yet, I heard a woman crying last night. I heard it very distinctly. And it sounded like it was being carried by the wind from a distance, or through a tunnel, or like it was coming up through deep water." She shrugged and shook her head. "That's not exactly right, but it's hard to explain. It's not just that I can't tell you where the sound of the crying was coming from. It's more that I can't tell you why I should have been able to hear it at all! Could someone have been using magic? I don't have any real experience with that sort of thing, but I don't believe for a second that what I heard last night was natural."

"And you're positive that you weren't imagining it? That you weren't influenced by your neighbor's story?"

She met my eyes again. "I listened to that sobbing for more than two hours, Mr. Southerland. It was very clear and very real. I'm not losing my mind, if that's what you're thinking. I know what I heard."

I nodded. "I believe you, Mrs. Teague. There are strange things happening. I wouldn't rule out the possibility that something unnatural is at work here."

Mrs. Teague took a deep breath and let it out. "Thank you, Mr. Southerland. Thank you for listening and understanding. But there's more."

I waited until she spoke again. Her eyes were closed as she struggled to calm her nerves. When she opened her eyes, she seemed to have regained some of her composure. "Every now and again, between the crying, the woman would speak. She'd ask 'Where are you?' 'Where are you?' Mr. Southerland, you can't imagine how terrified I was. The woman was looking for me! I'm sure of it! I couldn't move, because I was afraid that if I did, she would find me! And I didn't know what she would do!"

Mrs. Teague began to shake. I reached out and grasped her hand. "It's okay," I told her. "You're safe now. But I think that you're right not to stay here alone until this all gets cleared up."

She let out her breath and managed a thin, but sincere smile. "Don't worry about that. In spite of everything, I hate having to desert my husband. But I intend to be far away from here until this is all over. He'll know where I am if he wants me."

Gordo came into the room then. "Mrs. Teague? Sorry to interrupt, but your sister just pulled in."

Mrs. Teague smiled at Gordo and stood. I climbed out of the chair and stood, too. "Thank you for seeing me, Mrs. Teague. Have a safe trip."

"Thank you again, Mr. Southerland. I hope that we can see each other again in better times."

"That would be swell. I'll let myself out."

Gordo walked out with me. When we were outside, he stopped me. "You need to call Mr. Fulton."

"I will. I'm going to take a walk to the lake first. Want to come?"

Gordo shook his head. "No. Mr. Fulton wants me and Thunder to come back to the office as soon as Mrs. Teague leaves. He'll probably want you there, too, unless he fires you. Call him!"

"He won't fire me. Not after he hears my report."

Chapter Nineteen

"Where have you been? What have you been doing? Why am I just now hearing from you?"

Fulton was one of those guys who didn't have to raise his voice to let you know that he was pissed. The icy menace in his tone did the job just fine. I had waited until I was back in my office and sitting at my desk before calling him. I wanted him to stew a while. Maybe I wanted him to be mad enough to fire me. I felt like I could live with that.

"I just saw you two days ago," I reminded him. "What do you want, fuckin' hourly updates?"

"I want you to return my fuckin' calls!"

"I'm calling you now, aren't I?"

"I left you a message yesterday, asshole! Why didn't you call me back?"

"Yeah, about that. You called at an inconvenient time."

Fulton *did* raise his voice then. "What the fuck are you talking about, Southerland!"

I kept my tone businesslike. "I was in a meeting when you called. With Anton Benning. He sent a troll in a black luxury car to pick me up. Say, what is it with you big wheels, anyway? Why do you think you have to pick guys off the street? Can't you just call for an appointment like everybody else?"

I could hear Fulton controlling his breath before responding. "You talked to Benning? What'd he have to say?"

"Nothing much. He wants me to work for him on this Sihuanaba case. He knows all about it, by the way. He even knows that you only offered me half rates. He says that he'll pay me triple my standard fees and make whatever hold you have over me go away. I bet he could do it, too. He seems like a capable operator."

I waited for Fulton to respond, and when he did I could tell that he was suppressing rage like a dragon choking back a ball of flames. "What did you tell him?" I could almost hear his teeth grinding between clenched jaws.

"Relax, Fulton. I can't be bought off a case. You know that. Still, it's an interesting offer. And it's just good business to consider all my options, don't you think?"

"Fuck you, Southerland! Did Benning try to sell you on that 'we're just a family business' crap they like to dish out? Join our family and we'll look out for you and your loved ones for the rest of your life? Fuck that! They're the kingdom of the damned, and you're smart enough to know it. Quit trying to scare me. I know you. You'd never work for the Hatfields! You'd slit your throat before you let anyone own you, and if you took a job with the Hatfields—they'd own you, lock, stock, and barrel!"

"The way *you* think you own me? Listen to me, Fulton, and listen good! Benning tried to sell me on the idea that the Fultons and the Hatfields are just two rival teams, each with the same goals and playing by the same rules. I didn't buy it, of course. For one thing, you may be the biggest alligator in the political swamp, but the Hatfields transcend politics. They could swat you like a fly. And don't try to bullshit me by passing yourself off as the brave noble underdog standing up to the forces of evil! This isn't about good and evil. It's about expensive suits and shiny black sedans, and about enough raw power to light up a city. Only they've got more of it than you do—lots more!"

"Is that so? Then maybe you'd better join them before they crush you like the bug you are!"

"I told you, Fulton. I can't be bought off a case. But that doesn't mean I like working for peanuts, either. Tell you what. You pay my full freight, and I might be a little more forthcoming with my reports. I've already done you a favor by letting you know how far up your ass Benning is. If he knows how much you're paying me, then he's in there pretty deep. There's more, too. I've been working, and I've got some dope for you. You want it all? Or just half?"

Fulton didn't say anything for a while, and I let the silence grow. It was okay. I was comfortable with it. Finally, Fulton chuckled. "All right, you son of a bitch! You win. You can forget about triple your rates, though. I'll pay your standard fare, and that's it."

"That's all I ask. I'll call you back the minute you email me a signed contract."

I disconnected the call and leaned back in my chair. I even put my feet up on my desk. I would have lit up a cigar if I'd had one. I settled for taking a dusty glass and a bottle of cheap whiskey out of my desk drawer and pouring myself a drink. I held the glass up to the crow overlooking the desert and toasted him. "Here's to beating City Hall."

The crow continued gazing out at the desert. I didn't think he looked as impressed as I felt he should have been.

***

Ten minutes after I disconnected my call with Fulton, I had my signed contract: full rates plus expenses. I printed it out and filed it in my filing cabinet. Then I called Fulton.

He connected before the end of the first ring. "Okay, Southerland. Shoot! Whaddaya got?"

"For starters, I'm convinced that the Sihuanaba is tied to Zyanya's death."

Fulton cut in. "I told you to stay away from the Zyanya matter! The LIA have it well in hand. I don't want you butting in and fucking things up!"

"You mean you don't want me exposing anything to the public. Well nuts to that! You hired me to investigate the Sihuanaba, and, whether you like it or not, my investigation has led me directly to Zyanya. You want to hear the rest or not?"

Fulton fumed for a few moments, and I let him. Finally, he sighed into his phone. "All right, fine. Better give it to me now before Benning gets any wiser. Tell me what you know and we'll go from there."

I told him about Mrs. Teague's conversation with Loretta, the mother of the two kids who had washed up at the site where Zyanya's children had been found, and how the sounds of crying had awakened her that morning.

"And you think that it was the woman in white who was doing the crying?" Fulton asked me.

"I do. And I think that she drowned those two children."

"Why? There are a lot of people who live in that neighborhood, and a lot more who could have snuck in past the gate, or from the country club or one of the golf courses. Why does it have to be the Sihuanaba? That's not her style. She kills men, not children!"

"I heard the Sihuanaba crying, too," I told him. "On Wednesday night. Right at the spot where Zyanya and her children washed up. And I had eyes on her at the time."

"What? On Wednesday?"

"Yes. When I was at the lake with Gordo and his crew. Gordo, Thunderclash, and I had been investigating the site where the Sihuanaba had met Teague. I hung back for a while after they'd left. That's when I heard the sounds of crying. I hid in the trees and spotted her standing at the site where Zyanya had been found. She was looking out over the water, crying like she was in real emotional pain. That's when I first realized that there was something that linked the Sihuanaba to Zyanya's death."

"Did you tell Gordo about this?"

"Nope."

"Why the hell not?"

"Because I knew that he would tell you, and I didn't trust you. I wanted to get a better idea about why you had picked me up and pressured me into working for you. Besides, I didn't have a signed agreement from you yet, so I figured you could wait."

"You son of a bitch! You put your team in danger by withholding information from them!"

"Cut the crap, Fulton! The reason we were out there in the first place is because we were watching out for the Sihuanaba. We were already assuming that she was there! We wouldn't have been in any less danger if I had told them I'd seen her."

Fulton didn't back down. "You could have all gone down to the lake and hunted her down!"

"And leave the mayor unprotected? That would have been a swell idea! Besides, she disappeared. Vanished! I don't think that we could have followed her to wherever she went."

I waited for Fulton to finish processing what I'd told him. Then he asked, "So you think this really is some kind of ghostly spirit? I'd been hoping that someone was trying to pull off an elaborate gag. But you're telling me that she vanished into thin air?"

I hesitated. "I have to admit that I lost sight of her for a second." I didn't tell him why. He didn't need to know that I'd tripped over a tree root while backing away from the Sihuanaba in terror. "But it was only for a second. And when I looked again, she was gone."

"And there's no way you could have just lost her in the dark?"

"The sun hadn't finished setting yet. And I examined the spot where I'd seen her standing. There were no footprints leading away."

"What about that earth demon? He controls earth elementals, right? And he used one to disappear right in front of your eyes. Maybe he's working with the woman. He could have used an elemental to remove her from the scene."

"I suppose that's possible," I admitted. "But that doesn't change the fact that she's connected in some way to Zyanya's death. It's no coincidence that she was standing in that spot and crying."

"Don't you get it?" Fulton sounded exasperated. "What if she's some crazy stalker, working with that earth demon to undermine the mayor? She'd *want* to draw attention to Zyanya's death, and to the death of her children. First she terrifies the mayor by using some kind of magic mumbo-jumbo, and then she lets the knuckleheaded private investigator that I hired spot her where Zyanya washed up from the lake. And the earth demon uses an earth elemental to make it look like she vanished. They played you for a sucker, you dumb fuck!"

I had to give Fulton credit. It was an interesting theory. But I wasn't buying it, at least not yet. "You're grasping at straws, Fulton. And you're forgetting something. The mayor's wife heard crying from outside her house, which she says was sealed up tight enough to be soundproof. And she said that the crying had a weird, echoing quality to it, like it was coming through a tunnel or passing through water. Or maybe rising from an abyss? She wouldn't have heard some ordinary person crying from outside her sealed-up house, but she might have heard something more, I don't know, unearthly."

"You're talking through your hat, Southerland! I sent you to investigate some crazy stalker, and you're telling me ghost stories!"

"You hired me because I'd already run into the Sihuanaba! I've seen some other batshit crazy things in my life, too. A couple of months ago, some sort of demonic spirit with a hummingbird's head tried to slice out my heart with its three-foot long beak! And a giant shadowy dog with no eyes dragged me through a void to the borders of the land of the dead! I'm not smart enough to know all of the ways that the natural world interacts with the unnatural, but I know that it happens more often than most people know about. A bigshot slimeball like you? Who knows what kinds of otherworldly shit you've waded into during your sordid life! You might *want* this all to be an ordinary twist with some magic tricks and a dwarf elementalist at her side, but right now the evidence is suggesting something a lot less mundane."

Fulton was quiet then. He was still catching up. After a few moments, I decided to prompt him. "Mrs. Teague heard the Sihuanaba crying. That's a fact. The question isn't how, it's why. She suspects that the crying was projected by magic, or that it has a supernatural source."

Fulton responded to that. "You think she's in danger?"

"Her sister came for her while I was there. I think she's probably safe now. Maybe the Sihuanaba was trying to drive her away."

Fulton mulled that over. "Why would she do that?"

"To get her away from her husband? The Sihuanaba targets men. Maybe she didn't want her target's wife to get in her way."

Fulton snorted. "Are you saying that this demon has a little angel in her?"

"Think about it, Fulton. She's a demon to men, but to a woman who's been hurt by a man she might seem more like an angel."

"Sure she would. Until she starts drowning children."

"Yeah, well, I've got a theory about that, but you're not going to like it."

"You're going to tell me anyway, though, aren't you."

"Of course. That's what you're paying me for." I shifted in my seat and transferred my phone to my other ear. "Okay, bear with me. The Sihuanaba is some sort of unnatural creature. A demon, or an angel of vengeance, or something like that. In the stories, she targets philandering husbands and boyfriends, or men who harm women in some way. I think that she has some kind of connection to the women who have been victimized. Maybe they call to her."

"You mean with a summoning spell?"

"Maybe. But I think it's more likely that the Sihuanaba is attracted to the emotional pain that these women are feeling. Either way, there's a connection. Think about it! Teague dumped Zyanya just before she died. Zyanya was in a bad emotional state. The way you describe her, she was close to the edge at the best of times. Throw in drug abuse and rejection by the man she loved, or at least desired, and she went over the edge. She's in so much pain that she drowned her own children so that Teague would share some of that pain. Or maybe somebody else did it. It doesn't matter. Either way, she's experiencing an enormous amount of grief at the death of her children, and in her crazed state she lays all the blame on Teague. All of that grief and pain attracts the Sihuanaba, who then goes after Teague."

I paused to collect my thoughts. The truth was that, although I'd been tossing these ideas around for a while, I was still trying to fit it all together.

Fulton spoke before I could go any further. "Sounds like you've got a screw loose, Southerland. How much have you been drinking today?"

"No more than usual. But let's say that I'm right, or at least on the right track. It means that there is a strong connection between Zyanya and the Sihuanaba. Now hang in there, because here's where it gets really wild. From what you've told me, and from my own experience watching her perform, Zyanya was a highly charismatic and strong-willed individual. I think that at some point, Zyanya began to, I don't know, *push* her way into the Sihuanaba, to influence her will to some extent."

Fulton interrupted me. "Wait a minute! Zyanya is dead!"

"What does that really mean, Fulton? I've had a glimpse of death myself. It's hard to explain what I went through, but I can tell you that during that business with Madame Cuapa I was close enough to death to smell its breath. I'm not convinced that I *wasn't* dead, at least for a while. What do we really know about death anyway? Maybe when that switch goes off, the light doesn't really go out, at least not all the way, or not all at once. What if the connection between Zyanya and the Sihuanaba didn't disappear when Zyanya died? What if the Sihuanaba doesn't play by the same rules as we do? I mean, what *is* the Sihuanaba? Where does she come from?"

"I don't know. Maybe she's hellspawn."

"Maybe, but I don't think so. Think about the hellspawn species we know about, trolls, gnomes, dwarfs, even dragons…. They *feel* different than the Sihuanaba. She's not like them, and I think that she comes from…somewhere else. I don't know where, but there's something very unearthly about her. She's more like the things I ran into when I was working with Madame Cuapa. More like the things she described as spirits, or even gods. We know that there are a lot of places that exist outside of our own plane of existence, but we don't know how many, or how many of them interact with ours."

"Let me stop you there, professor. I'm not interested in a lot of speculation about the nature of the cosmos. It's time for you to come back to earth!" Fulton sounded impatient.

"Okay, let's back up then. Let's just say that the Sihuanaba, a supernatural spirit of unknown origin, responded to some part of an emotionally-charged Zyanya, maybe to something in her mind and memory as she was grieving over her dead children, and she was influenced by it. Maybe Zyanya imprinted herself on the Sihuanaba in some way. Mrs. Teague said that she listened to a woman crying for two hours. But she also heard the woman speak. According to Mrs. Teague, the woman called out 'Where are you?' several times. It terrified her, and she couldn't move because she was afraid that the crying woman would find her. But what if it wasn't Mrs. Teague that the woman was looking for? What if the Sihuanaba, influenced by Zyanya, was looking for her children? Zyanya's children, I mean."

Fulton was still skeptical. "What are you talking about, Southerland? Have you gone batshit?"

I ignored him. "The way I see it, whatever happened to Zyanya's children, she couldn't accept it. When the Sihuanaba connected with her, she connected to a powerful impulse to reclaim the lives of her children. And the Sihuanaba eventually began to search for them. She found two kids, a boy and his younger sister, and lured them away to the lake where Zyanya's children had been found. But they were the wrong kids. So she drowned them. And she's continuing to search."

I stopped then, waiting for Fulton to respond. I got what I was expecting. "Southerland, I think that working with witches scrambled your noodle! Remind me, have I actually paid you anything yet? You're crazy as a bedbug! You keep drawing from that tap and they're gonna lock you up in the loony bin and throw away the key!"

"Why? We both know that the Sihuanaba is an unearthly spirit of some kind. All I'm suggesting is that she is attracted to emotional pain and anguish in women, and that she can be influenced by the women that call her to our earthly plane. It's actually pretty logical when you think about it."

"You don't say! Well, here's another theory, and mine makes a lot more sense. Our woman in white isn't the Sihuanaba at all! She's a deranged stalker out to get the mayor. She learned a few magic tricks, maybe, or she has a magic dingus or two, enough to scare Teague out of his shorts, and she has a partner who controls earth elementals so that she seems to vanish. Five will get you ten that she's working for that son-of-a-bitch Benning, and that it's all a plot to steal the election!"

Leave it to Fulton to make everything about his business. "You don't just go out and learn a few magic tricks, and magic items don't fall off trees."

"So she's gifted! You don't have to be special to be gifted. Hell, you're an elementalist! That proves that *anyone* can be born with a gift! And maybe she's got dough, or at least enough to buy an enchanted item. Sure, real magic ain't cheap, but neither is a diamond necklace, and my wife expects me to buy her at least one every couple of years! And if Benning is behind this, and I'll bet he is, then he'd have no trouble finding a gifted practitioner or some useful magic items."

I forced a smile into my voice. "Maybe so. Maybe I'm all wet. But I don't think you really believe that. We'll see how it plays out. In the meantime, let's just say that I think Teague needs to watch his step. Since the woman in white, or whoever she is, attacked him, two children that resemble his own with Zyanya have been murdered, and someone put enough of a scare into Mrs. Teague to drive her out of town."

"Teague's as secure as I can make him. With his wife gone, Gordo's whole team can babysit him in his apartment. The place has all kinds of security."

That might work against an "ordinary" deranged stalker, I thought to myself. I wondered how secure the place would be from an otherworldly spirit of vengeance. But I let it go.

Fulton continued. "What about this earth demon? Got anything on it?"

"I'm pretty sure that it's something called a nirumbee. A bunch of them live in villages in Lakota, and I found a van at the lake with Lakota plates. The floor pedals were built up so that a very short person could drive it. I found enough evidence to indicate that someone drove it there from Lakota in a hurry. I don't know how the nirumbee figures into this, though. I haven't found any direct connection to the Sihuanaba, but I find it hard to believe that he's here by coincidence."

Fulton grunted. "Hmph. Well, keep digging. And call me when you find anything! Don't withhold information from me!"

"Right, chief."

"Yeah, fuck that. I want you at the apartment tonight. Four-hour shift. Get there by eight."

"What for?"

"Because things are going on, and I don't understand them! I'm not ready to buy your story, but I can't afford to just toss it out, either. You're right. I hired you because of your experience with the Sihuanaba, and because you've got a strong mind. A little unconventional, but that's something I need around me when the situation calls for it. You're a stubborn motherfucker, and I'll never forgive you for not selling me that box that Graham smuggled in, but I value your perspective, and I'd be crazy not to listen to your theories, even if my instincts tell me that they're hooey. But listen to me, and listen good! Nothing you've told me convinces me that the woman in white, whoever she turns out to be, has anything to do with Zyanya's death! You've got an interesting theory, and, loony as it sounds, I'll pass it on to the LIA. But it's their case, and I don't want you sticking your nose into it. You hear me?"

"Fulton—"

"You stay away from it, Southerland! It's got too much potential to damage the mayor. Benning already knows too much about your activities, and I don't want to give him any more ammunition than he's already got. Let the LIA handle it! That's my final word on the subject!"

I made a show of giving up. "All right, you're the one writing the checks."

"And don't forget it! Focus your investigation on the woman and the runt. Mostly what I need right now is more manpower. I don't want this stalker thing to blow up in our faces, and I'd rather apply a little overkill than lose because I was stingy with my resources. I want you to check in with Gordon and then man the lobby. See who goes in and out. Check out the perimeter from time to time, see what's up. You got it?"

I sighed. I was hoping to see Edie's show again that night, but maybe I'd still be able to catch the end of it and see her afterwards. "Okay. Eight o'clock. I'll be there."

"Wait! You still there?"

"I'm still here."

"There's something else." I waited for Fulton to continue, and, after a few moments, he did. "Benning knew about my contract arrangements with you. Only one person knew that I'd offered you the job at half fare."

I thought back. "Gordo."

"He was in the room when I hired you, and I didn't tell anyone else. I never wrote anything down, either. You emailed me a contract, but it was for your full rate. Only you, me, and Gordon knew about my offer. I didn't tell anyone about it. Did you?"

In fact, I had told two people. I'd told Kalama, but she was solid. I couldn't imagine a scenario in which word of my business dealings with Fulton would make its way from the detective to Benning. We hadn't known each other long, but I felt like I had a good sense of her integrity. The idea that she would betray a confidence to the Hatfield crime syndicate seemed downright laughable.

I'd also told Lubank. We'd been through some things together, and I considered him to be a friend of sorts, but I also knew that I couldn't trust that slimy rat not to sell out his own mother if he could make money from it. Was there a way that he could profit by selling me out to the Hatfields? I couldn't discount the possibility. But I didn't think that Lubank would do it, not because of any feelings of sentimentality on his part, but because we had a mutually beneficial business arrangement that I didn't think he'd want to risk. I did investigative work for him, and he represented me in legal matters. We both charged each other for our services, but somehow or another I always seemed to owe him more than he owed me. To him, I was a source of steady income and would probably remain so as long as we were both in business. And besides, Gracie liked me, and Gracie was the only person, besides himself, that Lubank really cared about.

After weighing the possibilities, I said, "I'm ninety-nine percent certain that I'm not the source of any information that reached Benning."

"You're sure? I'd be happier if it was a hundred percent."

"I'm sure. I'll get back to you if I begin to doubt it."

"So that leaves Gordon."

"You think that Gordo is Benning's mole?"

"Not necessarily," said Fulton. "He's always been loyal, and I trust him as much as I can afford to trust anybody. But he may have let the information slip to someone on his team. Or to Teague, for that matter. Those boys haven't had much to do the last couple of days except drink, and liquor loosens lips."

"Gordo or one of his crew, then. I take it that you want me to keep an eye on them?"

"One of those four is a Hatfield plant. I'd stake my right arm on it! Find out which one for me and you'll have my gratitude."

"You want me to be your snitch? How much is your gratitude worth?"

"More than you can imagine."

Fulton disconnected the call. I put my phone on my desk, rocked back in my chair, and stared at the ceiling. I felt sick.

Chapter Twenty

I pulled my last frozen pizza out of the freezer and put it in the microwave. Somehow, it had survived the raid by the overgrown alley rat. I was going to have to find time to buy groceries soon, though.

I finished off the pizza without bothering to taste it, which was probably just as well. I'd barely slept the night before, but I was wide awake. At some point it would catch up with me, but I'd found that I didn't need as much sleep anymore since the elf had done whatever he'd done to me. In fact, I could go a few days at a stretch without sleeping at all. It was still early in the afternoon, and I wondered whether Edie was awake yet. While I was considering whether or not to call her, she called me.

"I'm surprised you're up," I told her.

"I'm too excited to sleep. I guess you kind of got to me, big man."

"You want me to come over?"

"I'd love it, but I've got to go rehearse with the band. One of them wrote a new song and we want to put it into the show tonight. Are you coming to see us?"

"I've got to work tonight until midnight, but I'll catch the end of your show and see you afterwards, if that's okay with you."

"Sure, baby. I'll hang around the club until you get there, and you can walk me home. I'll let you hold my hand."

"Uh-huh. That's how it starts."

She laughed, and it sounded nice.

We chatted for a few minutes longer, and after we disconnected I found myself grinning like a schoolboy. The crow in the painting looked like he was about to fly away in disgust. I stuck my tongue out at him and blew a raspberry. Then I set my mind on business.

I tapped an app on my phone and clicked on the photo of the gemstone that I'd found in the nirumbee's van. I was surprised at the clarity of the picture. I used two fingers to zoom in on the image and examine the pink and red veins in the crystal. I didn't detect any particular pattern to the colors, which seemed to blur into each other, like streaks of light shining through swirling water. I remembered how I'd been unable to look at the actual stone. Was it protected by magic? Perhaps a ward of some kind. Was it enchanted? The only magic I knew much about was elementalism, and that wasn't going to help me figure out this gemstone. I was out of my depth, but I knew someone who could help me, provided she was willing. Our last meeting had been less than warm, and it was likely that she'd find this matter to be beneath her.

Nothing ventured, nothing gained. I called up my keypad and punched in the phone number of the most powerful witch in western Tolanica.

A male voice answered. "Madame Cuapa's residence."

"Is that you, Cody?"

"Alex? The Madame told me that you might be calling soon. She said that if you did, you were to come over right away. She said to tell you that she only has about thirty minutes, but that it should be enough."

"How did she know…oh, right. She's a witch."

Cody laughed. "Best not to forget that, sir. See you soon!"

***

Madame Cuapa, the Barbary Coast Bruja, lived in a high-rent neighborhood on the west side of town. It wasn't far as the crow flies, but it took me an hour to navigate the beastmobile through the Saturday afternoon traffic. I hoped that I wouldn't arrive too late to get my full thirty minutes with the witch.

Cody answered the door when I rang the bell. I took one look at him and groaned.

"What—you don't like it?" Cody was beaming like a cat in a spotlight. Madame Cuapa's personal assistant was a young man in his early twenties, six and a half feet tall, with a mane of thick dark hair that hung past his shoulders, and eyes like black diamonds. His broad smile exposed a set of gleaming white choppers that looked like they could crush granite. He had the physique of a grizzly bear, with thick muscles that seemed capable of stopping bullets, and he moved with the grace of a jaguar. But what always made Cody stand out in a room full of people was his penchant for sartorial flamboyance. Today he was wearing a top hat, a tuxedo jacket with long tails that hung almost to the floor, and knee-length leather boots, all so black that they glowed. He wore no shirt under the jacket, which hung open like a vest and exposed his muscular chest and abdomen. His only other item of clothing was a pair of beltless dark red leather shorts that hugged his huge thighs and stopped two inches above the tops of his knees. "I threw this ensemble together after we spoke on the phone."

"You did that for me? What did you think I would do, dance with you?"

"I'll settle for the expression on your face when I opened the door. How have you been, sir?"

Cody held out his oversized mitt and we shook. He was a strange jasper, but I'd taken a liking to him during my job with his boss. "How's the Madame?"

"She's been staying awake nights restructuring the coven the last couple of months after that unfortunate dust-up. It shook her up pretty good. But she's managing. Come with me, sir. The Madame knows you're here, and she'll be down in a moment. As I told you on the phone, she doesn't have much time, but she's anxious to talk to you."

Cody led me into the living room, and, as I entered, I pulled up short. Curled up on the floor in the middle of the room, watching me with feral yellow eyes, was a four-hundred pound killing machine. His fierce lion's face was surrounded by a spiky mane. Leathery wings were folded against his reddish-brown and black-striped tiger's body. A segmented scorpion's tail swished back and forth on the floor. As he sized me up, the creature let out a low menacing growl that caused my back teeth to vibrate.

Cody smiled at the manticore. "Mr. Whiskers is happy to see you again, sir."

"Uhhh…. Hello, kitty! Umm…. Have you been fed today?" I didn't think that the manticore posed a danger at the moment. Apart from the swishing of his barbed tail, he wasn't moving. The creature knew me. I'd even ridden on his back high above the skyscrapers of downtown Yerba City, although that was a memory I didn't like to recall. Besides, he and Cody were bonded with a telepathic link, and I knew that as long as I was with the jasper, and not threatening him or the Madame in any way, I'd be safe. But, still—it was a fuckin' manticore!

Cody laughed at my obvious discomfort. He gave a nod toward the back of the house, and the monster rose to his feet and stretched. The growling continued, and I realized that he wasn't growling at all, but purring. I almost felt like scratching him behind the ears. Almost. The manticore gave me one last stare, licked his lips with a tongue that looked like a slice of raw beefsteak, and padded past me out of the room, bumping me in the waist with his massive forehead as he slid by. I felt my bowels loosen, but I managed not to embarrass myself in the living room of the region's most powerful witch.

Cody directed me to a chair, and, letting out a breath I hadn't realized I'd been holding, I sat down with as much poise and dignity as I could muster.

After another minute, time I needed to regain my composure, I stood again as Madame Citlali Cuapa entered the room. It had been less than three months since I'd last seen her, and her appearance hadn't changed, but I knew that she'd looked the same fifty years earlier, and that she would likely show no signs of aging for another fifty, at least. Five feet tall and fashionably thin, with auburn hair tied in a bun, and smooth caramel skin, Madame Cuapa wouldn't have struck anyone as out of place in any downtown office building. Sure, the intensity of her jet black eyes was unsettling, and, when not covered by her standard, if expensive, office attire, the exquisite tattoos that covered her skin from shoulders to feet would have revealed that the Madame was more than she seemed. But it wouldn't have been obvious to many that they were in the company of one of the most powerful humans on the planet. I knew some things about her, though, maybe too much, and I couldn't keep myself from shivering a little as she approached.

She smiled when she saw me, a businesslike smile, and extended both hands for me to take. I was pleased with myself for not flinching. I still had a vivid memory of snakes slithering down those outstretched arms, mouths opened wide to expose gleaming fangs dripping with poison. But I smiled back at the witch and gave her hands a brief clasp with my own.

"Mr. Southerland. So good to see you again. Please, sit down. You once again find yourself in deep waters, and you have questions. Let's hope that I can shed some light on these matters." She turned to Cody. "Bring tea, please. Some for yourself, too."

"How are you, Madame?" I asked as I reseated myself. Madame Cuapa took a chair near mine after repositioning it so that she could look directly at me.

"I'm doing as well as can be expected. I lost two dear friends, and I miss them. But the business of the coven, not to mention my responsibilities as chief executive officer at Greater Olmec, have been keeping me busy. But my time is limited. You need not explain your current investigation to me. I'm aware of the important points. But you come with one specific question, and maybe two, if the second occurs to you. Please. Ask me what you came to ask."

I took out my phone and brought up the photo of the gemstone. "What can you tell me about this?"

Madame Cuapa held out a hand. "May I?" I handed her the phone and she studied the photo.

Cody came in at that point carrying a teapot, teacups, milk, sugar, spoons, and napkins on a serving platter balanced on one hand, and three folded tea trays in his other. After he arranged it all, Madame Cuapa showed him the photo.

After a few moments, Madame Cuapa passed the phone back to me. "Where did you see this?"

"In a compartment under the dash of a van driven by what I think is a creature called a nirumbee. When I tried to look at it, I felt like I'd been blinded by the sun. But it radiates no light, and, as you can see, I was able to photograph it."

The Madame nodded, as if it all made perfect sense. "The crystal is known colloquially as a heartstone." She looked at Cody, who nodded in agreement. She turned back to me and continued, "My guess is that it is protected by a ward that keeps it hidden. I doubt that most people would have even noticed the compartment in which it had been placed. You have some special abilities that allowed you to detect that much, at least, but the ward prevented you from seeing the heartstone itself."

I'd never told Madame Cuapa that I'd met an elf, but she somehow knew about it, and she knew that the elf had changed me in some meaningful ways. I didn't know how precise her knowledge was, but it never paid to underestimate the Barbary Coast Bruja. She was probably more aware of the nature of the abilities that the elf had given me than I was. If that were so, however, she wasn't likely to reveal anything to me, even if I asked. I liked to think that I played my cards close to the vest, but she'd turned secrecy into an art form and parceled out only as much of the knowledge she'd gained over her long life as she felt necessary.

"How hard would it be to create a protective ward like that?" I asked her.

She shrugged. "It's a simple spell. Any competent practitioner could have done it. As for the heartstone itself, however, that's another matter entirely. These gems are rare and very special." She gestured toward my phone with her teacup. "The crystal in your photograph contains a living heart, most likely the heart of a nirumbee, though not necessarily. If you had taken a video, you'd be able to see the living heart beating inside the gem. I'm familiar with these creatures, though I've never known one to travel to this part of Caychan before. Nirumbee shamans have mastered the practice of storing the hearts of their fellow nirumbees in these heartstones. It's common to protect nirumbee warriors in this way, although there aren't many warriors among the nirumbees anymore. And the nirumbees themselves have greatly diminished in number in recent years. They were never numerous, and today I doubt that there are more than a thousand that still live. Maybe even half that number."

"Why would a nirumbee warrior want his heart stored in a gemstone?"

"Because, dear boy, as long as his heart was safe within his heartstone, that warrior would be impossible to kill! You could cut the warrior to pieces and grind the parts into paste, but in the morning he would be intact and as good as new. The only way to kill the warrior would be to find his heartstone and destroy it, along with the heart within it."

I whistled. "Wow! Neat trick! But how come he brought it with him? If my heart were locked inside a stone like that, I'd drop the stone into the middle of the ocean!"

The Madame smiled at me the way a first-grade teacher smiles at a child who has asked why monkeys can't talk. "Because then he'd never be able to retrieve it. And it wouldn't be safe there. The crystal would wear away in short order, and the heart would be destroyed. Also, the farther the warrior is from his heart, the weaker he becomes. If he were to deposit his heartstone at the bottom of the ocean and then travel inland, he wouldn't die, but he would fall into a deep sleep and be utterly useless to his tribe."

I thought that over. "How close does he need to be to his heart to be fully functional as a warrior?"

The Madame frowned. "I'm not entirely sure. No more than a few miles, I'd guess. Traditionally, the nirumbees never roamed far from their villages."

"That explains why he had to bring it with him. If only I knew why he was here in the first place."

"That is a question I cannot answer, I'm afraid."

I looked at her. "Can't, or won't?"

The Madame gave me her best poker face. "It is as you say."

Typical witchy response. But I couldn't complain. I'd learned a lot from her in a short time. I started to leave, but the witch didn't move. Then I remembered that she'd said something about a second question. I wracked my brain, but couldn't think of another question she'd be likely to answer. I thought about asking her for a hint. And then, in a flash of insight, it came to me.

"Speaking of gemstones," I said, and the Madame's smile told me that I had taken the right path. "I've run into a carving that puzzles me. I don't have a picture, but I can describe it."

Madame Cuapa took a sip of her tea and nodded. "Please do."

"It's a gem of some kind carved in the shape of a spider, about this big." I held my fingers apart about a half inch. "It's black with a dark green tinge that shows up when the light hits it a certain way. It lies in a web, well, a tattoo of a web, actually, spread on the…" I started to reach toward my own stomach, but stopped. "Well, never mind where I saw it. What's unusual about it is that the ornament lies on its back, so that the spider is facing upwards." I held out my hand, palm up and fingers curled. "Like this. It's got fangs, and something that looks like vines are growing out of its head."

Madame Cuapa's eyebrows arched, and her lips twisted into a sly smile. "The tattoo of a web? When you saw the ornament, was it, by chance, in the navel of an attractive young woman?"

I hesitated, and she stopped me. "Never mind, you don't have to answer that. I wouldn't need to be a witch to see the truth of it in your face." She and Cody exchanged a look. He was smiling, too. I felt myself growing irritable. I'd come here on business, not to be the focus of salacious gossip.

Madame Cuapa sensed my burgeoning ire and scolded me with her intense dark eyes. "Oh, please, Mr. Southerland. There's no reason for you to be embarrassed. We're all mature adults here, and your private life is not our concern. But I find the circumstances in which you found this jewel to be fascinating, and, yes, maybe a bit amusing, too. For one thing, the ornament was likely to have been placed, um, where it was… in order to facilitate procreation."

What? "What?" I felt like I'd been knocked for a loop, and I had to put my teacup on my tray in order to keep from spilling any of its contents.

Madame Cuapa's smile broadened, and it wasn't businesslike anymore. "It sounds like the gem was carved into a likeness of the nameless Great Goddess of Teotihuacan. In her days as the ruling queen of the Kingdom of Teotihuacan, the goddess assumed a number of roles. She was the protector of the kingdom, of course, and the defender of the capital city. In those capacities, she was a goddess of war and battle. But she was much more. She ruled both the living and the dead, and her kingdom was not just of this world, but of the underworld, as well. She was also a fertility goddess, and she was responsible for bringing prosperity to the kingdom, both in the fields and in the home. That all ended with the coming of Lord Ketz-Alkwat, who overthrew the goddess and destroyed and rebuilt Teotihuacan in his own image. Under the direction of Ketz-Alkwat, the name of the Great Goddess was forgotten, but some memories of her lived on. It was her role as a fertility goddess that lingered, and in Teotihuacan today it is popular for young women who wish to enhance the quality of their sex life, or, more often, to become pregnant, to place the carved image of the goddess face-out in their navels. As for the web, I'd have to see it for myself. It's probably just decorative, but maybe the young lady believes that it increases the potency of the goddess's power." The smile wouldn't leave her face. "If you are involved in an intimate relationship with this woman, I suggest that you use some protection, unless, of course, you desire a child."

Cody winked at me. "I hope you're ready to be a poppa!"

I felt the blood rushing out of my head. "Hang on a minute!"

Cody licked his upper lip with the tip of his tongue. "Was the sex incredible?"

Madame Cuapa turned to Cody with what was supposed to be a look of disapproval, but she made no attempt to hide the amusement in her eyes. "Honestly, Cody. You know better than to tease our guest like that."

Cody's smile disappeared and he looked thoughtful. "I hope that the baby looks more like his mother. Or *her* mother. *Especially* if she's a her!"

I'd been knocked off balance, and I most definitely wanted to ask Edie some pointed questions. I opened my mouth to say something, but my mind went blank, so I closed my mouth and attempted to regain my composure.

Madame Cuapa came to my rescue. "Pour Mr. Southerland some more tea, Cody. He looks like he could use some." Turning toward me, she amended, "Or maybe something a little stronger?"

I waved away her offer. "No thank you, Madame. I either need a bottle of the strong stuff or none at all. I know that you said you would answer two of my questions, but do you have time for one more?"

Madame Cuapa sat back in her chair and crossed her legs at the knees. "I have time to listen. When I hear the question, I'll let you know whether I have the time to answer it."

"Is it possible that a nirumbee warrior could summon and command earth elementals?"

The Madame all but rolled her eyes at my question, as if the answer were obvious. "Of course, Mr. Southerland—*all* of the nirumbees are born with that gift!"

Chapter Twenty-One

On the way home, I stopped off at the store on Wool and Summer. The shabby little market wasn't where I usually shopped for groceries, but I wanted to pick up some cartons of yonak. If leaving some of that slop in the alley would prevent the goat-headed raider from invading my kitchen, then it was worth the cost. Maybe I'd trap it one morning and send it off with Animal Control. While I was still in the parking lot, I took out my phone and called Gordo.

"Looks like I'm joining you guys tonight," I told him when he answered.

"That's what I hear. I'll be happy to see you. I'm getting tired of looking at these other lugs. Irondick and Mayor Teague have run out of stories about all the loose women they've met. They're just making shit up now and not even *trying* to make it sound convincing. Stormclaw's getting grouchy, and Thunder spends most of his time pretending to be napping. I know better, though. That motherfucker *never* sleeps! He's just bored. Stormclaw, too. I don't want to question the boss, but I think we're just wasting our time around here. At this point, we're actually hoping that the woman in white shows up! Anything to break the monotony!"

"Careful what you wish for," I told him. "I think that the woman in white killed those two children at the lake."

"Yeah? I was thinking that it might be that runt we saw there."

"Either way, I think that the mayor is in the middle of it all. You guys need to keep yourselves ready."

"Of course. We know what we're doing. The waiting isn't easy, though."

"You fellas stocked up on brew and hooch?"

Gordo laughed. "It never lasts long with this bunch! Especially with the mayor here. The trolls can pack it away all day and hardly feel it, but the mayor matches them drink for drink. I don't know where he puts it! When you come by you'd better bring some extra bottles. And maybe some pretzels for the mayor and me and some jerky for the trolls. Call it a necessary expense and put it on Mr. Fulton's tab."

"Sounds like a plan."

I heard Ironshield's voice shouting through the phone from somewhere in the room. "Is that Southerland? Tell him to bring the woman in white with him! The Iron Pole's greased up and ready for action!"

I heard Gordo groan. "When are you getting here?"

"Around eight."

"Bring a tranq gun. I want to fire a couple of darts into that Iron Pole."

In the store, I stood behind a rheumy-eyed middle-aged lady dressed in a flower-printed housecoat and slippers, her hair up in curlers. I concluded that there was no one in the store that she wanted to impress. When she got to the counter, she pulled two bottles of cheap red wine out of her basket for the cashier to ring up. I tried to convince myself that she had plans for a big Saturday night with a special someone. I had my own plans for the evening, and I unloaded a carton of eggs, a loaf of sourdough bread, a cube of butter, a jar of peanut butter, a premade submarine sandwich, a frozen pizza, two jumbo-sized bags of pretzels, a twelve-pack of brew, two quart bottles of the cheapest whiskey in the store, and five containers of yonak from my basket and placed them on the counter. The cashier rang them up and bagged them with veteran efficiency and a blank face. She knew better than to speculate or judge. I kept the receipt.

***

Teague's apartment was on the top floor of the Grand Pinnacle, a luxury complex located a short block away from the popular Midtown Square walking plaza, the most crowded shopping area in the city. Parking on the street anywhere near the towering complex was impossible, especially on a Saturday night, so I pulled the beastmobile into the building's underground parking facilities, paid a small fortune for the privilege of leaving my car there for a few hours, and took an elevator to the lobby. With its marble service counter, its walnut-paneled walls, and its modern furnishings, the expansive lobby of the Grand Pinnacle apartment complex rivaled those of the city's best hotels. It also featured a huge picture window that offered a clear view of the boulevard outside the building's main entryway. As surveillance sites went, it beat the hell out of spending the evening cooped up inside one of Fulton's black sedans with a bruiser and three trolls.

Teague's apartment was on the thirty-ninth floor, one floor from the top. I wondered about that. If the mayor of the city didn't rate a top-floor apartment, then who did? Lord Ketz-Alkwat's government agents? Doubtful. International dignitaries? Nah! Film stars and recording artists? Probably. Criminal kingpins? The heads of the Hatfield Syndicate probably could have scored a penthouse suite, but I knew that they didn't live in the top floors of luxury apartment buildings. In my experience, the more powerful organized crime heads tended to shun the limelight. They lived understated lives with their families in modest homes in the suburbs, where they held backyard barbecues on the weekends, and their wives were members of the local PTA. It was the more flamboyant and high-living criminal bosses that found themselves targeted by government probes and police task forces. There's no glory in going after shadowy crime lords that the public never hears about. Taking down the big-noise celebrities is what gets politicians and police commissioners the favorable attention that they seek.

These thoughts drifted through my mind like a meandering brook as the elevator whisked me up to the penultimate level of the Grand Pinnacle. I'd brought the beer, booze, and pretzels that I'd picked up that afternoon, and Ironshield was happy to see the bags of groceries when he opened the door of Teague's apartment.

"Southerland, you glorious son of a bitch! Just in time! I knew you wouldn't let us down!" The smiling troll swung the door open wide so that I could enter. "Come in, pal! Let me give you hand with those."

Ironshield took one of the bags and pulled out the two bottles of cheap rotgut. "One for me and one for the mayor! Those other ladies can split the beers. Hey, Gordo! Southerland brought snacks! Here, catch!" The troll tossed the two bags of pretzels across the room to Gordo, who caught them both.

Gordo ripped open one of the bags. "Grab a seat, Southerland. Have a beer before you go to work."

I took a good look at the mayor's suite. One enormous space, four times the size of my whole apartment, doubled as a living room and bedroom. A sixteen-piece sectional sofa with a few of the pieces pulled away from the others ran down one side of the room, and a king-sized bed dominated the far end of the suite. The adjacent kitchen area was the size of my bedroom. Picture windows on two walls of the corner apartment displayed spectacular views of the city lights and the bay, but the stark, quiet beauty of the vista was a sharp contrast to the squalid condition of the mayor's suite. Glasses and bottles, some half-filled, but most of them empty, cluttered the countertop of a recessed bar near the kitchen, and more bottles stood or lay on various tables and on the polished hardwood floor. Cigar smoke filled the room, and mounds of butts and ashes spilled out of the ashtrays scattered about on tables and on the floor. Foam food containers and paper wrappers, some of them still containing the remains of meals, had been left in random places throughout the suite. It was obvious that maid service had been put on hold for the past three days.

I shook my head. "I'd say that you jokers were pigs, but that would be an insult to pigs."

Gordo actually looked a little embarrassed, but Ironshield let out a belly laugh. "Haw haw haaaaaw! Can you believe this place? Look at that view! You can see through every fuckin' window in the city from up here! Especially if you use binoculars!"

Mayor Teague, a cigar in his lips and a bottle of beer in his hand, sat in the center of the sofa, his feet propped on a coffee table. He saluted me with the bottle. "Southerland, right? Good to see you again. Sorry for all the bother. I think that Fulton is overreacting. I had a minor breakdown the other day, but all I needed was a couple of nights of good sleep. I feel tons better now."

Well, wasn't that dandy. Reduced to madness by some kind of avenging spirit less than four days ago, Teague couldn't have been more relaxed than if he'd been spending the week trout-fishing at a remote mountain resort. Not a hair on his handsome face was out of place. His polo shirt and khakis were clean and pressed. The smile on his kisser was so self-satisfied and smug that I wanted to slap it off his face. But I forced myself to smile back at him and wave. It wasn't his job to worry about nirumbee warriors or angels of vengeance. It was my job to make sure that he wouldn't need to.

I nodded at Thunderclash, who was sitting next to the mayor on a section of sofa that he'd pulled away from the wall and turned at a right angle. He tipped his fedora in my direction and puffed at his cigar until the tip glowed as red as his eyes. I looked around the room. "Where's Stormclaw?"

I was answered by the sound of a toilet flushing. Then I staggered forward as Ironshield clapped me on the back. "I hope you don't have to use the toilet. You do *not* want to go in there after that old man has stunk it up!" His laughter rattled the windows.

I nodded a greeting at Stormclaw as he emerged from the bathroom. "Everything seems copacetic in here."

Teague smiled up at me. "Just a big party! All we need are some hookers, but that motherfuckin' Fulton won't allow it. Bastard!"

I couldn't stop myself from giving him a reminder. "It's that kind of thinking that's got you into this mess in the first place, Mr. Mayor."

Teague's smile disappeared. He took the cigar out of his mouth and knocked back a drink of beer.

Gordo walked up to me and leaned in so that he could mutter into my ear. "Ixnay on that kind of talk, Southerland. Mr. Fulton wants us to keep things stress-free for the mayor."

I nodded. "I should get downstairs."

Ironshield held up a bottle. "Sure you don't want a drink first?"

I reached into my coat pocket and pulled out a flask. "I'm set. You guys enjoy that one."

Gordo nodded at me. "Stormclaw will go with you. I think that Mayor Teague is right. Mr. Fulton is being over-cautious. My guess is that we're all in for another quiet night."

***

Stormclaw never said a word as we rode the elevator to the lobby. I indicated a couple of expensive-looking armchairs near the window. "I figured we could set up here."

Stormclaw nodded his approval. "You mind if I have a look outside first? I need some air."

"Sure, good idea." I settled into one of the chairs, and Stormclaw stepped over to the check-in counter. He had a brief word with the clerk, a bored-looking young man with thick glasses and the hint of a thin mustache. The troll pointed over his shoulder in my direction, and the clerk glanced at me and nodded without much interest. Having informed the clerk that I was there on legitimate business, Stormclaw walked out of the lobby. I watched him through the window as he walked up the street and disappeared around the corner.

I took off my coat and made myself comfortable. A stream of well-dressed pedestrians walked past the window to and from the plaza, looking happy to be alive and strolling through one of the most exciting cities in the world. The neon bulbs that lit up the entrance to the Grand Pinnacle blended with the colorful display lights from the restaurants, department stores, hotels, and bars that lined both sides of the boulevard. The white beams of headlights and the red blaze of taillights streamed from the vehicles cruising by, and amber-colored streetlights glowed at every corner. The interaction of light and shadow made the entire block seem like a crowded amusement park after dark, which, in many ways, is exactly what Midtown Square was, especially on a Saturday night. Most of the faces belonged to wide-eyed young adults in their twenties and early thirties, probably tourists or young professionals staying in the nearby hotels, or college students and suburbanites cruising the city streets for a good time. Yerba City's native population tended to gravitate to nightspots outside of Midtown that didn't depend so much on the tourist trade, places with more local character, as opposed to the big franchise establishments that could be plugged into the downtown districts of any major city in Tolanica. But Yerba City's Midtown District had a magical air about it that gave it an identity all its own. Maybe it was the cold salt-tinged ocean breeze blowing off the bay, or the ever-present fragrance of shrimp and deep-fried calamari that drifted in from the wharfs. Or maybe it was the city's colorful history as a city on the edge, not just on the edge of the continent, but on the cutting edge of social evolution and transformation. The city's position as a coastal trading hub made it a dynamic mixing bowl of international cultures where, on any given night, you never knew what you might see or what you might find yourself doing for the very first time.

  I kept a watch on the street and waited for Stormclaw to return. Twenty minutes later, just as I was thinking about going out after him, he walked through the door and lowered himself into the chair next to mine.

  I stared up at the old troll. "Have a nice walk?"

  "It was all right."

  "See anything interesting?"

  "It's all interesting. But I didn't see anything that we're looking for."

  I gave the boulevard a quick scan. "Gordo may be right. This could be a long, quiet night."

I didn't think that Stormclaw was going to respond, and I prepared to leave him to his own thoughts. But after a few moments he surprised me by asking, "What do you think of Gordo?"

"Gordo?" I shrugged. "He seems to be an okay joe. Why do you ask?"

It was Stormclaw's turn to shrug. "Maybe I shouldn't say anything." He turned his attention to the street.

I let it sit until I couldn't any more. "Well, now you've got me curious."

Stormclaw continued to scan the stream of pedestrians and didn't say anything for a while. Then he reached into the inside of his coat and pulled out a cigar that was smaller than my forearm, but not by much. He fired it up and puffed it into life. After blowing a thick trail of smoke toward the ceiling, he shifted in his chair a bit so that he could speak to me more directly. "You may not have guessed, because I've got such a handsome face, but I'm two hundred seventeen years old. Does that make you uncomfortable? I know how hard it is for humans to understand how anyone can live that long. Most trolls don't talk about their age when they're around humans. It tends to piss them off. They think it's unfair that trolls, gnomes, dwarfs, and the other descendants of Hell should live twice as long as they do. But I'm ancient even for a troll, and I'm much too old to care what anyone thinks about it. The fact that I'm older than most people ain't my problem, and there's nothing I can do about it, even if I wanted to."

The old troll took another puff off his cigar, and I wondered where he was heading with all this. Truthfully, I was stunned that he was talking to me at all. I'd been in the car with him for almost eight hours the previous night, and I hadn't heard him string more than a few short sentences together the entire time. I had him pegged as the strong, silent type, and I found myself intrigued by this sudden avalanche of verbosity. He had something he wanted to tell me, and I figured he would get to the point in his own sweet time.

Stormclaw kept his eyes on the street as he spoke. "I'm not going to tell you my life story. It would take too long. I've traveled in all seven realms. I've been on both sides of the law. I've worked for governments, and I've spent some of my life behind bars." The troll pulled his cigar from his lips and glanced at me. "I was rich for a little while. But I lost it after my Flavia died." He resumed scanning the street. "I went a little crazy after I lost her. Got involved in some stupid shit. Anyway, my point is that I've run into a lot of people from every walk of life. All types of people. Rich, poor, troll, human, gnome, dwarf, criminals, coppers, politicians, and ordinary slobs. I got where I can read people pretty well." He glanced back at me and smiled. "Well, I can read *men* pretty well. I've never been able to figure out what women are thinking. Gave up trying a long time ago." His gaze returned to the street, and he took a few slow puffs on his cigar. Then he removed the cigar from his lips and faced me directly. "I don't trust Gordo. You shouldn't either."

When he didn't elaborate, I said, "Because he's blindly loyal to Fulton?"

Stormclaw shoved his cigar into his lips and clamped down on it. "Is that what you think?" He turned away from me to peer out the window. "Me? I'm not so sure."

I had to admit that I was surprised. Like Stormclaw, I considered myself a good judge of character, even if the troll had more than a hundred eighty-five years of experience on me. I couldn't claim to know Gordo all that well, but we'd spent several hours together in close quarters, and I'd formed some strong impressions. I thought we'd hit if off well enough. But I had Gordo pegged as a loyal soldier, and the way I saw it, if Fulton ordered him to put a bullet in my head, the bruiser would pull the trigger without thinking about it twice. Stormclaw was giving me a different story. He was suggesting that Gordo might not be as loyal to Fulton as he let on. Could Gordo be Benning's mole? Or maybe Stormclaw was the mole, and he was trying to throw suspicion on Gordo. Either way, I wanted to keep the old troll talking.

"What do you think Gordo is up to?" I asked.

The troll shook his head. "I'm not ready to say anything except that you should watch him. And watch your back while you're at it."

I took my flask out of my pocket and tossed back a shot. I offered the flask to Stormclaw, but he shook his head.

"I've got my own stuff. That piss you humans drink is like water." The troll placed his cigar in an ashtray built into the arm of his chair and pulled his own pineapple-sized flask out from his coat pocket. He held the flask up to me. "Now *this* is a drink for a troll. Good old-fashioned home-stilled 'shine!"

I felt a cold chill in the pit of my stomach. "No thanks. I've *had* some of that troll shine."

Stormclaw's eyes widened. "And you're still alive? I'm impressed!"

I laughed. "A renegade troll cop forced some down my throat when he was torturing me. I thought I'd reached the end of the line, for sure. Funny thing, though. The second gulp was actually bearable. Not so's I'd ever want to try it again, mind you."

Stormclaw stared at me for a moment and then broke into a laugh. "Don't.... Don't worry, little man! I'd never do anything that cruel to you." He unscrewed the cap from his flask and knocked back a troll-sized gulp. "Ahhhhhhhh! It's a shame you can't appreciate good trollshine, but to each his own." He held out his flask, and I clinked mine against it as if they were wineglasses.

"To our own choice of poison," I said, and we quaffed down a healthy swallow of our respective brands of joy juice.

Stormclaw smiled down at me. "I'd offer you a cigar, but this one's all I've got at the moment."

"That's fine. I don't smoke much, and that one's a little big for me."

We both turned our attention to the street then, and I was afraid that Stormclaw was going to clam up on me. But it turned out that he wasn't done talking after all. Without taking his eyes off the stream of pedestrians, he asked me, "You ever see Zyanya sing?"

I glanced at him, surprised. Maybe the trollshine had loosened his tongue, or maybe he was just in one of those moods. "Couple of times."

"She could really belt out a tune."

"Sure could. Good looking dame, too."

"Poor judge of men, though."

Once again, I shot Stormclaw a glance. His face remained impassive, but I sensed that he had something more that he wanted me to hear. That was swell with me. Gathering information was my business.

"I take it you're not a fan of the mayor?"

Stormclaw continued watching the pedestrians stream by. "He's a damned jackass. They say that he made Zyanya's career. I think that she would have been better off without him."

"Sounds like she was pretty upset when he dumped her."

Stormclaw shot me a quick glance. Then he picked his cigar stub out of the ashtray, and, discovering that it had gone out, took the time to re-light it before speaking. "I'll never understand what goes through a woman's mind. It's not like she lacked alternatives. She had a ton of admirers to pick from. Any of them would have treated her better than Mayor fuckin' Teague." He drawled the last three words out, spitting them out with contempt.

I gave him a long look as he filled the lobby with cigar smoke. He seemed to know what I was thinking. "Don't look at me that way. She wouldn't have given an old-timer like me a tumble, even if I was human. Besides, I'm much too old to be interested in anyone in that way anymore. I've been done with all that bullshit since Flavia." The old troll gave me a sidelong glance. "Gordo, on the other hand.... He was in love with Zyanya."

I chewed this over a bit. "No shit?"

"Head over heels. And him with a pretty wife and two good kids." The troll placed his cigar back in the ashtray. "Just couldn't help himself, I guess."

"How'd she feel about him?"

"The songbird? Big star like her? She never gave him the time of day! Fulton had him watching her a lot there towards the end, but I doubt that she ever even knew his name. He was just one of Fulton's flunkies."

"Her death must have hit him hard."

Stormclaw nodded. "He doesn't show it, but, yeah, I think it did."

We both turned to the window. No two-foot earth demons popped up from the street. The Sihuanaba didn't walk through the doors of the Grand Pinnacle.

After a few minutes of silence, Stormclaw spoke again. "Funny how it works. Lots of people can sing, and a lot of people who can sing are good looking. Most of them wind up waiting tables. Some people with little or no talent stumble into the right situation, or meet the right people, and become big fucking stars. Doesn't seem to be any rhyme or reason to it. When it comes down to it, it's just dumb luck."

I nodded. "True enough."

Stormclaw took a sip from his flask. "Take Zyanya's sister, Nina. She's a cute little canary in her own right. Maybe if Teague had seen her first, she'd'a been the one headlining at the Gold Coast."

My heart skipped a beat as adrenaline shot through my system. Did Fulton know about Edie and me? Did Gordo and his crew? I decided to bluff it out. "Zyanya has a sister?"

"Sure! Cute kid, like I said. Good singer. I mean, I'm no expert, but as far as I'm concerned she's just as good as Zyanya was. She pops up at bars and small clubs from time to time. Gotta hand it to her for not trying to capitalize on her little sister's fame. I don't know that too many people even knew that the two were related."

"Her name's Nina?"

"That's what she goes by. It might be a stage name, though. She's trying to do the 'one name' thing, like Zyanya. It hasn't done much for her so far, though. At least she's not waiting tables, not as far as I know, anyway."

I sat back in my chair. If Stormclaw knew that I was seeing Nina—Edie—he wasn't showing his hand. "You say that Nina's pretty good? I'll have to check her out some time."

The troll looked at me and smiled. "She's a doll! Young man like you will definitely want to catch her act."

"You ever meet her?"

The troll's eyes widened. "In person you mean? Nah! I've just seen her from the audience. No reason a mug like me would ever get to meet someone like her."

"Why not? You met her sister, didn't you?"

"That was different. It was part of the job. But I didn't really *meet* the dame. I just happened to be there when the mayor was with her. I used to drive them around a lot." He shook his head. "Those two fought like animals!"

"Did he ever knock her around?"

"Oh yeah! And she used to give it right back to him. That dame could throw a mean hook, let me tell you! Then after a little of that she'd start in with the cryin', and he'd get all hangdog and start apologizing', and the next thing I knew they'd be tearing at each other's clothes and sucking at each other's faces like a couple of schoolkids. And me? I'd just be watching the road, Jack. Just watching the road."

I decided that I'd better get off the subject. "Speaking of watching, have you spotted any dark-haired women in white dresses out there?"

Stormclaw gave the boulevard a quick scan. "White dresses don't seem to be too popular among the youngsters these days. Short little black dresses seem to be the trend. It's a wonder those little girls don't freeze to death!"

We turned our attention to the pedestrians for the next hour or so. Stormclaw finished his cigar, and I sipped from my flask. We spoke little and said nothing of importance. As the hour approached ten, the traffic in front of the window grew thicker and noisier, both in the street and on the sidewalks. Horns honked and people laughed and shouted. At one point, a minor altercation broke out as a couple of inebriated young swifties tried to damage each other with wild haymakers and bear hugs while their pals cheered them on. No one suffered any lasting harm, and the skirmish quickly degenerated into a contest to see who could scream the least creative expletives at the greatest volume.

Stormclaw had watched the scuffle with a detached expression. When it was over, he turned to me. "Think either of those jokers ever saw combat?"

I scratched at the side of my chin. "Nothing that mattered."

The troll resumed watching the street. "I wouldn't be too sure. Those yay-hoos probably did their service time sorting mail and copying insurance forms, and I hear those interoffice turf wars can get pretty brutal."

"Everyone has a part to play in the Lord's service." I took a nip from my flask and put it away. It was already half empty and we still had a long night ahead of us.

"Very true." Stormclaw nodded in the direction where the scuffle had occurred. "Our little songbird could have taken either of those lollipops. She slugged the mayor harder than those bums hit each other."

"Think they'll kiss and make up?"

"Sure they will. And eventually one of them heroes will pull out a rod and the other one will wind up dead. It's all a big party until the iron comes out."

I nodded. "Seems like everyone has a gun these days."

The old troll picked at his ear with a taloned finger. "So many guns, so little sense. And they do the same amount of damage no matter who's pulling the trigger. Good thing Zyanya didn't own a firearm. Otherwise, she'd a put the mayor in the ground a long time ago, and this old troll woulda had to retire!"

I glanced over at him. "You don't want to retire?"

Stormclaw's lips parted in a smile. He indicated the vista on the other side of the picture window. "And give up all this?" He sat back in his seat, chuckling softly while he focused his attention on the bustle of the streets in Midtown on a Saturday night.

Chapter Twenty-Two

A few minutes later, I stretched, put my hat on my head, and stood. "My turn for a walk."

Stormclaw nodded. "Might want to circle the block a time or two."

"Sounds like a plan. Want me to pick you up anything while I'm out?"

"There's a cigar stand back that way up the street. Get me something long and thick."

He started to reach for his wallet, but I waved him off. "This one's on me," I told him, and I headed for the door before he could object.

Once out of the building, I stood for a few moments and breathed in the crisp night air. At some point, the fog had drifted in from the ocean and was starting to settle over the city. I pulled up my collar, made sure my hat was snug, and headed in the direction of the cigar stand with my hands planted deep in my coat pockets. I walked slowly, keeping both eyes on the milling pedestrians, looking for a tell-tale splash of white fabric in the multi-colored swarms of clothing. My attention was caught for a moment by a dark-haired woman in a white dress, but she was chatting and laughing with three female friends in a manner that was uncharacteristic of a spirit of vengeance. I saw another woman in a white coat, but it was unbuttoned at the collar and I saw that she was wearing dark blue underneath. I also saw a few gnomes and a couple of dwarfs, but none were built like the creature that had evaded us at the lake.

The open-air cigar stand stood two blocks up the street in the opposite direction of the plaza, and I reached it without incident. I bought the largest cigar in the place and decided to pick up a late-edition newspaper while I had the opportunity. I figured that if the night stayed quiet, Stormclaw and I could take turns reading it. Leaving the stand, I made my way down a cross street so that I could circle back behind the Pinnacle and come back up from the other direction.

The cross street was less crowded than the boulevard that ran in front of the apartment tower, and less well-lit once I passed out of the range of the corner streetlamp, although my enhanced vision worked as well in the dark as it did in the light. I decided to investigate a broad driveway that led to a loading bay in the rear of the Pinnacle. The driveway served as a service road for the trucks and vans that brought food and other supplies to the kitchen facilities, and it was closed to all but authorized vehicles. Anyone could walk in, though, and it occurred to me that someone trying to sneak into the building might try forcing his—or her—way through the access doors at the back of the loading bay.

Although a couple of cars were parked near the building, and the area was illuminated to some extent by a couple of overhead lamps that extended from above the metal sliding door at the end of the loading bay and the employee-entrance door next to it, no one was working in the area at the moment. A little casual snooping seemed to be called for, so I meandered past the parked vehicles, keeping my eyes peeled for anything out of the ordinary.

As I drew close to the loading bay, I spotted what appeared to be a small bundle of dirty blankets piled up against the side of the building near the doors. I studied the bundle from a distance and saw a pair of marble-sized orbs shining like the eyes of a jungle cat reflecting the moonlight. The eyes followed me as I stepped toward the bundle. Trying to give off non-threatening vibes, I put a smile on my face. "Good evening, brother. Feeling the cold tonight?"

A pair of hands reached up out of the bundle, and thick fingers pulled the blanket back to reveal a dusky round human-looking face framed by a head of matted black hair tied into a topknot by a thin hemp cord. I sensed no hint of uneasiness, much less fear, in the dark eyes that continued to study me from beneath a pair of arched eyebrows that rose to a point, like two inverted 'V's. As I came closer, I heard a quick sniff and watched the pug nose wrinkle. The blanket lowered a little farther, and I could see that the figure had no discernable neck separating his head from his broad shoulders. A feathered vest hung down from his shoulders, exposing a chest as thick and solid as a beer barrel. He looked a lot more formidable than the round-bellied nirumbees I'd seen in the article I'd read. A knife hilt carved from bone extended from a sheath attached to a thick leather belt. When I was within six feet of the figure, he rose to his full height, all thirty-some inches of him. The blanket fell to the ground, and I marveled at the creature's upper arms, which were as big around as grapefruits. The creature reached up and pulled a homemade cigar stub from his lips. He dropped the stub to the asphalt, where it joined a pile of identical burned-out stubs. Without taking his eyes from mine, the creature opened his mouth just wide enough to expose an impossible number of menacing pointed teeth, and a low growl began to emanate from deep within his chest.

I held up both hands, palms out. "Whoa, big fella. I come in peace."

A voice that sounded like a chain-smoking twelve-year-old emerged from the creature. "What kept you, Southerland? It's fuckin' freezin' out here!"

I tried to make sense of the creature's question. "You've been expecting me?"

"Either you or the old troll. Stormclaw, right? I assumed that one of you would've checked out this loading bay hours ago. This is a logical place for the Deer Woman to get into the building. Good thing *someone* around here has the brains to stake this place out." The creature reached for the blanket and wrapped himself in it. "Ho, bo—you don't happen to have something to take some of the bite out of this night air, do you? It gets plenty cold where I'm from, but I'll never get used to this fuckin' fog!"

Without speaking, I took the flask out of my pocket and offered it to the creature. He tossed a slug down his throat and immediately broke out into a fit of coughing. "Shit, bo! You drink this swill? It tastes like you distilled it in your fuckin' toilet!" He flung the flask in my direction and I used both hands to catch it.

The creature sniffed with a sound like a small motor, loudly cleared his throat, and spat a vile-looking blob to one side. He made a lot of noise for something the size of a teddy bear. I wiped the mouth of the flask off with my coat and returned it to my pocket. "Who the hell *are* you?" I asked.

The creature looked up at me from somewhere down below my belt. "You can call me Ralph."

"Ralph? Really?"

"Got a problem with that, Beanpole?"

"No, Ralph's a fine name. It's just not what I expected. You're a nirumbee, right?"

Ralph blinked in surprise. "Give the man a cigar! I'm surprised you've heard of us. We call ourselves the Awwakkulé, but for some reason other people call us nirumbees. I don't know why. Makes us sound fuckin' cute, I guess. Don't try to call *me* cute, though, or I'll fuckin' rip your arm off!"

I stared at the nirumbee for a moment, trying to keep my jaw from dropping. "That was you down at the lake, right? The one who was watching us and then escaped into an earth elemental."

The creature snorted. "I wasn't escaping you. I just didn't want to have to bust you up until I knew what you all were doing out there."

"That was your van at the boat launch. The white one with the Lakota plates and the empty cartons of yonak."

Ralph nodded. "Not bad! You ain't as fuckin' stupid as you look. Not quite, anyway."

"So what's your racket? What brought you here in such a hurry?"

The nirumbee sneered. "I already told you—the Deer Woman! Maybe you *are* as stupid as you look!"

I felt heat rising up the back of my neck. "You got a smart mouth on you, half-pint."

The nirumbee's eyes narrowed. "Yeah? Whatcha gonna do about it, skinny? Try something and I'll fuckin' break you in half!"

I don't know why. Maybe the frustration I'd been feeling over this case was getting to me. I didn't like anything about it. Two bigshot fixers were trying to pit me against each other, and I didn't give a fuck about either of them. Lack of sleep was getting to me, and I'd left my manners in my desk drawer when I left the apartment that night. Or maybe I simply didn't like this disrespectful homunculus treating me like I was some kind of joke. I hadn't cared for the way the creature had flung my booze back at me without so much as a "thanks anyway." Or maybe it was because I'd been knocked for a loop by the revelation that the doll I'd just met, and who already had me seeing rainbows and moonbeams, might be using me to get herself knocked up. Whatever the reason, I lost control. Without planning to, I aimed a kick at the creature, intending to plant my toe square in his midsection.

My foot flew through thin air. Even with my elf-enhanced awareness, I never saw what happened. Suddenly, there was a weight on my shoulder, and I felt the nick of something sharp on my right ear.

"Make a move, motherfucker, and I'll drive this pig-sticker up your ear canal, through your eardrum, and straight into your little pea brain. Get the picture?"

I froze. "Yeah, I got it."

"Good!" I felt the weight leave my shoulders as the nirumbee flipped over my head, twisted in the air, and landed on his feet, facing me. He re-sheathed his knife, but not before I caught a glimpse of its thin polished black blade. Flint, I guessed. Probably sharper than my shaving razor.

Okay, this hadn't gone the way I expected, and it was my own damned fault. It was time to readjust my attitude. I drew in a long slow breath and let my anger flow out of me as I exhaled. "Please allow me to apologize. It's been a long couple of days, but that's no excuse for me to try to take it out on someone I just met."

The nirumbee relaxed by a degree. "Not that you could have done nothing about it anyway."

"Guess not, Ralph. You're a quick little devil, I'll give you that!"

Ralph's lips widened into an openmouthed smile that showed off plenty of sharp teeth. "Too fast for an oaf like you, that's for sure." He stopped smiling and held up a hand. "Okay, sorry. I guess I *do* have a fuckin' mouth on me. Let's start over. We're on the same side. You're trying to protect that idiot mayor of yours from the Deer Woman, am I right? I'm after her, too. And I think she's gonna try something tonight, so we need to stop with the gab and make sure she doesn't get anywhere near your mayor." He looked me up and down. "Hope you're up for it. I don't trust those clumsy trolls to take three steps without tripping over their own feet."

I stared down at the nirumbee. "Deer Woman? That's what you call her?"

"Of course! Why? What do *you* call her?"

"The Sihuanaba."

"The see—what? I've never heard that one before."

"That's what they call her in the Borderland."

"Really! Didn't know she traveled in those parts." The nirumbee shrugged.

I looked the nirumbee up and down. "What do you know about her?"

"The Deer Woman? She's a fuckin' monster! Only a crazy man would get anywhere near her on purpose."

I nodded. "Right. We should go home."

Ralph spit to one side. "Probably. Can't, though. Gotta job to do."

I considered this. "Yeah, me too. Don't tell me that we're working for the same client."

An odd expression appeared on the nirumbee's face. "Who can say? But if you're asking if I take my orders from that shithead Fulton, then, no. That cocksucker can kiss my wrinkled old ass!"

I had more questions for Ralph, but they died on my lips as I saw his eyes dilate and focus on something behind me. I was aware of a sudden movement, but before I could turn I found myself lying on the asphalt in a heap with a dull throbbing pain just below my right ear. I heard a thud off to one side and turned to see Ralph sprawled on his face. I glimpsed a flash of white and looked up to see a dark-haired woman in a long white dress standing over the nirumbee's prone body. Her head whipped in my direction as I pushed myself to my hands and knees. Her hair, now transformed into a drab, almost colorless gray, flew to one side and revealed the hag's hideous horse-jawed face. Drool dripped off the two canine fangs that extended above her upper lip from her lower jaw. Her eyes gleamed purple in the reflected light from the street. She took two quick strides in my direction, pointing at me with a taloned finger. Her mouth opened wide, and I *felt* her shriek. I fell back to the asphalt, unable to do anything except cover my ears with my hands. The shriek continued, and I felt blood pour out of my ears through my fingers.

A voice from somewhere deep inside was screaming at me to move, but it couldn't break through the chaos in my brain to reach whatever button it needed to push. Curled into a fetal position on the asphalt, helpless as a newborn, I felt clawed fingers grip my neck. It occurred to me that death would be a blessing if it freed me from the Sihuanaba's torturous shrieking. I felt a burning sensation around my neck, as if I were being garroted by a white-hot metal wire.

Then, all at once, the onslaught stopped, and, although my neck still burned, I felt the claws draw back from my flesh. I looked up to see the hag standing over me, a scowl on her misshapen face. Suddenly, she shot to one side with Ralph's arms wrapped around her knees. The hag fell headlong toward the metal sliding door on the side of the building—and vanished!

***

"Ow." Ralph didn't sound so much pained as disgusted. The hag had blinked away without a trace, leaving Ralph with nothing to hang on to after his flying tackle. He'd fallen straight to the asphalt, face first, and, as a result, blood was leaking out of his nose and down his mouth and chin. He rose to his feet, retrieved his blanket, and pushed it against his face to stop the bleeding.

I was trying to process what had happened. Had the Sihuanaba escaped into an earth elemental, like Ralph had done back at the lake? No, she'd disappeared just before she would have fallen into the sliding door. Could an air elemental have whisked her away like that? As far as I knew, that wasn't possible, and I liked to think that when it came to air elementals I knew what I was talking about. No, the hag had vanished into thin air. I'd seen it happen. Fulton was wrong: whatever the woman in white was, she was *not* a human stalker with a handful of magic tricks or an enchanted device. And the nirumbee wasn't helping her. I filed the new data away for a later time. Right now, I needed to move.

I retrieved my hat, which had fallen from my head during the scuffle. "Ralph! I need to check on the mayor! Right now!"

The nirumbee waved me away. "Go! Do what you need to do. Use that back door—it's faster!"

I ran to the employee-entrance door and tried the handle, but it was locked. I looked back at Ralph, still standing where I'd left him. I detected no more than a blur, and suddenly Ralph was beside me at the door. Before I could open my mouth, the little runt leaped into the air and kicked the door right off its hinges. It fell back and hit the metal floor with a clatter. "Get moving!" he commanded.

More questions for later. I got moving.

As I ran through the inner loading bay, I noticed that the burning sensation around my neck had eased. I reached up, and my fingers fell on Leota's necklace, which I'd forgotten I was wearing. I had picked it up and put it on just before leaving my apartment. For luck, I had told myself, but in truth I hadn't thought much about it at the time. Now I was regretting my impulsive decision. The metal shells were hot to the touch, and the skin beneath them was raw. I didn't think I'd suffered any serious damage, but it was still painful.

I pulled the necklace from around my neck and stuffed it into my pocket. It occurred to me then that the burning sensation I'd felt when the Sihuanaba had grabbed my neck had not come from the hag, but from the necklace. I replayed the attack in my head. Had Ralph driven the Sihuanaba off me? No, I remembered. The hag had pulled back from me, and *then* Ralph had tackled her. I reached into my pocket and fingered the shells, thinking. A memory from my first encounter with the Sihuanaba at Zaculeu came flashing back to me, the memory of waking up on the rooftop with a burning sensation on my skin where Leota's necklace hung from the back of my neck. I stopped running and stood in the darkness of the loading area.

According to the stories I'd heard in the Borderland, no man could look upon the face of the Sihuanaba and live to tell about it. It made for a good story, but I'd never taken it seriously. This was my third encounter with the Sihuanaba, and my second time seeing her face. I was still living, so what made me special? Maybe it wasn't *me* that was special, but the necklace. On the two occasions when the Sihuanaba had actually put her hands on me, the necklace had heated up and the hag had let me go. Had the necklace been enchanted in some way? Leota had never said so, and I couldn't think of any reason why he wouldn't have bragged about it if that were the case. Perhaps there was a simpler explanation.

An idea began to form in my brain. Could it be? I cast my eyes about the loading area, studying the floor and the walls of the modern forty-story structure. I stepped to the nearest wall and rapped on it in several places with my knuckles, listening hard. I recalled the ramshackle apartment building in Zaculeu as best I could. I remembered climbing up the rickety stairwell, hearing noises from the apartments through the thin walls, kicking in the door to the rooftop, watching the old wood paneling splinter....

I stood in the loading area for ten minutes, testing the idea in my mind and thinking about what to do with it. Finally, I searched the area until I found the door to a men's room. I stepped in and examined myself in the mirror. After using a paper towel to clean some grime off my face and to wipe off my coat, I appeared to be none the worse for wear. I left the men's room and exited the building the way I came in, walking over the fallen door and emerging into the outer loading bay.

Ralph was nowhere to be seen. Even his blanket was gone. A small pile of cigar butts was the only sign that the nirumbee had ever been there. I left the loading bay and resumed my circuit around the building, as if nothing had happened. I kept an eye out for the Sihuanaba, just in case, but I didn't think that I would see her again that night. A few minutes later, and without further incident, I made my way back to the front entrance of the Pinnacle.

***

I crossed the lobby to Stormclaw and handed him his cigar. "Anything happen while I was gone?" I asked.

Stormclaw reached for his lighter. "Fella's hat blew off, and he had to chase it down. He kept grabbing for it, and it kept on blowing away from him. It almost made me smile. Other than that, it's been quiet. How 'bout you?"

I plopped down into the cushioned chair. "Nothing. We're wasting our time, old sport. Nobody is going to bother the mayor while he's holed up in a thirty-ninth floor apartment surrounded by bodyguards."

Stormclaw brought his cigar to life and blew smoke toward the ceiling. "I called Gordo a few minutes ago. The mayor's sleeping like a baby. So is Ironshield. Me? I don't sleep much these days. Some old people want more sleep after they get older, but the closer I get to the end, the more I want to be awake for my final days."

I pulled the newspaper out of my coat pocket. "I hope that most of your final days are a little more exciting than this one."

The troll tipped his cigar in my direction. "They're all exciting if you look at it the right way. What could be more exciting than sitting in the lobby of a luxury downtown apartment building and smoking this here fine cigar?"

I laughed at that. "I like your attitude. I wish I could share it." I began to skim the front page of the paper.

I had no intention of telling anyone in my new crew about Ralph and our dustup with the woman in white. I had little doubt that we were all safe from her for the evening, at least, and probably for as long as Fulton kept Teague stashed in his apartment. And if I was wrong, well, so what? I was working for a corrupt asshole to protect a slimeball who wanted to know why he couldn't have some hookers delivered to his downtown luxury suite now that his terrified wife had been driven out of town by her concerned sister. What did I care who sat in the mayor's office? Let Fulton and Benning fight that battle. And with no further obligation, I'd be free to look into Zyanya's death, which was the case I actually wanted to pursue, even if no one was paying me to do it.

I found an article about the two children who had washed up on the shore of Ohlone Lake on page two, and there was no mention of Zyanya and her children. According to the article, the LIA already had a suspect in custody, a transient with a history of child molestation. The article also noted that the local police were continuing to patrol the neighborhood out of "an abundance of caution." Fulton had probably dictated the article word for word.

As I flipped through the paper, I found another item on the goat-headed alley rat on the back page of section three. It was basically a repeat of the earlier article with an additional warning that the creature had broken into a resident's apartment and eluded capture, and that the area's residents should be sure to lock their doors at night. I chuckled to myself. Fat lot of good *that* would do!

I got Stormclaw's attention and pointed to the article. "Hey, Stormclaw—you see this?"

I handed him the paper and waited until he'd finished reading the piece. "Ever see anything like that?"

"Nope."

"More than two hundred years old, traveled all over the world, and you've never run into it?"

"Nope."

I folded the newspaper. "I guess it really *is* rare!"

***

I stayed at the Pinnacle until midnight. Stormclaw and I each took two more circuits around the block, but neither of us ran into the nirumbee or the Sihuanaba. Everything remained quiet upstairs. As far as Gordo's team was concerned, it had been an uneventful night, and I said nothing to make anyone believe otherwise.

Chapter Twenty-Three

I managed to catch the last half hour of Edie's show. She saw me walk into the joint, and her next song was the new one that the band had added to their set. She kept her eyes on me for the entire song, a bluesy torcher that I guess she'd written herself. I don't remember the lyrics all that well, something about a detective, a real private eye, who is searching for answers, the who, how, and why.... I was flattered, and I guess I was grinning like an idiot all through the number. Eric, the bartender with the handlebar mustache, handed me a beer in the middle of it and patted me on the shoulder. He thought I was an all right gee.

Truth is, I was nervous about seeing Edie after the show. As I watched her perform, I couldn't take my eyes off the spider jewel in her navel and wondering what was going on behind it. I was still trying to figure out how I was going to ask her about it when her set ended and she disappeared with her band through the door behind the stage. I drank down the last of my beer and pushed myself off the barstool to follow her.

Edie threw her arms around me as soon as I walked through the door. I hugged her back and lost myself in the scent of her hair and the thin layer of moisture on the back of her neck. After a few long moments, she pulled her head back and pressed her lips against mine while holding me close. Then she jumped away from me, eyes glowing with excitement. "What did you think of my new song?"

"It's my new favorite. I hope you'll sing it to me solo in a more private setting."

Edie hunched her shoulders and let out a squeal. She reached up to put her hand on my cheek. "Come on! I have to get my stuff. It's our last night, and I need to clear it all out of here." She turned and led me back to her makeshift dressing room.

This time, she didn't make me wait outside the room while she changed into a blouse and slacks, and I was surprised by how aroused her nearly nude body in the overhead light of the makeshift dressing room made me. I decided not to ask about the jewel until after I'd walked her home. I suppose that I wanted to delay the conversation as long as possible. We passed a bottle of rye back and forth while she packed her clothes and her makeup. We left the unfinished bottle behind when we walked out the door.

She chatted at me during the walk to her apartment, and I was mostly silent. Most of what she told me didn't register, but she seemed happy, and that was good enough for me. I hoped that she would still be happy after we started to talk for real. When we entered her apartment, she grabbed me by the tie and began leading me to her bedroom, but I wrapped my hand around her wrist and stopped her.

"Hold on, Edie. Can we sit down? There's something I need to ask you about."

Edie rolled her eyes. "Can it wait? I've kind of been looking forward to this all day!"

"Me too, believe me! But, I really need to talk to you first. Please. Can we take a minute?"

Edie's smile disappeared, and she released my tie. "Okay, spoilsport. Be that way!" She walked to an overstuffed couch and plopped down on it, pouting.

I started to follow when I felt some resistance on the side of my leg. I looked down and discovered that Sunny was pressed up against me, head and tail held high as she greeted me.

"Look!" Edie laughed. "Sunny approves!"

Taking care, I stepped around the cat and joined Edie on the couch. Sunny leaped up and curled herself on Edie's lap.

Edie scratched the cat's head between the ears and gazed at me through narrowed eyes. "Okay, mystery man. Hurry up and ask your questions so that we can get down to business."

I plunged in. "It's about your jewel." I dropped my eyes to her midsection, where the spider jewel hid behind Edie's blouse.

Edie looked down and then back up at me. "What about it?"

I hesitated. "Can I see it?"

Edie smiled, and her eyes grew mischievous. "I get it. Got a little bit of a fetish?" She lifted her blouse and exposed the jewel.

I stared at the green-tinged spider, at the vines emerging from its head, the tiny exposed fangs, the outward curling legs. "That's an image of the Great Goddess with no name, right? From Teotihuacan?"

The mischief left Edie's eyes as she glanced down. "Yeah, wow! I'm surprised you know about that. I guess you've been around!"

"How long have you had that?"

"It was my mother's. My parents were from Teotihuacan, and she wore it every day until she died. She left it to me, and I've just started wearing it recently. In her memory, mostly, but also because it looks good on stage."

I met her eyes. "The spider is a fertility goddess, isn't she?"

She shrugged. "That's right. She represents fertility and sexuality. I know it looks strange, maybe even ugly, but I think it's kind of a turn on. Especially with the web. Hey, it might not be your cup of tea, but I kind of got the impression that you liked it. Am I wrong? Is it too weird? Does it put you off?" Her eyes grew round with worry.

"No, no, that's not it. Just the opposite, in fact, which, if you want to know the truth, surprises me quite a lot. But it's...a *fertility* symbol! As in, you know...*fertility*!" I wanted to kick myself for how ridiculous I sounded.

Edie's mouth snapped open and her eyebrows arched. Then she laughed, and Sunny leaped out of her lap to the floor. "Holy moly!" She put a hand on my thigh and held it tight. "Oh, you poor man! You think I'm trying to…. Oh my! You've got it wrong. You poor man." She stifled the last of her laughter and let out a breath. "Ohhh, honey! Oh, you poor dear! Don't worry. The unnamed goddess *is* a fertility goddess, that's true. But it works both ways. Think of her as fertility *control*. She makes you fertile or infertile, depending on how you want it. But I don't know if this one's even got any magic in it. I just wear it because I like it. And besides, I'm on the pill, so you have nothing to worry about, darling! Believe me, the last thing I want at this stage in my career is to be anchored down by a baby. Maybe someday, but now is definitely *not* that time!"

Edie slid her body into mine, and I felt a surge of electricity running through my nether regions as her breasts pressed against my chest. She raised her eyes and gazed into my own. I reached up and cupped the back of her head, and lost myself in her scent as my lips met hers.

***

Sometime later, as we lay together, exhausted, between her black silk sheets, and I was relishing the sensation of her warm, firm skin pressed against mine, Edie raised her head from my chest and asked me, "What would you have done if I had told you that I wanted your baby?"

I reached down to stroke her hair. "I would have let you try to talk me into it."

"Would I have succeeded?"

I thought about it. "I guess that depends on how well you argued your case."

Edie laid her head back on my chest. "I was serious when I said that a baby is the last thing I need in my life right now. I'm not sure I'll ever want children. I had to finish raising three after my mother died, and I'm not anxious to start from scratch." She slid her leg over both of mine. "I hope you're not disappointed."

"To be honest, it's hard to imagine myself as a father. I hope *you're* not disappointed."

Edie giggled and nipped at my chest with her teeth. "Maybe I'll just get you a pet. You like cats?"

"Not especially."

"Have you ever had one? I can see you as a cat person. Sunny likes you."

"I'm too much of a loner to have a pet. Although…. Well, there's this odd creature that wandered into my alley a couple of days ago that seems to want to move in with me."

Edie turned her head to look up at me. "Really? What kind of creature?"

"An ugly one. I caught it going through my garbage cans. I chased it away, but then I left some food out for it the next night so that it would leave my trash alone. Big mistake! It not only ate the food, but it somehow managed to get through my locked door and spend the night in my laundry room."

"What'd you do?"

"I called Animal Control. They sent a team over to pick it up, but it got away. And then this morning it came back, got through my locked door again somehow, and ransacked my refrigerator! The little bastard did a real number on my kitchen."

Edie sat up cross-legged in the bed, favoring me with one of the better vistas I'd experienced in my life. "Holy moly! What the fuck *is* it?"

"I don't know. It's like some kind of deformed goat. It has the head of a goat with long curved horns. But it has spikes down the length of its spine and a long hairless tail, like a giant rat. It's got what look almost like human feet and hands, except that it's got sharp talons on its fingers and toes. And it can walk upright when it wants to. Oh, and its eyes are red, and they glow like a troll's, which makes me think it might be hellspawn."

Edie stared at me openmouthed as I described the creature. When I was finished, she said, "It sounds like the Huay Chivo!"

"The why what?"

"Huay Chivo! Except that's impossible!"

"Animal Control says that it's rare."

"Rare! There's only one!" Edie's eyes were wide. "My mother used to tell us stories about it."

I braced my pillow against the headboard and sat up. "What kind of stories?"

"Stories she learned from *her* mother, my grandmother. My grandmother was a bruja in Teotihuacan. Well, maybe she was a bruja. She might have been a fake. But she sold charms and amulets to people in her neighborhood. She gave this Great Goddess jewel to my mother, and my mother gave it to me." Edie reached down and rubbed the ornament in her bellybutton. "Anyway, according to my mother, a long time ago this powerful sorcerer-king used to rule a kingdom somewhere in Qusco. And then the Dragon Lord Manqu showed up and claimed authority over the whole continent. This sorcerer-king tried to resist, and he sent his army against Manqu. But he was defeated, and Manqu transformed the sorcerer-king into this goat creature and banished him from Qusco. He wound up in the region of Teotihuacan. After that, he was called the Huay Chivo, which means 'sorcerer goat.' According to the stories, he can kill livestock by staring them in the eyes, and after he kills them he drinks their blood."

"Some joker from Animal Control wanted to know if I had looked into the creature's eyes and whether I was sick. And then this blowhard came out and wanted to examine me."

Edie stared at me. "And were you? Sick, I mean?"

I shook my head. "No. I remember that I felt a wave of nausea when the creature first looked at me, but it passed, and after that I didn't have any trouble with it. At least, not *that* kind of trouble. He's a pain in the ass, though. I should never have left him food. I can't figure out why my locks won't keep him out."

"He's a sorcerer! Or at least he was. According to my mother's stories, his mind's all messed up. He's like a really smart animal now, or like a very insane shell of what he used to be."

"Well, I think he's gonna be hanging around for a while. I left food out for him again tonight. Or last night now, I guess. It was the only way I could figure out how to keep him from making a mess of my kitchen again."

Edie smiled. "So you *do* have a pet! What are you going to name him?"

"He's already got a name, right? Huay Chivo?"

"*The* Huay Chivo. That's not really his name. It's just what he is."

"Well, once I can catch him, he's going off with Animal Control. He smells like shit, and I can't have him driving away clients."

"Awwww…." Edie protested. "That's no way to treat an ancient sorcerer who wants to be your friend."

"Tell you what. *You* can have him!"

Edie squealed. "No way, buster! He'll eat Sunny!"

I sighed. "I hate to say this, but I've got to work today. Believe it or not, I'm going to be the mayor's caddy."

"You're going to what?"

I couldn't help but chuckle. "I know, right? The mayor's going golfing this afternoon. I've been hired to help protect him, and he wants me to be his caddy."

Edie stared at me openmouthed. "You're going to be Teague's bodyguard?"

"One of them."

Edie's mouth closed, and she frowned. "So he's going to be golfing. Galindo Arms?"

"Yup. Pretty classy digs for a working class stiff like me, right?"

"Uh-huh, I suppose." Edie seemed distracted.

It struck me that I might have made a mistake telling Edie that I was going to be protecting the man that she blamed for her sister's death, and I decided that I'd better change the subject. "Anyway, I need to go home and get some shuteye. Maybe I'll catch the Chivo and get him hauled away once and for all."

"What, you've got to go *now*?" Edie lowered her head into my lap. "Are you sure about that, big man?"

It turned out that I was wrong. I didn't have to go home right away after all.

***

"Smokey, meet Edie."

"Greetings, Edie. How's trickssss?"

Edie squealed "He's adorable!"

"*It's* adorable. Elementals don't have genders."

During a lull in the action, Edie, impressed by Badass, had asked me about my ability to summon elementals, so I'd introduced her to Smokey. She pulled her hand from beneath the sheet and flattened her palm. "Can I touch it?"

"Smokey, stand on Edie's hand." Smokey drifted over to the palm of Edie's hand and whirled like a two-inch twister.

Edie's grin spread from ear to ear. "That's so crazy! It tickles! Does he do tricks?"

"It's not a pet. Smokey's my associate. When it isn't spinning, it's an invisible puff of air. It sees and hears everything, and it's got an excellent memory. Pretty handy to have around in my line of work."

"Well, I hope you pay him well."

"That's the best part. It doesn't need dough. When it's not working for me, it hangs around in the rafters at the Minotaur Lounge, soaking in smoke and whiskey fumes. Not a bad life when you think about it."

"Well, I wish he could live with me when he's not working. He could chase Sunny around the apartment and give her some exercise. I bet they'd have a swell time together."

I scooped Smokey off the palm of Edie's hand and lifted the elemental to my shoulder. "Speaking of work, I haven't had any sleep and I think that the sun is going to be coming up soon. I wish I could stay, baby, but…."

Edie sighed. "I understand." I felt her leg drape over mine. "How about one more for the road, big man?"

***

Later, when I was dressed and getting ready to leave, I sat on the bed next to Edie, who had drifted into a doze. I studied her for a while, letting my gaze linger for a few moments on the scar under her left eye and the sideways bend in the tip of her nose. When Edie was in my arms, it was easy to forget how little I actually knew about her. I doubted that she was born with that scar and a crooked nose, and I wondered about the violence that had caused them. She'd never spoken of it, and I hadn't asked. Did I want to know, and, if so, why? Because I wanted to know this fascinating woman more intimately? Or was it because she was part of my investigation into her sister's death. As a professional, I knew that it was a mistake to become romantically involved with a person of interest in a case. As a man, I'd been willing to take my chances, and I had no regrets. Not yet, anyway. I leaned down and kissed Edie's forehead. If I was making a mistake, I'd fix it later. For now, being with Edie felt right.

Edie moaned, but kept her eyes shut. "I'm leaving now," I whispered. In response, Edie, eyes still shut, turned on to her back and kicked off the covers, exposing her nude body.

I looked down at her and shook my head. "Sorry, baby. There's nothing left in the tank. I'm beat!"

Edie's lips curled into a pout. "Ohhhh," she protested. "You're no fun." Her eyes were still closed, and I wasn't sure that she was even awake.

I took one more long slow look at her body, wanting to memorize every gorgeous detail so that I could remember this moment for the rest of my life. When my eyes fell on the spider jewel, I smiled to myself, remembering how apprehensive I'd been when I'd come to the club to walk Edie home. My eyes drifted across Edie's bare midriff and over the tattooed webbing surrounding the jewel. And then I leaned down to get a closer look. For the first time, I noticed a trace of red, like an inflammation, along the edges of some of the webbing.

"Edie, how long have you had this tattoo?"

Edie turned her head in my direction, but still didn't open her eyes. "Dunno," she muttered. "Week..., two mebbe." She reached out and grabbed the inside of my thigh. "Come back to bed, baby."

I kissed her on the cheek and gently pulled myself out of her grasp. "Can't, sugar. I'll call you this afternoon after I've finished babysitting the mayor."

***

I found the Huay Chivo in my laundry room curled up on a folded blanket that I'd laid on the floor next to the washing machine. He'd brought the carton of yonak into the room with him, and it had been licked clean. The creature's eyes were closed, and he was making soft snoring sounds. Sleep sounded like a wonderful idea, the most wonderful idea in the world. The overgrown alley rat didn't seem like he was going to cause any problems, sacked out like he was. He still smelled like a combination of dead possum and wet carpet, though, so I summoned two elementals and instructed them to funnel the odor out through the open window. Satisfied for the moment, I left the room, closing the door softly behind me.

Soon, I was in my own bed and under my own covers. I found myself missing Edie's silk sheets and thought I could get used to them in a hurry. On the other hand, I thought that I might have a better chance of getting some actual shuteye now that I was alone. Not that I'd be able to get much—it was a little late in the morning for that! I decided to allow myself four hours of sleep, and, after making sure that my shades were closed tight to prevent the light from the upcoming sunrise to disturb me, I set my phone's alarm accordingly. That wouldn't give me a lot of time before I was supposed to caddy for the mayor, but I'd have to make it work. I closed my eyes and searched for the gates to dreamland.

My brain insisted on wrestling with puzzles, however, so while I'd hoped to grab forty winks before the alarm went off, I wound up having to settle for about fifteen. I turned off the alarm and rolled out of bed right away so that I wouldn't be tempted to sleep in. I opened the shades and let the sunshine fill my room. It was already shaping up to be a fine day, good for golf. Whatever questions my subconscious had been trying to answer dissipated into the air like smoke from the tip of a cigarette. I took a deep breath and stretched. Shortchanged as I'd been, I felt like I could get through the day, at least once I'd consumed a quart of coffee.

I checked on the Huay Chivo and found him still sleeping off his dinner in the laundry room. The elementals had succeeded in reducing the stench to a bearable level, so I released them from their service and sent them off to rejoin the world of winds and breezes. Turning my attention to the sleeping alley rat, I considered my options. I could call Animal

Control, I told myself, but then the blowhard would send his soldier boys charging through my office, and then he'd try to give me a physical examination, and the creature would be gone by the time they searched the house, and who needed all that hoopla anyway. Besides, I had matters that I wanted to take care of before I was scheduled to leave for the golf course. I wasn't looking forward to going, and I was hopeful that if things fell my way I'd be able to get myself out from under that obligation. I decided that if Chivo didn't bother me, I wouldn't bother him.

I turned to walk out of the laundry room, when I noticed that one of the elementals that I'd dismissed was still hovering a few feet above my dryer. It had stopped spinning and was drifting like a fat bubble. "I released you from my service," I told it.

The voice that emerged from the bubble was deep and sonorous. "This one will stay."

That was curious. "Why?" I asked.

"This one fits here."

I scratched my head and yawned. "If I need you later to blow the smell out of this room, will you be available to serve?"

"This one will be ready."

I shrugged. "Fine. Stay as long as you like."

"This one will. This one fits here."

Okay, I could live with that.

The next order of business was breakfast. After some fried eggs, sourdough toast, and two cups of coffee, along with a promise to myself that I'd have at least two more before I left the house, I went down to my office and fired up my computer. I kept the "Closed" sign up on my front door so that I wouldn't be disturbed by any walk-in business, not that I got a lot of that in this age of the internet. I figured that I had less than two hours to find what I needed in order to get myself out of carrying the mayor's golf clubs. First on the agenda was to find confirmation for the theory that I'd formed about the Sihuanaba. I sifted through internet sites for more than an hour before I found what I was looking for. An academic working in something called the Quscan Ministry of Culture had written an article comparing the folk tales that had been told by the indigenous people of Qusco to the stories still told by the farmers and working people in the Borderland. The obvious intent of the article was to strengthen Dragon Lord Manqu's claim to the disputed territory by showing that the culture of the Borderland was rooted in the traditions of Qusco. Ignoring the political bullshit, I skimmed through the article until I found a short section on the Sihuanaba. The author had only devoted three paragraphs to the woman in white, and I was already familiar with most of the details, but one of the paragraphs provided me with the clue I'd been searching for. I stopped and reread the passage: "According to one story, only the farmers of the Kingdom of Cholula were able to withstand the Sihuanaba. To get rid of her evil intentions, these farmers would bite on the blades of their machetes, which would make her disappear instantly." After a few more minutes of digging, I knew that I had something.

My research showed me that Cholula was an advanced pre-Dragon Lord kingdom located in the highlands of what would become southern Azteca. Although Cholula's roots predated known history, the ancient society hadn't long survived the coming of Dragon Lord Ketz-Alkwat, who claimed the entire northern continent as far south as the Isthmus for his new realm of Tolanica. Much more recently, with the development of large-scale ocean trade and transportation, Lord Ketz developed a desire to have a canal carved through the narrow land of the Isthmus in order to connect the Nihhonese and Atlantis Oceans. At that point, Lord Manqu declared that his realm of Qusco had originally extended much farther to the north, and that he had tolerated Ketz-Alkwat's impertinence long enough. Manqu's real target, of course, was the Isthmus, but, figuring that if he was going to lay claim to a little territory he might as well lay claim to a lot, he declared himself to be the rightful ruler of all the land up to the Cutzyetelkeh Peninsula. Thus, the Borderland was born. The ruins of ancient Cholula, located in the northern part of the disputed region, were destroyed in the conflicts between the forces of the two Dragon Lords, and the old kingdom was all but forgotten. But I happened to know someone who had done some archeological work in that part of the world, and I was hopeful that he could tell me what I needed to know. I took out my phone and punched in a number.

"Hello?"

"Is this Dr. Kai Kalama?"

"Speaking."

"Hello, Kai. This is Alex Southerland."

"Oh, the gumshoe! Are you trying to reach Laurel? Unfortunately, she got called in to work."

"They never let her rest, do they. Actually, though, I was hoping that I'd catch *you* at home today."

"Me? What can I do for you?"

I'd never met Detective Kalama's husband, nor had I ever spoken to him on the phone, but the detective had told me a lot about him. Dr. Kalama was a history professor at Yerba City U, specializing in the ancient settlements of pre-Dragon Lord Tolanica. He also supervised a couple of archeological digs in Azteca outside Tenochtitlan. I knew that he spent a good part of his summer breaks at the digs, and I was glad that I'd been able to catch him at home.

"I'm working a case that involves some old stories from the Borderland. I was hoping that you might be able to shed some light on them."

"The Borderland? It's a little out of my area of specialty, but I'll try. Whatcha got?"

"How much do you know about the Kingdom of Cholula?"

"Ahhhh, Cho-*luuu*-la! Fascinating place! It's a damned shame that we can't get access to it anymore. I've dreamed of sneaking into the militarized zone and doing some digging. It's just a hop skip and a jump from my site outside of Tenochtitlan, but with the conflict going on there it may as well be on the moon! You know about the pyramid of Cholula, right? Excavated just ten years before the fighting broke out. I think that one of the reasons Lord Manqu extended his claim as far north as he did was because he wanted Cholula in his realm. But the pyramid didn't survive the first year of fighting. I'd give my right arm to be able to go there and see what's left." He paused for a moment. "Sorry, Alex. You know how we professors are. We get all carried away over things that no one else gives a damn about."

"No problem, Kai! I happen to be interested in Cholula right now. It touches on a case that I'm working on."

"What do you want to know?"

"I'm interested in their tools and weapons. Specifically, I want to know about the materials they used to make their blades."

Kai didn't answer right away. When he did, I detected a note of suspicion in his voice. "Why do you ask? If you've run across some sort of artifact, I'd like to know about it, and what you intend to do with it."

"Nothing like that, professor. We're not talking about a smuggling operation or anything criminal. It's just that I've run into something out of the ordinary. I don't want to get into specifics at the moment, but I promise to tell you about it when things settle. Right now I just need to know whether the Cholulans had any special technology that other people in the area didn't have access to."

"Hmmm." Kai still sounded skeptical. I gathered that he was sensitive about historical objects falling into the hands of private collectors. He went on with some reluctance. "We-e-ell, the obvious feature of Cholulan culture that set them apart from their neighbors was their use of iron, but other than that I can't think of anything unique."

"Iron? Didn't all those old kingdoms use iron?"

"No, not at all! Iron is very rare in that part of the world." Kai sounded less reluctant now. An opportunity to lecture had presented itself, and his professor instincts kicked in. "Copper, silver, and gold are much more common in Southern Tolanica, both then and now. Now, farther south, in pre-Manqu Qusco, copper smelting was fairly common, but mostly for jewelry and other ornaments. Not so much for functional objects, like swords or plows. Those were almost universally made of sharpened stone, such as flint. They certainly didn't have access to iron. But up in Southern Tolanica, copper smelting was almost nonexistent. The big exception was the Moche, who smelted copper with gold, silver, and arsenic, but, again, mostly for jewelry." Dr. Kalama paused for a beat. "A lot of that jewelry was highly pornographic, by the way. If you ever run across any samples, I'd be pleased to know about it—for professional reasons, of course!"

"You'll be the first person I call, I promise. But getting back to Cholula…."

"Yes, yes! Sorry. I *did* warn you, right? Anyway, Cholula…. Unlike the rest of the settlements of Southern Tolanica, the Cholulans discovered a substantial deposit of iron, perhaps from a large meteorite, and learned how to smelt it from the ore. They used the iron for jewelry and other trinkets, but also to make weapons, armor, and farming implements."

"Like machetes?"

"Like machetes, certainly!" The professor was rolling now, as he found himself in his element. "It was their use of iron for functional objects that made them culturally unique, not to mention powerful. They fought with iron weapons and armor when all of their neighbors were still using wood, stone, and tree bark. The location of their iron mines was a closely guarded secret, and the Cholulan kings controlled all of the production and distribution. By monopolizing the iron, the Cholulans dominated their neighbors and constructed a fairly sizable kingdom that lasted for several hundred years. Maybe a thousand. It's tricky pinning anything down in these old communities. Unfortunately, the deposits proved to be finite, and, eventually, the Cholulans tapped it out. The kingdom grew weaker after that, and then Lord Ketz arrived and mopped them up. Much about Cholula is a mystery today, and anything from there that still survives would be of great academic interest, not to mention incredibly valuable to dealers and collectors. If you've run into rumors of an iron machete from that period...."

I laughed. "I assure you that I haven't. But, thanks, that information confirms a theory that I've formed regarding the case I'm working on. You've been very helpful, and I appreciate it."

"Thanks! It's not often that anyone finds a practical use for the esoteric knowledge that we gravediggers uncover. I'm glad you called. Laurel isn't a fan of private investigators, but she says that you have more integrity than most. We should meet for a drink some time."

"Thanks, Kai. That sounds good. I've never been much of a history buff. The present gives me all I can handle. But I've been running into a lot of old stories lately, and I bet you've got some interesting ones of your own that you could tell."

"Tell that to my students! Anytime you want to talk about the history of ancient Tenochtitlan, let me know. Just tell me when you've heard enough. Laurel says that I don't know when my audience is getting bored."

I thought about Edie's spider ornament. "Just for the record, how valuable would a trinket from the pre-Dragon Lord period be? I mean, it would have to be more than six thousand years old, right?"

When I didn't get an immediate response, I thought that the professor had disconnected the call. "Kai?" I asked. "You still there?"

"I'm here," came the response. "I'm just considering my answer to your question. You're assuming that Lord Ketz-Alkwat established the Realm of Tolanica about six thousand years ago. That's what they told you in school, and that's what all the history books say."

I was confused. "What are you saying, Kai?"

"I'm not saying anything. Especially on the telephone. But keep in mind that every school curriculum and every history book is carefully vetted by the Dragon Lord's offices in Aztlan. Most people think of history as a collection of unalterable facts, but, in truth, it's anything but. History is a fragile thing, Alex. It's easily molded by the people who control the flow of information."

I thought about that. "Kai, I'm really looking forward to that drink."

***

After we said our goodbyes, I leaned back in my desk chair and enjoyed some moments of satisfaction. Iron! That was the Sihuanaba's weakness. And steel, too, which is mostly iron with a little carbon mixed in. The farmers of Cholula drove the Sihuanaba away with their iron machetes, by biting on them according to the Quscan academic, but that seemed doubtful, and I suspected that those farmers put their blades to use in a more traditional way. The steel-jacketed shells in Leota's necklace seemed to react to the Sihuanaba's touch, repelling her and growing hot in the process. And, although she'd been able to climb to the top of the wooden apartment building in Zaculeu, she'd vanished into thin air when she was about to crash into the steel sliding door of the Grand Pinnacle. The framework of the Grand Pinnacle was made of steel, too, of course. It was no wonder that every time Teague had seen the woman in white she'd been out in the open rather than inside the steel structures of the modern city, and when she'd wanted to confront Teague she'd lured him away to the lakefront. The Sihuanaba seemed to be able to pop in from nowhere and vanish at will, like some sort of unearthly spirit. It was almost impossible to predict where she would appear next. But I was certain that the mayor would be safe from her as long as he was inside his modern high-rise apartment building.

This was it, then. The way I figured it, once I gave this information to Fulton, my job would be done. He'd hired me to stop the Sihuanaba from troubling his boy, and, once he knew about her allergy to iron, he'd be able to eliminate her as a threat. Thank you, Southerland, job well done! No caddying today! I'd walk away from my client in good conscience, free to investigate Zyanya's death whether Fulton wanted me to or not.

Chapter Twenty-Four

The fixer answered on the first ring. "Fulton."

"It's Sunday, Larry. Go home!"

I heard a sigh. "I wish I could. I can't talk the mayor out of this motherfuckin' golf game! He says he's bored! It's been almost a week since he was attacked by that crazy dame, and he thinks he's as secure as a government bond. The man is a fuckin' child!"

"You sound sad, Larry. Cheer up, pal. I'm about to make your day."

"That right? Did you get a photo of Montavious Harvey drowning a puppy?"

"Sure I did. But I'm gonna sell it to Benning. I figure I can get more dough from him than from a cheapskate like you."

"Fuck you, Southerland. I thought you were going to cheer me up."

"Would you feel better if I told you that the Sihuanaba has a weakness that will take her out of the mayor's life for good?"

There was a pause on the other end of the line. "I'd be happier if you told me that the woman attacking the mayor is just an ordinary stalker."

"Can't do that, buddy. She's the Sihuanaba. But I know how you can protect the mayor from her."

Fulton paused again before asking, "Is this on the level?"

"Of course it's on the level! The question is, how badly do you want it?"

"Don't play games with me, Southerland. You got something, spill it! If you're fucking with me, take a hike! I don't have time for your bullshit."

"No bullshit, Larry. I know how to stop the Sihuanaba. And I'll tell you what I know. But first, I want my gun back."

Fulton snorted. "You really think you can put the touch on me? Don't make me laugh! You're small change."

I felt my temper rising, and I didn't feel like standing in its way. "I'm sorry you feel that way, Larry. I hope the mayor enjoys his golf game this afternoon. You've got nothing to worry about. I'm sure he'll be fine."

Fulton's voice rose a few decibels. "You can't back out on me now, Southerland! We've got a contract!"

"And I want to honor it voluntarily and of my own free will. I'm tired of you pointing my own piece at me! Stop treating me like your flunky, Fulton! I'm sick of it!"

"You *are* a flunky, Southerland! You're a two-bit peeper in a cheap suit with one foot in the gutter. If I snap my fingers, you'll lose your license. You won't be able to get a job as a fuckin' security guard in this town!"

"I was thinking of moving anyway. This town's starting to smell. It must be all that rot at the top."

I held my phone away from my ear as Fulton's voice rose to a shout. "You aren't going anywhere, motherfucker! Pack a bag and I'll pin you with the rap for the songbird's murder!"

"Yeah? And whose coattails are you going to grab on to when the Sihuanaba kills your boss today? You're nothing but a flunky yourself, Fulton! The difference between me and you is that you get paid more than I do, but you're the mayor's pet gorilla, and I get to call my own shots. The election is only four months away. Good luck trying to find another candidate to run against Harvey at this late date. And good luck convincing him to let you be *his* pet gorilla after your failure to keep Teague breathing."

Fulton had no immediate response, and I let my finger hover above the disconnect icon. I decided to wait and see if he would disconnect first.

Seconds passed, and then Fulton broke the silence. "What the fuck, Southerland. This is getting us nowhere. Look. I don't want to extort your services from you. I *like* you, damn it! Maybe I've been going about this all wrong. I have…trust issues. I've got moles on my staff, and I work with people who sell their services to the highest bidder. But maybe you're different. Maybe I can play it straight with you. First things first, though. Let's get the mayor through his golf game. Do a good job for me and we'll talk about the pistol afterwards. Deal?"

I wanted to keep pressing the issue, but I sensed that Fulton wasn't going to relent, at least not yet. "Okay, Fulton. But we *will* talk about it. You can take that to the bank!"

"Fine by me. But don't think I'm going to let you get away with those pet gorilla cracks—those were low blows!" I heard him sigh as he collected himself. "All right, shoot! What's this about a way to stop the Sihuanaba?"

I let out a breath. "Iron," I told him.

"Iron?"

"Iron." I laid it out for him, from my first run-in with the Sihuanaba on the roof of the wooden apartment building in Zaculeu to my recent confrontation outside the Grand Pinnacle. I told him about Leota's full-metal-jacket necklace and filled him in on the history of Cholula. I told him about Ralph, too, but I left Kai Kalama out of it. There was no need to put the professor on Fulton's radar. By the time I was done I knew that I'd told Fulton enough to make my case.

When I was finished, I let Fulton consider the information that I'd given him. After a few moments, he asked, "So you think that this earth demon…this…nirumbee? Ralph? You think he's on our side?"

"He's trying to take down the Sihuanaba for reasons of his own. Think of him as an enemy of our enemy."

Fulton grunted. "Hnh. I don't like wild cards in the mix, but at least he's not working against us. All right then. How do you propose that we protect Teague on the golf course?"

"That's up to you. I've done the job you hired me to do. We're quits."

Fulton didn't like that. I didn't figure he would. "Guess again, Southerland! We're quits when I say we're quits!"

I sighed loud enough so that he could hear me over the phone. "We're not going to do this again, are we? Look! You hired me to provide my perspective on the Sihuanaba. I've given you all the dope you need in order to protect the mayor. Gordo's crew can handle it from here. You don't need anything more from me."

Fulton was as tired of shouting as I was. He bit back on his anger and tried for a soft sell. "You don't give yourself enough credit, Southerland. You're right: you've provided me with valuable intel on the Sihuanaba. And, after hearing your story about last night's attack, I'm willing to concede that it really *is* the Sihuanaba who is going after the mayor. But she's still out there, and that means that the mayor still needs our protection. Gordon and his operatives are the best in the business, but you've faced down the Sihuanaba twice, and they haven't. And one of them is betraying me! I know it! I want you on the team until the threat to the mayor has been neutralized. I need you there. You might be a pain in the ass, but at least you aren't working for Benning."

"And you'll threaten me with my gun to keep me in the game, is that it? I wouldn't overplay that hand if I were you. I might decide to take my chances in court."

"It wouldn't get that far, and you know it. You know how the game works. You'll walk into an LIA field office and that's the last time anyone would ever see you. Then they'd go to work on your past, and in a month you'd be erased from history. Your own mother would forget that she'd given birth." Fulton sighed. "But I don't want to play it that way, Southerland. I want your full cooperation." The fixer paused for a couple of breaths, and then offered a concession. "Tell you what. I'll double your rate."

"Sorry, no dice."

"Now isn't the time to be pigheaded. I know you better than you think. The Sihuanaba killed your pal in Zaculeu, and you're not the kind of guy who forgets something like that. You'd go after her for nothing!" He paused to let that sink in. "I get it, Southerland. You've got your principles. I respect that. I'm offering you double your usual rates. You think I'd offer that to anybody?"

"Benning offered me triple."

"And I'm offering double. Take it or leave it, peeper."

What could I do? Fulton knew that I wasn't going to work for Benning at any price. It was double rates versus stubborn pride, and I wasn't rolling in so much dough that I could afford to turn down good business. I gave in. "All right, Fulton. I'll send you a new contract."

"Good! Then it's settled. The mayor and Thunderclash will be at the Galindo Downs clubhouse in an hour. Be there to meet them! I'll see that you're all outfitted with gats and steel-tipped bullets. If the Sihuanaba shows up, finish her for keeps!"

Fulton disconnected the call, and I slid my phone across the top of my desk. The fucker couldn't even be bothered to say goodbye. But he was going to pay me double rates now, and I told myself it was a victory, even if it didn't feel like one. As for the gun, well, I figured that if I could help get rid of Fulton's Sihuanaba problem I'd have time to come up with a way to solve the gun problem, too.

I looked up at the painting on my wall. The sandy hills looked like a vast minefield to me, and all the mines were primed to explode. The crow seemed to know that something was up, and he glared down at the landscape, daring it to erupt. I stared at the painting, waiting for something to happen. Nothing did, and I shook my head. I told myself that it was just a drawing of a bird in the desert. Anything else I saw in the painting was nothing but a product of my fevered imagination.

***

I needed to hustle if I was going to get to Galindo Downs on time, but my phone rang while I was getting my things together. When I saw that it was Detective Kalama, I connected the call.

"Detective? What's up?"

"Two more children went missing this morning at Galindo Estates." Kalama sounded like she was holding back rage.

"Shit." I sat on the edge of my bed.

"Leea took the case, of course. Motherfuckers! I'm at the Estates. How soon can you get over here?"

"I'm headed for Galindo Downs right now. The mayor's got a tee time, and I have to be there." I hesitated. "I'm, uh, I'm going to be his caddy."

"Excuse me? We must have a bad connection. I thought I just heard you say that you were going to caddy for the mayor."

"I'm part of a protection detail. That means I'll be nearby. What do you need me for, anyway?"

"Leea has chased all our officers out of the neighborhood." The detective spat out the words like they were choking her. She sounded tired, and more than a little frustrated. "They said that if we couldn't protect the residents we might as well go home. Well, fuck that very much! I'm at the lake trying not to get noticed. I want you to come over and give me some cover. No bodies have turned up. Yet. Maybe I can…. I don't know, probably it's already too late, but if I can be in the right place to prevent another tragedy…. Damn it! I've got to do everything I can." Kalama didn't sound hopeful.

"Don't give up, detective. You won't be alone out there. The golf course is on the lake, so maybe *I'll* be in the right place at the right time. I'll be watching for the Sihuanaba anyway; that's what I've been hired to do. If she's the one taking these kids, and I think she is, then I'm as likely to catch her and stop her as anyone. If it's not too late, that is."

Kalama let out a breath. "Okay, gumshoe. Make sure you've got your phone on you. It's all one big sucker bet anyway, but as long as there's any chance at all that those children are still alive I'm gonna stick around the lakefront. Until Ieea kicks me out, anyway. And even then I'll sneak back in."

"Any chance you can get some of your fellow coppers to slip into their civilian gear and come out to give you some help?"

"On their day off? Without pay?"

"Okay, forget I asked."

"Actually, I might be able to convince one or two. But they all pretty much think it's a lost cause. Maybe they're right."

"Maybe. But hang in there, detective. I've gotta go, but I'll stay in touch. I think that the Sihuanaba is still after the mayor, so there's a fair chance I'll see her today."

"Yeah, maybe. If you're right about the Sihuanaba, I should head over to that side of the lake myself."

"That's a good idea. Stay close to the waterline. If she took those children into the lake, that's likely where she'll be. By the way, the Sihuanaba has a weakness. She can be driven away with iron or steel. If you've got any steel-tipped bullets, use them!"

"Figures. I've got plenty of silver-tipped, but no steel. Maybe I'll get over to the clubhouse and confiscate some clubs. Plenty of iron in those club heads. That's something you might want to keep in mind."

"Thanks. Actually, I hadn't thought of that."

"They call them irons for a reason, egghead. The shafts might be made of graphite or aluminum, though, so put your faith in the club head. Even the woods are likely to have steel club heads. Stay away from the putters. You probably won't be able to do much damage with them."

"Terrific. As soon as I figure out what club is what, I'll be ready to rumble."

"I'll make it easy for you, gumshoe. Just grab the biggest club you can get your hands on and whack away!"

***

The bright sunny morning was on its way to becoming a bright sunny afternoon. Traffic heading west was stop-and-go until I passed a sports car on the side of the boulevard with its hood up and steam shooting out of the radiator. It was going to take me another half hour to get to the Galindo Downs, and my thoughts drifted toward Edie. I was anxious to see her again, and not just for the obvious reasons. Little details that had been tickling my brain when I was trying to sleep began to percolate back up from the depths that I'd forced them into. I was relieved that Edie had not been using the spider charm to make herself a mother—and me a father!

I pushed those thoughts aside and forced myself to think about something else. Stormclaw had told me that Gordo had been in love with Zyanya, and that I shouldn't trust him. The old troll didn't strike me as a gossip, but what was he trying to tell me? That Gordo saw himself in some kind of triangle with Zyanya and Teague? That Gordo blamed Teague for Zyanya's death and was trying to get even with the mayor? Fulton believed that someone in Gordo's crew was a mole, although Fulton didn't seem to think that Gordo himself was the culprit. Maybe the fixer was wrong about Gordo.

Fulton wanted me to find the mole, but I didn't have enough information to make a guess. It occurred to me that the mole might be nothing more than Fulton's paranoid fantasy, but I dismissed that idea for two reasons. First, Benning knew far too much about my contract arrangements with Fulton, not to mention the nature of my investigation. Someone was reporting to him, and I couldn't accept that it was either Kalama or Lubank. It had to be someone close to our operation, and that almost certainly meant Gordo or a member of his team. Second, Fulton was right: embedding moles in the enemy camp was something that operators like Fulton and Benning did as a matter of course. I knew well enough how it worked. I'd been hired several times to infiltrate businesses in order to uncover improprieties or to steal a file or two. I didn't know all that much about Gordo or his crew. I'd gathered impressions of them during our nights of surveillance, but I needed much more in order to find out which of them was snitching. If I got through this golf match, I'd have to start doing some real digging.

I turned my attention to my most immediate concern. Would the Sihuanaba come gunning for the mayor this afternoon? The golf course was a perfect spot for an attack: plenty of open space and no steel skyscrapers. It was daytime, and so far I'd only seen her at night, but my research into the stories about the Sihuanaba indicated that she had no aversion to daylight. If the stories were true, she'd attacked Cholulan farmers while they were out working in their fields. I couldn't assume that a sunny day would keep the woman in white away. I'd prepared myself as best I could. I was wearing Leota's necklace under my shirt, and I had the knife I'd taken from the curly-haired bruno clipped to my belt. I hadn't brought a rod because Fulton was going to see that I got one with steel-tipped slugs. I was also going to have access to a bag of golf clubs. I smiled. Bring the Sihuanaba on—the bitch didn't have a chance!

Finally, I thought about Detective Kalama, and the despair in her voice when she'd told me about the two missing children. Kalama had been in homicide long enough to know the score: when children disappear in the night, the ending is almost never a happy one. The detective was as tough as they come, a legit hard number. But she was also a parent. I thought about what Gio had said about looking at his kids and only seeing the babies they used to be. I didn't doubt that when Kalama had seen the two children who had washed up out of the lake on Friday, she had seen a little of her own daughter in their faces. I'd never had children, and maybe I never would. I had some inkling of what Kalama was feeling as she fought to keep alive the hope that the two missing children would be found safe and sound, but I knew that she was feeling it more deeply than I ever could. Hard as she was, I knew that if these children were found dead, a little piece of Kalama would die, too.

I pulled the beastmobile into the parking lot at the Galindo Downs Country Club under an early afternoon sun and blue skies highlighted by long feathery wisps of clouds, a Chamber of Commerce kind of day in Yerba City. And yet, somehow I found myself shivering as I climbed out of my car, feeling a chill that the bright sun couldn't dispel. I shook it off, along with all thoughts about moles and spider gods, children and Cholulan farmers, and even torch singers with crooked noses and skin as smooth as silk sheets. A job needed doing, and I was on the clock. I pulled the brim of my hat down over my forehead against the summer breeze and headed for the clubhouse.

Chapter Twenty-Five

As I was crossing the parking lot, I spotted Thunderclash standing outside the clubhouse. The troll waited for me to join him and then handed me a shoulder holster, complete with a semi-automatic nine millimeter pistol. "It's fully loaded with fifteen steel-tipped rounds. No extra magazines, so don't waste them."

I took off my jacket and strapped on the holster. "You have one, too?"

Thunderclash shook his head. "I don't like pistols. That's not a weapon for a troll." He patted at the side of his coat. "And I've never run into anything that I couldn't bring down with a shotgun."

"The Sihuanaba isn't like anything you've ever run into. I don't think that little lead balls will bother her much."

Thunderclash's eyes glowed like red-hot coals as he glowered at me from under the brim of his fedora. "Good thing I've got you to protect me then, little man. Come on. Let's go see the mayor."

I followed the troll into the clubhouse where I found Mayor Teague chatting with three middle-aged men in sweater vests, denim slacks, and plaid newsie caps topped with pompoms. I assumed that these were the bigshot campaign contributors that Fulton had mentioned. The mayor didn't bother introducing his three boosters to me, and I began to think of them, for no particular reason, as Pete, Zeke, and Elmer.

A few minutes after I entered the clubhouse, Teague broke away from the boosters and walked up to me with a broad smile. "Southerland! So you'll be caddying for me today, right? Glad to have you along."

I shook the hand he extended in my direction. "You sure you want me? I don't golf. I don't even know much about the game."

Teague patted me on the back. "No problem, son! I'm a scratch golfer and I know this course like the back of my hand. Just drive the cart, give me the club I ask for, and we'll be fine."

That relieved me a little, although I bristled at being called 'son' by this pompous asshole. Teague went back to join his colleagues, and I followed Thunderclash out of the clubhouse so that he could show me to the mayor's cart. Three other carts belonging to Teague's contributors were parked near the mayor's, and Thunderclash introduced me to the other caddies, who were already sitting behind the wheels waiting for their bosses to emerge from the clubhouse. After some brief 'hello's' and 'pleased to meet you's,' I took a short stroll to scan my surroundings, noting the vast expanses of grass and trees. Protecting the mayor in this open battleground was going to be a nightmare. What kind of dope puts himself in such obvious danger? A dope who's too much of a dope to realize what a dope he is, that's who. Or one who believes he's too important for his underlings to allow him to suffer any harm. Well, as one of his underlings, at least for the afternoon, I was going to have to do my best to prove him right. I let out a slow breath. Why had I agreed to this shit show? But I had no time for those kinds of questions. I resolved to do my job and worry about the meaning of life some other time.

When I made my way back to the clubhouse, I saw that Teague and his pals were getting into their carts. "Hey, Southerland!" Teague called. "You done with your nature hike? Let's get a move on, son! We've got some golf to play!"

The mayor climbed in the passenger's seat of his cart. Thunderclash was already sitting in the back of the cart with the clubs. After I was seated behind the wheel of the cart, I turned to the mayor. "Let's get something straight, Teague. I'm here to protect you from the woman in white while you dazzle those well-heeled suckers over there with your pretty teeth and sell them on pouring more of their dough into your campaign. You want me to drive you around and carry your clubs? That's fine. That won't get in the way of me doing my job. But if you keep ordering me around and calling me 'son,' I'm going to take your three-iron and knock the caps off your teeth. You understand me, Mister Mayor?"

Teague scowled. "Now see here," he started. But he must have seen something in my eyes, because his lips widened into a smile. "Ah, skip it. It's too nice a day and I'm in too good a mood. Okay mister driver, sir. Let's go play some golf." He sat back in his seat and looked up at the blue sky. "What a great day to hit the links!"

Sure, I thought, as I stepped on the petal and propelled the cart up the path to the first tee. And I'll try to make sure that nothing hits you back.

***

I'd tried to play golf exactly one time. My parents had never belonged to a country club, and I'd had little desire and even fewer opportunities to "hit the links." When I became a private investigator, a client had taken me out to a course and tried to teach me the game. It was a disaster. Let's just say that I had no gift for hitting a ball in the direction I wanted it to go. I saw a lot of the course that day, every grove of trees, every sand trap, every water hazard—everything but fairway! We stopped keeping score after the third hole, and after nine holes we agreed to call it a day. This was going to be my second time on a golf course, and I was fine with spending it driving an electric cart through the pastoral countryside and keeping my eyes peeled for an otherworldly spirit of vengeance, as long as I didn't have to try to hit a golf ball.

Galindo Downs was a pretty patch of real estate, and the fifth hole was the most scenic of all. It was a short, downhill par three that was loaded with hazards. A thick grove of cypress trees lined both sides of the narrow fairway. The green, which was pushed right up to the edge of the lake, tilted toward a huge sand-filled bunker that rose up to meet it from the right. A stroke that hit the green stood a fair chance of rolling off into the sand trap, but the biggest danger was driving the ball over the green and into the water. That's what Zeke did, and he did it again when the mayor, in a grand display of magnanimity, gave him a mulligan.

"Forget about it," the mayor told him with a broad smile. "We'll give you a one-shot penalty and you can drop a ball on the edge of the green."

Pete put his shot in the bunker, and Elmer's drive put him on the upper edge of the green some fifty feet from the hole. Then Teague, who was by far the best golfer of the group, used a nine-iron to drop one right down the center of the fairway, a few feet short of the green.

"Pretty conservative shot," said Elmer. "Just what we want from our mayor, right boys?" Pete and Zeke laughed.

"That right there is a perfect lie—right where I wanted it!" the mayor shot back. "That's the way to play this hole. You boys come down and watch me chip it in for a bird."

I drove Teague to his ball and handed him his pitching wedge. Thunderclash strolled off toward the trees on the left, looking for threats. The mayor was away, and Pete, Zeke, and Elmer, along with their caddies, all pulled up behind him to admire his stroke. After making sure that he had an audience, the mayor lined up his shot and put the ball next to the pin, leaving himself a one-foot putt for par. The boosters and their caddies all applauded, but the mayor looked up at them with a mock grimace. "Pushed the motherfucker!" he exclaimed. "Oh well, looks like a gimme for par." He turned to walk up to the green, and the others followed. I took Teague's putter out of his bag and stepped out of the cart.

While the others were waiting for Pete to blast his ball out of the bunker, I walked to the edge of the green and looked out over the lake. It was a dazzling sight. The lake's surface sparkled under the afternoon sun. A calm breeze cooled my face and neck as I listened to the gentle waves lapping up against the narrow belt of sand separating the green from the water. I closed my eyes and focused on the sounds carried to me by my elf-enhanced awareness. I listened to the seagulls calling to each other as they flew over another part of the lake, to Teague and his pals as they muttered advice to one another while they sized up their putts, and to the movement of the water as it glided over the sand. I opened my eyes, and it struck me that the waves were increasing in size and advancing further over the sand than they should have been, especially since no boats were nearby to create a wake. I watched a wave crash over the sand and roll up to edge of the green. The next wave rolled all the way to my feet, and I took a couple of steps backwards to avoid getting my shoes soaked.

A cold sweat began to form on the back of my neck, and I felt my heart begin to pound as adrenaline was pumped into my bloodstream.

I raised my eyes and saw the top of a head break through the surface of the lake just off the sandy strip, too close to the shore, in fact, for the water to be more than a few inches deep. The head continued to rise above the water, and I saw long dark hair obscuring a woman's face. Her neck and shoulders cleared the water's surface, and as she continued to rise from the lake I stared at the soaked white dress that was clinging to her breasts and torso. The woman's arms emerged, and I saw that she was bearing a burden: two small children, limp and unmoving, eyes shut, lake water draining from their slack mouths, and more water streaming down the sides of their tiny arms and legs, which were hanging limp as seaweed from their drenched bodies.

I continued to back away as the woman stepped up from the water and onto the green, whose surface was now flooded by water from the lake. She stopped ten feet in front of me and shook the hair out of her face, revealing the monstrous hag-like features of the Sihuanaba. A sob burst from somewhere deep in her chest, and she roared, "These are not my children! Where are my children?"

I didn't wait another moment. I reached inside my jacket for my pistol, but the woman moved faster than my eye could follow, and before the gat had cleared my jacket I was on my back skidding across the smooth surface of the green. A heavy wet sack was lying on my chest, and I found myself staring up into the waterlogged face of a drowned child. Choking back a sudden wave of nausea, I threw the body off to the side and scooted away from it.

"Where are my children?" The wail was followed by an explosive blast, and I turned to see Thunderclash with a smoking shotgun. The hag's dress was now tattered and blackened over her chest, and the body of the child she was still holding in one arm was torn and ragged. But the hag was still standing. She turned to Thunderclash and pointed a taloned finger at him. Then her jaws opened wide, like a snake's, and, although I couldn't hear her shriek, the troll's eyes widened as he dropped his shotgun to the ground, covered his ears, and sank to his knees.

A quick glance over my shoulder revealed that Pete, Zeke, and Elmer, along with their caddies, were doing the most sensible thing imaginable—they were taking it on the lam as fast as their feet could carry them! Teague, for some reason, was standing at the edge of the green, rooted to the spot. I wanted to grab him by the collar of his sweater vest and chase off after his pals, but Thunderclash needed help. Spotting my nine-millimeter a few feet away from me, I made a lunge for it, but the body of the second child struck me in the shoulder like a cannonball. I rolled away emptyhanded and scrambled to my feet.

The hag was now standing between me and the gat. I glanced at Thunderclash, but the troll was on his knees, and, although he was no longer covering his ears, he had the vacant, dead-faced look of someone whose mind had retired from the battlefield. A stream of drool poured from the corner of his mouth. I drew my knife out of its sheath, but a backhanded slap from the hag sent it flying across the green, where it sliced into the turf and buried itself up to the hilt. The sleeve of my jacket hung open where a talon had torn through it, and I felt a burning sensation on my wrist.

The hag opened her misshapen mouth and bellowed. "Where are my children!" I backed away, stepping over the unmoving body of the lifeless child lying behind me. The hag streaked toward me, her movements a blur. "Where are my children!" She raised an arm and pointed at me. The strength drained from my legs, and I sank to my knees. The hag's mouth began to part, and I knew what was coming next. I'd been living through versions of this in my nightmares for ten years. Feeling helpless, I found myself raising my eyes against my will to gaze into hers. And I felt…something wrong. Something about her eyes. It hit me then: the eyes of the Sihuanaba I'd seen on the rooftop in Zaculeu, and countless times in my dreams, were black as pits. The eyes I was staring into now were a deep violet, and, despite the circumstances, pretty!

"Zyanya?" My voice was little more than a whisper. "Zyanya? Is that you?"

The hag's mouth closed, and her arm fell to her side.

"Zyanya? Can you hear me?"

The hag stood still as stone.

"Zyanya. Let me find your children for you. Would you like that? Would you like to see your children?"

The hag frowned for a moment and seemed confused. But then she scowled, and her violet eyes opened wide. "My children are dead! They're dead!" Her mouth widened, and it was like I was looking into the depths of the abyss. Before I could make another sound my senses were overwhelmed by the Sihuanaba's shriek, bringing with it all the anguish of every woman who had ever cried herself to sleep at night knowing that the man who claimed he loved her was wrapped in the arms of another woman; by the unbearable pain of every woman who had suffered through the blows of a drunken brute as he unleashed his rage and fury on her because, while the world was too much for him to handle, he could bruise her and bust her up as much as he wanted; by the frustration of every woman who had to pretend that she enjoyed the attentions of rude, loud-mouthed creeps who tried to get a rise out of her with their ill-mannered japes because they were 'just joking,' or who touched her and stroked her because they were 'just being friendly,' and who forced her to endure it all in silence because she needed the job; by the overpowering desperation of each woman who had given her body to a man she loathed because she needed the money or the support, or because he had taken her by force, or because she had grown weary of the never-ending and unwinnable struggle to find justice and self-worth in a world determined to deny it to her at every turn. The screams of every tortured women penetrated to the core of my being, too intense to register as sound, too powerful to resist, too agonizing to ignore. I had nothing to fight back with except my will, and my will was a leaf in a tree at the edge of a hurricane. I felt myself slipping away into oblivion.

Just before my consciousness slipped away, I heard the sound of a voice. "Zyanya? Is that really you, baby?"

The sonic pressure that had been battering my senses ceased. I became aware of Mayor Teague approaching from behind me. I heard his voice again. "Zyanya? It's me, Darnell! Is that really you?"

I looked up to see the hag staring at Teague with her violet eyes opened wide. A shaky voice that didn't sound like the Sihuanaba's said, "Darnell?"

I scrambled to my feet and stretched my arm in front of the mayor. "Stay back, Teague!"

Teague seemed entranced. "It's…. It's Zyanya! How…?"

The hag raised an arm toward Teague, and the shaky voice said, "Darnell? Where are our children, Darnell?" And then a stronger voice, the voice of the Sihuanaba shouted, "Where are our children!" The hag extended a taloned finger and drew it back to slash at Teague. I threw myself in front of the mayor and brought up an arm to absorb the attack.

Before she could strike, a streaking nirumbee crashed into the hag like a missile and sent her tumbling. Ralph, lips curled to expose his wolf-like predator's teeth, had the hag's shoulders pinned to the turf. Moving faster than my eyes could follow, he raised his flint knife above his head with both hands and plunged it into the hag's forehead. It didn't have the effect that Ralph was hoping for. The hag grabbed the nirumbee by his topknot and flung him twenty feet through the air. He plowed face first into the manicured grass, tearing loose a four-foot divot in the green before somersaulting to his feet. The hag sat up and yanked the knife out of her forehead, which, somehow, wasn't even scratched. She hurled the knife at the nirumbee, who reached up and caught it by the hilt.

Watching these two creatures in action, it was clear to me that I had no business being mixed up with either of them. I turned to the mayor. "Teague! We've got to get you out of here!"

"But that's Zyanya!" His eyes were shining, and a tear was falling down one side of his face.

The hag screamed. "Where are my children!"

"It's not the Zyanya you remember," I told Teague, and began forcing him away from the hag.

Ralph, charging like a rabid badger, hurled himself into the hag and sunk his teeth into her thigh above the knee. The hag reached down and lifted the nirumbee into the air with one arm. Ralph, blood dripping from his teeth, twisted in the air and kicked the hag just below her ear. He wrapped his legs around the hag's neck and, in a blur of motion, began pounding at her ears with both fists. His attack was savage, but it had little effect on the hag. She reached back and slashed at the nirumbee's face with her talons, leaving long bloody streaks across his cheek and nose. Ralph grabbed at his face and dropped from the hag's shoulders to the turf, landing flat on his back. The hag fell on him with her knees and began slashing at the nirumbee, over and over again, shredding the flesh of his muscular chest.

I pushed the mayor away from me and ran toward the nine millimeter lying on the grass about ten yards up the far side of the green. The hag spotted me and cut me off before I could reach the gat. I didn't see the backhanded slap that sent me flying. My head hit the ground, and darkness began to descend. I tried to sit up, and I felt two hands helping me. Turning, I found myself face-to-face with Detective Kalama.

She stared into my eyes, checking to see if I was conscious. "Are you all right?"

"I don't know. How do I look?"

"Like you should throw in the towel. This must be the Sihuanaba."

I turned and saw the hag standing over us. She seemed angry, like the way a lion is angry when you've been poking at it with a stick. Her jaws parted, and I think I managed to groan before my brain was hammered with the blast of a million soundless screams.

Kalama stood, and I marveled at the fact that she could. Tears streamed down her face as she stared into the hag's eyes. Then she spoke, and I heard her through the pressure beating down on my temples and filling my senses. "I understand. Believe me, I get it." The detective held up the machete-like knife that she'd plucked out of the green on her way to help me. "But you murdered children." She plunged the steel blade straight into the hag's chest.

A different kind of shriek came from the Sihuanaba, a roar that I could hear loud and clear. She wrenched herself away from Kalama and lowered her eyes to stare at the knife buried up to its hilt in her chest. She grabbed at the hilt and tried to pull the knife out, but the blade wouldn't budge. She screeched non-stop without a breath as she continued to try, and her body began to fade, like a light growing dim.

I staggered to my feet, reeling a bit as blood struggled to reach my brain, but managing to stay conscious. I was aware of Teague standing at Kalama's side. The three of us stared at the ghostly figure of the Sihuanaba as it seemed to shimmer and recede into the daylight.

As we watched, our wonder turned to horror as the hag finally plucked the blade from her chest. She held it up into the air, and I watched the iron blade melt away. The hag crushed the hilt in her hand like an empty beer can, and she tossed it aside. She stopped fading, stopped receding, and her form grew more substantial.

"Oh, shit," Kalama muttered, speaking for us all.

The hag's eyes fixed on Teague, who staggered back a step. And then the Sihuanaba's face began to change. The elongated jaw shortened, her lips thickened, and the two canines rising from her lower jaw shrunk into her mouth. Her skin smoothed, and her straw-like gray hair transformed into soft black waves. Tears sparkled in her beautiful violet eyes. We were no longer staring at the hag.

"Zyanya!" cried Teague, stepping toward the figure. "You're alive!"

"Darnell!" Tears rolled down Zyanya's cheeks. "Darnell! Where…"

Teague had been reaching for Zyanya, but something in her expression made him stop. "Zyanya?"

The face of Zyanya hardened, and the tears stopped. "Where…. Where. Are. My Children!" She screamed the last two words.

Before any of us could move, Zyanya grabbed Teague and lifted him off his feet. She crushed him to her body in a bear hug. "Your children need their father! We have to go to our children!"

Teague screamed, and it seemed to release me from a spell. Knowing what I had to do, I reached under my shirt and pulled Leota's necklace over my head. I stepped toward Zyanya and dropped the necklace around her neck. Immediately, the necklace glowed red and began to burn into Zyanya's skin.

Teague continued to scream, and Zyanya screamed, as well, a human scream at first, but then her scream changed into a demonic roar that began to recede and echo as if it were falling into a well, or a pit with no bottom. At the same time, the figures of both Zyanya and Teague became translucent, and then transparent. Soon, the screams faded into silence, and Zyanya and Teague grew more and more transparent, until, after what seemed like an eternity, but was probably only a few seconds, they disappeared from sight.

Kalama and I stood in the bright light of the afternoon sun, stunned, openmouthed, neither of us moving, listening to the silence. A high-pitched voice that sounded like gravel brought us back to our senses.

"Well, that went well." The detective and I looked over to see Ralph sitting cross-legged on the turf, covered in blood, but smiling.

Kalama was the first to react. "You're alive?"

The nirumbee chuckled. "I don't die that easy, sister."

I met his eyes. "You must have a strong heart."

Ralph opened a pouch hanging from his belt and pulled out a child-sized hand-rolled cigar. He put the cigar between his teeth and pulled a wooden match from the pouch, which he flicked to life with his thumbnail. As Kalama and I watched, he lit up his stogie and sucked it into life. Then he winked at me and smiled.

Kalama let out a breath. "Okay, I'm going to call in a team. You two stick around for questions."

Ralph blew a cloud of smoke into the air. "'Fraid not, Detective." He reached back into his pouch and pulled out a badge. "LIA. This is my scene now."

Chapter Twenty-Six

Kalama scowled at the buzzer in Ralph's hand. "You've got to be shittin' me!"

"Sorry, sister. Good work with the knife, but I'll take it from here."

While the two of them were sorting things out, I went over to take a look at Thunderclash. The troll's face was dull, and his whole body was shivering.

Ralph glanced my way. "Is he okay?"

"Physically, there's not a mark on him. But mentally, I think he's checked out. He needs help."

Ralph put his badge away and pulled a phone out of his pouch. "I'm calling in a team. They'll be here in a few minutes."

Within a half hour, a dozen silent professionals were securing the scene. Thunderclash was in an ambulance, which had been driven right up to the green from over the fairway. The course managers were going to have a fit. The two children had been whisked away to who knows where. Kalama and I were sitting at the edge of the bunker with our backs to the green. Ralph came up behind us, and we turned to see what he wanted.

The nirumbee's teeth were clenched on one of his child-sized stogies. "This is what happened here today. The mayor was playing golf with three of his campaign boosters when he had a fatal heart attack. Although it hadn't been reported, Mayor Teague had been suffering from heart problems over the past six months. It caught up to him today. The three boosters have issued prepared written statements to the media expressing their condolences to the mayor's family and have no further comments. The mayor will be cremated, in accordance to the terms of his will, and his urn will be carried into City Hall for an official ceremony before being given over to his wife. The two missing children were discovered in the lake, and, in accordance with the wishes of their parents, they will be cremated in a closed private ceremony. The grief-stricken parents will be moving out of state immediately. A transient has been detained by the LIA and charged with the murders of four children in the

Galindo Estates neighborhood. His identity has not been disclosed, but the LIA has closed the case and will issue no further statements on the matter."

Kalama and I listened in silence. I nodded at the nirumbee. "So it's over, all wrapped up and tied with a bow. Nice and neat. That just leaves the two of us. Are we going to disappear into the system and never be heard from again? That will be easy enough with me, but the detective has a family."

Ralph blew smoke out the side of his mouth. "Don't be a nincompoop, Southerland. The detective has nothing to investigate, and you're an inconsequential private snoop. The LIA isn't interested in either of you. Forget about all this and go home. It's over."

Kalama glared at the nirumbee. "Is it? How do we know that the mayor is really gone? He disappeared, but that doesn't mean he won't reappear."

Ralph glared back at the detective. "Nobody comes back from where he went."

"Zyanya did," I said.

Ralph turned to look at me. "Did she? All I saw was the Deer Woman."

"It might be more complicated than that. And what about the Sihuanaba, the Deer Woman, as you call her? We drove her away from the battlefield, but how do we know that the war is over?"

Ralph spit a tobacco-laced glob to one side. "She got what she came here for."

"She didn't get her children."

Ralph pulled the cigar from his teeth. "I think maybe she did. You'll have to trust me on this, Southerland. We've seen the last of the Deer Woman in these parts. If I'm wrong, and she shows herself again, I'll be here to meet her. Seems that I'm going to be stationed in this city for a while. I'll probably be seeing you around." He looked back at Kalama. "Both of you." With that, the nirumbee stuck his cigar into the corner of his lips, turned, and walked away.

Kalama and I stood. "What now?" I asked her.

She sighed. "Guess I'll go home. I've got nothing more to do here. How about you?"

"Me? I was supposed to protect the mayor. Now that he's succumbed to a fatal heart attack, I guess my job's over. Once I clear things up with Fulton, I'll only have one thing left to do."

"What's that?"

"Find out who killed Zyanya, and why."

Kalama gazed out over the ruined green. "You missed your chance."

"What do you mean?"

The detective turned back to me and shrugged. "You could have just asked her."

***

"What are you trying to pull, Fulton!"

"Sit down, Southerland!" Fulton was leaning back in his desk chair with his hands clasped in front of his chest. "You were supposed to protect the mayor, and now he's dead. You didn't fulfill your part of the contract. I don't owe you a stinkin' dime!"

I glowered down at Fulton from the other side of his desk. "I was supposed to protect him from the Sihuanaba. It's not my fault that Teague had a bad ticker."

Fulton jerked himself forward and slammed the flats of both hands down on his desktop. "That's a load of hooey and you know it! Lord's balls, Southerland, who do you think you're talking to? You think I can't smell LIA bullshit when it's waved under my nose? You let the woman get Teague and now the LIA is sweeping the whole thing under the rug!"

"I didn't *let* the Sihuanaba get Teague."

"You didn't stop her, either. I don't pay for failure."

I had a feeling that this was a fight I wasn't going to win, but that didn't mean I wasn't going to go down swinging. "You hired me to investigate the Sihuanaba, and I found you some legit dope on her. I advised you to keep Teague in his apartment, where he would have been safe. If you couldn't talk him into it, then that's your failure, not mine. I did an honest job, and my services don't come with a money-back guarantee. You owe me, you chiseler! Pay me or I'll see you in court. Lubank is going to be all over your ass!"

Fulton smiled. "Lubank is a good lawyer. He's going to tell you that you don't have a case."

"The official word is that Teague had a heart attack. Nothing in my contract covers heart failure."

Fulton's smile grew broader. "No court is going to hear your case. It will be thrown out as a nuisance lawsuit. You have my word on that." Fulton stood. "I think we're through here. If you'll excuse me, I'm a little busy. My boss died, and I've been asked to clear out my office. If you're going to insist on sending your lawyer after me, he'll have to track me down. If you're lucky he'll hire you to do it for him. I hear you could use the dough."

A wave of weariness swept through me, and I felt my shoulders slump. I was tired. Tired of the grimy game of politics and tired of grubby political fixers that cared more about winning than they did about people. Tired of shadowy government agencies that cared more about maintaining order than solving crimes, and that could make inconvenient people disappear as if they had never lived. And I was sick to death of squabbling over money with rich self-important lowlifes in expensive suits with fancy offices and fleets of black sedans just hours after tripping over the drenched and broken bodies of lifeless children. "Benning was right about you, Fulton. You're a small and mean little man. You never gave a shit about Teague. He was nothing to you but a ticket into City Hall. Without him, you're just another lawyer in a city that's full of them. In a year you'll be chasing ambulances and passing your card out at funerals."

A single chuckle escaped through Fulton's tightened lips. "I won't be passing them out at yours. Who would come?"

I left then. We didn't shake hands.

***

"Forget it, Southerland. You ain't got a case."

"Don't tell me that, Lubank." I switched my phone from one side of my head to the other and reached for the bottle of beer on my coffee table. "Fulton signed a contract, and I fulfilled my side of it. You're supposed to be a hotshot lawyer—are you telling me that you can't handle a simple breach of contract case?"

"Didn't you hear what I just told you? There ain't no fuckin' case!"

"Why not?"

"Because no judge will hear it! Fulton fuckin' owns them."

"Even with Teague out of the picture?"

"Teague! Who's he? Teague never had nothin' to do with it. Fulton owns the judges. He put most of them in their positions, and he's got dirt on all of them. He's a cold, ruthless bastard, and he's got contacts inside the LIA. Hell, a lot of people think that he *is* LIA!"

"Okay, but without Teague, he's through. We're going to have a new mayor in a few months, and Fulton is already cleaning out his office."

"He'll turn up in Angel City, or New Helvetia, or, who knows, maybe even fuckin' Aztlan! The local judges will be happy he's gone. Th'fuck, Southerland! They aren't going to hit him with a judgment over some fuckin' breach of contract suit that they know won't be enforced. Forget the money! Just be happy that he didn't use that fuckin' gun of yours to frame you for a murder before he left town."

I sat back on my sofa and gulped down some brew. "So you're saying there's nothing you can do?"

I heard Lubank sigh. "Let me see what I can come up with. I'm billing you for this call anyway, so I guess I should put enough time into it to make it worth my while."

"Gee, thanks."

"If you really want to stick it to Fulton, why don't you find some proof that he was responsible for the murder of that songbird, Zyanya? He won't be able to run from that. Probably not, anyway. She was too fuckin' popular."

"I'm still looking into it. Nobody's paying me for it, though."

"I think I heard that she has a sister somewhere. Find her and see if she'll hire you."

"I've already found her. At this point I'm looking into Zyanya's death as a favor to her."

"A favor! She must be some dish! Wait'll I tell Gracie about this!"

"The sister, Edie, isn't buying the official story that Zyanya's death was a suicide. She thinks Teague or Fulton did it, or that Fulton had it arranged. She may be right. Fulton was afraid that Zyanya would raise a big stink and cost Teague the election."

"A stink? A stink about what?"

"You know, about getting dumped by the mayor after he'd fathered her two children. I gather that she didn't take it well when Teague broke it off with her."

"Lord's balls, Southerland! Th'fuck you talking about? Teague was too pussy-whipped to break off his relationship with that canary! Fulton was pressuring him to do it, but Teague told him to go to Hell!"

"Wait—Teague never told Zyanya that they were through?"

"No! Is that what Fulton told you? He's a lying sack of shit! If I was a betting man—and, as it happens, I am—I'd lay a grand that Fulton had Zyanya whacked because Teague wouldn't let her go!"

***

I needed to see Edie, so I called her up.

She answered on the first ring. "Well hello, sweetie. I was just thinking about you."

"Hi, baby. Hope I didn't catch you in the middle of a rehearsal."

"Nope! I'm home by my lonesome. The band's taking the day off. We need a rest after that last gig. We'll probably be back at it tomorrow, though."

"Need some company?"

"I'd love some, sugar! How soon can you be here?"

"In about thirty seconds. I'm parked across the street."

"What? You're kidding me, right?"

"Take a gander for yourself."

I looked up at the upstairs window and saw a face peek through the blinds.

"I don't see…. Wait a second! Is that tank yours? It's big as a bus!"

"That's mine all right. I call it the beastmobile."

"Cute name! It looks like it's ready to eat that little number parked in front of it."

"It won't unless I tell it to. I'm coming up now." I got out of my car and gave Edie a wave before putting my phone in my shirt pocket.

I walked through Edie's front door without knocking, and she fell into my arms. Her body was warm and inviting, and I gave her a gentle squeeze. I detected a floral scent in the air, with a slight metallic tinge lurking beneath. I thought I caught a hint of burning wood, too, but that could have been my imagination.

Edie pressed her lips against mine, and I let her. "Are you hungry?" she asked me. "You could take me to dinner. Unless you want your dessert first." She ran two fingers down my chest over my heart.

I extricated myself from her embrace. "Let's sit first. I want to tell you about my day. It's a lulu of a story, and I think you'll be interested in it."

Edie lifted an eyebrow but didn't say anything as I led her by the hand to the sofa.

"First, I have some sad news," I told her when we were seated. "Two more children were taken in the Galindo Estates neighborhood. I was one of the people who found their bodies."

Edie's hands flew to her mouth. "They...were killed? Oh no! Do you know who did it?"

"You haven't heard the news?"

"No, I don't listen to the news much. It's too depressing."

I wasn't surprised by this. As a professional entertainer, Edie kept odd hours, and most of those were spent looking for gigs, rehearsing with her band, working on the details of her stage act, performing, and unwinding from her performances. She lived in a bubble, and news from the world outside her bubble didn't always find its way inside. She'd only heard about the death of those first two children when someone from her band happened to mention it to her.

I filled her in. "You're going to hear that the LIA has arrested and charged some transient with kidnapping and murdering those children. It's all hooey. This so-called transient doesn't exist. We know who really did it."

I waited for Edie to ask me who, but she sat in silence, and a tear emerged from the corner of her eye and dripped down her cheek.

"You told me that your grandmother was a bruja in Teotihuacan. And that she told your mother stories, and your mother told those stories to you. Did your mother ever tell you the story of the Sihuanaba?"

Edie wiped the tear from her eye, and she nodded. "Yes. It's a popular legend in our culture."

"A legend? Maybe. But a very real one. You don't have the witch's gift, do you?"

Edie's eye's widened. "No, of course not! I'm not sure my grandmother really had it, either. She told everyone that she did, but my mother gave me the impression that she was an old fake-a-loo artist."

"She had enchanted artifacts, though, didn't she? Like that spider that you wear in your navel?"

Edie's voice, shaky when she'd heard about the children, had regained its strength. "She had artifacts that she *said* were enchanted. It's more likely that she was a hoopla spreader, and the charms were just part of her racket."

I nodded. "Maybe so. But your sister, Jenny.... *She* had the gift, didn't she. I saw her perform. She didn't have any more talent than you have. I mean, you're good, and she was good. Talent definitely runs in your family. But there was something special about her when she was in the spotlight. Something beyond her looks and her ability to sing. Something more than just her unusual violet eyes. She had something that wasn't quite natural."

Edie shook her head. "I don't know what you're talking about, mister."

"Come on, Edie. Look at me. You can trust me. You know you can. But you've got to be straight with me about this. It's important." I put my hand on hers, and she didn't pull it away.

Edie raised her eyes to meet mine. Then she looked away and nodded. "There wasn't much to it, just a little thing. She wasn't a real bruja. She couldn't cast spells or anything. But there was something, a light that you could sense in her. She was always everyone's little darling. It used to drive me crazy! Mom used to say that she had an angel in her. When Jenny was on stage, when she was being Zyanya, she would turn that angel loose, and everyone would love her."

I nodded. "I heard that Gordo had a thing for her."

Edie smiled without looking up. "That big palooka used to chase after her like a lovesick puppy. He was harmless, though, and no worse than any other mug that fell under her spell."

Edie turned back to me. "But let me tell you, whatever that thing was in her, it was no angel! When she turned on that light, she could get away with anything. Jenny and me were always getting into trouble. We were a couple of little rascals, her and me. We'd pick flowers from the neighbor's garden when no one was looking. We'd boost stuff off the shelves in stores—nothing big, just candy and stuff—and when we'd get caught, I'd get all the blame! I was the oldest, but that wasn't it. It was that thing in her. She'd smile and turn on that light, and Mom would tell her that she had to be better next time, and I'd get whacked with a big ol' leather belt for getting my dear little sister into trouble. Afterwards, Jenny would look at me with those purple eyes, and I'd forgive her." Edie's lips spread into a rueful smile, and she shook her head. "And I could never be mad at her. I loved her, and I still love her." She laughed, and tears ran down both cheeks. "The little shit!"

"And when her career took off, did you still love her then?"

Edie frowned at me. "Of course I did! I was happy for her. Hell, I was her biggest fan!"

"But you didn't like Teague, did you."

Edie shuddered. "Hell no! He liked to take credit for Jenny's success, but he didn't have much to do with it. About the only thing he was good for was that Jenny never had to fuck her way to the big stage. No one except him, anyway, but she was cool with that. He wasn't just a sugar daddy to her, either, no matter what everyone says. He might have been a world-class heel, but Jenny loved him. I don't know why, but she did."

"I hear they used to fight a lot."

"Yeah? So what! Everyone fights. And Jenny gave as good as she got, let me tell ya! She really knew how to hurt him, and not just with her fists. Teague might be a smooth operator around everyone else, but he was a real moony-eyed sap around Jenny. She had him wrapped right around her finger."

I nodded. "But you think he killed her?"

Edie's eyes went cold. "I *know* he did! Or if it wasn't him, it was Fulton, or someone who works for that snake. See, things were getting real bad there between Teague and Jenny at the end. Jenny wanted Teague to leave his wife and get married to her. She wanted to be an honest woman, and she wanted her kids to have their father at home with them. He kept telling her that it would be bad for his political career. She accused him of loving his career more than he loved her, which was true, of course. They had some real knock-down drag-outs over it. And then there was *her* career. She wanted to go to Angel City. Yerba City's okay, if you want to be small time all your life, but Angel City is where the stars are. And Jenny wanted to be a real star! Teague wasn't having none of it. He was mayor of Yerba City, and he didn't have enough imagination to aim any higher."

"And Jenny started doing drugs?"

Edie pulled her hand away from mine. "That's a dirty lie! Sure, she drank a little. Maybe more than a little. But she wasn't no juice head! She smoked cigarettes and a little dope from time to time. She dipped into the nose candy sometimes. Lord's balls—she was a fuckin' entertainer! That's part of the life. But she didn't abuse pills, and she didn't never shoot nothing into her. She didn't like to lose control."

"Fulton says it got worse at the end."

"Fulton is a filthy liar! He wanted Teague to break it off with Jenny. He said she was bad for his career. He tried to convince Teague that Jenny was some kind of junkie, but it was all bunk! And he kept hounding Jenny, trying to get her to leave Teague alone. It drove her crazy! It drove both of them crazy!"

"But Teague never did break if off with your sister, did he?"

Edie shook her head. "Teague was hopeless. They fought like cats and dogs, but Teague was more puppy than dog. He was Jenny's as long as Jenny wanted him. That didn't mean he didn't stray whenever he got the chance, though. That's what led to a lot of their fighting."

"That must have hurt Jenny."

Edie didn't say anything. She wrapped her arms around her chest like she was trying to keep her heart from escaping.

I didn't say anything for a while, either. The silence settled on us like a weight. When I felt like it had dragged on long enough, I broke it. "I wonder, though. I mean, wouldn't she have been better off without Teague? With Teague out of her life, wouldn't she have been free to go to Angel City and further her career?"

Edie shook her head. "Don't you think I told her that? But Jenny was stubborn. She wouldn't listen to reason."

I plunged forward. "Fulton told me that Teague broke it off with Jenny, and that Jenny went a little crazy because of it."

Edie's eyes widened. "That's a lie!"

I nodded. "Yes, it was. I talked to someone today who thinks that Fulton gave up trying to get Teague to free himself from your sister and switched to Plan B, instead. He killed Zyanya, or he had her killed."

Edie's eyes flared. "Yeah! That's right! That *must* have been what happened!"

I stared at Edie without speaking. After a few seconds, she tilted her head and shrugged. "What's the matter?"

I shook my head. "I don't buy it. It's an attractive idea, but it doesn't quite add up. Maybe Fulton would have had Zyanya bumped off to ensure that his man got re-elected, but I don't think he would have done that to her kids. He's a cold, heartless bastard, but he has limits. I think that your sister drowned her children. I think that something upset her enough to drive her over the edge. Teague wasn't going to leave her, and even though it wasn't in her best interests, she was willing to stick it out with Teague. I guess she really did love the little weasel. Who knows what makes people feel the way they do, but she didn't want to let him go. Until something happened. Something big enough to make her snap."

I looked at Edie. Her eyes were pinched shut, but tears escaped in streams that flowed down her cheeks and down her neck.

"Teague raped you, didn't he. And Jenny found out about it."

Choked sobs rose from Edie's throat and burst through her lips. She opened her eyes and stared at me. "How long have you known?"

"I didn't, not for sure. Not until just now. But it makes sense. Jenny really did kill her children, didn't she."

Edie nodded. "It was my fault. I met her and her kids one evening at the Country Club, and we all walked out to the lake. She loved that lake. We let the kids go running off, and we argued about Teague. I had to try one more time to convince her to leave him, to take the kids and go to Angel City, to stop letting him hold her back. I told her that he was never going to leave his wife for her, and that she was a fool for thinking that he would."

A strained, choking sob escaped from Edie's throat, and then her face hardened. "I hadn't planned to tell her what Teague did to me, but I lost my temper. It had happened a couple of nights earlier, and I was still shook up. Teague had been in the audience at one of my shows. He and Fulton. They stayed for the whole show, and when it was done, Fulton came backstage and told me that Teague wanted to talk to me about Jenny. So I came out to the lounge. But Teague was drunk. He started pawing at me, telling me that I was prettier than Jenny. I slapped him and went backstage to change and go home. Teague and Fulton waited a few minutes and then followed me. I was in my panties when they burst into the room. Fulton left the room and closed the door behind him, leaving me in there with Teague."

Edie's eyes were dry as she told me the story. She'd done all the crying she was going to do.

"He broke your nose, didn't he."

"Yes. He was very rough. I fought back, but he hit me in the face until I couldn't fight back anymore."

I nodded, straining to keep a grip on the rage that was growing inside me.

"Afterwards," she continued after a pause, "he got off me and walked out the door. Fulton was waiting for him. He'd been standing guard. Fulton came inside, and I thought he was going to take a turn. But he just knelt down on the floor next to me and told me that if I ever breathed a word to anyone, he'd kill me, my sister, and her children. He looked me right in the eyes when he said it. I had no doubt that he meant every word of it."

"So you kept quiet."

"Yes."

"Until you told your sister."

"Yes. I thought it would show her what a creep Teague was, and that she would leave him. But she went nuts! She screamed at me and accused me of lying. Then she accused me of trying to take Teague away from her for myself."

Edie sniffed and wiped her nose with her sleeve. "Jenny couldn't handle the truth. Something came over her. It was like she'd been on the edge of a cliff, and this pushed her over. I didn't even recognize her anymore! People always thought that Jenny was strong. She had that glow! But that wasn't really her. Let me tell you something. I knew Jenny better than anybody, and she was the weakest person I've ever met. Everyone loved her, and so they always took care of her. No matter what happened, or what she did, somebody was always there to fix it and make it better. She never had to fix anything for herself, and she was never blamed for anything she did wrong."

"What happened at the lake?" I prompted.

Edie's eyes seemed to cloud as she recalled the events. "She was screaming at me. Her children came up to her, crying their little eyes out. I tried to calm her down, but it was like she'd left and some awful creature had taken her place. Something monstrous!"

Edie looked like she wanted to clam up, but I wasn't going to let that happen. "What happened, Edie? Give me all of it."

Her voice sunk to a whisper, but I could hear it just fine. "When she saw her kids, she got quiet. It was very strange. She'd been screaming bloody murder, and then she just...stopped. She knelt down in the sand so that she could hug her children. She told them that their father didn't deserve them, and that she was going to take them away from him. She told them that he was never going to lay eyes on them again. I thought that she had decided to run off with the kids to Angel City like I'd told her to do. But then she scooped up the kids and went running with them into the lake. I followed her, of course. I grabbed at her, but I couldn't stop her. It was like her madness had given her strength. She threw me off her, and I fell. She carried the children out into the water and held them down. I went after her. I tried to save them. I really tried." She shook her head.

"What happened then?"

Edie's breathing was unsteady, and she started coughing. I put a hand on her shoulder to help calm her. When her coughing fit subsided, she took a deep breath and resumed her story. "Jenny walked out of the lake. I tried to find the children, but I couldn't. It was dark, and their bodies had floated away. It was no use anyway. I knew they were dead." Edie's eyes fell, but she continued. "When I got out of the water, I found Jenny sitting in the sand. She was just sitting there, not crying, not shouting or anything. I said, 'Jenny, what have you done?' She looked up at me, and I'll never forget her eyes. They were cold, like they were dead. She said, 'I killed them, Edie. What have I become? What kind of monster kills her own children?' Then she looked out over the lake and said, 'Where are they? Where are my children?'"

I felt a shiver go up my spine at those words, but I didn't say anything. The dam had broken, and everything that Edie had been holding inside since the death of her sister was spilling out. I wasn't about to stand in the way.

Edie continued. "She wanted to run back into the lake after them. I think that she wanted to drown herself. But then she stopped and asked me if I still had the gun that she knew I carried in my bag. I told her that I did, and she started begging me to shoot her with it. It was horrible! I told her that she was being ridiculous, but she pleaded with me. She said that she couldn't live without her children, and that she wanted to join them. But she said that she was too weak to do it to herself. She told me that I had always been the strong one, and that I would have to do it. She said her life was over anyway, and that she'd never be able to go on. She begged me and begged me." Edie paused and took a deep breath. "And then…and then she smiled at me and looked me in the eyes the way she would do when we'd gotten into trouble. She looked at me with those violet eyes that always made me forgive her. I saw the hurt in those eyes, and I saw her future in them, the pain that would never go away, that would haunt her forever. I took the gun out of my bag. I tried to hand it to her, but she wouldn't take it. She stood in front of me, smiling."

Edie looked up at me. "I don't even remember doing it. To this day I don't remember it. All I remember is seeing her lying in the sand, and blood pouring out of her chest. I remember the ringing in my ears. I remember the gun in my hand, and the smell of the gunpowder. I stood over her for a long time. And then, I put the gun in my bag and walked away."

Chapter Twenty-Seven

Edie slid up against me and buried her face in my shoulder. I wrapped my arm around her, drew her close, and listened to her muffled sobs. I offered no comforting words. I didn't have any to give, and, anyway, they wouldn't have helped. Her grief was nothing I could fix, so I held her in my arms while her body shook and convulsed as she cried. When she was finished, and her breathing had calmed, I said, "But there's more to the story, isn't there."

Edie's body stiffened, and she lifted her head off my shoulder to stare at me with her tear-stained eyes. "What do you mean?"

I studied the scar under her eye, the bend in her nose, and the tear streaks on her cheeks, and concentrated on keeping my emotions under control. "I mean that it didn't stop there. You killed your sister. I'm not here to judge you. You loved her, and I can't imagine how horrible you felt once it all sunk in. And it was all Teague's fault. Your sister loved him, but he was a louse who was only interested in himself. And then he raped you. That was unforgivable. And when your sister found out, something in her snapped. She killed her own children, and she knew that she'd never be able to live with that. She begged you to kill her, and you did. You might not have been in your right mind yourself when you did it, but that's neither here nor there. The point is, it was Teague's fault. It was all of it his fault. And you wanted—you needed—to get even. Have I got it right so far?"

Edie drew away from me. "You crummy bastard! What are you trying to say?"

"I'm saying that you needed to kill Teague. You needed to do it for your sister and for yourself. And you succeeded. Teague is dead."

Edie's eyes grew so wide that I thought they would pop out of her head. "What? How...."

"The Sihuanaba took him to whatever abyss she comes from. I was there. I saw it happen."

Edie rose to her feet. "He's dead? He's really dead?"

I thought about that. "He's as dead as it matters. To tell you the truth, I'm not even sure what that means anymore."

Edie's eyes blazed, but then her features relaxed as her mouth broke into a smile. "But you said that I succeeded. What did you mean? You don't think that *I* had something to do with it. I mean...do you?"

"Of course you did. You summoned the Sihuanaba. You used the avenging spirit to get even with Teague."

"Me? Don't be silly, darling. I don't know how to summon spirits. And anyway the Sihuanaba is just a story."

"Oh she's real enough. This wasn't the first time I've run into her. And you brought her here."

Edie's smile disappeared, and she put her fists on her hips. "Why are you talking to me like this? I thought we had a little something good going on between us. Why are you doing this to me?"

Edie knelt on the floor next to the sofa and took my hand in both of hers. Her face was composed, and when she spoke, her words were measured and reasonable. "Honey, I don't know what you're going on about. You've had a rough day, and it's making you say crazy things. But you gotta believe me! I had nothing to do with whatever happened today. You're tired. Why don't you stretch out on the sofa and get a little sleep. I won't bother you. And when you feel better, we'll go out and get something to eat. How does that sound, darling?"

I gave her hands a squeeze with my own. "It sounds wonderful, sugar. It really does. I could use a rest. But it's not going to happen until you come clean with me. Because it's not just Teague. As far as I'm concerned, he got what was coming to him. He was a shitheel, and the world is better off without him. But the Sihuanaba killed four innocent children, and their deaths are on you, too."

Edie pulled her hands away. "Don't say that! That's a shitty thing to say to me! I never wanted those kids to get hurt. How dare you lay that on me!"

"You summoned the Sihuanaba, and the Sihuanaba killed those children."

"That's a lie!"

"It's not a lie. I know everything, Edie."

"Oh yeah? You think you're so smart! How can you know anything?"

"You seem to forget, Edie. I'm a private detective." I held my hand out palm up. "And I've got an associate."

I saw Edie's jaw drop as Smokey whirled itself into a visible funnel and descended on to my palm. Edie stared at the elemental and then jerked her head in my direction. "How long...?"

"Smokey has been here since late this morning," I explained. "I sent it over after I heard about the two kids who disappeared last night. After I drove here, I summoned it to my car for a chat right before I called you. It followed me back in. You never saw it because it wasn't spinning like a whirlwind, picking up dust and distorting the air around it. It was drifting, a tiny puff of air, calm and invisible, until just now. But it heard and saw everything."

Edie stood up and backed away from me. Her face grew pale, and she clasped her hands in front of her stomach.

I lifted my hand and let Smokey hover above the sofa. "Smokey, I'm detecting a scent in the air, like burned flower petals. Can you show me where it is coming from?"

"Smokey can!" The elemental drifted toward the bedroom and zipped under the closed door into the room. I rose from the sofa to follow.

"Wait!" Edie grabbed me by the arm. "Don't go in there!"

I shook her off and opened the bedroom door. Smokey was hovering above the incense burner. Edie followed me into the room.

"From what Smokey described to me," I began, "it sounds like you conducted a ritual earlier this afternoon. You burned some twigs and herbs in this burner. I guess you haven't gotten around to cleaning up. The ashes are still in there. Smokey says that you had something on this grill. He described it to me: a rock carved in the shape of a spider."

I let my eyes drop to Edie's midriff, covered by her blouse. "That gem is still warm. I felt it when you were hugging me."

Edie frowned. "How can you feel that? It's already mostly cooled, and we're both dressed."

"My senses are keener than most people's. It's a long story. Hopefully, I'll have a chance to tell it to you someday. I can smell the herbs that you used for your offering. And I can smell something beneath that fragrance, too. Something metallic, like copper. I know that smell. It's blood."

I turned to Smokey. "Where did this human get the blood?"

The elemental shot toward the bedroom door. "Smokey will show you."

Smokey led me out of the bedroom and into the kitchen. It hovered in front of the refrigerator. "Blood is in cold box."

I opened the refrigerator door, and spotted an unmarked plastic food container on the bottom shelf. Inside the container was a stoppered glass tube filled with a dark red liquid. I retrieved the tube and held it up in front of Edie. "Jenny's blood?"

Edie's eyes dropped, and she nodded. Then she turned and walked into the living room. I returned the tube of blood to the refrigerator and followed after her. When I reached the living room, Edie was hunched over on the sofa, head in her hands.

I lowered myself on the sofa next to her. "Your grandmother may not have been a bruja, but some of the items she had were enchanted. That spider goddess ornament was one of them. A friend of mine owns a jewelry store, and he's taught me a few things. If I let him examine that stone, five will get you ten that he'd tell me it was something common and ordinary, like quartz. That ornament would have little value if it wasn't special for some other reason. But your grandmother passed it to her daughter, and she passed it to you. Maybe the ornament has sentimental value in your family, but I'm guessing that it's more than just a keepsake. I'm guessing that it's enchanted."

Edie looked down and placed her hand on her stomach. She didn't say anything.

I went on. "After you shot your sister, you started thinking about how you could get even with Teague. A man in his position is well protected, and with Jenny gone you weren't going to be able to get anywhere near him. You had to strike from a distance. Somehow you learned how to use your enchanted stone to summon the Sihuanaba. This wasn't something you knew how to do. I'm guessing that you've never done anything like this before. It took you a few weeks to learn the summoning spell, and you had to get a new tattoo to make it work. That incense burner is new, too. Summoning the Sihuanaba required a Nahuatl spell. I was hired by a powerful Nahuatl bruja a few months ago, and during that case I learned a little bit about how Nahuatl magic works. It involves negotiations with ancient Azteca spirits, and what these spirits want most is blood, especially human blood. Anybody's blood will do, but today I saw something that made me believe that there was a strong connection between the Sihuanaba and your sister. Something that led me to believe that the blood you used to summon the Sihuanaba came from your sister. I didn't know it for sure, though, until I asked you."

Edie glanced at me and then looked away again. Her face was blank, but I knew that she was listening. I continued, "Yesterday I had a meeting with that bruja I told you about. She was the one who told me that a lot of women in Teotihuacan use that spider image when they wanted to become pregnant. But she also told me that the nameless Great Goddess of Teotihuacan had once been much more than just a fertility goddess. Before the coming of the Dragon Lords, she was worshipped in Teotihuacan as the ruler of the realms of both the living and the dead. I think that you knew this. It's something that your mother would have taught you. So once you learned how to do it, you used your enchanted image of the Great Goddess to reach into the realm of the dead for an avenging spirit, and you turned the spirit loose on Teague. How am I doing?"

Edie shook her head. "You got some of it. But I wasn't trying to summon the Sihuanaba."

It struck me then like a bolt of lightning, and I wondered why it had taken so long for me to see it. "You weren't trying to summon the Sihuanaba! You were trying to raise the spirit that lived in your sister! What did you say earlier? Something about how that thing in her wasn't an angel? You knew your sister better than anyone, didn't you. And you knew that whatever was in her was powerful. So you decided that you would call it back from wherever it had gone and help you get revenge on Teague."

Edie shut her eyes against a renewed onslaught of tears. She wiped the tears away and sniffled. "Jenny told me once that if anything happened to her, I could use her blood and the enchanted spider stone to communicate with her in the land of the dead. When she told me that, I thought she was joking, or being dramatic. She was a very melodramatic kind of person. But when I saw her lying in the sand, with blood streaming out of her chest, I remembered. I gathered up as much of her blood as I could into a plastic bag. I bought a glass tube and used it to store the blood in my refrigerator. And then I learned everything I could about the Great Goddess, and how to use the stone. I talked to witches, and I read books. I got the tattoo and I mounted the ornament in my navel. I needed to do that so that the spider goddess would bond with me. And when I thought that everything was in place, I performed the ritual to unlock the magic from the stone."

Edie shook her head, and then turned to look me in the eyes. "I didn't know that it had worked! And then Gordo came to see me. He said that Fulton had sent him. He asked me what I knew about a woman who was stalking Teague. I told him that I didn't know anything about it, but then he told me how the woman had taken Teague down to the lake near where my sister had died, and that the woman had done something to Teague. He said that she had screamed at him, but it was a scream that no one could hear. And that the scream had fucked up Teague's mind. I knew right away from the stories that my mother had taught me that he was describing the Sihuanaba. And I knew that it was my ritual that had summoned the Sihuanaba."

"And that's when I came to see you at the Turbo. And you told me that Teague or Fulton had killed your sister."

Edie nodded. "Gordo told me that if I talked to anybody about what had happened with the woman and Teague that Fulton would not be happy. I knew what that meant. You looked to me like someone who could handle himself, so I sent you after Teague."

I felt something cold in my stomach. Something was beginning to make sense. "And you brought me home with you hoping that you could 'encourage' me to prove that Teague had killed your sister."

Edie's expression hardened. "Well? What do you expect? You thought you'd won me over with your big arms and your pretty face? I wanted you to be on my side! I may not have my sister's 'inner angel,' but I still know how to get what I want from a man! So I led you on, and you followed right along." Her expression softened, and her eyes welled. Just a bit. She might have been out of tears. "But then something happened that I wasn't counting on. I fell for you, you fuckin' bastard! I fell hard!" She crouched down and covered her face with her hand. "That wasn't supposed to happen. It wasn't part of the plan."

I felt something warm rising up inside me, but I forced it back down. "What did you do when you found out that you had summoned the Sihuanaba?"

Edie took her hand away from her face and looked up with a broad grin. "I laughed! I poured myself a drink and celebrated! I knew that the Sihuanaba was exactly what that motherfucker Teague deserved! I didn't know whether I wanted the bitch to kill him or drive him insane, but I hoped that it would be slow and painful!"

"And then you found out that the bitch had killed two children."

The grin on Edie's face disintegrated, like it had stepped on a land mine. "Yes." The word was little more than a squeak that she'd managed to squeeze out of her throat. "Those poor children! If I had known.... I would never, never, in a million years...." She brought her hand up to her face again. "But the worst part of it was that I knew.... I knew that it was Jenny. I knew that the Sihuanaba had come from Jenny. Somehow it was the spirit in her, and it was looking for her children." She looked up at me again. "But how can that be? The thing in Jenny was a light! It made people love her! It wasn't an angry monster, like the Sihuanaba. It never tried to kill anybody."

I shook my head. "Edie, I can't pretend to know about these things. It's way beyond me, and way beyond you, too. You were meddling with things you don't understand. I don't know what the Sihuanaba really is, except that she's connected with women. All women maybe, all the women who live now, and every woman who came before. Maybe she's a part of every woman, or at least something that wakes up in them when they've been wronged by men. She's something universal, like love, or anger. Maybe she's stronger in someone like Jenny, who was gifted with that inner light. And when you called on Jenny's inner light for revenge against Teague, it was the Sihuanaba that answered. That's the only way I can explain it."

Edie shot to her feet. "I need a drink!" She crossed through the living room and into her kitchen. She emerged a few seconds later with a bottle and two cups. "Will you pour it?" She asked. "My hands are shaky."

Edie put the bottle and cups in front of me on the coffee table and plopped back down onto the sofa. I splashed the rye into the bottom of each cup. She grabbed one and tossed it down, so I poured her another shot. I raised my cup and took a sip. "I need to tell you one more thing, Edie. Today, when the Sihuanaba went after Teague, I was there, along with some other brave people, to defend him against her. We wounded her. She has a kind of allergy to iron, and one of the people with me stabbed her with the knife that I'd brought." I smiled. "It was the knife those thugs wanted back from me when they ambushed us on Friday night. Anyway, after the Sihuanaba was stabbed, she changed. She became Jenny. I think what happened is that when you cast your ritual and hooked the Sihuanaba, some part of Jenny, that inner light of hers maybe, came along for the ride. You're right, Jenny was trying to find her children, but she wasn't the Jenny you knew. She looked like Jenny, and she had some of Jenny's memories, but she was something more otherworldly, something a lot like the Sihuanaba herself. When the Sihuanaba was stabbed, the iron in the blade sent her back to where she'd come from, but whatever was left of Jenny stayed behind. I saw her grab Teague, and the two of them vanished. She took him…somewhere. Somewhere that's not here. I don't think we'll ever see either one of them again. At least, I hope not."

Edie put her cup down on the table. She drew in a breath and let it out. Then she raised her eyes to meet mine. "So now what. I suppose you're going to turn me over to the cops?"

"You're responsible for those kids, Edie. You should go down for that."

Edie crossed her arms across her stomach and nodded.

I leaned back into the sofa. "Don't worry, sugar. No wants to hear your story."

Edie looked up, surprised. "You're not going to give me up?"

"To who? The LIA has closed their investigation. They're not interested in you. Leea is far more interested in order than truth, and they've already wrapped this case up in a nice tidy package. The YCPD isn't interested in you, either. The last thing they want to do is cross swords with the LIA. It wouldn't change a thing, and it would probably cost some people their jobs. As matters stand, any lawyer in this city would tell you to do the same thing: keep your mouth shut tight and go on with your life."

"Then…." Edie hesitated as she considered what I was telling her. "Then, it's over?"

"As over as it's going to be," I told her. "For you, it will never really be over. You'll have to live with what you've done for the rest of your life. But you know how to handle yourself. I'm sure you'll get by."

Edie laid a hand on my arm. "But you'll be there to help me, won't you? I mean, what we've got between us, that's still good, right?"

I sighed. "I need to sort some things out."

She squeezed my arm. "Stop! I know what you're going to do. You're going to line up a list of reasons why we should stop seeing each other, and a list of reasons why we should stay together. And then you're going to weigh one list against the other and tell me that staying with me isn't the reasonable thing to do. But that's not how it works, darling! How do you *feel* about me? How do you feel about *us*? That's what counts. Don't let your head talk you out of a good thing!"

I put a hand over hers. "I don't know, baby. My heart says yes. But my head still gets a say in this. Maybe if you'd been honest with me from the start. I think you're a swell kid, and life with you would be a thrill a minute, but I'm not sure I could ever trust you."

Edie's eyes teared up again, and she pulled me into an embrace. "Don't say that, baby. Don't say anything. Just hold me."

So I held her. One thing led to another, as they say, and I stayed with her until night fell, and then long afterwards. We didn't say a lot to each other; we let our hearts make their case. It was close to midnight when I left, promising that I would call in the morning.

***

On the drive home, I turned the radio on to a station that played hot tunes from Azteca, heavy on the horns. I turned off my thoughts and let the music fill my head. I dropped the beastmobile off at Gio's lot and set off for the walk home, humming the melodies that I'd been listening to, still thinking about nothing. I trudged down the sidewalk on legs filled with lead, while my helium-filled head wanted to drift away into the night. I was all too aware that I hadn't had any sustained sleep in days. All I wanted to do was crawl between my own plain cotton sheets in my own familiar bed in my own cozy room and fall headfirst into a long dreamless slumber.

I spotted the black luxury sedan parked in front of my house from a half block away. My first thought was, "Lord's balls! How the fuck do these guys manage to find parking places so close to where they want to be?" My second thought was, "What now?" I was getting tired of these big black cars popping up every time I wanted to go home and wind down after a rough day.

When I reached the sedan I saw that it was unoccupied, but it was the same make and model as the ones Fulton had in his motor pool. At least I wasn't going to be plucked off the street this time. The blinds covering my office window were lit from behind by a light that I knew I hadn't left on. I walked up to my front door and turned the handle. As I expected, it was unlocked.

I stepped into my office and found Gordo and Ironshield seated inside. They seemed as comfortable as a couple of boardinghouse lodgers as they drank the coffee that they'd brewed in my coffee maker. Gordo nodded at me as I entered. "About time you got back, Southerland. We were thinking about having some pizza delivered."

"I don't remember leaving my door unlocked."

Ironshield's thick ruddy lips broke into a grin. "If you didn't want someone to pick your lock, you'd get yourself a better lock."

I walked past them to my desk and sat down. "I see the two of you found the coffee."

"You want me to pour you a cup?" Gordo asked.

"Might as well. Black."

When we were all settled in, I asked Gordo what was up.

He got right down to business. "Mr. Fulton sent me to ask you if you'd work for him as a permanent employee on his security staff."

I blew on the surface of my coffee to cool it. "Why would I want to do that? He's stiffing me for the job I just did for him."

Gordo pulled an envelope out of the inside pocket of his coat. "Mr. Fulton was pissed off when you saw him earlier. You can understand why. He'd just found out about Mr. Teague. But after a while he started thinking about things in a different light. Also, I think he got a call from your lawyer." Gordo put the envelope on my desk. "There's a check in there that should cover your time and expenses."

I stared down at the envelope without moving.

Gordo took a sip of his coffee. "I hope you'll consider Mr. Fulton's offer. Thunder took a bad beating today, and it looks like he's going to be on the shelf for a little while. Maybe longer. So you'll be part of my team, at least to start with. If that's okay with you, I mean. I'd love to have you on board."

I shoved the envelope back in his direction. "Tell Fulton that I don't like the way he does business."

Gordo sighed. "Be reasonable, Southerland. Even if you don't want to work for him, Mr. Fulton is a good man to have on your side." He waved a hand at the envelope. "That's good dough. Take it."

"I don't want his money. He wanted me to protect Teague, and Teague's dead. Tell him that he was right, I failed to live up to my side of the deal."

Gordo made a point of looking around my office. "Pardon me for saying so, Southerland, and I don't mean no disrespect, but this doesn't look like the office of a man who can afford to throw good money back into a client's face, especially a powerful client, like Mr. Fulton."

"Fulton's through, Gordo. Teague was his meal ticket."

Gordo shook his head. "You're wrong about that. Don't worry about Mr. Fulton. With his connections, he'll always be in the center of things. He was on the phone this afternoon with Governor Tatanka. With Mayor Teague gone, Mr. Fulton might actually wind up in New Helvetia somewhere high up in the provincial governor's office. It would actually be a step up for him."

I had to smile. "Figures. The world always seems to have a place for smooth bastards like Fulton. But I'm still not interested. I like it here in Yerba City. New Helvetia is too far from the ocean for me. And besides, I like working for myself. My boss might a little tight with the jack, but we get along, and I make enough to keep my head above water."

Gordo seemed confused by that, and he turned to Ironshield for illumination.

The troll smiled. "Southerland is his own employer. He's saying that he doesn't make a lot of scratch, but he can live on it, and he doesn't have to constantly be butting heads with some jackass boss."

Gordo turned back to me. "I see." He set his coffee cup down on my desk and tapped his fingers on the desktop a few times. "Anything I can say to change your mind?"

In response, I picked the envelope off my desktop. Without opening it, I held it in both hands and ripped it in half. I put the halves back on the desk and shoved them toward Gordo.

Gordo nodded. The corners of his mouth drooped, and he looked sad. Then he sucked in a breath and clapped his hands in front of his chest. "Well, I'm sorry you feel that way. I like you, Southerland. Too bad you're so stubborn. I guess that's it, then. Mr. Fulton will be disappointed."

Having said his piece, Gordo picked the two halves of the envelope off the desk and stuffed them into the inside of his jacket. When his hand reemerged, he was holding a pistol. A big one, probably a forty-four. He pointed it at the center of my chest.

Chapter Twenty-Eight

"Let me guess," I said, staring down the barrel of Gordo's forty-four. "Fulton told you to make sure that if I wasn't going to work for him, then I wasn't going to work for anybody."

"He thinks that you're going to go over to the Hatfields. He thinks you'd make a bad enemy."

I glanced over at Ironshield. The troll tilted his head and shrugged. Thanks a lot, I thought.

I turned back to Gordo. "Is that what he told you?" I shook my head. "That's bullshit! He said that because he knew that we were getting along, and that he was afraid that you'd hesitate to pull that trigger. He was trying to give you some motivation. Not that you need it. You'd do what he told you to do, no questions asked. You don't even mind that he killed Zyanya, and we all know that you were soft on her."

Gordo's eyes narrowed. "Who told you that? I mean, what are you talking about? Wait a minute. Fulton didn't kill Zyanya!"

"Sure he did," I assured him, pressing my bluff. "She was going to cost him the election. Fulton couldn't allow that to happen. So when she drowned her own children to spite Teague, Fulton shot her and tossed her into the lake. Why do you think he never wanted me to investigate Zyanya's death? Why do you think he turned the whole thing over to the LIA? He knew they'd cover it up for him. The LIA wanted Teague to be reelected. They were used to him. They don't trust Harvey. You know how the LIA is. They're always on the side of the status quo."

It was all bunk, but it was plausible bunk. I was stalling, trying to find a way out. I had a gat in my desk drawer, but I knew that Gordo would drill me the moment I made a move for it. I thought about Badass, but the elemental would never reach me in time, and, besides, Gordo would hear it coming. Badass was anything but subtle. No other nearby elemental was going to be able to help me against both Gordo and Ironshield. All I had were words, and I was running out of them. I hoped that I'd had enough left to give Gordo second thoughts.

Gordo nodded as he thought about what I'd told him, and I began to think that I had a chance. But then his eyes narrowed, and I knew that my time was up. "You may be right about Mr. Fulton. Maybe he did kill Zyanya. But if he did, then he had a good reason to."

I sighed. "Gordo, you're the most loyal joe I've ever met. And I don't mean that in a good way. Nothing personal."

"No," Gordo agreed. "Nothing personal."

A deafening blast echoed through the room, and I flinched and shut my eyes at the sound. A few seconds later, when I realized that I wasn't dead, I opened them again in time to see Gordo's arm drop to his side. The gun in his hand fell to the floor. Gordo didn't look right to me. His eyes were wide open, but they didn't seem to be looking at anything. His wide mouth was slack, and there was something wrong with his ear. My senses were strangely dull, a combination of shock and lack of sleep, but it finally came to me: Gordo's ear was missing. It had been replaced by shreds of blackened skin and pieces of bone, and blood was leaking out of a hole the size of a silver dollar in the side of his head. And then Gordo collapsed. His head bounced off the desktop, and he fell to the floor on his back, arms and legs extended at odd angles to either side.

"Lord's balls! Yap, yap, yap!" Ironshield was still extending a pistol toward Gordo's body. "I thought he would never shut up!" Without rising from his chair, the troll fired another shot that ripped a hole in Gordo's chest. "When you're going to shoot someone, just shoot him! Don't give the fucker a chance to try to talk his way out of it. Plug him full of lead and move on!"

I stared at Ironshield, trying to control my breathing.

Ironshield got out of his chair and leaned over Gordo's body. He put a finger on his bloody neck, feeling for a pulse. After a few moments, the troll picked up Gordo's pistol and stood. He put the pistol under his coat, pulled a handkerchief out of his shirt pocket, and used it to wipe Gordo's blood off his finger. Then, without putting his own gun away, he returned to his chair and sat down with a grunt.

"You've probably got questions," Ironshield said.

I drew in a breath. "A few."

Ironshield chuckled. "I thought you might. Did Fulton tell you that he thought Benning had embedded a mole in his organization?"

I nodded. "It came up."

"Yeah? Well, you found him. Benning came to me about a year ago and convinced me that I'd be better off working for him."

"You mean for the Hatfields?"

Ironshield shrugged. "Sure, why not? Fulton's problem is that he's a fuckin' cheapskate! He doesn't know the value of a good soldier. He got spoiled by Gordo and the others. Do 'em a favor or two, and they're yours for life. Me? I want to get paid. And no one pays like the Hatfields."

Ironshield was still holding the gat. "So you shot Gordo because the Hatfields paid you to do it?"

The troll glanced at the gun in his hand. "Not exactly. I shot Gordo because he was about to shoot *you*. Benning doesn't want you dead."

I puzzled over that for half a second. "He still wants me to work for him."

Ironshield's lips widened into a smile. "Yep! Benning's a smart cookie. 'Wait till Fulton's man is about to kill the dick and then save his bacon,' he tells me. Now, you owe him. You owe him bigtime!"

I stared at the troll. Actually, I stared at the gun in Ironshield's hand. "That's not the way I see it," I said. "Benning set this all up. Why did Fulton think I was going to join Benning's team? He knows me better than that. He knows that I like being my own boss. Like you said, I treat myself pretty well, and I don't have to answer to some jackass. Benning must have let it out that I was thinking about coming to work for him." I paused, as a thought struck me. "It was you, wasn't it! Benning told you to tell Fulton that I was going over to the Hatfields."

Ironshield chuckled. "You're a smart egg, Southerland. It wasn't quite that simple. Benning told me how to handle it. I took Gordo aside and told him that you'd let it slip that the Hatfields had their hooks in you, and Gordo ran to Fulton with the news, just like we knew he would. So Fulton sent Gordo to sign you up with his team for keeps, and he told him to take you out of the game if you refused."

I nodded. "Sounds about right. But it was a setup. My life wouldn't have been in danger if Benning hadn't arranged the pieces on the board. So he didn't really save my life, and I don't owe him a thing."

Ironshield's smile vanished. "Gordo would have iced you. That would be you on the floor if it wasn't for me. I stopped him. Bottom line, pal. You're still breathing because of me."

I shook my head. "Nope. Go tell Benning that it doesn't work that way. He can't both set the trap and then expect me to be grateful when he stops it from springing. That's hooey."

Ironshield shook his head. "Whatever you say. Both of you are a couple of bobble heads. Me? I like things black and white. So here's how it's going to work. One, I take you to see Benning, and you and him come to an agreement. Or two, you join our pal Gordo."

Ironshield raised the pistol and pointed it at me. "You recognize this piece? Fulton says that he took it off you a while back. Nice gat! I like something bigger and noisier, like a shotgun, but this little 'ol thirty-eight can do a real number on a guy." He glanced down at Gordo's fallen body and then looked up with a smile. "As you can see!"

The troll reached under his coat with his free hand and drew out Gordo's forty-four. "Now this is a serious piece of iron! A shot from a piece like this will take your head off! So here's what's going to happen. You've got an offer on the table. You can work for Benning and the Harvey campaign. Once Harvey is elected, which is pretty much a lock now, then Benning will have other jobs for you to do. I don't know, a smart joe like you? You might wind up heading his security team! From there, who knows? Once Harvey is mayor, the Hatfields will run this city. My advice? Take the offer. Join them. The sky will be the limit for a tough mug with brains and ambition."

"And otherwise?"

Ironshield's upper lip twisted into a sneer. He held up the thirty-eight. "This firearm is registered to you. Funny thing. The other day, you talked to a jeebo who works in the Hatfield Syndicate. A drugmaker named Kintay. You asked him if he could find someone to hack into the Central Firearms Registry and make the entry for this pistol vanish. I guess you and Kintay go way back. Problem is, Kintay is a little loose with the lips. He wanted to help you out, but he talked to a guy who talked to another guy, and, well, you know how these things go. Eventually word got to Benning."

I suppressed a groan. "Let me guess. Benning told you to find the gun."

"Would you believe that Fulton kept it in his own weapons stash? It was just sitting in there, begging to be taken! I guess he didn't think it needed to be put anywhere more secure."

I nodded. "It didn't occur to him that anyone except me would want it."

"Yep!" Ironshield agreed. "And no one would have if you hadn't talked to Kintay about it. So this is all your own fault."

"Gee thanks, dad. So let me see if I've got this. If I don't come with you to go see Benning, then you are going to plug me with Gordo's roscoe. Then you'll put my thirty-eight in my hand, maybe even wrap my fingers around the trigger and fire off a round to leave behind some residual powder burns, and it looks like Gordo and I shot each other."

"Him with his gun, and you with yours. Open and shut case, just the way the coppers like it."

Ironshield leaned forward and pointed the forty-four at my forehead. "So what's it going to be, Southerland? You join the team and maybe we go out on the town together from time to time and score us some prime poontang? Or I feed you a lead sandwich."

I let out a breath. "Can I have some time to think about it? It's a big decision. You might even call it life-altering."

Ironshield smiled. With that curl in his upper lip, it still looked like a sneer. "Sure. I'll give you ten seconds. And keep your hands on the top of your desk where I can see them. Ten... nine... eight..."

"All right, fine. I was hoping to get some shuteye tonight, but you might as well take me to see Benning. It wouldn't hurt to talk to him."

Ironshield's smile broadened, though it still looked like a sneer. "Good man! I knew you'd listen to reason." He gestured at me with the gun. "Get up and let's go."

"What about Gordo? He's bleeding all over my nice throw rug."

"Don't worry about it. I'll take you to Benning, and if everything is jake between the two of you, he'll arrange to have a couple of his boys come over here and clean up. Let's move!"

We both stood, and I reached for my coffee cup. "Mind if I top this off? If I don't get more caffeine in me, I won't make it to the car."

Ironshield hesitated. "All right, but no games! I've still got this rod on you, and I'll pop you the second I think you're up to any funny business."

I stepped around my desk to the coffeemaker that I kept on a table against the wall. "You want any?" I asked.

"Nah, I'm good. Quit wasting time!"

I kept my voice bland and steady. "Fly up the troll's nose and spin as fast as you can. Suck the air out of him."

Ironshield frowned as he took a second to process what I'd just said. A second was more than enough time for the elemental that I'd summoned moments before from the laundry room to stop drifting unseen above my head and shoot up Ironshield's nostril, where it started whirling like a motherfucker in the troll's throat.

The effect was dramatic. Ironshield's body jackknifed as air whooshed out of his mouth and nose. I grabbed the half-filled glass coffeepot from the coffeemaker's hotplate and slammed it into the side of the troll's skull. The glass shattered, and boiling hot coffee splashed over Ironshield's face. The troll grabbed at his scalded face with both hands, and the pistol fell from his fingers to the floor.

Ironshield wasn't as tall as most trolls, but he was broader and heavier. He was almost three times my weight, and it was all rock. I had no intention of trying to tangle with him toe-to-toe. I ducked past him and reached down for the forty-four. But Ironshield got lucky. Either that, or he was just that good. He lunged and caught me across the back with a massive forearm, and it felt like a tree had fallen on my shoulders. I crumbled to the floor and rolled away just in time to miss the full force of the kick that Ironshield aimed in my direction. As it was, the troll's foot grazed my elbow, and my arm went numb from my shoulder to the tips of my fingers.

The elemental was still doing its work in Ironshield's head, and the troll's face was turning purple. He grabbed at his throat and opened his mouth wide, trying to draw air into his lungs. I spotted the forty-four and made a lunge for it, but, even inconvenienced as he was, Ironshield was too fast for me. Before I could get my mitts on it, the troll kicked the gun to the far side of the room. Long knobby fingers grabbed for me, but I rolled away in the nick of time.

Ironshield was in a bad way. He began to pound on his chest, trying to dislodge the elemental from his throat. He was no longer fighting me, but he was standing between me and the forty-four. New plan. I turned and scrambled for the door leading out of the back of my office. It didn't work. Trolls are quicker in small areas than you'd expect, and Ironshield, who had been a martial arts instructor in the military, was quicker than most. Striking like a jungle cat, the big troll seized me by my coat collar and lifted me off my feet. He held me in the air for a moment and then flung me across the room. I tried to scramble to my feet, but a piercing pain shot through my ankle, and I collapsed.

I was paralyzed with pain for a moment, and I would have been helpless against another attack, but Ironshield was too preoccupied with trying to breathe to take advantage. I watched the troll's chest expand. He gathered his strength, and his upper body convulsed as he forced out an explosive cough. The effort seemed to drain Ironshield. He fell to his knees, and I thought he'd reached the end of the line. But in desperation, the troll threw back his head and, with an earsplitting wheeze, sucked air deep into his lungs. Then he lurched forward and let out a tremendous sneeze. The whirling elemental, spraying goo into the air in all directions, flew from the troll's nostril like it had been shot from a cannon. Ironshield didn't hesitate. He scrambled to his feet, reached beneath his coat and drew out the thirty-eight.

"Call it off!" the troll bellowed. "Call if off, or I'll plug you!"

I let out a breath, and Ironshield shouted, "Now!"

"I release you from your service," I told the elemental, not without some reluctance. The elemental's spinning slowed to a stop, and the film-covered bubble drifted to the back of my office where it disappeared past the edge of the hall door.

Ironshield kept the roscoe pointed at my chest as he pulled his handkerchief from his shirt pocket and wiped his face. "Get up!"

I tried, but my ankle had other ideas. "I can't. I think I broke my leg."

Ironshield sneered, a real sneer, and not a smile that looked like a sneer. "Then you'll get it where you're layin'." He raised the gun to point it at my head.

"Wait! You're supposed to shoot me with Gordo's gat, remember?"

Ironshield's face twisted in confusion for a moment, but then he brightened. "Oh, that's right. I've got to set the scene. Let's see…."

Ironshield reached down and wrapped a giant paw around the back of my neck. He picked me off the floor like I was a kitten and carried me past my desk before dropping me into my chair. I watched him step across the room and pick Gordo's forty-four off the floor. Grinning his sneering grin, he moved to stand above Gordo's body and gave me a good look down the barrel of Gordo's gat. I didn't do a single thing to stop him. I was out of ideas and out of time.

The hall door behind me flew open and slammed into the wall with a bang. Both Ironshield and I whipped our heads around at the sound. The Huay Chivo, standing on his hind legs, was framed in the doorway, staring into the room with his hellish red eyes. Ironshield didn't think twice; he turned Gordo's gat on the creature and fired. As I watched, amazed, I saw the slug stop an inch in front of the Huay Chivo's chest. It hung in the air for a second, and then fell clattering to the floor at the creature's feet.

The overgrown alley rat dropped to all fours and raised its goat-like head. He glared into Ironshield's eyes, and the troll began to make choking sounds, as if he was struggling to breathe. He dropped the gun and sank to his knees. He closed his mouth, and his cheeks swelled. Then his mouth flew open, and a bile-colored stream of liquid came spilling out like brackish water from an open fireplug. My own gut began to rumble, and I fought down the urge to empty it.

Ironshield collapsed to all fours and let loose a second torrent of vomit. The stench in the room was threatening to knock me out for the count, but I slowed my breathing and kept my senses. The Huay Chivo continued glaring at Ironshield, who was gasping for air like a man going down for the third time. The creature lowered his head and charged, butting the troll in the top of the head with his ram's horns. I heard bones crack, and Ironshield fell face down in his own puke.

The Huay Chivo sniffed at the troll. Satisfied, the creature opened his jaws and plunged his teeth into the troll's neck. Troll blood sprayed out from the sides of the Huay Chivo's mouth and mingled with the vomit on the floor. I shut my eyes to keep from getting sick, but the sounds of ripping and chewing proved to be too much. I retched, and the contents of my stomach spilled out onto the top of my desk.

When I forced myself to open my eyes. The Huay Chivo had one clawed hand around Ironshield's dangling neck. With his other hand, he grabbed Gordo's corpse by the arm. The creature turned and looked me in the face. A long thin tongue slipped over his bottom lip and licked at the blood that was dripping down his whiskered chin. He stared at me for a few seconds, his eyes glowing red and bright. For one brief moment, I thought I saw the hint of something human in his stare, a kind of mad intelligence, as if I were gazing into the eyes of a lunatic. Then it was gone, and I only saw the feral eyes of the mangy goat-headed alley rat. The creature turned and dragged the two stiffs through my back door. Soon, I heard the door to the alley open and shut, and I knew that if I were to go check it, I'd find the inner deadbolt firmly in place.

I sat up in my chair and tested my ankle. I was afraid that it might have been broken in the skirmish, but it was just sprained. I knew that with my elf-enhanced ability to heal, it would be good as new in a few days, especially if I taped it. I took a long, slow breath and, with great care, rose to my feet.

My office was a disaster. Benning wouldn't be sending his cleanup crew, so it would be up to me to deal with it. I wondered if being my own boss was worth the trouble. Over the past few days, I'd been plucked off the street by powerful lawyers with political connections, I'd been tossed around by a demonic spirit of vengeance, and I'd almost been shot by a man that I respected and even liked. I'd seen my death coming from the barrel of a big gun pointed at me by a big troll. I'd been played for a sucker by a beautiful dame, and I was pretty sure that I was in love with her anyway. I'd lost my dinner, I'd made no money, and I needed a shitload of sleep.

Bracing myself on my desk, I took a few tentative steps. Pain lanced through my bad ankle, and I knew that the stairs were going to give me trouble, but I told myself to stop whining, that I was a tough sonuvabitch, and that I could handle it. The mess in my office would keep until morning. It was time for some shuteye.

I made my way past my desk and picked Gordo's forty-four off my ruined throw rug. As I started to make my way to the stairs, I spotted something lying on the floor just inside the back door. I limped over to it and picked it up. I smiled as I gripped the familiar handle of my old thirty-eight. For too long, Fulton had been holding it in reserve, waiting for the day when he could use it to force me to march to his tune like a toy soldier on his political game board. Benning had tried to use it on me, too. Two bosses, and both wanted me to be part of their crew of minions. I guess I was supposed to be flattered.

I examined the thirty-eight. Fulton had kept it clean, so that was a small point in his favor. I had little doubt that the high rolling fixer would navigate the murky halls of power in New Helvetia and find a prominent place for himself in the inner circle of some new chosen one with capped teeth and a pretty face. I wished him well. Why not? Caychan's provincial capital was a hundred miles from Yerba City. I ran my fingers over the iron barrel of the weapon that Fulton had been holding over my head for the past year. Then I opened my safe, placed the piece inside, and locked the door.

Epilogue

The bodies of Gordo and Ironshield never turned up. I didn't see the Huay Chivo for three days, and then one morning I woke to find him sleeping on the blanket that I'd left out for him in the laundry room. He slept without moving for six days straight. After that, he would disappear during the evening and walk back through my locked door every morning to eat a bowl of yonak and sleep next to my washing machine in the new basket that I bought for him. I never thought of Chivo as a pet. I thought of him as a boarder, free to go about his business as he saw fit. I kept him supplied with yonak, which was good news for the neighborhood cats and dogs, and I gave him a place to bunk during the day. It was the least I could do. As far as I was concerned, he had already paid for a lifetime of room and board in advance.

Chivo shared the laundry room with Siphon, which is the name that I gave to the elemental who had nearly choked out a troll. Although regular meals and a comfortable place to sleep it off worked wonders for Chivo's overall health—his mange eventually cleared up completely—the overgrown alley rat still gave off a reek that could stun a grizzly bear. To be fair, since the laundry room doubled as my home gym, and I tried to maintain a regular schedule of lifting weights and punching the shit out of the homemade heavy bag that I'd hung from the ceiling, Chivo wasn't the room's only source of foul odors. I kept Siphon busy every day sucking the stench out of the room and blowing it out the window. Siphon seemed happy serving me in this vital role. The elemental told me that the task was a good fit.

**

After nine hours of first-class shuteye, I grabbed a mop and a bucket and faced off against the mess in my office. I was going to have to replace my coffee pot, and the throw rug was a total loss, but after a couple of hours of hard work I felt like I could receive clients again.

When I felt that the time was right, I called Edie. I'd been dreading our conversation, but it turned out to be pleasant enough. We didn't talk long—Edie said that she had to go rehearse with the band—but her voice was light, and she invited me to meet her later that night at the Turbo. She wasn't performing, but said that she had grown to like the joint, and that it would be a nice place for a few drinks and a longer conversation.

I arrived at the Turbo at nine, but Edie wasn't in sight, so I pulled up a stool at the bar to wait for her. Eric with the handlebar mustache spotted me and poured me a shot without waiting for me to order. He also brought me an envelope with my name on it and told me that Edie had left it for me.

I knew the news wouldn't be good, so I downed the shot before opening the envelope. I pulled out two items. The first was a letter from Edie. The second was the spider goddess ornament that she'd mounted in her navel. I laid them both down on the bar and started reading the letter:

My dearest Alex,

>We had some fun, didn't we? I wasn't lying when I told you that I fell for you. I never thought that something like that would ever happen to me, and if I ever wanted to spend my life with a man, you would be the man I would want to spend it with. But it would never work out, my darling. I've got plans! Big plans! I'm going to be someone special! And I can't do it in Yerba City, and I can't do it if I'm tied down to a man, not even a good man like you. So Sunny and I are moving to Angel City. By the time you read this, I will already be on my way. Tuvi, my bass player, has a contact there who he says will introduce us to an agent. I am going to get myself noticed and then I am going to do what Jenny wouldn't. I'm going to do it for her. Baby, I'm going right to the top!!!
>
>I left you something to remember me by. You were wrong when you said that the stone wouldn't have any value if it wasn't enchanted. It is very old, like REALLY old! It goes back to the ancient times in Teotihuacan when the Great Goddess still ruled over the lands of the living and the dead, before Ketz-Alkwat came and threw her out and destroyed everything. Take it to your jeweler friend and he will tell you what I am talking about. It is probably worth a lot of money,

but I don't want it. I think you will understand why. It is better off with you than with me.

I am really very very sorry, baby. If things were different I think that I could have been very happy getting to know you better, and, well, who knows what might have happened. Trust me, you will be better off without me. But hey—come catch my act when I am famous! I will make sure that you and some lucky dame gets a front-row table for NINA!!!

I will always, always, always remember you and what could have been. Maybe I am making a big mistake. Believe me, I know how hard it is to get a break in this business, but I am determined and ready and willing to do whatever it takes!!!

Don't you ever forget me, sugar!

Forever yours!
Edie

When I was finished reading, I folded the letter and stuffed it back in the envelope. I picked up the ornament, laid it in the palm of my hand, and studied it. It was damned ugly, but it was enchanted, and Edie claimed that it was ancient. I thought about letting Crawford give it a once over. I considered giving it to Madame Cuapa. But then I decided to give it to Kai Kalama, instead. I figured that it might be dangerous for Crawford to have around, and I thought that the world might be better off if I kept it away from Madame Cuapa. Dr. Kalama, professor of Azteca antiquities, seemed like the safest bet to act as the stone's guardian.

When I was finished studying the ornament, I put it in my pocket and thought about Edie. At first I was miffed that she hadn't broken things off with me face-to-face, but, after slamming back another shot, I changed my mind and decided that she had made the right play. If she had come in person, we would have wound up between those black silk sheets. And then what? We were at the intersection of two different streets, and we could only linger there for so long. She had somewhere she wanted to go. Whether she'd ever get there didn't matter; either way, she was going to give it her best shot, and woe betide the joker who tried to stand in her way! And what about me? Where was my street taking me? I had no idea.

Maybe I wasn't going anywhere at all. Maybe I was stuck in the intersection. That was fine—for me! But not for Edie. Not for Nina.

I finished my drink and left Eric a generous tip. I put on my hat, buttoned my coat, and left the bar. It was a nice joint, but I doubted that I'd ever go back.

***

"I'm sorry, Sergeant! I thought I'd been careful." Kintay's regret sounded genuine. "I never thought word would leak back to my bosses, at least not that fast. Somebody stooged on me, and when I find out who it was..."

"Forget it, Corporal. No harm done, as it turns out. I just called to tell you that I won't be needing anyone to hack into the registry after all."

"Are you sure? Because I think I've got a guy..."

"Sure you do. He's probably the one who ratted you out."

"You think so? I'm gonna..."

"You ain't gonna do nothing, Corporal. It's more trouble than it's worth."

"Well, okay. Hey, you and me are still good, right Sarge?"

"Sure, Corporal. Your bosses don't like me much right now, but that's not on you. I'm a little surprised that I haven't heard from them lately, though. If you happen to hear anyone dropping my name, I'd appreciate a head's up."

"You bet, but no one talks to me. Not about shit like that."

"That's right. You just produce product, right?"

There was a pause on the other end of the line. "You still there, Corporal?"

Kintay's voice was hesitant. "Yeah.... You know, I probably shouldn't say nothing, but..."

"But what? You got something you need to tell me?"

"Well, I don't know. I don't know what's going on, but..." I waited, knowing that Kintay couldn't stay quiet for more than a couple of seconds. I heard a cough, and then, "Something's happening around here. Something big. They've given me some stuff to work on, but it's not a drug project. Actually, you know what it reminds me of?"

"No, but I bet you're going to tell me."

"Remember that box you brought to me about a year or so ago? The cold pack with the trick lock? Well, the stuff they've got me working with looks an awful lot like the stuff that was in that box."

That stopped me like a stiff jab to the chin. "What do you mean?"

"I mean that they've got me working on these stem cells, and they're a lot like the ones you gave me that time, except a little different. More…evolved, I guess you'd say. It's weird shit, man! And I don't know what to make of it. I mean, they've taken me off everything else! Off the designer drugs! That stuff makes zillions for them, but they don't want me producing any of that shit right now. During an election year! It doesn't make any sense! Unless…"

"Unless there's even more money in these stem cells?" I finished for him.

"Exactly! But they don't have me using them to produce product. They've just got me…testing it, studying it. Writing up fuckin' reports. And nothing online, either! No email! All my reports have gotta be hand-written and delivered to a special courier who comes around once a day to take them from me in person. It's bizarre! It's like the Hatfield Syndicate has given up on the drug trade and turned itself into a clinical lab! Where's the dough in that?"

I thought for a moment. "That's the kind of stuff that usually gets funded by the government."

Kintay laughed. "Well, you can rule *that* out. The Hatfields don't work for the fuckin' *government*! The fuckin' government works for the Hatfields! I mean, am I right, or am I right!"

***

The display scrolling across the top of my cell phone screen told me that the number of the incoming call was unknown. Hoping that the caller was a potential client and not someone trying to sell me an extended warranty for my car, I connected the call.

"Southerland Investigations. Alexander Southerland speaking."

"Do you recognize my voice, Southerland?"

"You sound like a pre-teen delinquent who needs to quit smoking."

"I get that a lot. We need to talk, but not over an open line, and not in a crowd. You know the place where you met with the fisherman? Can you be there this afternoon at three o'clock?"

"I can be there."

"Good! Come alone and make sure you're not followed."

The call disconnected. It was eleven thirty. Agent Ralph of the LIA had given me plenty of time to get to the abandoned Placid Point Pier, the place where I'd first met the old elf, and where I'd met him again to give him the hybrid stem cells. I wondered at the fact that the nirumbee knew about those meetings. It had to mean that Ralph and the elf had some kind of connection. What had Ralph said when I'd asked him if we were working for the same client? "Who can say?" It had been an odd response, especially after he'd made it clear that he wasn't working for Fulton.

I spent some time testing my phone to make sure that it was still off the grid when I wasn't using it. When I went to retrieve the beastmobile, Gio, Antonio, and I checked the vehicle over to make sure it hadn't acquired a fresh bug since the last time the mechanic and his boy had inspected it. The two of them were pretty good at making sure that my car stayed clean in every possible sense of the word. I summoned Badass, and the big elemental helped me check the area for suspicious air spirits. I summoned Smokey, and the tiny elemental helped me check the area for anyone who might be watching me drive off the lot. Satisfied that I wasn't being observed, I drove in the general direction of Placid Point, taking a meandering route and checking for tails. I reached the old pier at three o'clock on the dot.

No cars were parked in the decaying lot, and I left the beastmobile a little down the street so that it wouldn't be any more conspicuous than it was. I walked into the lot and spotted a short, squat figure wrapped in a blanket at the far end of the wharf.

"You look cold," I told the nirumbee when I'd reached him.

Ralph's teeth were clenched on one of his child-sized homemade stogies. "It gets a lot colder than this in Lakota, but this ocean wind is brutal! I don't know how you stand it!"

"You're stationed here now. Stick around long enough and you'll get used to it."

Ralph pulled his blanket tight around his stubby frame. "I hope so. No one followed you, right?"

"Far as I know. I suppose that someone could be watching us by satellite."

"Don't look up." The nirumbee's voice was bland.

I leaned against the rail overlooking the water. "What's with all the secrecy?"

"I'm LIA. It's our nature to be secret."

"Come on, Ralph. Does this have something to do with the elf?"

Ralph pulled the blanket all the way up to his chin as he shot me a glance. "The elf sent me here. Well, he arranged it so that the agency would send me. I don't know the details. That old boy has his hands in everything. I've been reporting to him since I joined the agency."

"You're a mole for the elf in the LIA?"

Ralph's eyes crinkled as his lips widened into a wry grin. "Sounds crazy, doesn't it? If my superiors ever find out, I'll disappear for good. So, yeah, I'm a little cautious."

I watched a wave roll under the pier. A flock of pelicans crossed the sky, searching the water for an afternoon snack. A gust of wind whipped past me, and I pulled my hat brim down low on my forehead. "What's this about, Ralph?"

The nirumbee plucked his cigar out of his teeth and killed its glow with his fingers before pulling it inside his blanket and stuffing it somewhere. "The elf says that you turned over some smuggled stem cells to him a few months ago. Those cells caused quite a stir. The elf launched some kind of operation."

"What kind of operation?"

Ralph glanced up at me. "A secret one."

"That right? That's jake with me. Tell the elf he can shove his secrets up his ass. I guess we're about done here." I pushed myself away from the railing and turned to leave.

"Don't go running off, Southerland. We're talking about the elf. You owe him."

I stopped. "For what?"

"For that little red crystal he shoved into your forehead. Yeah, I know about that. He did the same thing to me. Pretty handy, isn't it?"

I had to admit that it was. It was after the elf had implanted the crystal sliver in my head that I'd gained my enhanced awareness and everything that came with it. I had done a service for the elf by giving him the stem cells that I'd taken from Captain Graham, who had acquired the merchandise for Fulton, but Ralph was right. I was still in the elf's debt. Apart from the crystal dingus, the elf had also helped return me from what was supposed to be a one-way ticket to the land of the dead. "Okay, but I'm still not gonna be kept in the dark. Give me the dope, and make it straight."

The nirumbee sighed. "All right, I'll tell you what I know, since we're gonna be working together on this. You know about what the elf wants to do, right?"

"Yeah." I knew. Ever since the Dragon Lords had taken control of the world from the elves some six thousand years ago and nearly driven them to extinction in the aftermath, a handful of surviving elves had been plotting to take the world back from the Lords. It wasn't something I wanted to be involved with. It looked like the elf had other ideas.

Ralph nodded. "Well, those stem cells are going to help him get it done. Don't ask me how, 'cause I'm not party to the big picture, but he's going to be using the Hatfields as his agents here in Yerba City."

I'd suspected something along these lines after my conversation with Kintay, but the news was still hard to take. "Why the Hatfields? The elf doesn't understand humans very well if he thinks that working with the Syndicate is a swell idea."

Ralph chuckled. "If you think that the Hatfields are a match for the elf, then you don't understand *elves* very well. The Hatfields are going to provide management, facilities, lab personnel, and security for the elf's project. I don't know much beyond that, except that I'll be keeping the LIA off their backs."

I shook my head. "I'm not going to work for the Hatfields."

"You don't have to. Just try not to work against them."

I thought about that. "I don't get it. What does the elf want from me?"

In response, Ralph slid a brown paper bag out from underneath his blanket.

"Really? A brown paper bag?"

"There's a metal box inside. Take the bag. Don't open the box."

"What's in it?"

Ralph paused for a breath. "Do you know what a heartstone is?"

I nodded. "Yeah."

"Did you find it when you were searching my van?"

I just grunted.

"Thought so. Were you able to get a look at it?"

"Not directly, but I got a photo."

Ralph smiled. "Cute! That was clever. The heartstone is warded against sight, but not against *artificial* sight. Bit of a flaw, if you ask me, but I didn't have anything to do with that."

I frowned. "What do you mean? Isn't it yours?"

Ralph shook his head. "Nope."

I stared at the nirumbee. "Then whose is it?"

Ralph looked up at me. "I don't know. But you're going to help me find out. And we don't have a lot of time."

***

The Sihuanaba appeared in my dreams that night. As always, we were on the roof of the apartment building in Zaculeu. Cable had toppled over the edge, and the ghostly woman in white was glaring at me with her wild eyes in her corpselike face. Her misshapen jaws opened wider than a human mouth is capable of opening, and I was battered by her scream, too loud and too shrill for even my elf-enhanced hearing to register. But it was different this time. Instead of fighting against the scream, I embraced it. I kept my breath even, my heart still, and I let the scream take me. I couldn't hear the sonic blast, but I felt it rattling the bones in my temples, behind my ears, and in the back of my head until I thought my skull would shatter. I lay my head back in my pillow and endured it. I felt the hurt and the anguish in the Sihuanaba's shriek, the pain of every woman who had ever been forced to endure mistreatment from men, in all of its forms, physical, mental, and emotional. I didn't ignore the pain, I didn't let it wash over me. Instead, I listened to it. I didn't try to answer it, I just listened.

After a time, the shriek of the Sihuanaba began to recede into the back of my mind. It didn't disappear, but it ceased to overwhelm my senses and bury me under its weight. When I woke, I was still aware of that shriek, but as a kind of passenger in my brain, content to lurk as a background presence for the time being, but riding just under the surface, and not so deep that I would ever forget it was there. I knew that it would be quick to rise in anger if circumstances dictated. If I were ever to, say, break a woman's heart by cheating on her. Or to humiliate or belittle her out of envy or spite. Or to come home drunk and slug her. Or to deny her the respect that she deserved. I never again dreamed of the Sihuanaba, but her anguished shriek stayed with me as an ever-present memory of an eternity of agony and pain that accompanied me wherever I went, soundless, but not unheard. I had to admit to myself that no one was asking anything from me except a little common decency. All in all, I thought it was a square deal.

The End

Thank You!

Thank you for reading A Hag Rises from the Abyss. If you enjoyed it, I hope that you will consider writing a review—even a short one—on Amazon, Goodreads, BookBub, or your favorite book site. Publishing is still driven by word of mouth, and every single voice helps. I'm working hard to bring Alex Southerland back, and knowing that readers might be interested in hearing more about his adventures in Yerba City will certainly speed up the process!

Acknowledgements

I wrote my first book as a personal challenge. Since then, I've come to know and appreciate a great deal of meaningful support and input from a number of other folks. I'd like to thank my parents, Bill and Carolyn, and my sisters, Teri and Karen for their years of unwavering care and support. I'd also like to thank Cousin Juliana, who is practically a sister.

I owe a lot to Assaph Mehr for showing me the ropes and for promoting my works. Assaph is a tremendous supporter of the indie author community, and the author of the fabulous *Togas, Daggers, and Magic* series featuring Felix the Fox. I'd like to also thank Richard Knaak, author of the excellent *Black City Saint* series for his encouragement.

A very special shout-out goes to Duffy Weber, the fantabulous producer and narrator of the audiobook versions of the books in this series. He's been a joy to work with.

My thanks and appreciation go out to my oldest friend Kevin, and to Anita, Paul, Tim, Mira, and Whitney.

I thank anyone who ever gave me the slightest bit of encouragement or support. If I left you out, please let me know. I've received a lot of great advice, and, if I didn't take it, that's my fault, not yours.

And finally, I want to send a very special thanks, along with all my love, to Rita, my partner for life, not to mention my *de facto* editor, without whom none of this would have been possible—or nearly as much fun!

About the Author

Dr. Douglas Lumsden is a former history professor and private school teacher. He lives in Monterey, California, with his wife, Rita, and his cat, Cinderella.